I Looked Over Jordan; and other stories

by Ernie Brill

South End Press   Boston MA

Cover design by Nick Thorkelson
Publishing and production work
done by the South End Press

Printed by the workers at Maple Vail Press in York, PA.
They are represented by the Allied Printing Trades Council

ISBN 0-89608-117-6 paper
ISBN 0-89608-118-4 cloth
Library of Congress Card Number: 80-51042

**South End Press, P.O. 68, Astor Station
Boston, MA**

DEDICATION

This book is dedicated to:

My father, Leon Brill, who's taught me that strength resides in the warm and the gentle,

My mother, Bessie Brill, who's showed me to swing and sashay,

My sister, Debbie Brill Coplon, the one who is always there, and to George Leys,

and Stacie.

ACKNOWLEDGEMENTS

The author is lucky to have known some very special people. Thanks are given to:

Jim Willems, Paul Yamazaki, Fernando Barreiro, Robin Roth, Eli Shul, John Levin, Dan Cassidy, John Curl, Leslie Simon, Roger Taus, Dan Georgakas, Peter White, Mary Ellen Churchill, Kutay Kugay, Amy Jackson, Peter Jackson, Dennis Cohen, Ava Wolfe, Beverly Leys, Vicki Lynn Jones, Ron and Laurie Nardinelli.

To Jack Conroy, Fred Whitehead, and my Midwest and Foolkiller friends.

And to the families Piccioto, Dillon, Dann, Morse, Kutchins, Spero-Kassahoun, Epstein, and my many other friends in the Bay Area.

Special thanks to the South End Press Collective, and Billy Pope.

Special thanks to the following artists for their inspiration and sustained eloquence:

the writers: Leo Tolstoi, Damon Runyon, James Joyce, Richard Wright, Ranier Maria Rilke, Andre Malraux, Albert Maltz, Chester Himes, Theodore Roethke, B. Traven, Sterling Brown, Meridel Le Sueur, Carlos Fuentes, Ishmael Reed, Ousmane Sembene, Ronald Fair, Alex Laguma, Toni Cade Bambara, Thomas McGrath, James Allan McPherson, and Miguel Angel Asturias.

the painters: Vincent Van Gogh, Edward Munch, Emil Nolde, Edward Hopper, Marsden Hartley.

the musicians: Duke Ellington, Sidney Bechet, Coleman Hawkins, Buster Bailey, Chu Berry, Roy Eldridge, Lester Young, Billie Holiday, Johnny Hodges, Ben Webster, Charlie Parker, Wardell Gray.

the filmmakers: Charlie Chaplin, Roberto Rosselini, Vittorio DeSica, Akiro Kurosawa, Andrezei Wadja.

PREFACE

These stories are drawn from my experiences over ten years working in hospitals in San Francisco and Boston as an orderly, ward clerk-receptionist, and industrial claims clerk.

Among the more notoriously unsung groups in the United States are hospital workers—those who soothe terror, wash bodies, bring food, make beds, mop floors, hand-deliver charts, take x-rays, and change wounds. The work is paradoxically fascinating and monotonous, dirty, intense, extremely low-paid, and emotionally exhausting.

This collection gives a different dimension to the usual presentation of hospitals as the exclusive and immaculate domain of doctors. The reader will encounter a fuller, nitty-gritty view of a world seldom seen, rarely mentioned, and insufficiently appreciated.

Although there is not room to name all the remarkable people I've met, I'd like to mention a few: all my friends in the Hospital and Institutional Workers Local 250 of Northern California, and especially—Nina, Ken, Colleen, Blanche, Joe, Jing, Taffy, Dolly, Ruby, Kathy, Toni, Frank, Laverne, Linda, Ladean, Doris, Lavelle, Lauray, Mary, Debbie, Percy, Flora, Alice, Louis, Sean, Bill, Annie, Buck, Gloria, Bea, Joseph, Harold, Charmaine, Willie, and Henry.

I'd also like to note that these stories took place in the turbulent sixties and the more subtly seething seventies; they reflect conflicts and dreams that remain with us.

Crazie Hattie
Enters the Ice Age

We could hear Lodge and Crazy Hattie going at it. The three of us were trying to eat our lunch and at the same time listen to the muffled angry voices in the closed conference room across the hall. I was sympathetic; Hattie'd been pretty nice to me when I became the floor's wardclerk. ("Main thing you wanna do is always be on top of things when the patients need somethin'. Next thing is helpin' the peoples what come visit, and keepin' 'em offa our behinds so we can take care of their kin properly. You'll understand more of that when you're here a spell. Remember, the paperwork you can do anytime. Paperwork don't puke.") Hector, the Filipino orderly, aggressively supported Hattie. Often at the end of the shift, Hattie would put her arm through Hector's, smiling, "This here's my main man. He gonna ditch his wife and kids, and we gonna elope to Manila and live offa coconuts and roast goat balls." Hector would smile and with a wink add, "And love." Hattie would howl. As for Janie, she disliked Hattie ever since Hattie dubbed her "Chicken Little", explaining, "She ain't a bad nurse, 'cept every little

1

thing goes wrong, we got a disaster movie on our hands." All three of us—Janie, Hector, and me—strained to hear the arguing voices rise, then drop in loaded silence.

"They are INTO it," Hector grinned grimly.

I nodded. Janie smoothed her blond tight curls, then opened a yellow tupperware bowl, and began eating salad. She ate rapidly with decreasing daintiness as hunger overtook form.

Suddenly, Luann, the aide at the other end of the floor, walked in, her dark-brown face frowning, her large hands pushing back her sweat-wetted, bunned hair. She went over to the sink, splashed her face with water, and dried herself, turning.

"That Hattie screamin' in there?"

We nodded.

"Hm. Hope when I get her age I'll know when to get out while the gettin's good."

"Why you say that, Luann?" Hector asked, an almost hurt look on his face. I stared at Luann.

"Nothin'. Skip it."

"Hattie would retire if she could afford it," I put in.

"Well," Luann sighed, "that's a real problem now. Too tired to step it up, and too broke to step down."

Janie leaned back in her chair, squinting at Luann, who eyed her.

"You know," Janie began carefully, "If you're really going to be honest about all this, you'll admit Hattie can't do the work she used to do. And she's becoming a real problem."

"How's that?" Luann asked.

Janie sighed, "You tell me."

"I can tell you this," Luann snapped, "that Maggie McDermott what been here goin' on two hundred years now and goes around talkin' to bedscales, they kept her on and she's the laughingstock of this place and been that for three years now with her Memorandum Coordination Service jive they set up just for her, only she's administration AND white —so you don't see no one evaluatin' her now, do you?"

"We're not talking about Maggie, Luann," Janie maintained. "We're talking about Hattie."

Luann folded her arms and moved toward the door. "Hell, I'm not even supposed to be in here. I just came to wash up."

"You know," Hector said, turning toward Janie, "Hattie gets her work done. So she's a little slow. If you really cared, you'd help figure out how we can maybe lighten up the work for her, you know?"

"Hattie don't need no charity, Hector," Luann snapped.

"Hey, I'm not talkin' about charity. Shit." Hector shook his head, disgusted.

"Everyone gets their daily assignments," Janie persisted cooly. "And if that's too much to handle each day, then something's wrong, and that person should be man or woman or whatever enough to admit it to themselves."

"From all I can see, Hattie does her work," I threw in, "and other peoples' too."

"Like when?" Janie scowled.

"Like the time she hung that I.V. pole when you had your hands full and the I.V. nurse hadn't gotten here yet, that's when. And she got a whole lot of shit for that."

Janie scowled. "Well, Josh, I think there's also alot you don't know and don't see."

No one said anything.

"O.k.," Janie nodded, "so she does help when someone needs help. But it slows her own work up, and she's not fast enough to do that. And she's always taking forever—FOREVER—with her charting and her temperatures and all of her paperwork. She's slow and there's just no getting around it."

"Right. She's the slowest sixty-five year old here," Hector remarked bitterly.

"Look," Janie said. "What it really boils down to is: can she do the work, or can't she?"

No one spoke. Across the hall, something slammed. Hector nodded toward the closed door and the sound.

"She can do the work if people quit breathin' down her neck all the time."

Luann frowned, silently taking out a pack of cigarettes and going toward the door. Janie, smoothing her blond curls, shrugged.

"Well, maybe she could transfer. To a different shift other than days. Or something."

Luann lit up.

"You're quiet all of a sudden, lady," Hector remarked.

"Way I see it," puffed Luann, "it's Hattie's business. She don't need advice from any of us, leastways from me. Hattie knows what's best for Hattie. Let's leave it at that."

Luann suddenly left the room. The tension lessened. I wondered if Hattie would last, wondering too if there was any place in the hospital for someone who slowed down a step. The voices grew louder across the hall. The door opened. We heard first the voice of Judy Lodge, the sixth floor supervisor.

"I want to speak to you Hattie. I'm not finished."

Hattie very slowly walked out of the conference room, gripping her brown lunch bag in one hand and in the other hand her black rhinestoned purse—her fabled trademark ever since the 1968 strike when she wacked a Tactical Squad officer with it across the head so hard he fell off his motorcycle. Hattie wore green surgery "scrubs", green tops, and green pants—her favorite outfit from the days when she had been training as a surgical technician, though they had long since cancelled the program. She walked down the hall slowly, staring straight ahead, erect, muttering.

I concentrated hard to hear her mumblings. Her face seemed to pout permanently, a strong dark black face with large-lidded deep brown eyes, a small nose, and a full mouth with the bright red lipstick she sported, bragging, "Never know when some fine man gonna get tired of all these silly young things and ache for someone with experience." She'd wink with her large brown eyes, which were like a shot deer —full of red veins. When she wanted to "put a fix on folks," she spoke monotonously, her eyes focusing on a pen in a shirt, a ring on the finger, a nearby chart. She babbled, then silently stared straight into the eyes just as she reached her point. It distracted the nurses and aggravated the doctors, especially the ones who wanted her to kowtow. If a doctor, giving orders for a patient's treatment, added, "How does that sound to you?" mechanically consulting Hattie, he'd be abruptly jarred by the slow, firm answer, "Don't sound too good," followed by the famous, "Now, the way I see it—"

I watched her proudly trudging, with Judy Lodge right on her heels, the voice whiney, tight.

"Hattie, I want you to sign this."

Lodge sighed, persisting, too tightly encased in a yellow uniform. Pink flowers merrily spread down the wide shoulders and sides, below a thick neck and a strained white freckled face. Lodge was built broad and squat. On her five foot three inches, her two hundred pounds looked like a huge square.

"Hattie!"

"Stomachs don't know paper," Hattie muttered, staring at the floor. "Not a thing. Stomachs don't."

Luann watched from the far end of the corridor. Hector smiled slightly. Janie greeted Lodge with a wave of the hand that Lodge acknowledged while turning toward me.

"Josh, isn't your break at one o'clock?"

"Well, yes, but things seemed slow so I thought I'd—"

"Take your lunch when it's scheduled from now on," Lodge snapped. "If you want to change it, ask me."

She moved down the hall after Hattie, almost on the backs of her shoes. "Hattie. Hattie."

I slipped behind the desk to my chair and started looking busy. Hector was slowly moving toward the lunch carts, trying to stay close. Luann hadn't moved a muscle. Staring, Janie almost collided with one of the dietary aides bringing up the lunch carts.

"Hattie, I'm talking to you," Lodge persisted, waving the paper.

Hattie turned and blinked. She frowned, then walked over to one of the lunch carts and took a packet of salt and a packet of pepper. The phone rang. I grabbed it, trying to hear Hattie as she approached Lodge.

"Is there a Mr. Kitchener in room 669?"

I rapidly scanned the patient list, and muttered, "Went home yesterday."

"Hah?"

"Yesterday. He went home. Bye—" I whispered, hearing a faint, "Well, thank you anyway." Still, I missed hearing Hattie—only saw her,with a tired look on her face, hand Lodge the packets of salt and pepper.

Lodge's reddening face jutted out as if she didn't believe what she was seeing and hearing. Hector laughed out loud. Lodge glared at him. Luann choked on her cigarette and grabbed her side with her free hand. Even Janie tried to stifle a smile.

Hattie headed toward the break room, gripping her lunch bag and her black rhinestoned purse. Just before going in, she turned and said to no one in particular, "I'm on break. Anyone needs me, you know where to find me."

II

NURSING MEMORANDUM: *CONFIDENTIAL*
FROM: Judy Lodge, R.N. M.S. Assistant to the Director of Nursing, Six South Supervisor.
TO: John Booth, R.N. M.B.S. Director of Nursing Services.
SUBJECT: Perkins, H.
TITLE: Nursing Assistant.
LOCATION: Six South.
SPECIFICS: Employee performance evaluation and employee reaction.

The following are my summary notes of a discussion I had on June 14, 1976 with Ms. Hattie Perkins concerning a mutual talk we had about her most recent employee performance evaluation.

Ms. Perkins, as you know, has been at the Medical Center now for over thirty-five years. She has had a consistently good work performance, excellent attendance, and has gotten along reasonably well with her co-employees and our housestaff. She has been quite popular with many of our patients, and at times has epitomized our credo: "The patient comes first.'' Therefore, it is all the more regrettable that in recent months, it has come to my attention, as well as to other employees on the floor, that several factors are adversely affecting Ms. Perkins' work performance to the point where it has become seriously questionable as to whether or not she can continue to function in the manner and standards we expect of our employees in the deliverance of patient care.

Ms. Perkins' patient care is dangerously erratic. She has difficulties in performing the simplest tasks. Just this morning I found her nearly unable to complete the simple task of helping a patient back into bed. Of a graver nature is the recent incident concerning the near-drowning of a patient who was left unattended by Ms. Perkins. Fortunately, the patient himself talked his own family out of filing a malpractice suit. These bouts of ''forgetfulness'', as Ms. Perkins has called them to other employees (she won't admit this to me), have, as you can see, reached a frightening point.

Ms. Perkins has also become noticeably slower, nearly to the point of painful embarrassment. While this is to be expected of someone of her age, it is reaching the stage where she cannot keep up with her work, particularly the increasing amounts of written work given to the aides in an attempt to begin in-service training and upgrading, such as more charting in the patient notes to free the nurses for more leadership responsibilities throughout the hospital.

Ms. Perkins also tends to argue with her superiors regarding the quality of care. She has, on several occasions, illegally performed the work of registered nurses, and then asked to be monetarily reimbursed for working in the registered nurse category. This is not only impermissible, but unlawful. Ms. Perkins has been seen putting up intravenous poles for patients. Again, this could lead to a potential situation of considerable harm to the patient as well as the hospital (again, in terms of malpractice). Ms. Perkins claims it is "common practice" throughout the Medical Center, due to what she claims is "understaffing". I might add that she has received several previous warnings about hanging I.V. poles, and that this particular item is being grieved through the union grievance procedure by Ms. Perkins and several other aides and orderlies.

I mainly mention the above to illustrate Ms. Perkins' attitude. I feel Ms. Perkins assumes that her length of service with us entitles her to privileges and freedoms unavailable to other employees in her job category. This seems to be part of a growing truculent attitude on her part. More than several of the housestaff have complained about her attitude towards them—she contradicts their orders and often calls them "children". Indeed, while most of our house staff are much younger than Ms. Perkins, housestaff, residents, and interns are, in the majority, grown men with wives and families of their own, and certainly deserve to command respect among all of our employees.

Before sitting down with Ms. Perkins, I offered her our new procedure where she could write up her own evaluation of herself, explaining how this was to encourage employee input and feedback into the evaluation process. She refused. Again, today, after showing her her evaluation, I told her she could write her own reply in the designated space on the employee performance evaluation sheet. Again, she refused. This is the second time in less than a year that Ms. Perkins has refused to sign an employee performance evaluation. When I informed her of this, she simply agreed, and said, "So what?"

In short, I find that Ms. Perkins' work performance and attitude have grown increasingly unsatisfactory. I also feel that she is taking advantage of the fact that she has been with us for a long time, and is somewhat personally popular with many employees, particularly other minorities like herself.

This brings me to an important and delicate point. Ms. Perkins has openly accused me of being a "racialist". I replied that if I was a "racialist", would I have been given so many different positions of increasing responsibility in such a relatively short period of time? I think my record speaks for itself. When I first came here three years ago, I was a floor R.N., and within three months volunteered to be team leader. By the year's end, I took the responsibility for supervising the entire sixth floor. Six months ago, I assumed the position of Assistant to the Director of Nursing, while also maintaining most of my duties as sixth floor supervisor. I have also served as treasurer for the Christmas Club Committee, secretary of the Credit Union, and most recently, as Director of the March of Dimes Fund Drive. In all instances I have tried to be fair to all, regardless of race, creed, or religion. I think that most of my employees would say I was more than fair, and that Ms. Perkins' criticisms were unwarranted.

My main concern is to inform you of a very difficult situation. We are, at present, forced to keep on an employee whose performance and attitude I find basically unsatisfactory. I would appreciate a conference with yourself and several of the other supervisors concerning this problem, which I consider somewhat representative, in that the improper resolution could set a negative precedent, particularly in regards to the handling of our senior employees.

I might add that Ms. Perkins has threatened "to go to the union first thing in the morning." I told her that, according to our contract with the union, that was her privilege according to the second step of the grievance process, since the first step—meeting with the immediate supervisor, myself—will obviously prove unsatisfactory. I felt at a loss to say anything further for fear of jeopardizing our future case. I think it would be an excellent idea at some future date to have a workshop concerning this.

This brings me to another point. There occurred a small incident at the end of today's discussion about Ms. Perkins' employee performance evaluation that I consider to strongly border on insubordination. However, it was unclear to me when and under what circumstances—exactly—an employee can be charged with insubordination, other than the obvious instances of outright slander and physical assault. This area, too, could merit a workshop with yourself, the four assistants to the director, the head of personnel, and someone from labor relations. I would even be glad to make it a coffee and cake evening at my house, if that would be found suitable and agreeable.

Well, not wishing to take up any more of your valuable time, I remain,

Sincerely yours,
Judy Lodge

cc: Orville Larson, Administrator.
    Ike Howes, Personnel.
    Larry Shields, Labor Relations.

ATTENTION FILES: MATERIAL MARKED "CONFIDENTIAL" SHOULD NOT BE PLACED IN EMPLOYEE FILE.

III

She kept wavin' that piece of paper like she thought she was God and that little piece of paper was the Ten Commandments. And I wanted to say hey we ain't up on Mt. Sinai bitch; and I coulda played crazy but she was lookin' so like she thought she was God, I had to set her straight and play the hand out and tell her what for.

I seen her kind come and go, and I think her kind oughta just as soon as they get here go right down to the Man, pull his pants down, and start right in. Why pussyfoot around with all that polite shit. I mean that's what they here for—to move up that ladder like there was a house of cheese at the top. All this noise about patient this and service that. I seen her from the get. That's why she hates ol' Hattie—'cause she knows I know what she's about. She knows I had her number before it was on the board. Only what she don't know is I got her number on MY board. I got one of her hairs. Just in case. Though I don't know that much about what to do with it— just the stories—but if it gets to that I can find out. I got that hair all right. I caught her actually doin' some work one day. She wiped her forehead and this hair got loose and twisted and she pulled at it and wiped her fat self with a towel and put it in the dirty linen and I headed straight for it and held my breath and got that towel and that hair, plucked it right off that nasty thing and into a paper towel. I washed my hands for twenty minutes afterwards.

She make me mad enough I might get some more hair. Might have to pull on that bitch's head until I see some brains. And that might be a long, long time. Maybe I pull her head open and there's nothin'—just a bunch of memos and maybe a purse fulla that Godawful lipstick like what French whores wear or like she thinks she's a eighteen year old heifer and not a fat way-over-forty cow the Army got tired of. And don't know she's not in the Army no more, that we don't salute here. We just do the work—the salutin' you can forget the minute you walk in here 'cause I ain't saluted for twenty some years and ain't about to start now, all my yessin' and maamin' is over with cause I waited and seen alot and seen the union, and when folks say the union's fat I tell 'em you kids try workin' without it, honey, and you'll find out just how skinny you can get—to the bone—and I don't want to hear nothin' else about it.

And the look on her face when I said, "Well, I guess I'm gonna have to go to the union again," and tomorrow first thing after I soak these bones and shower, I'm gonna get dressed up and see my business agent before he gets the sleep-crust outta his eyes—he gonna SEE me—and we'll see who's goin' to be signin' what, 'cause I'm a dues payin' member goin' on thirty-three years. Maybe I could try and get HER ass fired. Maybe I could make up an employee performance for that do-nothin' bitch what talks and walks around doin' nothin' 'cept spyin' on people and botherin' everybody with this evaluation and that memorandum b.s. Talkin' all this shit like she couldn't just come out and say, "Hattie, you're too old."

And I woulda said, "You think I enjoy this? Draggin' my bones here everyday, cleanin' cranky old people's ass-holes, seein' folks cry cause their kin dyin' or ain't never gonna be the same? Gimme a decent pension and I'll be outta here so fast, you can blink and I'll be home fixin' dinner."

Only everyone here knows that our retirement plan is the joke of the world, and when I was at Spencer's—Spencer he makes good money as a longshoreman, they have a pension you can live on instead of take one look and wanna lay down and die—Spencer he heard how much we got and leaned closer, frownin' like his eyebrows was gonna shake hands, "Did I hear you right, Hattie? You know, I pride myself on my hearing, Hattie, but I don't think I heard you right."

And I said, "You heard right. Eighty-five dollars a month."

And Spencer said, "Hattie, this is 1976."

And I said, "That's what the calendar say."

And Spencer was like he couldn't believe where he was for a minute. Poured himself a new drink. Yelled at his kid five minutes later. For nothing.

And I wish I could get outta here 'cause they don't appreciate a thing you do. Like you try to do someone nice, and all of a sudden they got you as a murderer, and don't want to hear a word from you about it.

I brought this man in for his bath and everything was fine. I washed him and he smiled and asked me could he stay in the tub longer, and I said, "It says twenty minute bath," and he said, "Come on, please Hattie, my roommate's a royal pain in the ass." "Didn't I know it," I said. "Tell me about it, honey, I been carin' for that sucker for two weeks and if he ain't one of the funkiest, crankiest sonsabitches I ever run across, my name ain't Hattie Perkins." And the man laughed, "Then you understand what I mean," and I say, "Sure, stay as long as you want." And he say, "Thanks alot Hattie, you're a lifesaver." And I say "Just dry yourself good when you get out so you don't catch cold."

And how was I to know his family'd come lookin' for him, and he be startin' to doze off and got a few bubbles of water up his nose, and his family screamin' and fussin' to wake the dead about how come he was all alone, was we tryin' to drown the man, what negligence, and who was it. They wrote it up. How could we leave him by hisself the senile old man, and I said, "Senile my ass, he just wanted to have himself some privacy." And the resident gettin' huffy as hell sayin', "I said short baths, Mrs. Perkins," and I said, "I was usin' my judgment. It was a matter of judgment or do you think judgment is reserved only for you." And he said, "That's not the point," and I said, "If that ain't the point, then I don't know what is."

And the next day he and Lodge had their heads together like they was playin' football and she kept slidin' her weasel eyes over towards me thinkin' she was so slick, only I forced her to keep them on me 'cause I stared at her straight out and said, "Yeah?" (pretendin' she didn't see me, who did she think she was foolin'?)

And now that all gets translated into I tell doctors what to do and hates 'em all, which at times ain't too far from the truth, but the truth too is the ones treat me decent we get along fine—like that Dr. Hartman, now me and him are great friends. Maybe I should have him see that pack of lies she wrote up, maybe he could straighten her out since she just goes ga ga over any doctor, practically gets down on her hands and knees and tries to get her name legally changed to Fido.

So when she was wavin' that paper I thought of all that and then some. And once I sat down and read what she had put down I was mad. I was so hot I wondered if I said anything would there be flames comin' out of my mouth I was so mad. I told her she must be crazier than even I thought she was if she thought I was goin' to sign that mess—all those lies, up and down, unsatisfactory this and doesn't meet requirements that. And I been workin' here 30 years goin' on 40. She said sign it and write whatever you want in this little itty bitty space over here. And I said I didn't hire on here as a writer, besides if I do start writin' what I think of what you

wrote here, we gonna be here til after dark and I got grand-
daughters to see and grandchildren to visit and neighbors
what need my advice on things. So I ain't signin', I ain't
writin', and that's all there is to it.

And that bitch made me so upset sayin' things just
weren't done like that, and in a way I was glad 'cause I could
see I was messin' her up—she wanted it all wrapped up tight.
So I just walked away 'cause I was gettin' tired of her jawin'.
And I walked past all these folks—Hector, Josh, Janie, and
saw Luann down the hall, and the other aides and folks from
the kitchen with the food. And she was followin' me callin',
"Hattie, Hattie," like she thought sooner or later I was
gonna have to sign that paper. I just shook my head. I was
tired of it. I had all to do to not just turn around and flatten
that fat bitch, only my legs was hurtin' so bad I didn't know
if my joints would make the turn. I reminded myself to take
me home some rubbing alcohol and take a nice warm bath, a
long hot soak.

And I thought of how earlier on in the day she seen me
tryin' to help that poor old man Moore back into his bed
where for a second I thought neither of us was gonna make it
and we was gonna both land up on the floor. And she just
stood there watchin' me so she could write down on that
piece of paper that Hattie Perkins can no longer help move a
six foot, 200 pound man back into bed all by herself. And she
didn't move a muscle but stood there with her fat bitch self in
the doorway, while I liked to kill myself twistin' and turnin'
that old man Moore who had a bad back to begin with.

Yeah, well they'll be throwin' snowballs in hell before
they get me to sign. They can come to my grave with a five
dollar Papermate, and I'll just turn over.

And that's when I grabbed some of that salt and pepper
offa the lunch wagon and turned to her as best as I could turn
and said, "Here, Judy, maybe you actin' funky and peculiar
'cause you're hungry. Why don't you just pretend that piece
of paper is a steak, and go on and chew it up. Just chew slow
so you don't make yourself sick now." And folks started
laughin', some was coverin' their mouths so she couldn't see
'em laugh, and I just kept on goin'.

And didn't look back neither, 'cause I don't need anyone or any piece of paper to tell me I'm not as fast as I usta
be. Only who appreciates what a 65-year-old woman can do,
'cause I can do things in less time than it takes these girls what
every time they give a bedpan almost or change a wound, they
fussin' and raisin' up a storm. And if they did less fussin' and
runnin' and fidgetin' and ohmyGodin', they'd get it done a
whole lot faster. I try to tell 'em, but some folks you can't tell
them a damn thing. And they call me Crazy, just 'cause I like
to say a few things to remind myself about this and that. They
say, "No Hattie, you crazy 'cause you talk to yourself." And
I just say, "Hey, you find me someone who's more
interesting than me, and I'll talk to them." That tickled
them. They had a good laugh behind that. And what can you
tell some kid who's got her figure and knows she's fine, and
sees me as her grandma what should be in some old folks
home anyway? What are they gonna listen to me for? Though
there used to be a time when they did listen. But when they in
a jam who you think they come to? When there's some mess,
who you bet even these college nurses run to? 'Cause no one
said much about what happens when someone collapses on
the floor bleedin' and shittin' all over theyselves while they at
the other end of the floor helpin' someone who can't breathe.
And when they want me to help 'em lift, or clean someone
shitted up themselves, well all of a sudden no one's callin' me
crazy then. And once I pointed that out. And no one said
nothin'—suddenly everyone got busy writin' and foldin'
linen and lookin' real hard at their fingernails.

　　　And it's like all these years, one after another, they be
runnin' up, "Oh Hattie, Hattie you're the ONLY ONE can
help me," which always seemed strange to me seein' how
there's so many of us around, yet year after year I'm the
ONLY ONE, yet now they don't seem to need the ONLY ONE.
'Cause maybe they gonna get someone else to be the ONLY
ONE. And maybe that person don't know they been selected
yet to become the next me, and instead of Ol' Hattie, it gonna
be Ol' Luann, or Ol' Hector, or Ol' Johnnie.

　　　And oh the look on her face that time last evaluation
when I said in front of everybody when she said, "We only

have your best interests at heart, Hattie," and I said, "So what you gonna do now? Take me to the Colonel, and buy me the Ten Dollar Bucket?" And Luann and Hector and Josh was gigglin' and I kept on, "See? I rate. They takin' me to The Colonel. Money's no object. Nothin's too good for ol' Hattie. And they gonna guarantee me no wings, and no backs. How about THAT?"

And I remember that 30 year anniversary party, and that was nice for real. Real nice. They got us all front row seats at the Venetian Room in the Hilton, and there was the twenty-year folks, and the twenty-five year folks, and three of us thirty-year folks—me, Irish Katy what works in the kitchen, and Capek the old engineer from Slovokia or one of them countries where it rains all the time. And they got me and Irish corsages. She got red roses, and I took the yellow roses 'cause I was wearin' my green silk evenin' gown, and it went with it. They gave us gold pins. I have it at home. And we talked into the microphone and I said, "I'm not Johnny Carsons or anything, but thanks alot." And later on J.J. who been there almost long as me said I did that so slick and to such perfection that he was gonna call up Johnny Carsons himself and tell him watch out for Hattie Perkins, Johnny, she's a real comer. And that's what I like about J.J. 'cause he's always sayin' stuff like that to me make me feel good even if it is a complete lie—only it's different, like a fib or stretchin' things a bit, or a tall tale, like a lotta things.

And not a real lie a complete lie a white lie, say a white lie weighin' about 220—if she ain't wearin' her wig today. If she's wearin' her wig now, that probably ups it to 230. Where she got it I'll never know, all I know is it fits bad and makes her look like she stole if offa some orangutang, the bitch, and I could even see her real colors her ugly roots in my ear, "Sign, sign, sign, Hattie, Hattie."

And I got to thinkin' how you always think and say, "Now that's *cold*," and me always tellin' these kids, "I seen it all" and "That ain't nothin'," and yet how I can never get used to it. Never.

Like Spence sayin' about the pension, "This is like the Stone Age. This is some cold shit." And me sayin', "It's the

Ice Age is what it is." And Spencer saying, "Yeah, yeah. And the Ice Age was all white, wasn't it now." And Spencer's wife laughin', "Well, I don't recall seein' any black Eskimos. In fact, I don't recall seein' any Eskimos whatsoever." And I said, "That's 'cause everybody froze to death. Every living thing froze to death."

And for a second just a second when I come to work that mornin' in the rain last week and that wind was blowin' that rain, "Hattie," I said to myself, "what in the world are you doin' fightin' this rain and this wind to walk into THIS fool place?"

And that same day that fat cow started in with this, "Here's your pre-evaluation form, Hattie. I want you to look it over. You'll see that you can evaluate yourself and put in whatever comments you'd like. So, feel free." It was some new bullshit. I saw that right off—'cause she wanted me to write down about myself so she could take it and study on it, and I just said, "Do I have to do this? Is this in the union book?"

"Well no," she say, "but it's a new procedure and—"

And I didn't let her finish, told her straight-off, "If it ain't in the book, then forget it." And the blue in her eyes got so dark they looked like they was snowin' razorblades and she stomped off.

And later in the rain I was thinkin' of them animals what you see in the museum, old and funky and trapped in the ice, with them long teeth like what elephants got, and they say these was kin to the elephants—their great, great grandfolks goin' way back, and so big the elephants was like little bits next to these mothers.

And I couldn't get that outta my mind. I told my daughter and she said, "Ma, you got more to do than to worry about them old time animals," and I just said, real quiet, "Do I? And how else are they dealin' with me?" And she didn't say a word, but just hugged me. And I wanted to tell her how I dreamed I was on break and lookin' through the National Geographic and saw a picture of one of them mammadons in the ice. And the picture got bigger and bigger and the ice got big like a mirror, and I saw my face and my skin with these wrinkles and these bad teeth, and I felt like I was inside an icecube and woke up shiverin' chilled to the bone on a night you don't even need a blanket, and all around me it was white and cold, and Hector handed me a serape and said, "Take care Hattie, it's real cold out," and I was scared like when I was five years old and you wouldn't think I was 65, and then I woke up for real, and right there in the dead of night was cookin' at three o'clock in the morning, and hungry like I hadn't eaten a decent meal in weeks.

And I'd like nothin' better than to be able to get out of it. I wouldn't be one of these peoples you hear about what retires, then goes off and dies straight off 'cause they don't know what to do with themselves—like when the wardclerk and Hector they asked me, "What would you do Hattie?" And I said, "First thing, I'm gonna buy me a motorcycle, and come back here and ride 'round and round. Maybe run a few people over." They started laughin' and I went on.

"And if they give me enough money I'll travel. I'll go dancin' down in Rio—Rio de Janeiro where they got the biggest Mardi Gras in the world, bigger than the one in New Orleans even. Yeah, I'll hit all them festivals in Brazil and Mexico and Africa—I'd like to see Africa, they say they got some of the oldest civilizations in the world. Yeah, I'll travel my ass off, get to all them places, go to Europe and have 'em show me around all them famous museums and things, and go to Egypt and hit the Pyramids, and India with all them fancyassed temples—" and they was all laughin'.

And suddenly I got hot 'cause I figured here I was again runnin' my fool mouth and where the hell was I goin' anyway and whose business was it anyway, and I said, "Their business is to give me enough of a pension so I can do it, and maybe we should stick to that, because without that all this is so much BULLSHIT, I mean I'll probably be lucky if I get enough to eat three meals a day and make the rent," and just sayin' that made me feel like I was on the floor and out in the rain again and I felt hot and said, "Yeah, its all so much shit."

And all of a sudden no one was askin' about what I wanted to do or would do, and Josh was lookin' down at his papers, and Hector got that hurt look on his face like he gets sometimes, and Luann lit up though I been tellin' her them smokes gonna cut her heart out, so I figured the hell with it and smiled to myself and said, "Hey, and'you know what else?" They were still solemn-like but they looked at me, and I said, "The main thing is, if I get what's comin to me (and they started to smile but half a smile like they weren't sure what was comin' next cause with me its true you never know), "I'm gonna party me up a storm. The last you'll hear about me I'll be drinkin' the finest rum in the world at midnight in the Caribbean Islands, the real stuff, the real homemade brew. That's the number one choice when you get down to it 'cause in the Caribbean—and I know 'cause I was there on my honeymoon if you can believe that — in the Caribbean they got water so blue and so clear you can see clean through it, yet that water is cool and at the same time warm as a bathtub 'cause they about as near the sun as you can get—they call it The Torrid Zone and that's where you can write me, Hattie Perkins, care of The Torrid Zone—"

They was all laughin' now and sayin', "Sounds great," and stuff like that, and I said, "You damn right it sounds great. 'Cause they got evenings there where the stars are dripping like they was split open melons, that's how they look— it's like the whole sky was like my purse only brand new and a whole lot bigger—and maybe I'll find me some magician stud, some magic man, who can turn these rhinestones into diamonds and who appreciates and respects a woman of my bearing."

And they was going back to work slow and shakin' their heads and smilin', "Crazy Hattie", and I said, "That's me."

Linc's Door

I first met Linc the morning he destroyed his locker and decided to transfer off graveyards.

Me and Stoney were getting dressed in the orderlies' locker room, trying to unbend our uniforms and put metal clip buttons through the starched shut buttonholes. The single window in the basement was going from dark black to dark blue. Stoney cursed, his dark brown fingers straining.

"Jesus, wha'd they do—sit these things in tubs of starch all night? I worked with concrete looser than this shit."

We heard the night orderlies down the hall—Old Tobey, "Yeah, it's a bitch, um hmm," and a louder furious voice insisting, "So I just hafta stand there while this doctor, this dildo, finally shows up and breaks this guy's ribs. Only one small problem: guy's already dead. Then he blames me and the night nurse for not gettin' someone sooner. Sooner—when we been callin' around for three hours! Then he gets mad at me when I tell him it's tough titty all around. HA!"

Harsh laughter slammed the locker room door open, a

strong pink hairy arm shot it back. The furious voice was a redfaced sweating man in his early thirties with thick brown hair, a walrus mustache over a jutting jaw, and green eyes burning like pissed off emeralds. He was about my 5' 9", more muscular, and held himself like an up and coming boxer, hungry and ready to take on all comers. Old Tobey, a slender elderly black man with smooth ashy skin and arms that looked full of wires, nodded silently to me and Stoney, as furious voice continued.

"And it didn't have to happen, that's the goddam shame of it all. All he needed was a steady dose of oxygen. I told them that last week for Chrissakes, and again three days ago —same damn doctor too. I told him I don't know how many times to get a fuckin' oxygen tent in there."

"You did the best you could, son," Tobey yawned, shaking his head.

"Mornin' fellas," Stoney greeted them, still pulling on his uniform.

"Yeah," furious voice nodded, "you guys hear what I'm saying?"

Old Tobey took an offered puff from Stoney's held-out cigarette.

"Bad night?" Stoney whispered.

Tobey just nodded, exhaling smoke. Silent, he began unbuttoning his shirt. My watch read 6:30 a.m. The sky through the window was getting lighter blue.

"Three fuckin' days ago I told 'em what he needed," furious voice repeated, "only he's just a poor bastard they found lyin' in the park so he don't count. They'll get to him one of these days. Only it's a day too late. It's all over. One more wino out of the way. Slab 'em, dab 'em, and goodbye Charlie."

No one spoke. Stoney offered furious voice his cigarette; he waved it off.

"I've had it up to here."

"Umm hmm," Tobey nodded, peeling off his shirt blotched grey with sweat.

"This time I mean it." Furious voice suddenly spied the uniforms. "What the fuck's this?"

"New uniforms," Stoney grinned. "Find me some wooden slats, and I'll make some right nice night tables out of 'em. They're strong enough, I know that."

Tobey laughed with me.

"Can't even launder uniforms!" Furious voice sneered. "Am I right?"

"You right."

"Yeah," I agreed.

"Who the hell are you?" Furious voice asked me.

"New day man," Stoney said. "Dov Jacobs, Linc Burns, Linc, Dov. Linc here's King of the Graveyard—All Around Trouble Shooter. I personally trained him."

"The fuck you did," Linc laughed shortly, nodding. "We need some help around here."

I shook his offered hand. His strong grip gave the feeling of greater strength, withheld, poised. He stared at the uniforms, remembering something; his body stiffened.

"And tellin' me" he reddened, "tellin' ME that I shoulda been there sooner! They must think I got a fuckin' rocket up my ass. I'm supposed to take care of all emergencies, run around half the hospital cause no one wants to give enemas— as if I was nuts about them—"

Stoney and Tobey laughed.

"Then put up an oxygen tent I warned 'em about three days ago. In the nick of time. Like I'm the Lone Ranger!"

His face grew redder, his eyes, wild. He spotted the starched-shut uniforms. "Well that's bullshit! Crap! It's all fuckin' bullshit!'"

He slammed his fist into the locker, then reared back and kicked the locker. His workshoe dented the metal door, caving it partly in from top to bottom. Before we could blink, he ran out into the hall, returned with a broken bed frame, and swung it for all he was worth against the dent, crushing the caved-in metal deeper. Stoney grabbed his waist as Tobey grabbed his arms. I froze, awed. Linc, surging forward, backhanded the broken bed piece against the locker.

"Easy fella," Stoney gasped, "easy."

"Had it," Linc panted. "had it."

"All right now, son," Tobey crooned, sweating, "all right."

Linc dropped the broken bed frame, then kicked it angrily across the locker room. Tobey and Stoney eased him onto the bench.

"It's bullshit, Tobey, ain't it."

"Nothin' but."

"But it's gonna be o.k.," I smiled, regretting my words instantly, as Linc's face went wild.

"No it ain't! 'Cause I ain't gonnna let it!" he yelled, rising and scrambling for the siderail. Stoney grabbed him solidly around the waist this time. Tobey just smiled. Linc didn't move.

"Now you calm down before you get us all booted outta here," Stoney ordered.

"Lemme go," Linc panted. "It's my fuckin' locker."

"Ain't nothin here yours," Stoney said.

"Leggo."

"Now, just...take it...easy," Stoney breathed.

"O.k. Let go. You're cuttin' off my circulation."

Stoney let him go. Linc rubbed his ribs.

"O.k.?"

Linc stared at Stoney. "You're in the wrong business. You shoulda been a goddam wrestler."

Linc slumped to the bench and slowly unbuttoned his clothes, staring at the concrete floor. "I gotta get off nights. Start livin' like a human being. Shit."

"Thought you wanted nights," Tobey smiled.

"The fuck I did. I was doing Jack a favor. He's married, got a family. Then he goes and quits."

"Well, you got some seniority,' Stoney suggested. "Put in for it—you never know."

"I'll see."

Linc studied Stoney curiously.

"What's up?"

"How long you been workin' in this hole, Stoney?"

"Nine years goin' on ten."

Linc yanked his buttons open, disgustedly. "You're nuts."

"I'm workin'."

Stoney paused, then grinned and punched Linc lightly in the arm. "Keep tellin ya, ya gotta let some of this shit slide offa you."

"I'm a human being," Linc snapped, "not a fuckin' duck."

Stoney laughed. "Yeah, well you sure let them puff your feathers up."

"Y'all better slide over here, and see what we gonna do about this here locker," Tobey drawled, studying the caved-in metal. "It's lookin' like Godzilla was tryin' to find his tieclip."

None of us could budge the door.

"Yee-aah," Tobey pronounced, "if this door was human, it woulda bled to death by now."

"Won't open a bit," I said, tugging at it.

"It better open," Linc gritted. "My clothes are in there."

He grabbed the siderail and began prying at a crack near the door's middle.

I pulled on some jutting metal at the bottom.

"Now hold on," Stoney ordered, "you clowns ain't makin' no sense at all."

We stopped.

"No call for everyone to bust their nut over this. Look, you just—" Stoney reached into his locker, pulled out a Phillips screwdriver, and with a few strong twists unhinged the door, which clanged to the floor as Linc's neatly hung clothes stared at us.

"See?" smiled Stoney, "easy as pie."

As Linc hurried into his clothes, me and Stoney checked our watches. It was 6:55. We usually hit the floor around 6:35 —to go over charts and check new patients. Stoney cursed. Late for Stoney was twenty minutes early for everyone else. He explained once that he arrived places early to get a jump on life because life was always trying to jump him.

"Look," Linc said, slipping into a red and black plaid jacket, combing his thick hair, "don't say nothin' about the locker. Let me handle it. I did it, and I ain't hiding a goddam thing. I'll pay for it too, if I have to. So, if they ask you or give you any shit, just have 'em call me. Fuck it. I'm definitely gonna transfer to days. Before I go nuts.''

"Get some sleep, fella.''

"What the hell did you think I was gonna do?''

"And go easy on the stuff,'' Stoney added.

"Sure,'' Linc laughed, licking his lips, "I'll go nice and easy.''

Unsmiling, Stoney followed Linc out with his eyes, then turned and tapped me in the chest, "Well, let's go up and see today's good news.''

The good news was the usual: they put Stoney "on house''—like Linc, he went all over the hospital wherever he was needed. I took the cancer ward. Neither of us got a break until eleven o'clock. I spotted Stoney entering the break room as I sat drinking coffee. He poured himself a cup, paid for it, brought it over, and knocked on his cigarette pack, taking out a smoke and lighting up. He whooshed the smoke out, then sipped his coffee. "How's things, kid?''

"Busy.''

"Tell me about it,'' Stoney laughed softly, whooshing smoke out.

The sun through the windows warmed the cafeteria. The place was empty except for Stoney, me, and some of the dietary people who were eating their lunch before the 11:15 rush of the first lunch breaks. They ate fast, joked, and waved to us to join them. Stoney waved back, "Tomorrow, got some business today.''

I looked at him curiously.

"Don't feel like bein' around alot of people today.''

I nodded.

"Anyone ask you about that locker yet?''

"Nope.''

"Well, they gonna. So we might as well have our stories straight. Just tell 'em it was like that when you got there. I'll do the same.''

"Fine.''

"If Linc wants to tell 'em he did it, he'll hafta tell 'em himself.''

"Fine," I agreed.

Stoney smiled, stretching his arms. "You're lucky you're only workin' here for a while, son."

I didn't say anything. I knew it never paid to rush Stoney. He blew some smoke rings, looking around. "Wonder if I should grab me a Danish? Ah, forget it. Need to lose some weight."

I waited.

Stoney suddenly leaned closer, staring at me. "Know Linc's problem?"

I shook my head.

"You can't let this shit get next to you. If you do, you gonna wind up out in the cold, inside a bottle, or down on the farm."

"Farm?"

"Funny farm. Or a combination of all three."

"Yeah."

Stoney's eyes softened. "Believe me son, I ain't talking to hear myself talk."

"Hmm."

"This place can get to people. Bad."

"Sure," I agreed, looking around. The cafeteria itself was depressing. On one side was the steamtable with its overcooked eggs, reheated bacon, day-old salads, cellophaned sandwiches, and tired desserts leading to a cash register near the coffee machine. The other side was simply ten tables and chairs around them with a few benches along the wall and a battered red Coke machine. The floors had the same green-grey linoleum that gleamed dully throughout the hospital. The walls were the same cheaply painted colors popularly used in projects, jails and schools—pale green like pond scum, tan-beige like light shit, or dreary brown like stale cocoa. In such rooms the patients lay and sat, fretted, worried, and sometimes prayed—"Oh God let me be all right." I closed my eyes and thought of how the patients had to lay there and look at the walls and the linoleum. I opened my eyes to find Stoney staring at me.

"Now Linc's a prime example of lettin' the shit get to him."

"Yeah?"

"Uh huh," Stoney smoked slowly. "He's a funny cat. Screams at the nurses, screams at the docs, screams at the patients. Curses out everyone. But you know, you'll look a long time 'fore you find someone good as him. I've seen alot of 'em come and go, and Linc—he knows his stuff. Cold."

Stoney's voice lowered; he looked around, then stared at me as if weighing my brains and ability at secrecy. "Linc was a medic in Korea. You should hear him talk sometime about all the stuff he did. Operations, even. Lotta stuff he wasn't supposed to do, understand?"

I caught my breath, nodding.

"Dam shame he ain't got the money to go to medical school. Anyways, he's gettin' very edgy, like the shit he pulled this morning."

Stoney's voice got lower, his mouth hardly moving, as if he were practicing ventriloquism. "He's playing it way too close to the vest."

"I see."

"Do you?"

I nodded.

Stoney smiled sadly. "Maybe you do," he sighed, looking at his watch, and downing his last drop of coffee. "Just didn't want you to get the wrong impression. But you'll see what I mean when you work with the man."

He spun the empty cup into the trash.

When I returned to the floor, Gilly, the head nurse, motioned me over.

"Yes."

"Mr. Jacobs, do you know anything about a broken door in the orderlies' locker room?"

"Yes. I saw it when I came in."

"Who did it?" she asked softly, as if I worked with someone named Who.

"I don't know. It was that way when I got there."

She looked at me, then called over to the wardclerk, "Becky, put in a page for Mr. Stoneham."

Three minutes later Stoney strolled down the hall, twirling his stethoscope. "This better be good. I got three people on bedpans, and three more goin' to x-ray in about ten minutes. What's up?''

"The door in the orderlies' locker room. Or should I say, what was once a door.''

Gilly smiled icily, "You wouldn't know anything about that, would you?''

"Not much. Came in, saw a door a little bent out of shape, if that's the one you mean.''

"I'm talking about the door to Lincoln Burns' locker, Mr. Stoneham. The door that is crushed and completely off its hinges,'' Gilly snipped out each word.

I struggled to keep my face as motionless as Stoney's.

"Vandalism?'' Stoney suggested, his dark brown face completely serious.

"I doubt very much if it was vandalism. Very few juvenile delinquents get up at 6:30 in the morning.''

Stoney shook his head. "What's this world comin' to? When I was young, I always made a point of bein' outta the house by 6.''

Gilly ignored him. "And you, Mr. Jacobs, know nothing except it was that way when you arrived?''

"Right.''

"How convenient.''

Stoney sneaked a look at his watch; Gilly saw him. "I'm not finished, Mr. Stoneham.'' We waited.

"Did Lincoln have anything to do with this?''

"Why ask us,'' Stoney shrugged carefully. "Ask him.''

"I will. He doesn't seem to be home at the moment.''

We didn't say anything.

"You wouldn't happen to know where I could reach him, do you?''

Stoney laughed.

Gilly reddened. "Am I missing something?''

Stoney smiled, moving his fingers and staring upwards. "Last count, there was 300 bars in Boston.''

Gilly watched Stoney smile, then pressed her lips primly. "That door is going to cost, Mr. Stoneham. Either the culprit fesses up, or all orderlies will have an amount of money deducted from their next paycheck—as financial remuneration. That's straight from downstairs.''

Stoney stopped smiling. Gilly stared, thin and steady. "That's not so funny, is it?"

"No," Stoney glared, his cheeks puffing up.

"Does that help refresh your memory?"

"Memory of what?"

Gilly stared.

"Look," Stoney said, leaning forward slightly and sticking his finger out, "I didn't have a thing to do with that door, and there had better not be one dime missing from my next check."

"We shall see what we shall see," replied Gilly.

"You can count on it," Stoney shot back.

The rest of the day I saw Gilly stopping people, mainly orderlies and aides, and one male nurse, asking them about the door. In a few hours word spread throughout the hospital.

"So who broke the door man?"

"Don't know. Heard Linc did."

"Can see that. Man's outta his mind."

"Come on. He got a temper, but he ain't that bad. And I'll work with him over anyone 'cept Stoney."

"He may not have a temper? You seen that door?"

"No, you?"

"Yeah."

"What does it look like?"

"I don't know. But it sure don't look like no door no more."

"He's too much."

And on other floors: "Yeah, and if they don't find out who did it, the bread's comin' out of everyone's check. To make things equal."

"Ohh, *now* they talk about things bein' equal, huh?"

"I ain't payin' for nothin'."

"Me neither."

And in the break rooms: "So what do we have to do with it? It happened in the mens' locker room. What's that got to do with us?"

"Not a thing."

"But we gonna have to pay just the same, is that it?"

"That's what they say."

"What who say."

"Downstairs."

"Yeah, well downstairs better lock their doors, they so much as touch my money, honey. They worryin' about broken doors, I'll give 'em somethin' to really worry about they take anything out of my check."

"Yeah. They'll be prayin' broken doors is all they get."

"Mmm, hmmm."

"All cause some hotheaded fool."

"Now, we don't know that."

"Don't we."

"Lincoln's o.k. He just gets outta hand."

"Outta hand? Those doors are all metal, chile. That's more than outta hand. That's one man you don't want to get near."

Toward the end of the day I ran into one of the evening people, Ron, arguing with Stoney and our floor's aide, Thelma.

"Can't you see what they tryin' to run by you," Stoney scowled, arms folded. "Are you blind?"

Ron came right back. "All I know is, there's gonna be some money comin' out of my check. The word is—Linc did it. Now what Linc wants to do here, or at home, that's fine, that's his business. But when his business becomes *my* business, and what's more, when his business starts *costin'* me, well, then that's not fine. That's not fine at all."

Stoney made a face, stubbing out his cigarette. "Well, it would sure be nice if just one person, just one, would stop and ask themselves, why, if it was Linc that done it—and mind you I ain't saying' it is—"

"Sure."

"It would sure be nice if someone just stopped and thought for a minute and asked themselves WHY Linc—if it was him—would get mad enough to kick in that door? Now tell me *you* never felt like that."

Ron was quiet. Thelma moved closer to Stoney. "We all get mad, Sto'. But even if I did get mad enough to demolish some door—and that happens just about every day—I promise you this: I won't leave anyone else holdin' the bag. If someone wants to start some business, they should be able to finish it, without dragging a whole lot of folks into it. Now, tell me that ain't right. Go ahead. Tell me.''

Stoney stood silently, his arms folded.

"And another thing," Ron put in, "if they even so much as thought it was you or me, we'd be out on the street and no questions asked."

Stoney tensed. "What're you tryin' to say?"

"Forget it," Ron said suddenly looking at me. "I'm just mad."

Stoney moved closer to Ron. "No. You wanna say somethin', say it."

"I think you know."

"Well, I ain't too sure about that. You may be right, and you may be wrong."

Ron just looked at Stoney, then at his watch. "Well, I better get crackin'. See you manana."

"Sure," Stoney smiled sourly, "manana," nodding, "Thel," as Thelma walked off. "Hell with it," Stoney said, staring after Ron and Thelma. "I can only do so much. Fuck it."

Down the hall Thelma began heatedly talking with another aide, seeming taller than her five foot two inches; the other aide nodded sympathetically and put in her two cents. Ron hustled past with an armful of linen and I stopped him.

"What if we call Linc up, and tell him what they're doing?"

"Doing what?" Ron snapped.

"Well, like what Stoney was sorta sayin'—how they seem to be playing him off against everybody."

"That's shit. You don't know what you're talkin' about. They just told us what happened. That's all. Don't make it into somethin' more than it is. Ahhh, what am I doin' still talkin' about this shit?" Ron stomped off.

I went down with Stoney to the locker where we washed up in silence. Stoney washed quickly, whistling rapidly like he often whistled when upset.

"You really think they're playing him off against everybody?" I asked, unsure.

Stoney nodded grimly. "Yeah. They'd love to get rid of Linc. Only he's like me—just too fuckin' good, and works his butt off." Stoney snorted. "But I've done all I can. That dumb sonuvabitch really had no fuckin' business gettin' outta hand. It's fine for him to go off smashin' shit up, but then who has to pick up the pieces?"

Stoney toweled himself vigorously.

"We could call him and tell him what's going on."

Stoney exhaled deeply, and started buttoning his shirt. "Son, I been telling people all day what's going on. People been comin' up to me and askin' what's going on since lunchtime. I'm off. I ain't callin' nobody."

"Yeah, nobody has his number probably," I put in, hoping it wasn't true and Stoney had it.

"Yeah, well, Linc kinda keeps to himself."

"Maybe I could look it up in the phonebook."

"Maybe. Lotssa phonebooks around."

"I'll do it," I decided, feeling like I was getting in over my head.

"Fine," Stoney yawned, leaving and not looking back.

Fifteen minutes later I walked into a bar near the hospital. A bunch of old men in suits and middleaged men in work jackets turned and stared. The one woman in the bar served drinks at an improvised dining room table in the back of the bar where some of the neighborhood patriarchs and leading drinkers sat in stuffed lounge chairs. Other than the strange dining room set, it was a standup bar.

"You got a phone, please?" I asked, standing on the rail.

"You hear that?" grinned the bartender. "Please!"

A few of the old men cackled. All nodded approvingly. Some gazed at me like I was a toucan bird just come in from South America.

"Sure, sonny, right over there."

"Right over there" was by the pinball machine where two oldtimers kibbutzed each other.

"You're shooting the balls too fast, Harry. You're not giving yourself enough time now."

"Shutup."

I looked in the phonebook under Burns and found the number right away.

"That's your main flaw, you know Harry. You always been an impatient bastard."

"It's my nickel, so fuckoff."

I dialed. The phone rang once. I almost felt the deep rough voice before I heard it.

"Yeah?"

"Linc?"

"Yeah, who's this?"

"Dov. Remember me?"

"Sure. Well fuckin'A, what the hell are you doing? I mean, how the hell are ya?"

"I'm fine thanks, but—"

"Whatcha got?"

"They're telling everybody at the hospital about the door, and Stoney and me think they're trying to play you off, and Ron even Thelma are pissed as hell, and we tried to explain it all over the place but it's like—"

"Now hold on. There's no one on the line for that phone is there? You callin' from a pay phone, right?"

"Yeah."

"And no one's on line?"

"No one."

"Good. There's no one on line here, either. So why don't you take it nice and slow, and tell me the whole goddam thing."

I told him the "whole goddamn thing". He said nothing, just listened so quietly I wondered if he had dropped the phone, or if we'd been cutoff.

"Hello?"

"I'm here."

"Well."

"Well, shit."

"Well, I thought I'd call you and let you know, seein' how you're off tomorrow."

"Yeah, I'm off."

"Just thought I'd let you know."

"Well, thanks kid. I appreciate it. Really do. Ha, gotta

go to the bank tomorrow, ain't that a bitch? Run around doin' all kind a' fuckin' errands on your day off?''

I began wondering if maybe it was true—maybe everyone was right, and Linc was just crazy.

"They can't give us normal days like everyone else you know. You know I've worked that rathole five fuckin' years and you know what, I got Tuesday and Thursday one week, and Monday and Tuesday the other week and they say I'm lucky cause every week I got Tuesday off. Ain't that a kick in the ass?''

"Great for the social life, huh?''

"No.''

"You're fuckin'A right, no.''

I held the phone, waiting.

"Well, look kid. Appreciate the call. Say, how much do you think that goddam door's gonna cost them?''

I shrugged, "Oh, I'm not good at this stuff. Sixty dollars? A hundred?''

Linc whistled.

There was a silence again. I wondered if I should offer to loan Linc some money. But I hardly knew him.

"So I suppose it's all over the place, huh?''

"Yeah.''

There was a silence again. I decided to chance it. "If you want, I can loan you some money.''

"Shit. You just met me. Besides, if I want a fuckin' loan, I'll ask,'' Linc growled.

"Uh huh.''

"Look, I gotta go. I got some food on the stove, and it's startin' to stink up the place. My food's bad enough without me lettin' it burn up, o.k.?''

"Yeah.''

"And don't worry. Everything's gonna be fine.''

"Yeah.''

"You bet. See ya soon.''

"Right.''

"So long.''

"Bye.''

I saw Linc sooner than I thought. The next day just at

the shift change, Linc strolled in. He looked different in streetclothes, without the orderly whites. He wore a leather jacket, a soft blue shirt, new blue dungarees, and worn dark brown boots. On his wrist was a beautiful silver scrolled watch that he caught me staring at.

"My grandfather gave this to my father who gave it to me. I wear it on special occasions," Linc laughed, winking.

"What are you doing here?"

"Can't stay away," he winked, clutching his breast. "Got a few things to take care of. First, let's go say hello to the folks."

I got the strong feeling Linc wanted to avoid running into Gilly as he quickly ducked into the cancer ward. I began introducing him to the patients, "Linc, this is Tim Slattery. Tim has a real bad leg—". I stopped, as I suddenly realized that everyone was politely smiling at me. Linc laughed and slapped me on the back.

"Hey kid, I know all these fuckin' goldbricks. I know Slattery, I know Reiner shammin' the bad lungs when everyone knows he's hidin' out from his father-in-law cause he owes him money."

"Up yours," Reiner smiled sweetly.

"Devlin over there—he really is a little sick, and O'Reilly and Ed are just two old farts who think they know how to play chess."

I stood there with my mouth hanging open, astonished at Linc's mockery of the patients, mentally re-listing the severity of their illnesses. Slattery's thrombophlebitis was so bad he'd thrown one clot to his lungs already; Reiner's chronic pleurisy had grown into multiple lung biopsies; Devlin had multiple sclerosis so severe he often shuddered uncontrollably. Not to mention the two cancer patients— O'Reilly with half a bladder and Ed with a malignant throat. All the men had had major operations; Ed alone had gone through twelve grafts to his throat over a three year period.

I turned angrily towards Linc then noticed that all the patients had perked up—Reiner and Slattery waving, Devlin laughing weakly, Ed muttering, "How ya been, young fella?" and O'Reilly sneering and clearing his throat. I raised my eyebrows: O'Reilly loathed most people, usually staring in glum silence, tolerating a few here and there with scowls and mutters, and only on very rare occasions, sneering and speaking. He looked at Linc and cleared his throat again.

"Jesus, look at him, will ya. He's in civies. Almost looks human."

"Real comedian," Linc remarked.

"Thought you was like the vampires," O'Reilly jeered. "Thought you only came out at night."

"You thought nothing of the kind, you old fuck. I don't think you've thought anything in the last ten years. Your brain's pickled in whiskey and gambling schemes. That's why your pecker's so bad—drinkin' and screwin' and runnin' around."

"Hooooo—look at the pot callin the kettle black now," chuckled O'Reilly. "Why I'll be thinkin' more thoughts when I'm six feet under than yourself from the day you was born til the Apocalypse itself."

"You ain't going into the ground," Linc shot back. "That's the devil's joint. And he told me himself, 'If I let that sonuvabitch O'Reilly in here, I'm gonna be out of a job'."

The ward cracked up. O'Reilly tried hard to feign indignance. Linc sat down on his bed and peeked at the gallon bottle connected to his catheter which contained O'Reilly's urine. The half full bottle was blood red.

"So how you doin?"

"Same."

"That's what I like to hear about you. Don't have to worry."

Linc tapped O'Reilly in the arm, then rose and studied the room.

"Well, all you loafers look all right. I'll see ya later."

"How come you come in today?" asked Devlin, wincing slightly.

"Wanted to check it out. I might transfer back to days."

"Oh shit," Slattery groaned, "now we're in for it."

"That's right," Linc laughed, " 'cause if I get back here on days, I'm gonna make you bastards work. You ain't gonna lie on your asses all day and bother the ladies tryin' to make a livin'. The joyride's gonna end, but fast, Sergeant Burns is gonna drill you. Get the flab off. Get the flab off fatsos like Ed here.''

Linc slapped the siderails on Ed's bed. Ed, five foot two inches and ninety pounds, grinned weakly, his neck heavily bandaged from his latest skin graft. "Heh, heh, just watch who you calling fatso, pal.''

Just then Stoney walked in. "Hey Dov, it's time to—'' He stopped, spotting Linc. "Well look what we got here.''

"Hi.''

"What the hell you doin' here on your day off. You're crazier than I thought.''

"Gotta see some folks about some things,'' Linc winked.

"Well, what are you waitin' for,'' Stoney smiled, his eyes gleaming in anticipation.

I followed them out, puzzled.

We walked into the nurses' break room where most of the day shift and the evening shift sat amidst a shuffle of papers, coffee cups, clipboards, charts, and index cards in leather casings. There was a general intake of breath on Linc's entrance, as well as an ensuing hush. Gilly rose, frowning.

"Can we help you with something, Mr. Burns?''

"I heard alot of people are upset about a door that was broken in the orderlies' locker room. I busted it, so I'm here to pay for it.''

Linc reached into his shirt pocket and brought out a black wallet, peeling off a wad of bills. Someone whistled. Linc reached into his right pants pocket; it jangled heavily, loaded with change.

"Ha—I just hope if I'm ever busted up and broken, people get this upset over me, ha ha ha,'' Linc laughed, harsh, short, then stopped abruptly. "So how much is it?''

Gilly stared at Linc, her lips tight. "This is overdramatic and inappropriate.''

"I don't think so. I heard people say a door was broken. I heard the money for it was gonna come out of everyone's check. I heard everyone was highly upset. Don't blame 'em. I'm just here to straighten everything out. So, how much?''

Gilly flipped papers on her clipboard, and squinted. "Seventy-nine dollars and eighty-nine cents."

Linc peeled off three twenties, a ten, a five, and four ones. He jangled his pants and came out with a fistful of silver and dealt out three quarters, a dime and four pennies.

"Right on the nose," he grinned. "I give it to you— that way I know it's in good hands."

"Thank you, Lincoln," Gilly smiled thinly. "Let's hope it doesn't happen again."

"At eighty bucks, let's hope so."

"I'll have the wardclerk write you a receipt."

"Fine," Linc smiled.

Everyone breathed a sigh of relief as Gilly started packing up, the signal for the meeting's end. Then Linc touched Gilly's arm. She jumped. "One more thing."

"What, Mr. Burns?" Gilly sighed, exasperated. "I'd like to get home if that's all right with you."

"Where's my door?"

"What?"

"My door. I paid for it. I want it."

"It's, it's, well, it's probably down in the basement, if it hasn't been taken to the dump yet. Look in the broken equipment area. That's the best place I can think of. Good night."

The floor emptied out, the dayshift going home and the swing shift beginning their afternoon work. Some people waved to Linc; others ignored him.

Thelma looked at Linc and shook her head. "Lincoln, you are something ELSE."

"Thelma baby, the only time I'd make you pay for something I did is if I took you out on the town and blew all my money and you wanted something and I didn't have my checkbook with me."

"Listen to him," Thelma laughed wryly.

Ron was studying Linc. "What you gonna do with a broken door, man?"

"I don't know," Linc shrugged. "Maybe I'll make a cocktail table out of it, and have you all over for drinks. You can drink on my hand made table. Rare—only one of its kind."

Ron laughed.

"Then again, maybe I'll give it to some wino to live under."

Thelma shook her head.

"Or," continued Linc, "I could throw some ketchup on the fucker, and have an exhibition. A one-man show. Call it Blood Of A Bent-Out-Of-Shape Lamb. Only 500 bucks, and cheap at the price. Or I could call it Untitled But Thinking Real Hard. Or 500 Degrees Fahrenheit, or some bullshit like that."

"500 Bedpans," I giggled.

"And then again," Linc smiled, his eyes darkening, "I might just throw it into the first garbage can I can find."

"Now you're talkin'," Stoney said.

"Main thing is—it's mine, and I can do whatever I want with it, and I'm takin' it outta here."

"Need some help?" Stoney asked.

"Nah," Linc grinned, "besides, I don't want any of you to get a rep for bein' crazy. I want to carry it outta here all by myself. I'm gonna walk real slow, and savor the sonuvabitch. And I hope that everyone that had the slightest doubt about me is standin' at the windows gettin' neckstrain."

Linc kept his word. Me, Thelma, and Stoney went down with him to the basement where he found his door. We stood outside on the hospital entrance steps in the crisp autumn air, watching and laughing a little.

Linc carried the crushed door on his head, his raised arms perfectly balanced, his body happily erect and gently swaggering. Every five steps his right arm gripped the door tighter, and his left arm waved magnanimously at the hospital. We watched him until we couldn't see him, until even his loud harsh laughter accompanying the waving slid into the late afternoon's cold air and dark brown-orange leaves.

Gersh

I first heard about Gersh when Stoney filled me in Monday morning. "Well I hope you had two nice days off, son, 'cause we got a treat for you today."

"Uh oh," I winced.

"This one's about as fucked up as you can get, boy. Cancer of the ass, plus he fell down some stairs, and broke his elbow and messed up his hip. Hard to turn 'cause he got a long-arm cast on. Don't take pain too well—you sneeze and he's dyin'. One more thing—he's incontinent."

"Well, we've had patients like that before," I said, trying to sound nonchalant like I'd worked there ten years like Stoney instead of three months like me.

"You don't understand, little friend. This one shits like rabbits eat carrots—whenever and wherever. Hardly knows he's doin' it. But *you* know. Your *nose* knows. I mean, until you take care of this man, you don't know what incontinent is." Stoney smiled, his dark brown skin crinkling; his brown-grey eyes serious, sympathetic.

I didn't say anything, beginning to feel weighted down, staring at the ward clock reaching 6:58. I pictured the hands at 6:58 p.m.—I'd be home three hours, eating supper. Stoney lit up a cigarette, checked his watch, then exhaled. "And what's more, you got to bathe the man, feed the man, plus keep on changing him. You got to do it all. And better make sure the door's shut so everyone out here don't have to be running to the john holding their mouths. And be real careful. You move him half an inch the wrong way and he screams. Sometimes he screams in English. Other times he screams in Jewish talk—watcha call it—"

"Yiddish."

"Yeah. Sometimes I swear he's cursin' me out in Yiddish."

"Some damn good swear words in Yiddish."

"Yeah? Well, he knows 'em all, and then some. And he's hurtin' enough to make up a whole messa new ones, that's for damn sure."

"Sounds like it," I said.

Gersh was in a private room. I dreaded going in, so I just breezily opened the door and gasped. The room smelled chock full of rotting vegetables mixed with hair-spray, rubbing alcohol, and old towels. There was a faint touch of mint and lemon. I recognized the lemon and the hair-spray as the Lemon Chiffon spray we used to "freshen" rooms. On the crumpled bed of twisted blankets and sheets lay an old man with a long chin and irritable grey eyes. His skin, urine-yellow, shone dully. His head was bald like a baby sparrow. His chest was lean and hairless. Although his shoulders were broad, the pale yellow flesh hung loosely goose-pimpled, like the flesh on chicken wings. His eyes, alert and alive, clutched at me. "Orderly," he gasped.

"Yes?"

"Orderly, I want some water."

I quickly went to the sink, grabbed his water glass from his night-stand, washed it out, then filled it full of cool water.

"Give," he whispered, holding out his hand, sitting up slightly, revealing a huge plaster cast on his left elbow. He tried to make himself comfortable by supporting himself on his good shoulder and turning his casted arm to the side as he offered up his good arm to take the glass.

"Here you go," I said, handing him the glass. His hand shook, sloshing the water onto the twisted blankets, sheets, and his pajamas. Not a drop went into his mouth. His good hand shook trying to hold onto the glass. I poured another glass, sat down on the bed, and, tilting his head, let his lips touch the water.

"Ahhh," he whispered. He opened his mouth wider. I poured the water slowly down his throat. He still had sleepy-crust in his eyes. I wiped his chin with a washcloth. The sun was now out, warming up the room. Gersh blinked, his lids heavy like pale walnut halves. He smiled as the last water slid down the hatch.

"Goot. Goot," he whispered.

"More?"

"No no. Enough. Fine. Thank you."

"You're welcome."

"Your name?"

"Dov. Dov Jacobs. I'll be taking care of you today."

"Where is the Negro man?" Gersh asked.

"Stoney? He's around," I said, seeing him smile. "Want a bath today?"

"No, not today. I did not sleep well. Later maybe."

"How about some breakfast?"

"Eh?"

"Breakfast. This is a new week. What we do is we fill out menus for the week. Want me to help you?"

He stared, wheezing. I wondered if he was also hard of hearing.

"Yes," he whispered, "you do it." He lay back on his pillow.

"Sure." I took out the menu card, and began reading to see what he preferred. "O.k. I tell you what. Why don't we take it one day at a time. Today for breakfast we have oatmeal and fruit, or scrambled eggs and bacon, or—"

"Feh! No! No pork."

"Oh, o.k. Or a Western omelette."

"Western? What's that?"

"It's good. Eggs and lots of vegetables."

He made a face. "Does it have pork?"

"I don't think so."

"Find out. Maybe I'll try it. And get some salt. This place, they think salt is gold."

I made a mental note to see if he was on a salt-free diet. He sat up slightly, gesturing.

"Would a pinch of salt hurt anything? You'd think at seventy-four I could have a little salt. Is that so much to ask?" he whined, grabbing my arm. Suddenly he made a face, his lip curling, his eyes looking away from me.

"Oh-oh, orderly, uh-oh."

I reached quickly for the cabinet by the bed that contained a bedpan, and tried to stick it under him just as I heard the plop-plop-plop-plapibbleplapibble.

A dense smell of rotting vegetables filled the room; the sheets looked full of chocolate ice-cream. Gersh clenched his mouth, the bottom of his cheeks twisting, "Aiii-yeeeee." The stench hit me in the face: I gagged.

"Oii-gevalt," Gersh moaned, "Ohhhh. Again and again."

I turned him over and wiped his ass with some toilet paper. He moaned. I turned him quickly, lifting. His hip bunked the night-table—he howled as if I'd stuck him with a foot-long needle.

"OY VAYERZ ME A OY," his whole face winced.

"Sorry," I gasped. I tried to pretend I was swimming underwater, holding my breath for as long as I could. I tried turning him back slowly, trying to hold his cast carefully and push him with my shoulder. The cast felt like it weighed a ton.

"Oh," he murmured. On pure reflex, he clenched his teeth, but since he had no teeth, his dentures clacked. The smell grew stronger: I eased out the bedpan. He moved suddenly, tipping the pan onto the sheets and part of my hand, filling the sheets with stinking warm chocolate ice-cream.

"Shit!" I muttered, wanting to run and not look at his

shit on the sheets and the blanket. I washed my hand vigorously, gasping. Then I put the pan on the night-table, and propped him up against his pillows.

"Hold on, Mr. Gerson, I'll be right back."

He studied me through his wincing, his eyes anxiously measuring me.

"Don't go away," I smiled, trying not to gag.

His face sweated slightly.

I whisked out of the room looking for Stoney. He was on the main ward where they put some of the poorest patients —winos and men found lying on the street or in transient rooms. I could hear his voice needling the long and short terms. At that second I wished I could trade anything I had so I could work the ward and switch with Stoney for as long as Gersh stayed in the hospital. Stoney's voice dominated the room: "If you clowns don't like the food here, you can go someplace else. No, we don't got no T-bones, and we don't got no Jack Daniels. When you chumps gonna get smart and start gettin' into the scrumptious cuisine around here? Chow down on these wonderful powdered scrambled eggs and these cereal specials. We got hot and cold. My kid loves Frosted Flakes. Says the Tiger's real friendly. I know you can't eat friendship, who's askin' you to? Now, hey, that's kinda, you know—you oughta go up there to Harvard soon as they throw you outa here for malingerin' and show those professors up there just what it's all about—I mean you're pretty sharp for an old rumbucket. What? No, that ain't Friday's bacon. It's as fresh as guess who's underwear." Laughter filled the ward, hearty laughter, wheezing laughter. Stoney strolled out, clutching a handful of menus, his head turned over his shoulder, "Be back in five minutes, and I want the rest of these suckers filled out."

"How's things?" I asked, adding, "Got a minute?"

"How's things?" Stoney mimicked, "Don't you mean, help me with that old man who can't hold nothin' in? Sure I got a minute. Got nothin' but time."

"Thanks."

"Now that I got all them winos in there to decide what their Highnesses want. You know," Stoney frowned, lowering his voice, "just between me and you, son, I wouldn't feed my dog the shit they serve here."

"Yeah," I agreed.

"And you know what else?" Stoney said, leaning closer. "What?"

"I don't even got a dog."

I laughed. Stoney nudged me.

"And you know why I don't got a dog?"

"Why?" I laughed, looking around to see if the head nurse was on the floor yet.

" 'Cause my landlord told me, 'You're lucky to get a place outside of Roxbury. So don't push your luck.' "

He smiled broadly, but his eyes studied me. I didn't laugh. He punched me in the shoulder. "Let's go see what's what with Pops."

I nodded.

When Gersh saw Stoney he smiled.

"Ahh, it's you," Gersh wheezed.

"Yeah, it's me again," Stoney said, pulling back the covers. "and," he sniffed, looking down, "it's you again."

Gersh shrugged sadly.

"O.k.," Stoney said briskly, "now what we're gonna do is you're gonna slowly lift him up and grab his good elbow and his good hip, and I'll clean him up right quick then slide a donut underneath his butt so we can turn him more easily and get these shitted-up sheets outta here."

"Why the donut?" I asked.

"Did he scream when you moved him?"

"Yeah."

"When you lift him up, check out his butt."

I lifted him up. Stoney wiped Gersh quickly, professionally. Gersh moaned, "Oy VAY. OY GEVALT."

"You hurtin', grampa?" Stoney said.

"AHH AHH OOO!"

"Yeah," Stoney wiped quickly, "You hurt like hell."

"Don't touch," Gersh moaned, "Don't touch. Ahhhii." He was sweating more, a trickle dripped halfway down his cheek.

"O.k. kid, now look at his asshole. Quick."

Looking, I saw a bright-red circular wound the size of a half-dollar.

"That's a bad one."

"Know why he hurt so much?"

"Why?" I shrugged, as Stoney, not even waiting, murmured, " 'Cause inside his whole asshole is like it's covered with them fuckin' things."

I winced.

"O.k." Stoney signalled, "now on three you turn him towards me and lift up on the donut and I'll grab him and take him and you get the rest of the sheets, bag 'em, then grab those clean ones on the table and start 'em on your side. Then I'll give him back to you and finish the bed on this side. One—"

I lifted Gersh up gingerly, firmly holding onto his good elbow and hip, turning.

"Two—"

"Ohhhhh," Gersh moaned.

"Three." I pushed Gersh toward a grabbing Stoney who took the weight. I grabbed the filthy sheets and rolled them up and stuck them in the dirty linen bag along with the dirty blankets. Then I grabbed the clean bottom sheet, put it on the bed, tucked in my side, then rolled it up so Stoney could unroll it once I took Gersh back to my side of the bed.

"Ahhhh," Gersh groaned.

"You don't hurt that much now," Stoney crooned. "You don't hurt that bad. C'mon now, it's almost over."

I took Gersh back, lifted up the donut, as he bunked against the nighttable, banging his casted arm as Stoney quickly unrolled the sheet and finished tucking it in.

"AIEEEE," Gersh moaned.

"Nearly done. You don't hurt. That was nothin'. Nothin'," Stoney panted.

Gersh breathed deep, whispering, "Water."

I gave him some water as Stoney finished up the bed with a new top sheet and new blanket. He then fluffed up Gersh's pillows.

"How's that? Feel like a new man?"

Gersh nodded weakly, his face glum.

"Good," Stoney said, nudging me, his voice lower, "Come outside a minute."

Outside the room Stoney put his hands on his hips.

"Well, wha'd I tell you?"

I nodded. My chest felt moist through my uniform. I started taking the dirty bag out. Stoney punched me lightly.

"Let's wash up some."

"Thanks a whole lot, Stoney."

"Go on," he scoffed. We washed up and he leaned against the sink, smoking a Camel.

"Thanks again."

"Go on. I'm gonna finish this smoke."

Half an hour later I fed Gersh oatmeal and orange juice. He didn't like the oatmeal, but I found some raisins in a package left by his family and put the raisins in the oatmeal. He liked what he could eat. I spooned it into his toothless gullet. He greedily smacked his lips, murmuring, "Goot. Goot." And suddenly his face changed again. His mouth opened, surprised, a little exasperated, as if he was tiredly re-rehearsing lines for a bizarre play.

"Oh-oh, orderly, oh-oh!"

I moved to grab the bedpan I'd replaced, but it was too late to even try to slip it under him.

"Shit," I cursed, "God-dammit. Fuck!" I caught his eyes looking at me angrily, hurt.

"Oooooooi yuy yuy," he groaned. "Ooooi."

"O.k. now, easy does it," I said. "I want you to move over a little."

He lay there, not moving an inch.

"*Move!*" I ordered, pushing on his good hip and arm.

"Oyyyy," he said, not budging. The stench almost felt like a hand squeezing me.

I went to find Stoney. He was nowhere in sight. I saw Thelma, an aide.

"Thel, where's Stoney?"

"He's up on seven. They needed him to help put up an oxygen tent."

"Jesus, can't they put up their own fucking tent?"

"Easy, Dov. I didn't send him up there, you know? I didn't know what and where, you know?"

"Sorry, Thelma."

"Need some help with that poor old man down the hall? C'mon."

As we walked down the hall, I felt bad, like a spoiled brat, studying Thelma, so small and wiry, willing to help when she had ten patients of her own.

As we moved Gersh, I could see her muscles straining when she turned him, her motions quick, nearly effortless, quiet.

"Thanks," I said, tying up the dirty bags.

"No problem, Dov," she smiled. "You've done the same for me. It's just the easy way to do things."

"Well thanks anyway. He's not easy."

"He's easy," Thelma smiled, adding, "It's his family what's the hassle."

I met the family after lunch. They arrived just as I returned from my break. Three women and two men—Mrs. Gersh, her son, daughter, and in-laws.

Mrs. Gersh—"Hello, I'm Esther Gerson, Zev's wife"—was a small woman, barely five feet with enormous forearms carrying a bag full of food, smelling like chicken and honey-cake. She wore a simple dark blue dress under a well made grey coat. She wore a silver wedding ring and strong black shoes. Her daughter, Naomi, dressed simply too. Under her fur coat she wore a wine-colored dress and matching high-heels. Naomi, definitely Gersh's daughter, had the same sharp grey eyes. Her husband was introduced by Mrs. Gersh as Herschel, who smiled, "It's Hank, you can call me Hank." Hank was in sales. I felt like saying I was in oars. I also rubbed my fingers from his handshake. Hank looked like he should wear a captain's hat with a gold anchor instead of the fedora that didn't go with the brown and orange plaid sport jacket with wide lapels and deep blue pants. I smiled to myself: he was definitely out to sea.

"Where is Mr. Stoneham?" Mrs. Gersh asked.

"He's here. He's helping out on what they call 'The House.' He goes all over."

Mrs. Gersh nodded seriously, "There's a great deal to do."

"Yes," I nodded. "So I'm taking care of your husband." The word husband for Gersh seemed somehow strange to me.

"And how is he?" she asked, her face tightening, "How is he today?"

"Good. He ate breakfast."

"And did it stay?" she asked, unblinking.

"Some of it did," I nodded, hoping I looked hopeful.

Mrs. Gersh studied my face, smiling. "How old are you?"

"Eighteen."

"Ahh," she smiled, "you're young." She turned toward Naomi and Hank and said, "Wait here a minute. I'm going in to see him for a little bit—just me. All right?"

"Of course Ma," Naomi smiled.

"Whatever you want Esther," Hank piped in, "just say the word."

I opened the door for Mrs. Gersh. The stench hit our faces, almost like a nasal archway where you ducked under as you entered the room, automatically crouching. Gersh tried to rise, smiling as much as he could with all his pain. His smile spread through his face, his toothless mouth looking like a small black-red canoe.

"Ha!" Mrs. Gersh gleamed, brushing past me—surprisingly spright — moving to the bedside.

"Nice," Gersh wheezed happily. "you look very nice." His eyes gobbled her up.

"You like?"

He grinned.

"Guess what I brought you?" she said, putting down the bag next to the Lemon Chiffon spray.

"Vhat?"

She reached into the bag and raised up a large bowl. "Chicken like you like: paprika."

"Ahh," Gersh cried, his fingers stretching to clap his hands, wincing, then smiling again.

"And honeycake."

"You're a gem," Gersh pronounced.

"Annnnnd, a present. And not more flowers either—" She reached into the bag and produced a beautifully ribboned purple pink box with mahogany colored squares flying through a beautiful sky full of green leaves and brown birds. "Denise went to New York and I made a special point of asking her to get this box for me. It's Barton's chocolate cherries. Your favorite."

"Wonderful," Gersh smiled. "Come sit," he added, patting the sheet next to him. He took a deep breath, tired, content.

"So how's things?" Mrs. Gersh smiled, smoothing a place on the bed next to him, looking all over his face, his shoulders, chest, nightclothes.

"Things are things," Gersh smiled weakly. "Me, I feel terrible."

She nodded, running her hands through her hair, smoothing it.

"This is Dov, Esther. A very nice young man."

"We met."

"Look," I said, "I've got to see some of my other patients, but if you need me, I won't be far away."

"Don't worry," Mrs. Gersh smiled. "After forty-three years I can handle anything where this one's concerned."

Gersh made a face, debating whether or not to debate her. As I left, the two other relatives appeared—Gersh's son Joseph and his wife Judy. Joseph smoked a pipe and dressed in a tweed suit with a very expensive rust cashmere turtleneck similar to the black one Judy wore with her tweed jumper full of charcoal grey with orange, white, green and yellow dots. Trenchcoats draped over both of their arms. The pipe smoke puffed daintily around Joseph's neatly trimmed beared. He kept checking his watch. I noticed a frostiness between Mr. and Mrs. Hank and the Tweeds. They barely nodded to each other. Mr. and Mrs. Tweed nodded at Hank and Naomi. They nodded back. Joseph and Naomi looked at each other with a tense sadness. Hank shuffled his feet.

"So you managed to get away from your classes, Joe?"

Joseph nodded. His wife glared at Hank.

"He'll be glad to see you," Hank remarked.

"Stop it, Hank," Naomi warned.

"Look, don't think for a minute that just because you come here every single day that...that..." Judy stammered.

"It's o.k., honey," Joseph puffed, "it's o.k."

"Look everybody," pleaded Naomi, "Let's take it easy for once and not fight. Hank?"

Hank cleared his throat, then stayed quiet. He saw me: his face got smaller.

"You got something to say, kid?" he asked, frowning.

"No."

I left to check my other patients. I gave some baths to a few patients. The rooms warmed up in the autumn sun. I returned to check Gersh—the foursome still stood outside the room.

"Kids in school?" Hank asked.

"Mm," Joseph puffed.

"Why ask a question you already know the answer to, Hank?" Judy said.

"Oh nothing," Hank mumbled.

"Jude, stop it," Joseph puffed.

"You never say anything for nothing," Judy snapped. "Talk is money, isn't it Hank?"

"Stop," Joseph puffed mildly, calmly watching his wife and brother-in-law.

"Come on now," Naomi pleaded.

"If you're so worried about the fucking will, *adopt* some kids," Judy hissed.

Joseph's eyes gleamed, then hooded over calmly. Hank took out a pack of spearmint gum, furiously unwrapped two pieces, and stuck them in his mouth, chewing vigorously. "You got it all wrong, Jude. You really got me all wrong. I've been here every—"

"I know how much you've been here," Judy interrupted. "That's wonderful."

"You're interrupting me again."

"Stop it! Both of you just stop it this goddam minute,"

Naomi yelled, nearly crying.

"Nome," Joseph puffed, awkwardly sticking his arm around his sister's shoulders.

"It's bad enough when the others are here," Naomi wept. "But us—"

"It's o.k.," Joseph puffed, holding her stiffly, "it's o.k."

Just then Mrs. Gersh walked out of the room, her soft smile changing abruptly.

"Honestly," she frowned, "I leave you alone for two minutes and you're at each others' throats."

"Sorry Ma," Joseph said.

"Sorry," Judy added.

Hank and Naomi nodded.

"I don't want you to be sorry," Mrs. Gersh said. "I want you to think of something other than yourselves for more than five minutes. It has been done. Other people do it on occasion. You don't have to be an Einstein to know that."

They looked down at the floor. No one spoke. Mrs. Gersh looked from face to face, then down, then up.

"So what's so pretty about linoleum all of a sudden?"

"Nothing," Hank smiled. "In fact it's ugly."

Mrs. Gersh made a motion as if to strike her forehead, halted in mid-air, and pretended to fix her hat as she motioned Joseph and Naomi over.

"Look, go in and try to act civilized. Naomichka, why don't you and Herschel go first. Then Joseph and Judy. O.k. Now that's settled: let's all try and act like a family."

She sniffed, opened her purse, took out a handkerchief, and blew her nose.

"Ma," Joseph said, touching her arm.

"Go on. I'm fine. It's chilly here."

I entered the room with Hank and Naomi.

"Hi Pa," Naomi smiled, "How are you?"

"Ahhh," Gersh smiled, "much better. How couldn't I be better when my daughter comes to see me?"

Hank smiled, reaching into his jacket pocket.

"Look here, Pa," he grinned.

"Not now, Hank," said Naomi.

"Oh come on. Lookit, Pa."

"What's this?"

"My new card. My promotion, remember? I'm now assistant vice president in charge of sales. My own office. I'll be home more."

"I see. So you call yourself Hank now?"

Hank's face reddened suddenly.

"Something wrong with Herschel?"

"No."

"So why not Herschel?"

Hank pretended to adjust the many flower arrangements on the night-table.

"Now c'mon, Pa," Naomi crooned, "let's try and have a nice time. Look what I brought you." She lay down a package of homemade fruitcake. "Ahh!" Gersh said. "Wonderful." He fingered the calling card absent-mindedly, his forehead sweating.

"Orderly."

"Yes, Mr. Gerson?" I said, trying to remember to call him Mr. Gerson in front of his family.

"Get me some water, orderly. Not from this sink. Get it from where Mr. Stoneham gets it. He brings very good water. Clean. That sink, I think something's wrong with it. It's too near some sewer." He turned slightly, scrutinized his son-in-law, then lay back wheezing.

"Tired, Pa?" Naomi asked cautiously, turning toward Hank and me, smiling. "He looks tired, doesn't he?"

I nodded, wondering where to go to get Gersh water, hoping he'd fall asleep and forget until I asked Stoney where "clean" water was.

"Maybe this is too much for him. Maybe we shouldn't all come at once. What do you think?"

I shrugged.

"You work here. How is it usually done?"

"It varies," I explained. "Most people sort of uh, feel their way. You know."

"You think we should leave?" Hank blurted, about to pop a Barton's chocolate cherry into his mouth and staring at it. "Think we're wearing him out?"

"No," I said carefully, "I just mean people just play it by ear. I mean, uh, you know him better than I do. You know," I said, trying to smile at Naomi who seemed friendlier, "family's the best judge."

"Judge?" Hank frowned.

"Judge of what?" Naomi snapped.

"Well, you can best figure out how tired your father is. That's all I mean. You've, uh, known him longer, and, uhh," I paused, wondering if I shouldn't just shut up.

"And what?" Hank persisted.

"And, uhh, you probably know what's better right now for your, uh, father, than me, as far as how he's, uh, doing in terms of people coming in and seeing him."

"He's not doing so hot," Naomi said. "Any moron with an I.Q. of ten can see that."

"But he's gonna be all right," Hank nodded. "He's gonna be just fine."

"Oh Jesus!" Naomi sighed.

I kept quiet. I washed out Gersh's water glass, then rearranged the food on the night-table, putting aside the dying flower arrangements sent by friends and relatives and going sweetly stale.

Suddenly Gersh sat up, muttering, "Oh-oh!"

"What is it, Pa? What?"

I dashed over to the cabinet, grabbed the bedpan just as the loud popping went off—like a bubble-gum machine gun —plopplipplopplipplopplip, with the smell of rotting meat filling the room.

"Maybe we better go outside," Naomi mumbled, trying not to gag.

Hank was already clutching his collar and heading for the door, muttering, "Right." He opened the door, took his wife's hand, and straightening his tie, smiled, "Let's let the orderly do his job and stay out of his way. That's the best help we can give right now."

I slid the pan under Gersh as the machine-gun of bubble-gum splattered again, the sheets full of chocolaty ice-cream and warm as I struggled to keep Gersh steady on the pan. He twisted uncomfortably. I gripped him. He tried to grit his mouth and hold his pain in, couldn't, and howled. I heard the plopplipplop with the stench thicker than ever. I grabbed for the Lemon Chiffon spray, trying to hold Gersh steady, and sprayed a little. The only thing that smelled worse than the spray was the stench. Gersh grabbed on to my chest, muttering, "Eeeeeeech! Oy!" and the spray can dropped to the floor as my arm bunked against the night-table and knocked off several bags and boxes.

"Ohh," Gersh moaned.

"Easy, easy," I said, lifting him up by putting my shoulder into his armpit, wiping him with a towel, and hoping no one would come in and see me wiping him with a towel. His eyes looked at me, and then at the floor. He scowled.

"My Kendy!"

"In a second," I gasped, struggling to keep him upright, remove the pan, then clean him up. He kept pointing to the floor, "My Kendy! My Kendy!"

"O.k. o.k." I gasped, "I'll get your goddam candy in a minute." I gasped again, and tried to imagine myself underwater as I tried to put the bedpan into a bag like we'd been told to do especially when visitors were around—recalling the words, "After all, it's not very pleasant for visitors to suddenly have to be confronted with the sight of a bedpan; well, we don't have to draw anyone here a picture now, do we?" Stoney, who was watching the training session, stepped forward and snorted, "Yeah, that's fine and dandy with a full staff, but we ain't got that. Besides, this is a hospital—it ain't the Hilton. I mean some of these people are all grown up, have kids and grandkids and shit themselves so what's the big dif? I mean it may be in a bag, but they can still smell it. Visitors people too you know. They know what the hell's goin' on, so why bullshit them all the time?" And the head nurse, eyeing Stoney like she'd eyed him every time he contradicted her—which was pretty close to all the time—smiled like she wanted to bite him, saying, "Well people have very different reactions to illness, Mr. Stoneham, as I'm sure you're well aware of. Here at the hospital we often tend to forget that not everyone is as accustomed and experienced as someone like yourself in dealing with these, er, matters, particularly in treating the terminally ill, being around them, and engaging in the many thankless and unpleasant chores we all go through.'' And Stoney muttering underneath his breath, so low only me and Thelma heard, ''Ain't that a kick in the ass? What you mean, bitch, you ain't given a bedpan in eight years. Ain't given an enema in ten.'' Adding louder, ''Don't worry about me doing my job.''

I bagged the bedpan just as Stoney showed me, tying the bag with two garbage ties so that as much as possible the smell would be lessened for the second it took to take out and dump. The stench in the room grew greater. I gasped, gagging. I grabbed for the Lemon Chiffon spray and squeezed. It was empty. Gersh angrily pointed to the floor with his good skinny arm, shaking. ''My Kendy!''

I threw the Lemon Chiffon can into the trash can, then reached down, got the candy, and put it back on the night-stand. Several chocolates were squashed: I could smell the cherry and the chocolate and the shit. I felt like my cheeks were gonna vomit. Gersh lay back smiling. I wanted to hit him on his bald sparrow head with the box of "Kendy." I stared at him, trying to imagine how he'd look with chocolate cherries leaking down his cheeks. He'd sit there stunned. Maybe he'd cry. As soon as I pictured him crying, the picture stopped.

''Thank you, orderly,'' Gersh nodded slowly, ''thank you.''

''You want some candy?'' I asked.

''No. No.'' He lay back, tired, waving his hands, ''Sleep.''

''No more visitors for a while?''

''No. Sleep.''

''Let me clean you up first.'' He was so used to the smell of shit and his illness, he could have slept right then and there. His head flopped drowsily.

I bagged the dirty linen and left the room. Mrs. Gersh toddled towards me.

''Thank you. Take care of my Zev.''

''That's what I'm here for,'' I smiled, wiping my forehead with the sleeve of my uniform.

"How is he now?"

"Sleeping."

"I'll just look in real quickly," Joseph muttered, stepping into the room before I could open my mouth. Just as quickly he came out, his nostrils quivering slightly. "We'll come back later," Joseph said, steadily looking at his wife Judy, "later when he's not so tired."

"You could wait a little while," Mrs. Gersh suggested, "I'm sure he'd love to see you, Joey."

"We'll be back later," Joseph repeated, trying to relight his pipe, checking the clock with his eyes while his mouth sucked on the pipe-stem.

"We're off," Naomi smiled, letting Hank help her into her coat.

"He's not looking too bad," Hank grinned.

"Goodbye, Ma," Naomi pouted, her lips wetly touching her mother's cheek.

"I'll call you later, Naomichka," Mrs. Gersh nodded.

"Ma," Joseph said, holding his pipe in the air while he pecked his mother's forehead.

"Try to be nice now. All of you," Mrs. Gersh said, holding Joseph tightly.

"O.k. Mom. Let's go," Hank said.

"I can drive her. We brought both cars," Judy said.

"It's on the way. No problem," Hank frowned.

"Enough," Mrs. Gersh said, waving, "I came with Hank, I'll go back with Hank. You want to drive me places —don't worry. There'll be lots of driving. Believe me, you'll get so sick of it in no time I'll be back on the busses and the subways again."

They all laughed, saying, "Oh Ma," "No such thing," "Don't be ridiculous." Laughing, they left, putting on coats, fixing hats, suddenly leaving me there with the bag of dirty linen and Thelma walking by nodding, "Well, wha'd I tell you?"

"Huh?"

She put her hand on her hip and motioned towards the elevator.

"Oh."

"Great bunch of folks?"

"Uh huh."

"Mm hmm."

I grinned.

"Good luck," she grinned.

"Thanks."

Just then the head nurse, Gilly, walked over to me. She wasn't smiling.

"*Mr.* Jacobs."

"Yes."

"How's everything with Mr. Gerson?"

"As well as can be expected. O.k., I guess."

"You guess? I just passed the room. It smells horrible. Like a slaughterhouse."

"Ohh."

"Make sure you spray consistently."

"I ran out."

"Mr. Jacobs, there is a large box of spray cans if you will take the trouble to look at the bottom of the closet in Mr. Gerson's room. It's a very adequate supply I stocked myself this weekend. Didn't Mr. Stoneham show you?"

"Yes," I said quickly.

"Yes?"

"Yes."

"So you *forgot*?"

"Yes. I was very busy."

"Well, please try to remember. I know you like to spend lots of time talking with the patients here, and I also know the families can be very trying, but please remember that it is attention to detail that is most important."

"Yes."

"You can go."

"Right."

I returned to Gersh's room. It was 3:30—time to knock off. Gersh slept. I looked in the closet. There was no box of spray cans—just Gersh's heavy shoes. I didn't see Stoney the rest of the day: they floated him all over the hospital.

"You know," Stoney smiled, "you never told me last week about Gilly jumpin' on you about that spray shit. Thanks for that. I hadda take that box outta there 'cause that family of his, 'specially that salesman and some of them cousins. They was gettin' kinda spray-happy." Stoney imitated them, holding his nose with one hand and a spray can with the other, going: "Woosh-woosh-woosh. Spritz-spritz-spritz. He's gonna be fine, just fine," his voice a serious, concerned, completely nasal tweaked sound. I laughed and laughed until my stomach started hurting. "Son, I thought they was gonna gas the poor old bastard to death and me along with him. They was spraying like that spray was the cure for cancer. I went to a party later on and didn't even want a lemon rind in my drink—that's how much that fuckin' spray got to me."

"Yeah, it doesn't smell good."

"You mean it stinks like a mother. 'Specially when it's mixed in with the rest of it. Pah! Sheee, I been workin' here over ten years and this is the first time I been considerin' wearin' a gas-mask."

I laughed. Stoney stuck his jaw out. "You think I'm kiddin', don't you?"

I laughed again. Stoney grinned. "You can laugh. You ain't takin' care of ol' Pops for awhile. You had it easy on the ward for one week."

"True," I nodded.

"Well, maybe we'll both have it easy. Pops is on his way home."

"What!" I said. "He's going *home*?"

"Religiously speakin', son. Home with the capital 'H'."

"Oh."

"Yep. He's gotten a whole lot worse this past week."

"Excuse me," interrupted a smooth voice. "Do you gentlemen mind if I interrupt your, ah, work for a minute?"

Gilly stared at us. Stoney smiled blandly.

"Sure, break's almost over, ain't it, kid?" Stoney smiled, checking his watch.

I nodded.

"I have a little problem," Gilly continued. "It looks like

Jackson's not coming in tonight and I was wondering if one of you would like to work a double. I'd really appreciate it—seeing how Lucy's on vacation—we'd really be in a bind if one of you can't come in.''

"Jesus fuckin' Christ,'' Stoney muttered.

"Hmm,'' I said. I was tired.

"I just worked a double yesterday,'' Stoney growled. "Why in hell don't you get some part-time people around this goddam dump? Come in every once in a while.''

"What can I tell you,'' Gilly moaned. "I don't hire people.''

"Yeah,'' Stoney replied bitterly. "You only make suggestions, and talk that jive about staffing patterns. Patterns, that's good for quilts.'' He made a motion like he was going to spit, and instead just bit his lip.

"I'll do it,'' I said.

"You don't have to, of course, Mr. Jacobs,'' Gilly smiled. "No one's forcing you to, you know.''

"I'll do it,'' I repeated.

"Good. You'll have Mr. Gerson and the ward, since you're familiar with both.''

"Gersh *and* the ward!'' I blurted.

"The ward's relatively no problem at all, Mr. Jacobs. Thelma can help you. And we may be getting some help from the evening house orderly.''

"Ha!'' Stoney chuckled.

"Something funny, Mr. Stoneham?''

"Help from the evening houseman—that's funny,'' Stoney said, not smiling.

"We're a little cynical today, aren't we?'' Gilly observed.

"You know what they say,'' smiled Stoney. "Seein' is believin'.''

"You don't *have* to stay here.''

"Don't I?'' Stoney drawled. "And if I split, you would be callin' me up every night, cryin' on my shoulder like you done before, after you tell me good orderlies are a dime a dozen. Sure.''

"*I* cry on *no one's* shoulder,'' Gilly said sternly.

"I know," Stoney agreed, studying her.

"You worry too much, Mr. Stoneham. You should be careful—with your high blood pressure. Your worrying might aggravate it someday."

"So? Some day they'll stick me in the ground," Stoney smiled. "And so what? Birds'll still sing, soap'll still float."

They gave me a half-hour break since I was working a double. When I came back, Gersh's relatives filled the waiting room: Mr. and Mrs. Tweed, Mr. and Mrs. Hank, and the Tweeds' children. The boy wore a brown tweed suit with a white shirt, a tan knit tie, and walnut brown Florsheim shoes. The girl, younger, shivered in a pink dress with patent leather shoes. Both children's faces glowed with the brightly-scrubbed look; their light brown hair shone too. The girl's long flowing hair was held back on both sides by two blue-bird barettes.

"Hello," I greeted the family.

"Dov, how are you?" Mrs. Gersh smiled. "These are my grandchildren—Jessie—"

"Pleased to meet you," curtsied the girl.

"Hi," I smiled.

"And my grandson, Michael."

"Hello," Michael nodded, a grim expression on his face as he stuck out his hand. "Are you my grandfather's doctor?"

"No," I smiled, "I'm just helping to take care of him."

"I thought I'd take the children in to see their grandfather," Mrs. Gersh said. "Me and Judy, that is—if you don't think that's too many people? My son wants a private conversation with his father. He hasn't said that, but you know how men are. They never say anything. I'm supposed to know by maybe sticking my finger in the air. Or what's that with the cells and the protoplasm? Osmosis. Out of the blue, or through some kind of water. Like that watchacallit —E.S.P. So what do you think?"

"I think four people is o.k. The kids, uh, that's fine."

"Not too long. We don't want to tire him out."

"Fine."

"We won't be interfering with you?"

"No, it's o.k."

We all went into the room. Gersh looked much thinner. Stubble covered his jaw and cheeks. His eyes seemed shrunken, less alert. I heard Mrs. Gersh and the children sniffling— the children's nostrils wide open. They looked at their grandma and nodded, as if wisely agreeing with what either she or their mother and father had warned them about. As soon as Gersh saw his grandchildren, his eyes brightened and grew more focused, as if he came from a long way deep within himself. He beamed, motioning to me with his good arm to help him sit up. I lifted him gently and placed two pillows behind his back. His grandchildren crowded around the bedside by his night-table.

"Hi Grandpa," said the boy.

"Hi Grandpa," said the girl.

"You look...ahhhhh. Let me look at you." He looked them all over—at their faces, their hair, their small ears, their necks, their faces again, their arms and legs, their suit and dress, and their shoes and their faces and hair again.

"You look wonderful. Like two angels. But better," Gersh smiled.

The children smiled shyly, "Thank you Grandpa."

The girl, her hands behind her back, shook her head slowly back and forth, and murmured, "I got an 'A' on my last math test."

"Goot," Gersh grinned.

"And Michael he got 'A' plus in Geography and the teacher told Mommy he was the best student she ever had. *Ever*."

"Excellent," Gersh crowed.

"And I ran the fifty-yard dash at school in six-point-seven seconds, Grandpa," Michael added.

"A scholar and an athlete," Gersh grinned, delighted. "A well-rounded boy."

"And my art teacher put up one of my pictures," added Jessie.

"You've seen her pictures," Mrs. Gersh beamed. "She's a real talent this one."

"Yes, I remember. What do you think I am? I remember

well." Gersh frowned.

"Of course, Zev," Mrs. Gersh whispered, looking down sadly.

There was a long pause. The two children studied their grandfather. The girl leaned over, put her hand on Gersh's, and looking deep into his face, said softly, "Grandpa?"

"Yes, tantala," Gersh smiled.

"You're dying, huh?"

Mrs. Gersh let out a little gasp. The two children stared at their grandfather, solemn, hushed, waiting for his answer.

"Yes," Gersh nodded, "I am."

The girl made a face like she wanted to cry, paused, then said, "I'm gonna miss you a whole lot Grandpa," and reaching over, hugged his good hip as Gersh patted her head, whispering, "You're a good girl, Jessie, you're a very good girl."

There was a silence again. Michael said, "You look— lighter—Grandpa."

Gersh stared at Michael.

"Lighter?"

He turned to his wife. "Interesting, no? Lighter?"

Mrs. Gersh shrugged, her eyes heavy, wet. Gersh lay back, whispering to himself, "Lighter."

Mrs. Gersh gathered the children, speaking low, "Let's go now and let Grandpa have some rest, children."

"Bye Grandpa."

"Goodbye you vonderfuls," Gersh smiled. "Come let me see you soon."

I got ready to give Gersh his bath. Joseph walked in, knocking his pipe on the door with an "Anybody home?"

Gersh studied him. "Ahh, the prodigal son!"

Joseph looked all over the room and glanced quickly into his father's face.

"Hi Dad."

"Come sit."

I made a move to leave and Joseph grabbed my arm: his grip was strong.

"Don't let me stop you from doing anything for my father." I looked at him. "We can talk while you do your work," Joseph said evenly.

"O.k." I said. "I was just going to give your father what we call a partial bath."

"Want a bath, Dad?" Joseph asked.

Gersh shrugged.

"Can take it or leave it, huh?"

I took the large plastic basin and began running water for it. I took out a washcloth and placed it near the night-table. I moved slowly, feeling worn out, still hearing Gersh's grandson whisper, "You look—lighter." I felt like an in-truder, even thought I could see myself washing Gersh, put-ting the warm wet cloth to his yellowing skin. He needed at least a partial bath—as Stoney would say, "He's overdue for some H_2O." Even though we'd been avoiding it—him and me—baths were important. I dreaded it because I knew movement caused him so much pain.

"So," Joseph said.

"So," Gersh said.

There was a silence. I shut off the faucets, tested the water. It was warm.

"So, how are your classes at the high school?"

"Fine. I'm teaching two American History classes and two Civics classes—just like last year. And one in World History."

"Voild history. A big job."

"Yes," Joseph laughed. "We have to go through it kinda fast."

"Like a whirling dervish," Gersh chuckled, grinning to himself and nudging Joseph. "Remember, remember when you were small what I told you?"

"You told me lots of things," Joseph said, looking at Gersh's bad elbow sadly.

Gersh gazed up at the ceiling, smiling faintly. "What I told you concerning chewing."

"Right," Joseph nodded, "Never bit off more than you can chew, but make sure also that you don't starve."

Gersh nodded, grinning as if immensely pleased with himself. "Yes," Gersh smiled, looking him in the eyes, "and you're teaching Voild history."

"At night. Brings in a little extra."

"That's good."

Joseph smiled.

"Excuse me," I said, "I'm going to wash you up a bit, Mr. Gerson."

"Fine," Gersh nodded.

I washed him, first his face, then his neck and shoulders, pushing aside his gown gingerly. I began washing his chest and his stomach, sponging him gently. I washed his armpits. He began sweating and looked at me. I put the basin down quickly, heard "Oh-oh, ohhhhh," as Joseph rose, backed up, saying, "What's the matter?" I grabbed the bedpan and signalled for him to help me lift up Gersh just as the bubble-gum machine-gun splattered off plipplopplable. Gersh moaned, "Ohhh no no no," and I could smell along with the rotting vegetables, rotten chicken, and something sweetly nauseating making my gut feel completely empty. I saw Gersh quickly turn calling "Joseph?" but the door was already closed. Gersh lay back. I heard the plipplopplable again and tried to lift him—he was like lead.

"If you can sit up just a little bit," I coaxed, "I can start cleaning you up."

Gersh lay back, still, his eyes so shut they seemed clenched or cemented.

"Mr. Gerson, can you hear me?"

He opened one eye, utterly glum.

"Yes. I have ears. Two of them. So vhat?"

"Hey," I said, gritting my teeth, "If you wanna lay there in your own shit and give me a hard time, that's fine with me. I don't have to take this."

"Yes you do," he sneered, his eyes narrowing.

"C'mon, let's not fight," I pleaded. "Let's be friends." I tried turning him: he lay lead-limp.

Suddenly his wife was there cheerfully rolling up her sleeves, "Need some help?" Before either Gersh or me could say anything, she lifted him up, smiling, "This is nothing— you should have been around before he lost weight!" as Gersh groaned, "Oh oy oy," spotting her and moaning, not knowing whether to order her to get out or cry for help. Before he could decide, we had him turned. I pulled out the filthy sheets, bagged them, and began a new bed while Mrs. Gersh held Gersh up with her bulging forearms crossed, murmuring, "Oh what a fresser you are, Zev Gerson, what a fresser. Between you and your son and your daughter, I'm lucky I'm not in the nut-house."

"There," I said, spraying a slight whiff of Lemon Chiffon spray.

"Done," Mrs. Gersh said triumphantly, rubbing her hands.

I sniffed, and sprayed a little more. The smell of rotten chicken remained. Mrs. Gersh, sweating, caressed Gersh's forehead: "Now you're snug as a bug in a rug."

Gersh lay back, utterly exhausted. I sprayed a little bit more.

"Enough," Gersh whispered, "enough."

"O.k." I went to open the window, and closed it just as I pushed it open: it was freezing. It was too cold to open the window even a crack without risking Gersh catching pneumonia. The radiator clanked on, instantly adding to the sweet spray smell and shit, the fat edge of stuffy heat. Mrs. Gersh fluffed up her husband's pillow.

"Please understand, Zev. Joseph loves you very much. He's just...just—"

"He teaches Voiled History," Gersh wheezed.

"Hmm?" Mrs. Gersh asked.

"You need to know a great deal to teach Voild History," Gersh wheezed in a tired voice.

Mrs. Gersh studied him. His foot stuck out from the blanket: she put the blanket over his foot.

"Well, Zev, I think we'll be going. You're exhausted. I'll come tomorrow."

Gersh nodded, stretching out his hand. She pressed it to her cheek.

"Be good. Take care."

Gersh nodded, his eyes shutting.

I walked out of the room. The relatives gathered around.

"How is he today?"

"The same."

"Is he all right?"

"He's the same," I told Hank and Naomi, my eyes seeking Joseph. He was sitting with his two children, watching the television in the waiting room.

"Can you do something about the uh, uh," Judy stammered.

"About what?" I asked.

"The smell," Hank blurted. "It must be extremely uncomfortable for him to have to sit there all day with that horrible smell all the time. I don't think he needs to be subjected to that kind of treatment."

"I didn't know you cared, Hank," Judy crooned sarcastically.

"We spray as much as we can," I replied.

"Isn't there something else that you can do?" Naomi asked, politely holding onto Hank's hand, her smaller fingers entwined in his larger ones.

I looked at her, Hank, Judy, and Joseph sitting with his children. I wondered if they asked out of concern for Gersh, or because they themselves couldn't stomach the room, the stench. I stared off into space, wondering if Gersh and the smell were separate. I saw them studying me. I blinked and wiped my forehead, trying to wipe away my sudden impression of their bodies avoiding the door to Gersh's room, their hips, shoulders, very glances and faces staring away to the window facing the street full of snowing—as if they wished they were out walking in the crisp cold snowing instead of having to step inside a cramped stuffy room and smell an old man, rubbing alcohol, lukewarm shit, lemon spray, and old wool blankets all mixed in with the smell of Gersh's most recent nibbling and the stale flowers they'd brought in and encouraged loads of friends and acquaintances to bring in to the point we threw some flowers out with Stoney muttering, "One more of these goddam things and people gonna think this is the fuckin' Botanical Gardens."

"We asked you a question, orderly," Judy said.

"Huh?"

"Is there anything more that can be done?"

"No," I said, trying to imitate Stoney, and stare at them coldly.

"There must be *something*," Judy said.

"Look," I said, trying not to get mad, "all of us here are doing the best we can to make your father-in-law's stay here as comfortable and pleasant as possible."

I wanted to add, "So just get off my fuckin' back," but instead, smiled.

"He doesn't seem too comfortable to me," Hank grumbled.

Just then Mrs. Gersh trudged out of the ladies restroom.

"He's as well as can be expected given he's a very sick man," she pronounced, as if settling again a running argument between her family and the world. "Now let's all go home and let this young man do his job."

"Thanks for everything," Joseph said.

"Just doing my job."

Joseph muttered something like, "Well, thanks just the same," and joined the rest of his family. I watched them leave, putting on their dark thick coats, readying their umbrellas for the sleeting snow. After they left, I took my break up in the cafeteria. It was 7:30 p.m.: the sky was dark, full of snow. I ate some split-pea soup, thought of Gersh, and gagged. I finished the soup by dreaming of green pine trees in the cold winds of Montana. I yawned and drank a cup of coffee, trying to figure how many hours straight I'd worked. I drank more coffee. Then I noticed the time and rushed back downstairs to finish my shift. Shaney came over and whispered, "Why don't you go home, Dov? I can handle the last few hours here."

"What about Gersh?"

"Don't worry. I'll watch him. What he needs is a special, only they probably figure it's too...well...I don't know."

"Too what?"

"Skip it."

"Too expensive?" I said mockingly.

"Now, Dov, don't get all hoighty-toity—I didn't mean that at all."

I didn't say anything.

"I just mean Gersh won't last the week so there's no

sense in having a special," she said softly.

"Oh," I said, feeling suddenly numb. I saw Gersh's face thinner, his chin more shrunken, and shivered.

"Look. Go home—I'll finish up here. You look like death warmed over. Fourteen hours is enough."

"Thanks, Shaney."

"Forget it."

"You really think he won't last the week?"

"Shaney never bullshits," Stoney nodded, "Old man's slippin'. And the more he slips, the more folks come to see him. You thought he had relatives before, hell, you shoulda seen his room yesterday—looked like a goddam airport with the hiyas and the flowers and the huggin' and the this and the that. One from Detroit, one from Philly. A brother from L.A. That old man has him some family."

"And they all brought flowers I'll bet," I cracked.

"Yeah," Stoney laughed, "I hear the florist downstairs is about to retire."

I laughed. Stoney smiled. "Glad you're in a good mood, 'cause you got Gersh today."

"Shit."

"You hit it. Hey, wanna trade? You take the house, I'll take Gersh. I'll clean him up and put up with his people, and you can run your ass off lifting three-hundred-pound old bags what need to leak every five minutes. And you can run around putting up oxygen for people who don't need 'em anymore 'cause they shoulda had 'em two weeks ago, and then you can stroll on over to the psych ward and hold down the loonies while they try and kick your nuts in."

By the door to Gersh's room stood a group of dark coats extending toward the waiting room. Mr. and Mrs. Hank and Mrs. and Mrs. Tweed were explaining different things to the relatives. I heard phrases: "No, no, that's o.k. We already have a lawyer." "Yes, he's very capable." And "Esther will be fine. There's a nice pension from his union—the Machinists, that's right—to go along with the Social Security. Yes, there should be something nice with all his years, you're right. Yes, well, there is and it's adequate." "So how's things in Cleveland, Harry?'' ''Altogether there's not as much as we first thought. The pension. Some savings. A few bonds. A little Social Security. Really not that much with today's prices.'' ''Well, I think this really isn't the time or place to talk about all this.'' ''She's right we should leave the man in peace. There'll be plenty of time to go over all this later.'' ''So tell me why Sheila left school? I don't understand it—so many young people leaving college? What is it?'' ''Chemotherapy? Well, I think it's a little late for that. Perhaps if they'd found it sooner—who can tell about these things?'' ''He's been taking it wonderfully. A little crabby lately, but that's to be expected. He's old. He's sick. It's not easy. It's not easy for any of us.''

Inside the room stood an older man who looked like a healthy version of Gersh—he was not yellow, but autumn-apple-red with wider cheeks and a fuller frame. He had similar sharp grey eyes, and shook my hand vigorously, as if, like my grandfather, he judged people by the way they shook his hand. Shook, not took, I thought to myself, thinking how Mrs. Gersh always took people's hands as if measuring something she held to be very valuable.

''Should I leave?'' the man who looked like Gersh asked.

''Stay, Sid,'' Gersh whispered.

''That's o.k.'' I said, ''I'm just going to wash him. You can stay.''

Sid talked and talked. He was a semi-retired newspaper man in L.A. He talked about the news, his editor, some of the cub reporters, laughing, gesturing, ''A real meshuginer, Zev, a real meshuginer. This snot-nose fresh out of nursery school and he wants to cover the Freedom Riders right away. He hates the police blotter. The new city editor—it isn't that he drinks so much, it's just that if he ever gave blood, they'd get a fifth of scotch out of him.''

Gersh lay there, his eyes shut, nodding, smiling, occasionally opening one eye.

Suddenly Sid grew quiet, studying the cold grey sky.

''Ha, I thought I'd miss the snow, but I don't.''

Gersh nodded.

"See, it's going to snow again, Zev. I can smell it. It'll snow like crazy. Remember our little joke? There's a crazy man in the sky whose brains are falling out?"

Gersh chuckled.

"Say," Sid stroked his chin, smiling, "wouldn't it be funny, Zev, if one December it didn't snow at all? Not a flake?"

Gersh opened both his eyes.

"No snow, Zev."

"Make sense," Gersh murmured.

"Not a flake anywhere. Just extremely cold weather. Cold and clear."

"Need a few clouds," Gersh murmured, "so you have a place to put your head."

"Just a thought," Sid smiled.

Gersh smiled back, "You were always a thinker."

"I was the thinker and you were the tinker. Nothing you couldn't fix."

"Ahh, I'm just a good tool and die man. With a lot of luck."

"Modest!"

"Nothing I couldn't fix? Some things," Gersh whispered, "some things you can't fix."

I washed Gersh. He smelled from sweat, urine, and spray. I washed his face and smelled the spray stronger. Without him or his brother noticing, I leaned closer, sniffing his face, ears, neck, and hair—all reeked of spray. I went to check the spray can on the table. It was empty. I cleared my throat: "Mr. Gerson?"

At the same time Gersh whispered, "Eh?" Sid leaned forward smiling, "Yes?"

I looked at Gersh: "Has anyone been, uh, using this can other than me or Stoney?"

Gersh grinned. His skin drew back from his lips. I realized he was sneering, not grinning.

"Anyone, orderly? That's funny. If you conducted a popularity contest between me and that spray can, I would place a distant second." He lay back, wheezing.

Sid looked at me, concerned. "I just got here, but if you

want me to make sure no one uses that, I can help. Just tell me what to do—that's what I'm here for." He leaned closer, whispering, "I couldn't get away until yesterday, but now I'm here for as long as it takes for me to be here."

Gersh waved me away when I went to wash him more. "No," he wheezed, his face sagging. "Wash me later."

"What would you like now? Some food?"

"Nothing. Rest."

"I'll go," Sid said softly. "I didn't mean to wear you out, Zev."

"Nonsense," Gersh whispered.

Sid leaned over and kissed Gersh's forehead. "Rest well, Zev."

"Shalom," Gersh whispered.

"Shalom." We left the room. Sid shut the door as if he were putting away a feather.

The relatives surrounded us.

"How is he, Sid?"

"Not so good."

"I think he's looking a lot better than he did last week. 'Course most of you weren't here," Hank said.

Sid pursed his lips, "Everyone's entitled to their own opinions. It's a free country." He walked away, toward the chairs in the waiting room, and plopped down next to Joseph. I strolled over there, pretending I was on my way to see other patients. Joseph and Judy were watching television with their children. "So what's on t.v.?" Sid blurted. "Anything of interest?"

Joseph puffed on his pipe. He took it out, then knocked it on the chair.

"Usual crap."

"Superman," Judy yawned.

On the television screen Clark Kent stepped into an alley between two tall buildings. He returned shortly as Superman, flexed his arms, and was suddenly flying over the tops of buildings.

"Oh," Sid yawned.

The children's eyes were glued to the set.

"I want a cape like that," the girl stared.

"Me too," nodded the boy.

"You can't have a cape," Joseph snapped, "so just watch the show."

The boy watched the show.

"Do you know what happened to Superman in real life?" Joseph asked his kids abruptly.

"What?"

"What?"

"He jumped off a building on purpose."

The children grew hushed, their eyes huge.

"Joey!" Judy hit Joseph's leg.

"Wha?" Joseph said, knocking his pipe on the edge of the chair again.

Judy leaned over, muttering, "I really don't like it when you take your own whatever the hell's bugging you out on your children. It's sick and unfair."

"Maybe you're right. I just don't like them watching this junk." He knocked his pipe savagely against the arm of the chair.

"It's just," he continued, "It's just you'd think television could have some shows of substance. About what goes on in the real world."

Sid nodded as Joseph scowled, mumbling, "This crap is just what people need to watch. Wonderful. Healthy." He knocked his pipe savagely again against the chair.

"Shit! I broke the bowl, dammit!"

"Joey," Judy said.

Sid stared at Joseph whose knuckles whitely clutched the pipe stem.

"Let's go home," Joseph said.

"I don't think we should," Judy whispered. "I think we should stick around."

Sid stared at the television—the credits flashed past. It began to snow.

"So," Sid said, "So everyone's sticking around? And flying in from everywhere? Very nice. Nice surprise. Everyone's here. Hail, hail, the gang's all here."

"Some people care," Judy pronounced.

"And some people live too long," Joseph blurted.

Sid's eyes boiled.

"And some people are lucky to have a tongue in their

head,'' Sid hissed.

Joseph looked down at the floor.

"Sorry, Uncle Sid,'' Joseph whispered, his pipe in his lap.

Judy stayed silent.

The watching children sat completely still, as if moving an inch might produce a catastrophe. Sid sighed deeply. He rubbed his hands, gazing at Joseph.

"Joseph,'' Sid smiled, "do you remember when you and your sister and me and your father and mother all went to the ocean in Maine with my Sophie?''

Joseph nodded.

"And do you remember those tidal pools? How we walked out and out and out and how you were the great scientist showing everyone and explaining about the life in those tide pools?''

Joseph nodded, silently laughing to himself, half-ironic, half worn-out.

"Do you remember how much you loved the starfish?'' Sid turned to Judy, and looked at me, beaming. "So many starfish!''

"So,'' Joseph urged, staring intently at Sid.

"So? Some things cling. Hold on. You know that expression—*hold on for dear life*,'' Sid enunciated, pronouncing each word as if talking to a child.

"I see,'' Joseph nodded.

"I know,'' Sid said. "A lack of brains was never your problem.''

They grew quiet. I left. I treated some patients in the ward. As I was bringing some new sheets, Joseph and Mrs. Tweed came rapidly toward me, their faces distressed.

"Orderly? Dov?''

"Yeah,'' I frowned, already knowing that Gersh had shat again. They were walking too fast for anything else, except if their kids had been hurt, and their kids were still watching t.v. I went into the room just as a group of relatives fled, gagging. Once they began recovering, I heard snatches of conversation: "They really need to do something!'' "Well, it's the room—obviously the room's much too small.''

"And knowing what his problems entail there's no one in the room?" "I never heard of such a thing!" "That's what's so incredible—I mean what kind of service is he getting?"

The relatives stared accusingly at me through the open door, studying me with a wary bitterness, yet standing a good distance away, steadily backing up, half the group holding handkerchiefs. In the room Gersh's wife was trying to lift him as he groaned, "No Leibshin, no, wait for the orderly. Please Leibshin, you'll hurt yourself." Naomi was trying to help her mother and at the same time avoid the shit on the blanket and sheets. Hank was spraying the blankets, the sheets, Gersh, Mrs. Gersh, Naomi, the bed, the nightstand, and all the new flowers and boxes of candy brought in by the relatives. I was about to take the spray away from Hank— trying to figure out how to approach him—when suddenly Gersh not only sat up, but made a move as if he were going to get out of bed, sticking one foot down and out toward the cold floor.

"Wha!" I said, staring at him.

"Get me up. I want to get up," he insisted, clenching his mouth. He bunked his casted arm and gritted his teeth, his mouth twisting as if he'd swallowed three lemons.

"You can't!" I said, grabbing his good arm.

"Zev!" Mrs. Gersh cried.

Gersh waved his arm, his nose scrunching up, waving his arm toward Hank and the spray. "Get away from me!" Gersh hissed. "Get that fa-shittin' spray away from me."

Mrs. Gersh clutched her chest, her eyes widening, "Zev!"

"Oooo, thank God I don't have a gun, I might shoot someone through the head!"

"Easy," I said, feeling his good arm, surprisingly strong, strain against mine.

"Fey! Get that meshuginer spray away! You want something sweet, eat some candy, but get that spray away from me!"

"Ahh, Zev," Mrs. Gersh sighed. Hank's hand was frozen in the air. He placed the spray on the table.

"Sure, Pop."

"Let them smell me. Let them smell. Hah!"

Gersh stared at the doorway, his eyes gleaming, stretching his neck to get a better look at the clustered relatives now joined by Mrs. and Mrs. Hank.

Through the flurry of coats pushed Sid, pressing forward with Stoney who, entering the room, looked around and muttered, "Now what's all this mess?"

"They want to pay respects," Gersh snapped, "Then they can smell me."

"Easy, Zev," Sid coaxed, "easy."

"Easy!" Gersh hissed, "Easy with vultures?"

Stoney leaned closer to me, muttering, "What the fuck's goin' on?—no, tell me later."

From the doorway Joseph and his wife stared. I could see his wife pushing back the grandchildren, and hear her voice, far-off, soothing: "Grandpa's not doing so well right now, Jessie. Why don't you and Michael go watch t.v. for a little bit?"

Gersh sat up, holding Mrs. Gersh's hand, the bottom of his face quivering, his eyes bright with fury, his neck veins trembling as his good arm pointed and shook at the doorway.

"Don't you understand I can't be sweetened! You think I don't know how I smell! Are you that stupid! You think something's wrong with my nose!" He paused, sneering, gasping for breath. He spied Stoney and reached out for him, his voice croaking urgently, "Tell them, tell them to take away their rotten flowers and their rotten sweets—ooo—their teeth should rot out and drop down their legs. And they can take back their get well cards. Who kids who?" Gersh fumed, "Their get well cards are drop dead cards!"

"Zev," Mrs. Gersh cried, trying to hug him, her cheeks wet. He collapsed into the pillows.

"O.k. Everybody out. Now," commanded Stoney. "We gonna clean this man up and see what's what." He gently took Mrs. Gersh away from her husband, his voice softening, "O.k. Ma'am, just wanna clean him up a little, and you can come right back in, right back."

Mrs. Gersh, sniffing, nodded. Stoney escorted her and Sid out as I got the new sheets ready. The door closed. Stoney sighed, then looked at Gersh and let out a long whistle. He winked at me, then poked Gersh.

"Hey Grandpa." Gersh lay still. Stoney poked him again. "Don't play possum with me. Not after that." Gersh opened one eye. Stoney stuck his hand out. "Way to go." Gersh opened both eyes, breathing tiredly. "I tell the world," he wheezed.

"You did great."

"I tell even you to go to hell if I want," Gersh frowned proudly.

"Sure," Stoney nodded, lifting him up so I could wipe him and start bunching up the dirty sheets, "but then if you say that and I do go to hell, I'm gonna come visit you and bother the shit out of you."

"Kha kha," Gersh cackled.

"All I gotta do," continued Stoney, "is sniff around when I get there—'cause you'll be in the place that stinks the most."

"Kha kha," Gersh cackled again, "Stink stink stink."

"You got it Grandpa."

"Kha kha," Gersh laughed weakly.

Stoney's forearms bulged. As he held Gersh, Gersh draped his good arm over Stoney's shoulder while I wiped Gersh with a generous roll of toilet paper, and then began bunching up the sheets.

"And," Stoney went on, his neck veins standing out, "when I come down there I'll bring you a whole case of Lemon Chiffon spray—just so you don't get lonesome."

Gersh chuckled. Stoney eased him back down, staring at Gersh intently.

Gersh saw Stoney's look, "Yes?"

"Ain't this somethin' anyway," Stoney grinned, "a millionaire havin' to lie in his own crap!"

"Ha!" Gersh grinned, "A millionaire! Great joke. Go back and tell my friends—tell that to the other machinists, oy, you'll need a truck so many of them will die laughing."

"Then what are you worth?" Stoney asked, folding his arms.

"What am I worth?" Gersh mused. "What's any man worth? Ha. I'm worth the two of you, no?" He laughed.

Stoney stared at him, not saying anything. I slowly finished bagging the dirty sheets, listening to the two men—Gersh's slow wheezing and Stoney's silence.

"Why don't you just put me out on the street and let me rot like I smell—like rotten food you wouldn't touch if you were starving? No, of course not. We are a civilized people. America. America is a great place, a powerful nation. What am I worth? I'm worth my children and my children's children. They come here. And the others come. Now, Esther—Esther is always with me. And Sid—Sid is my little brother, little Sidney with his head in the clouds. The others—they come here on Friday nights and Saturdays and Sundays or fly in. For some of them that's not easy. And believe me—it's not easy for me to see some of them." He grabbed for a Kleenex from his night-table and spat forcefully into it. Then he looked at Stoney. "So what do you think I'm worth, Mr. Stoneham?"

Stoney shrugged.

"No curiosity as to my value?"

Stoney shrugged.

"And you, wet-behind-the-ears," Gersh said to me, "what do you think?"

I shrugged.

"Ahh," Gersh smiled, "everyone's neck hurts today." He looked at me, then at Stoney, and back at me, pointing to Stoney.

"Watch him," Gersh instructed, pointing to Stoney, "This one—he's a very smart man. A man who knows when to keep quiet, and when to nudge. Rare." He lay back, exhausted.

Stoney motioned to me, and we left the room. Stoney smiled, "Well, that was quite a little rap."

"Yeah, but he didn't tell us how much he was worth."

"No?" Stoney smiled, "He said 'you and me.' You think on that. But don't think too much—we got some more work to do. 'Sides, he'll turn around and fall asleep now, or shit all over himself again."

I nodded sourly.

"They oughta pull the plug on that poor bastard,"

Stoney murmured.

I didn't say anything.

"Why keep him alive? Well, maybe he wants to stay alive. Shit. Just between you and me, son, 'f I ever get sick, I'm jumpin' off the nearest bridge. Somethin' quick. Ain't gonna catch me hangin' around, layin' in my shit and piss. Fuck that."

"Yeah," I drawled, real tough, "Fuck that."

"Yeah, he says," Stoney laughed, punching my arm, "little man of the world here says 'Yeah.' Well, you take care of Gersh, pardner, and I'll catch ya later."

"Bye Stoney. Thanks."

As I walked back to check on Gersh, Mrs. Gersh toddled over softly.

"Dov, I want to see my husband. I won't be long. Just a minute."

"Sure."

Gersh lay with his eyes half-shut.

"Zev?" Mrs. Gersh asked softly, her voice quavering.

"Yes."

"Is there something I should do, Zev?"

"Tell them to go home. Have Sid stay. And the children. The rest can go."

"And Joseph? And Naomi?"

"They stay—of course. But the rest—I don't want. Enough is enough."

He lay back, shutting his eyes again.

"They mean well, Zev. They mean well."

"Ehh."

Gersh's wife rubbed her hands as if they held a pain that wouldn't go away. She rubbed them modestly as if she didn't want anyone to notice. Her silver wedding band, extremely old, shone like the gleam of an antique that even in darkening sunset rooms still gives off its own thin light.

"You come tomorrow, Leibshin," Gersh whispered. "And bring the children."

"Yes, Zev," she whispered.

She left. Almost immediately, Gersh fell asleep. Quietly, I left the room.

When I gave my report at the end of the shift, the head nurse Gilly asked if there were any problems with the relatives. I told her no. She asked me and Stoney if we thought the family and relatives wore Gersh down. Stoney smiled and gave his look of "She's always right on the money right on time, ain't she?" I told the evening crew that fewer relatives would be around. Gilly said it really didn't matter since Gersh wasn't expected to last the week.

It snowed all through the night. In the morning it was still snowing. The hospital was dark and cold when I arrived on the floor. Stoney waved at me, drinking coffee with Thelma.

"Go see Gersh," he said. I looked in on him. He lay deep in the bed, moving a little.

"Is that you, Mr. Stoneham?"

"No, it's me, Dov."

"Ohh. Let me...let me know...when my...when my grandchildren come...right away..."

"Sure. Like a bath? Breakfast?" I tried pretending I was underwater again. I checked the sheets. They were clean. He hadn't shat: he just smelled bad. I gagged, trying not to show it, then realized he wasn't looking at me. I stared at him, wondering if he could see me. He wasn't looking at me.

"Something to eat? How about something to eat?" I asked.

"An orange," Gersh decided in a whisper. "An orange would be nice."

"An orange it is," I smiled. I tweaked his foot playfully, glad to be able to leave the room. "Be back in a bit," I said.

I strolled to the Nurses' Lounge in back of the medicine room and nodded to Stoney and Thelma.

"He's o.k. Wants an orange."

"Try the 'fridge," Thelma said.

I looked in the refrigerator, found an orange, and began rubbing it just as the other aides and nurses came in, followed by Gilly and the night nurse.

"Early breakfast?" Gilly smiled, studying me.

"It's for a patient. Mr. Gerson."

"Well, it's not quite the official breakfast time yet. And we do have to report."

"Just take a minute," gritted Stoney, staring at her.

"Very well," Gilly said. "Go ahead."

I walked down the hall, smoothing the orange, and walked into the room. I was about to say, "Here you go." Nothing moved. Gersh lay in the same position, only now he was staring past the ceiling, his ears in the same position as the bars in the siderail on the bed. The room was soundless. I stared at Gersh, then looked at my watch. It was 6:51. I stared at Gersh again. His eyes were half-open. He looked irritated, like he did when I'd feed him and he'd bunk his broken elbow or bad hip, and cringe. He lay there with his casted arm on a pillow, as if even dying he'd been very careful with his elbow, as if the healing and care he took with his elbow might hold back his cancer, slow it down, push it away —a long-shot cure counting totally on pure luck. His beard was stiff.

As I took the end of the top-sheet between my fingers and shut his eyes, it seemed as if he'd turned into a deep well and was looking down into himself at the same time he stared past the ceiling. The lids of his eyes felt hard like smooth rock. His arms and legs shone like sunlight on smooth rock. On the sheet his hands clasped together peacefully, fingers entwined like an obedient child school, or as if he'd been praying. I stared at him again: he was, in a way, no longer Gersh. I wanted him gone. I wanted nothing more to do with him, even more than the times I dreaded entering his room to clean him. I wanted the room cleaned—fresh, white, ready for someone new. I could see the motions unfolding: I announce Gersh's death. Stoney or me gets the morgue kit. One of us takes out the silken ties. The other gets the gurney. We lift him up onto it before he gets too hard— before rigor mortis takes hold. We tie his arms and legs with silken ties from the morgue kit. We tie his balls and dick to prevent his guts from leaking out. We put a sheet over him so no one sees his face gone dull yellow-white with a strange shine and a great stillness. Then we push him down to the morgue.

We take out the long lemon metal tray, slide his body into it, and slide the tray back into the freezer. Then we return and file away all his records and cards, writing across them: EXPIRED.

My watch said 6:55. I went over to the sink and splashed water all over my face. I ran cold water on my wrists. Then I walked back to the medicine room.

"Something the matter, Mr. Jacobs?" Gilly asked.

"Gersh—he's dead," I told Stoney. Stoney nodded and got up.

"You and Mr. Stoneham take care of it, Mr. Jacobs," Gilly said. "I'll give you your reports separately."

I started to go back to the room, but Stoney grabbed my arm. "Who's on call?"

"I don't know."

"Who's on call?" Stoney yelled over to the ward clerk at the desk in front of the medicine room.

"Vail, I think."

"Page him. He'll have to sign the death certificate."

"We're out of those, Stoney," the ward clerk said.

"Oh, that's perfect. Perfect. We should be in a fuckin' movie."

"I'll see if some other floor has some," the ward clerk volunteered.

"Never mind—when you page Vail, have him bring one." one."

"He won't like that."

"Tell him tough shit," Stoney snapped.

"You're sure?" the ward clerk said.

"I'll be responsible."

"O.k." said the clerk. "It's your funeral."

"My patient," Stoney said in a clipped voice.

"I'm sorry," the clerk said. "I wasn't thinking."

"Forget it," Stoney smiled, winking at me. "Well, it looks like it's gonna be a great day. Let's go."

Mrs. Gersh and the relatives arrived around noon. I dreaded seeing them, yet they all came—in dark coats, the men in dark suits,the women in dark dresses. Mrs. Gersh wore black, her eyes were red. Her hair seemed greyer, as if all the blue in the grey had vanished. I felt like laughing like an idiot: everyone dressed up for Gersh who was lying naked in a lemon-yellow metal tray in a cold room. I could tell how self-consciously some of the relatives were dressed. Hank, wearing a dark black suit with a white shirt and black tie, moved painfully polite, and smelled like ten bottles of after-shave—as if he were trying to uphold a sudden tradition. Anything connected now with Gersh demanded some kind of smell to announce the arrival of Gersh's people. The first part that heard was the nose. I stifled a big smile. The nose. How it goes. I tried to control myself. I braced myself and walked over. I could see Gilly and Stoney talking with Mrs. Gersh and Sid.

"I'm very sorry," I murmured, hoping I didn't sound like I was full of baloney.

Mrs. Gersh nodded. She barely saw me. It was as if she nodded more at what I said.

Hank stepped forward. "We're here for his effects."

Me and Stoney looked at Hank. We looked at Naomi and Joseph and Judy. Their children were there too. Sid stood very close to Mrs. Gersh, holding her up.

"You have my husband's things?" Mrs. Gersh whispered hoarsely.

"Yes," I said. "They're still in the room."

"Yes? I want to go to the room."

I opened the door and took her in. I brought out Gersh's stuff. His brown suit, his white shirt, his brown tie, his grey socks, his brown Florsheim's shoes, his watch, wedding ring, wallet, and keys to his house—all were in a brown valise. His hat, a brown Homberg, I'd placed in a fresh brown bag. I placed them on the nighttable and left the room, hearing the click of the valise snapping open. She'd have some time to look at the clothes she'd seen before and look at them again if she wanted to. I heard sniffing: the sniffing was wet. Soon she came out, looked around, and said, "Is there anything else I'm supposed to do?"

"No, that's about it," I said, staring over at Stoney who was giving Sid papers to sign.

"What? I can't hear you," Mrs. Gersh said.

"I said, No, that's it. That's fine."

"Yes," she breathed. "Well—" She started to hold her hand out to me, began shaking, and fell against Sid's chest. She steadied herself, and walked off, followed by her relatives and cousins trying to comfort and hold her. She shrugged them all off and took her grandchildren's hands, as if leading them to the first day of school or wanting to hold onto something fresh, young and vital, more than an old pair of socks and a suit, and less full of memories.

As the elevator door closed on them, a house-keeping team trudged up the hall toward Gersh's room, toting a bucket of disinfectant and a full bottle of PineSol. I waved at Tommy and Gloria. They nodded.

"No need to tell me which room," Gloria said. "I know exactly where it is."

I just looked at her. They wheeled their buckets and mops in, silently, professionally, and began mopping and squeezing with Tommy lining up the buffing machine. By the door I noticed the door slot still held a name tag. It was a simple strip of paper in a plastic holder on the door and read: Gerson, Z. I took out the strip, poking it with my pencil. I tore it into halves, then quarters, then eights, until I couldn't tear it any more. I let the pieces of paper fall into the trashcan like pieces of cheap snow.

"Well," grinned a passing doctor sarcastically, "having fun and working hard?"

"I always have fun," I said staring him in the eyes.

"Busy too, I see," the doctor stated.

"Uh huh," I said, wondering if he'd report me to Gilly.

"Come on," Stoney suddenly said, sidling over, "Let's finish the rest of our break with some coffee."

I looked at him, almost saying, "What? We haven't even gone on break yet." Then I saw the doctor watching us, eyeing Stoney, and I said, "Yeah, yeah, let's finish." The doctor left. By the t.v. in the waiting room stood Hank, with his coat on his arm, a smile suddenly appearing. He suddenly looked mournful and solemn. He took out his wallet.

"Well, men."

We stared at him.

"I understand that both of you took care of my father-in-law."

"That's right," I said. Stoney folded his arms.

Hank smiled at us, as if we all shared a secret.

"Well, on behalf of some of the family, we'd like you to have a token of our, um, appreciation for the fine job you've done."

He was holding out two fives.

Stoney coughed.

"Got a rule 'bout takin' tips."

"That's right," I said.

Hank winked.

"Well, you know the old saying, 'Rules were made to be broken.' Heh, heh."

"That's true," Stoney grinned, nodding his head, his hands in his pockets. "That's very true."

"Well?" Hank grinned.

"Only thing is, is sometimes rules're worth breakin', sometimes they ain't. This time they ain't."

"I don't understand."

"No?" Stoney said, smiling very softly, his hands deeper in his pockets. "Go down to the morgue and ask your father-in-law."

Hank's face reddened. "Well, if you don't want the money just say so."

Stoney smiled blandly. I stood there as Hank shoved his money back into his wallet, frowning.

"This is stupid!" he said, "Stupid!"

I didn't say anything. Stoney began whistling.

"Well it's no skin off my ass," Hank grumbled, putting on his overcoat.

I looked at Stoney. He whistled, smiling. Hank stomped over to the elevator, smacked the down button, paced back and forth, then flung the stairwell door open and clumped down the stairs.

Stoney grinned expansively. "How 'bout we take that break now? Seems like the perfect time. I'll buy."

"Broke as you are?" I said.

"Broke as I am, little friend, I got some," Stoney smiled, stretching his arms, "I got some."

A Routine Death

It was a raining autumn Sunday, and another "routine death." Another old man nobody knew was found unconscious in a cheap hotel room and brought in by ambulance to our emergency room with seedy clothes, a watch, a ring, and a wallet with a social security card and a six month old lottery ticket. He reached the ward in a coma; three hours later a member of the house staff pronounced him dead. That's when they called me and Stoney to take the body down to the morgue.

I met Stoney at the elevator, the morgue kit in my hands. I never got accustomed to the shiny brass box that looked like nothing special.

"Got everything, kid?"

"Yes," I nodded, holding the kit in the crook of my left arm, grabbing the end of a guerney with my right. I'd looked all over three floors for a guerney—the two from my floor were gone. We weren't supposed to use guernies from other floors, but since there was a shortage of guernies like everything else, we orderlies and aides took what we could find.

"Well, for starters, son, you can let go of that guerney. I ain't gonna steal it—we're workin' this one together, remember?"

"Sure," I laughed, reddening.

"Well," Stoney smiled, "let's get on down to the meat department and see what's on sale."

I nodded, shaking my head at Stoney's remarks, then I shuddered, remembering the wintry chill of the morgue.

707 was a two-bed room. The bed by the door was empty, neatly white. In the bed by the window stared the corpse with the peculiar hush that always jarred me. The corpse was a short, unshaven man wearing the standard flimsy pale yellow nightgown over his scrawny aged body. I moved closer, studying the small snowy-fringed balding head with the white tuft forelock like stuck-together chicken feathers above a rodent-like face: small eyes, a soft snarled nose with slightly flared nostrils, and a mouth protruding its upper lip into such a sour expression I wondered what the old man, dying, thought.

Stoney scowled. "I thought this sucker was supposed to be big. Shit. You can take him down yourself."

I shrugged. "They said he was big."

"They don't know," Stoney grumbled. "They don't know 'cause they never do it. Oho, wait a minute, now, wait just a minute."

"Huh?"

Stoney nodded, shaking my sleeve. "Remember what happened yesterday up on eight?"

"No."

"Well, they were busy as hell when someone kicked the bucket, and this poor little student nurse, who thought she had a patient that was no sweat—like she'd been told—well, she couldn't find no one so she tried to take down her 'easy patient' herself. Well, she never done this kind of thing before, and the stiff fell off the guerney, which was bad enough. What made it even worse was just as it fell off some visitors were walkin' down the hall. Seen the whole thing. Now that's bad. Reflects on the hospital, and alla that. Not to mention common decency, and alla that."

I whistled, and tried not to laugh.

"Anyways, 'causa that they want all bodies goin' down in twos for a spell. It's unofficial, but that's how they're playin' it. Who knows, it could start a whole new program. Maybe they'll get someone other than us to wrap these chops and put 'em in the freezer."

COLD – BUT HAVE TO BE

I frowned.

"See if that nurse had been usta it, like it's no big thing —it's like givin' a bedpan—well, she wouldn't have dropped it, see?"

"You mean cause it's all routine."

"That's right. You got it."

"Yeah," I said, staring at the corpse, "I got it."

Stoney frowned at me. "Hey son, you lived as long as me, and been doin' this for a while, and you'll see what I mean. People are meat, boy."

have to believe that

"People are human beings." *– no matter who you are – like*

"No argument there son, none at all. We are human *story* beings and meat. Light meat, dark meat, but don't fool your- *not it all* self—when it comes your turn, like this little shrimp here, no *greedy* one asks too much, and it don't make a whole lotta differ- *w/ cash* ence either." *worth not them*

"Well that's a mouthful," I said, feeling a little bad about arguing with Stoney, since he was simply trying to edu- cate me.

"Look at it this way, son, we are the proud kind of meat. We are thinkin' meat." *– bums don't think*

"O.k. O.k.," I laughed. "I get the picture."

"It's the same reason why rigor mortis is like the sun goin' down," Stoney smiled slyly.

"How's that?" I asked, feeding him.

"It sets the same for everybody," he deadpanned.

I tried to keep a straight face as Stoney slapped his thigh and chuckled.

"Yeah," I said sourly.

"I'm funnin'. You don't laugh a little you ain't gonna last too long around here." I didn't say anything.

Stoney strolled over to the corpse, smiled, and patted the bald head, "O.k., pops, it's almost time to go. Now I want you to make sure you got everything,'' and laughed again, this time out loud.

Then we both grew silent as I opened the morgue kit and took out the silken ties and the sheets. Stoney washed the body as I helped him lift the heavier-by-the-minute arms, the leaden jaw so he could wash the neck, the chilled rock-like sides to wash the back. I helped Stoney dry the body. Then Stoney tied the hands across the chest. I tied the feet at the ankles, just above the big bone. Stoney tied up the penis and testicles. I took one of the fresh sheets and put it over the guerney. I took another and folded it in half. We pushed the corpse to one side of the bed, then put half the sheet on the guerney and half on the bed. Then we rolled the corpse along the sheet, Stoney pushing back the guerney to the bedside and me at the head of the guerney turning the corpse's head and shoulders as Stoney strained with the legs and hips. Once the corpse was on the guerney side of the bed, I went to the other side, leaned, and pushed the corpse toward Stoney who caught the corpse with a grunt. Then I came around while Stoney held up the corpse. I took the part of the sheet on the bed, and pulled toward the guerney, as Stoney pulled the corpse. This last motion successfully pushed the corpse onto the guerney, with Stoney holding him, and me pulling the sheet off the bed and onto the guerney. We then draped the body with another sheet. I made sure the feet weren't showing. One time I had breathlessly done everything perfectly, and wheeling the guerney down the hall I was stopped by an aide who asked me to hold on a minute because she wanted to put some nail polish on the toes, winking quickly as she pulled the sheet down over the feet.

We wheeled the guerney toward the elevator. A few nurses passed us. Stoney winked at them. ''Mornin' ladies.''

''How are you, Stoney?'' one of them smiled.

''Fine, fine. Just me, the kid, and the filet mignon here.''

They stared at the guerney and frowned. ''You're horrible,'' the nurse giggled.

''Wanna come down with us? We can have ourselves a little par-tee. A little barbecue.''

"Really," said the other nurse disapprovingly.

"You're awful," the first nurse tittered.

Stoney wiggled his hips slightly. "Some nice cold cuts."

The elevator doors opened. As we wheeled the guerney in, Stoney shouted just as the doors were closing, "And don't forget Today's Special—a nice thick T-BONE," getting a last shred of giggling laughter and a glare from several doctors and nurses. Stoney, his face impassive, held the deadman's neck so he wouldn't bounce when the elevators stopped.

We were the last ones off—at the basement. I could feel the dampness. Stoney began whistling "When The Saints Go Marching In" as we wheeled the corpse down the hall.

"You're bein' pretty quiet, kid. This stiff here's makin' more noise than you."

I shrugged.

"You think I don't respect the dead, huh?"

"I didn't say that."

"Yeah. You didn't say that."

"I don't know," I shrugged.

"Boy, that's one of your favorite sayings there. For someone who's supposed to be smart, there's sure a lot you don't know."

He stopped, and thought a second. "Hmm, maybe that's what makes you smart."

He resumed the whistling. "You mind me whistlin'. Think that's awful, too?"

"No."

"You sure?"

"I'm sure."

"Then why dontcha whistle with me? Keep your mind off things. People like you thinkin', always thinkin' too much."

I started whistling, then stopped and looked around furtively.

"Don't worry," Stoney chuckled, "ain't no law against whistlin' yet. 'Sides, it's just us and the rest of it. Place is dead. Ooops."

"Maybe we can try whistling in harmony," I smiled.

Stoney started back up with "When the Saints Go

Marching In''; I followed, repeating him. I could see the light from the morgue. Even when unoccupied, a single light was kept on—in case someone needed to bring a body down.

We opened the big darkgreen door with the one white-painted word: MORGUE. Freezing air hit us, along with the medicinal stench of lysol, formaldehyde, and chemicals my nose couldn't place. In the middle of the room lay the long autopsy table, and behind it rose windows with frosted glass. Long ago, this part of the basement had been a warehouse, giving the impression now of windows below ground-level. Every time I entered the morgue I thought: how appropriate —the dead have frosted glass windows below the ground.

To our right stood rows of freezers: an entire wall of lemon-yellow lockers with shining chrome handles. Inside each locker was a long lemon-yellow tray with blue-grey insides, the color of cracked open pavement. To the left stood a huge cabinet supplying the mortician's tools and medicines. There was a filthy canvas cart where the morticians threw their used aprons.

On the long autopsy table lay a cut-open body. I gagged at the old woman with her throat slit. The slit went down her body's entire length. The brightly colored insides resembled an enormous chicken—dark purplish colored organs mixed in with yellow fat and red-orange smaller organs. I heard a fingersnap, twice.

"Hey, hey."

"Hmm?"

"Ain't too good to look too long at stiffs, son. I could tell you all kinds of tales my grandmother usta pass down to all of us, me, my brothers, sisters, and a mess of cousins, not to mention all the neighborhood kids, about what happens to folks who stare too long at the dead—if you believe in that stuff of course."

His stare twinkled. "Sometimes they trade places with you if you ain't careful. Just stories of course."

"Just stories," I nodded, feeling chilly.

"But then again, I heard these stories a whole lot of places. From a whole lot of people too."

I didn't say anything. Stoney studied the lockers, strolling around the room, appealing to various chrome handles. "Now ain't that right, folks? Ain't that right?"

He laughed, but eyed the freezers with bold caution, as if half-expecting that a freezer would suddenly slide open and agree, "That's right." Then he sighed. "Well, enough of that. Let's put this old-timer to bed, and get outta here." I opened one of the lockers and, reaching in, pulled the tray out easily. My hands were freezing. We turned towards the guerney to pull it closer.

The body sat up, the sheet dropping to the belly. The tufted bald head blinked sleepily.

"Haremph," the corpse muttered.

JEZUZZ FUCKING CHEEERICE!" Stoney gasped, his whole face bulging. My mouth felt like it was gonna land right on my big toe as I heard my own voice: "WHAAAA!"

The bald head frowned grumpily, trying by instinct to untie his knotted hands, prick, balls, and feet by wrinkling his nose and shoulders. The eyes blinked. The neck turned slowly towards the autopsy table. The old man stopped, sniffed, and coughed, tottering precariously. Stoney darted forward, straightened him, and jumped back. I tried to move, froze. The old man teetered again, the guerney sliding. Trembling, Stoney quickly shoved him into the center of the guerney, then stepped back as if scalded.

The old man cleared his throat. "Where am I?" he croaked, focusing on us, the locker, the metal tray. He shivered toothlessly, then spotted the autopsy table and brightly split-open corpse. He shrieked, shuddering, his gaping face going white, red, white. "AWWWWWAAAAHHH! AWWWWAAAHHH! OH MY GOD, BLEEDING JESUS MOTHER MARY! THEY'RE GOING TO BURY ME ALIVE! AWWWWAAAAHHH!"

I don't know how it happened, but we were suddenly backing up against each other, moving, running, rushing past the old man, past the gaping scream on the guerney and the gleaming single light bulb and the strong smell and freezing air, the lockers, the bald tufted head, the metal shining all over the chilled room, pushing past each other down the hall, turning the corner down another hall past empty used-up oxygen tanks, broken bed-parts, old carts, busted wheel-chairs, and smack into a waiting doctor and a nurse.

"What is this?" the doctor frowned. I recognized him—he was an endocrinology specialist. Glands. I snickered. A glands man.

Stoney gasped, trying to catch his breath.

"What the hell is going on here?" the doctor demanded. The nurse looked at us strangely. Down the hall we heard a faint scream.

"What's that?" asked the nurse, leaning her head forward to hear better.

"Simple," Stoney panted.

"Yes," waited the doctor, drumming his fingers on a clipboard in his hands.

"A man that was pronounced dead is not."

"I don't understand," the doctor breathed quickly, trembling.

The nurse raised her hand to her mouth.

"The patient is not dead."

"Oh my GOD!" the nurse gasped. "That's AW-FUL! How horrible! That poor man!"

"Yeah," agreed Stoney, "We just gonna go back now and get that poor old man and bring him back to his room."

I saw Stoney's hand shaking, even though he kept it behind his back away from the doctor and the nurse. I spotted it.

"This is a disgrace," the doctor said, gritting his teeth. "How could this happen! My GOD!"

I shrugged.

"You'll have to file an incident report immediately, if not sooner."

Stoney nodded.

"Go with them, Miss Delaney, and see if the patient needs any medication."

The nurse nodded.

As we returned rapidly to the morgue, the old man was tearing at his wrists with his toothless mouth and his nose. He saw us and shrieked loudly, "Murderers! Animals! OOOO, you'll lose your shirt over this! Mother Mary, I'll sue your asses off!"

He began sobbing. Miss Delaney rushed over to him, crooning, "There, there, Mr., Mr.," looking unsuccessfully for his nameband on his nude wrist.

"Finster" wept the old man. "Finster." His voice grew louder, "You hear me? MY NAME IS LEONARD FINSTER!"

He bawled, then screamed "LEONARD FINSTER" as if trying vocally to push his name above death and nudity. He wept into the nurse's soft breasts, noticed they were good full young breasts, and kept his face there, moaning mournfully, "My friends call me Finney," weeping with one eye open.

"What a pretty name," crooned the nurse, comforting him, patting the tuft on his bald head.

"We're t-t-terribly sorry," Stoney muttered, "sorry as hell, Mr. Finster. We're just glad you're alive, and we'll have you fixed up in no time, sir."

I stared at Stoney: it was the first time I ever heard him call anyone sir.

"I'll bet!" Finster snapped, staring at me and Stoney. "If you're so goddam glad, how come you was gettin' ready to deep-freeze me! AWWWWWAAAAHHH, Jesus, get me outta here!"

We wheeled him out of the morgue and back to the elevator, the nurse stroking his head, soothingly, walking along. Finster raved all the way up the elevator.

"Tying me up like I was a chicken! Tying up my dick! If you did anything to me down there, I'll kill you so help me God. You, Nazis, you were probably going to use me for some horrible experiment. Some work of the devil—Oh God in Heaven!"

As the elevator doors opened, nurse Delaney whispered, "He needs a tranquilizer BAD!"

"Let's get him into the room quick," Stoney whispered to me. We wheeled him fast; inside the room we moved to take him off the guerney.

He spat at us. "Don't touch me," he hissed. "Don't let him get me," he whined to the nurse. "They're gonna kill me, oooo," he wept again. "Can't a man even pass out drunk in his own place any more. Didn't you ever hear a man's home is his castle?"

Stoney folded his arms, leaned closer, and warily waited to see if he'd spit again. On Stoney's clenched fist, the jaw trembled. "Mister," Stoney began softly, "you were found unconscious. In a coma. All anyone wanted to do was take care of you. That's what we're here for. See you get better. They made a big, bad mistake. But that's over with now. And you'll be home before you know it."

Finster glared at Stoney, curling his lips as if to spit again. But before anything could happen, Stoney turned and stalked out of the room. I followed, hearing the nurse call, "I can handle him." I had to walk even faster than usual to keep pace with Stoney. The nurse called out to him, "Aren't you going to file an incident report?"

'When I get back. First thing," Stoney shouted without stopping. He opened the door to the stairs. "C'mon, let's forget the elevator. I'm sick of elevators anyhow."

Down in the dining room, Stoney got a cup of coffee, and pulled out his cigarettes, and lit up.

"Aren't you going to eat anything?" I asked.

He was quiet. He slowly drank the black coffee, smoked, and stared out the window at the grey wet sky. After a few minutes, he pushed the cup back, gently placed the cigarette in the ashtray, and put his head in his hands. Other orderlies and aides coming into the break room moved past him quietly, especially after I motioned some of them away.

"Hey," I finally smiled, "Know why I'm a genius?"

He silently rubbed his temples.

"Know why?" I repeated.

"No why?" he mumbled.

"I'm a genius cause I know something's wrong. Real wrong—right?" I smiled idiotically on purpose.

Stoney pushed his close-cropped hair back, and took a sip of coffee, grimacing. "We're lucky the coffee here's so nutritious seeing how this looks like lunch," I added.

"Um," Stoney grunted. He stared at the coffee.

"Don't you wanna get somethin' more to help you through the day?" I smiled.

"Ain't gonna be no rest of the day, son. I'm goin' home as soon as I finish this mud and have a last smoke."

I stared at him. He stared back crankily.

"And don't ask."

"I don't have to."

"Smart kid. Maybe some day you'll be as smart as me," he frowned, disgustedly.

"Hope so," I said.

He looked me straight in the eyes and smiled, embarrassed. Then he lit up, whooshed the smoke out, and nodded. "Yep, I'm gonna take a nice long walk. Think through some things."

"And have a few," I suggested, grinning, making a tilting-glass motion. Stoney glared at me.

"No. I'm goin' for a long walk. A real walk. You know, where one foot follows the other."

I watched him return to staring out the window, muttering how in all his years he'd seen a lot of things, a whole lot of things, then shaking his head. He rose, cup in hand. "Want some more coffee?"

"You buyin'?" I smiled.

"Do you want some more coffee or don't you?"

"Sure."

When he came back he drank his straight down without even blowing on it, and stubbed out his cigarette.

"Well, son."

"You still got fifteen minutes breaktime left."

"Yeah, but by the time I get back up there, write down what happened, and tell 'em I'm gone—if I do—" He stopped in mid-sentence

"Yeah?"

He went back for another cup of coffee, took a table closer to the window, and lit up.

"You o.k.?" I asked, coming over. He waved me back.

"Nothing's wrong. Just feel like being by myself for a few minutes. I'll see ya later son, don't mind me right now."

"O.k. Then I'll see you tomorrow."

"Probably."

When I returned to the ward, I filled out an Unusual Occurrence report. The head nurse told me the doctor had already informed Nursing Services, Administration, and the

Medical Chief, who was meeting with the young doctor who had pronounced Finster dead. There would be a further investigation once Mr. Stoneham returned from his unauthorized leave. Mr. Finster was presently in the ward, being treated to a special lunch of steak and a glass of wine, courtesy of the hospital. Some patients raised a slight stir when they saw Mr. Finster's lunch but had calmed down once his situation and special circumstances had been explained. I was told that under no circumstances was I to give out any information concerning the incident to anyone claiming to be a medical or legal representative of Mr. Finster. Apparently he'd threatened suit, even though he was just a South Boston derelict with no money and no friends, but just to be on the safe side. . . .

They also transferred my assignment away from his room, but around three o'clock it got hectic, and, as usual, they called me to help out in the ward. I was to take Mr. Finster downstairs and call him a cab.

I walked into the room. Finster, fully clothed, wore old grey wool slacks, brogans, a blue flannel shirt with a grey vest. Over his arm was a greasy grey coat and a yellow flannel scarf. In his hand he held a battered brown derby.

As soon as he spotted me, he began pointing excitedly. "There he is men, there's one of them gravediggers now!"

"That's just the kid," Reiner and Slattery laughed. "He's fine."

"You think so," Finster frowned. By his nightstand was a tray with a T-bone picked clean and an empty wine glass. All that was left was a sprig of parsley.

"Hello, Mr. Finster," I said cautiously. "I uh, uh."

"What?"

"Where's Stoney, kid?" Reiner asked.

"He went home. Personal business."

"They didn't can him did they?"

"No. Besides, if they fired him, they'd fire me too."

"No, I don't think so. Your college wouldn't like that. Have to check with them first. Besides, from what I hear it wasn't your fault."

"Whaddaya mean," Finster scowled, angry that for a second I was the center of attention.

"Len, Dov's going to take you to your cab," smiled nurse Delaney. "Is that all right?"

She stroked his head. He put his stubbled cheek against her chest and frowned. "Why can't you take me?"

"I have a million and one things to do."

"Too bad. They're gettin' me a cab, I could give you a lift home."

"Now, now, you've had a very horrible experience and you're still recuperating."

Finster frowned, nodding, "You're right. I am a little whoozy." He leaned against her as she gently disengaged him. Reiner winked at me.

Me and Delaney helped Finster into the wheelchair; I took the handles. "All set?"

"Yeah, just remember where you're takin' me this time."

Finster sneezed loudly, and nurse Delaney turned. "Are you *sure* you don't want to stay overnight?"

"Positive. You couldn't *pay* me to stay here. I'd stay up all night, wondering if someone was gonna come in while I was sleepin' and say 'Whaddaya know, that poor old guy is dead again'."

Reiner and Slattery laughed. Finster snorted.

"Yeah, it's funny now, but for a few seconds there I coulda been leg of Finster."

I took the handles and moved him out of the room, trying to see and imagine how just three hours ago he'd sat up. Time was a joke. It was not three hours, or a clock. Seconds could be years. Just a few years ago me and Stoney took down a dead man. Now the dead man was adjusting his flannel yellow scarf and surreptitiously picking his nose. He would soon take a taxi home to the room where he'd been found blotto, presumably in a deep coma. I felt exhausted. Neither of us spoke a word in the elevator, nor as I wheeled him to the emergency room exit and called a taxi. Although some sun brightened the grey November day, it was cold enough for him to pull his scarf tighter.

"You know," I sighed, "it really wasn't our fault," hoping I wouldn't set him off again, but needing to take the chance. I hated any patient thinking badly of me.

"Yeah. Just doin' your job. That's what Eichmann said, sonny."

"Hey—I'm Jewish, you know?" I snapped, wondering what the hell I was arguing about, why the hell I was trying to convince this old man I'd probably never see again.

"Maybe you are and maybe you aren't," Finster sneered. "All I know is — I'm alive, and no thanks to you."

I didn't answer. I just stood there silently, holding the wheelchair handles, waiting for the taxi in the cold autumn sun. I noticed Finster was also wearing a brown bow-tie. In his old rooster way, he looked dapper. The cab pulled up.

"Well," Finster snorted, "this sure beats a hearse, don't it?"

I nodded sourly.

"Here's hopin' they take you and your buddy off the stiff detail."

I nodded, watching the cabbie open the door and lean out to help Finster in.

I gripped his elbow as he rose. He scowled.

"I can manage," he said, pushing away my hand. As he was turning, his eyes caught the narrow strip of grass at the emergency room steps, between a sign along the side that said EMERGENCY ROOM and the steps themselves was a small purple flower on a piece of sunlit mud.

"Look at that goddam flower," Finster pointed. "Look at that purple sonuvabitch."

I looked.

"That's the purplest flower I ever seen."

"Pretty purple," I agreed.

"It makes sense, don't it, that old as I am, I saw it, and young as you are, you didn't see it."

I shrugged. Finster glared at me. In the background the cabbie fidgeted.

"You don't know what the hell I'm talkin' about do you," he scowled, turning and greedily looking at the flower.

"Yeah I do."

"Sure," he snorted, muttering, "in the dead of fall. Ain't that somethin'."

"Uh huh."

He turned, glaring. "Next thing you're gonna tell me is you're a botanist or a florist, hah?"

"The driver's waiting."

As Finster bent into the cab, the cabbie reached for his arm and helped him in, smiling, "How's it going old-timer?"

Finster was already reving up as he eased into his seat: "It's been a nightmare, buddy, let me tell you—I'm back from the dead."

I saw the cabbie's face change: he took a deep breath, sighing, bracing himself, and starting up the cab as Finney's voice picked up strength, "I'm tellin' you—Lazarus had nothin' on me, pal."

I smiled sweetly and waved as the cab pulled away with Finney leaning closer so the driver could better hear the whole story.

The day ended with people going off and coming on asking me what had happened. A few orderlies on the swing shift offered to give me and Stoney refresher courses, and laughed when I told them to get fucked. I told them they could kid me but to watch out for Stoney. An older nurse wanted to know how come we had assumed the man was dead after we'd been told to take him down—it was always best to check. I answered by saying maybe there should be a new procedure: throw five buckets of icewater on all dead bodies.

As I was getting ready to leave, I ran into Linc, an orderly, and Thelma, an aide — two of Stoney's best friends. Linc asked Thelma to take his pulse, then played dead, dying horribly and begging with me to take him down to the morgue. As Thelma placed her hands on his forehead playfully, he rose up instantly, grinning, "How'd you like to go dancing tonight, baby?"

Thelma looking slyly at me, smiled, "Sorry, honey, I don't go dancin' with corpses."

They both laughed and looked at me. I had to laugh too. Then Thelma grew serious. "They're mad as hell at Stoney for leavin'."

I shrugged.

"And he always tells me I take things too hard. Well, it finally happened to him. Ha," Linc laughed, his eyes serious.

"He just up and left? That's not like him at all," Thelma said.

"Well, they won't fire him," Linc said, "they need him too much."

I stood there, wondering if Linc was right.

And he was, just as he said, and just as Stoney said the next day. We talked early in the morning, dressing with the sky still dark. I asked him how his walk went. He sat there in his T-shirt and pants, smoking, quiet, calm-muscled, yet still in the hushed mood from the day before.

"You know, son, I've worked in hospitals almost twenty years now, including medic in the service, and that's never happened. I thought I'd seen it all. Then that sonuvabitch shrimp sits up."

He shuddered. I didn't say anything, just nodded.

"Do you know I got a certificate in Urology? Took a two year course at night. Studied hard. Old lady almost left me. Yeah, I worked for that sucker. It ain't no big time college degree, but it's two years, and certified. It's a legal document. And they know here I'm the best they got. Even some of the docs know that—the ones that can stand not being jealous of me for more than five minutes. But I might have to leave for awhile. Done it before. Sometimes I leave so these suckers wiil appreciate old Stoney."

"You gonna quit?"

"No. I thought about it. But not because I thought they'd try and can me and wanted to get the jump on 'em. They won't do that. Not even over this. They might have if this guy had had some big bucks, but, no, they won't do it over him. But, what I thought about for awhile when I was walking, among other things—I thought about a whole lot of things son, I wound up in Waterville—"

I whistled long and soft. Waterville was a good ten miles from the hospital.

"Yeah, hadda take three trains to get home. No, what I was thinking was maybe I should leave and get some rest. If I can't tell a man's dead or not, maybe I need a long rest."

"I don't quite follow you," I said.

"Son," he continued softly, "look at it like this: if we had just closed the door—just shut the shining handle—we woulda killed that man. You and me. Close that door like your frigidaire at home, and he's dead."

I shuddered.

"And I feel like I shoulda been able to sense some kind of life. That shoulda happened. It *shoulda*."

He said this while tying his shoes. He pulled so hard he almost snapped off the laces. I looked through the small basement window that almost reached the street. The dawn was starting: the sky no longer black, but pearly grey with bluish-white light.

Stoney smart have feelings

"But that's like sayin' there's some kind of sixth sense, or ESP or something," I frowned.

Stoney stared at me like he often did, wondering if I was a moron, a college kid, or both. "Yeah? So?"

"Well, I can't see it," I said, shaking my head.

"You can't see atoms or microbes either, son. Just cause you can't see it don't mean it ain't there."

"Maybe."

"So you might, could go for it?"

"I don't know."

"Well, I do. I've felt it, sensed it—like what I was tellin' you yesterday when...when...huh...hmmmm."

He suddenly bolted up, staring at nothing. I nudged him, he excitedly pushed my hand away.

"Let me think for a minute. Hold on now." His eyes, sad and dull before, shone like brown fire.

"What's up?"

"I been thinkin' about yesterday, but it only just now hit me."

"Huh?"

He slammed his fist into his palm. "THAT'S IT!"

"What's it? What?"

He laughed and lit up a fresh cigarette, blowing the smoke out of his nostrils, looking at me, and laughing some more. "You know, we're gonna get the brunt of this thing, right? And, look, I know yesterday I left you holding the bag and I'm sorry about that, though I did call some folks later last night just to make sure they hadn't landed on you too hard, or fired both of us outright or given us suspensions, but, well, I knew that wouldn't happen. But still, you know some of them damn doctors and nurses can damn near kill someone with a wrong shot or the wrong medicine, they can almost blow it completely and they're covered, but let someone like me or you make one goof and the shit will hit the fan, Jack. Only they take me back, even when I leave and don't tell 'em, even without a union, and you know why?'' He paused to catch his breath.

"Why?" I asked.

"*Think.*"

"They need you. You're good."

"Good nothin'. I'm the best."

He put on the top of his uniform and rubbed a towel along his shoes, spiffing them up. I waited.

'And what I just figured out—just now shootin' the shit with you—is that even yesterday I was still in there, right on target, without even knowin' it on a straight-ahead conscious level."

He laughed heartily and buttoned his shirt. I stared at him utterly bewildered.

"What are you talking about?"

He smiled, twisting and untwisting his stethoscope.

"I figured I saved that old fart's life."

"*How?*" I asked, almost angrily.

"Don't you see it, son?" What we were just *talkin'* about."

"Talkin' about what?"

"The ESP jazz."

"So?"

"So? So?" he grinned, twisting the stethoscope tubing around his wrists and gripping the silver cups like brass knuckles. "So remember when I was talkin' about Louisiana and the stories about all them bodies and stuff, and tellin' you not to stare too long at the bodies or they was gonna swap places with you? All them things I usta hear back home about comin' back from the dead and all?''

"Yeah, yeah.''

"Well I figure that old guy, in his own way, heard that shit. You hear me? HEARD it, in his coma.''

Stoney's voice was different now, possessing a sense of mystery and a growing assurance, as if he was deep-down trying to convince himself with each twist of the tubing and grip of the cups.

"Sounds reasonable,'' I said.

"*Reasonable*! There ain't nothin' in this shit reasonable! But it does make sense.''

I shrugged, yet suddenly remembering how people in comas could hear, as if a long way off, or underwater. I suddenly felt chilled.

"So I figure the old fart took heart, and somehow said to himself, ''Hey, shit, I ain't dead. They just think I'm dead. I'm just in the deepest goddam drunk I ever been in, and I better get the fuck out before they put me away for keeps. So up and at 'em baby'.''

My head hurt.

"And all that talkin' between you and me sorta prodded him into roustin' himself.''

"Yeah,'' I smiled, feeling a little crazy.

"So, you could say I raised that bastard from the dead.'' Stoney looked around the room, proud and cautious. "In a way you understand.''

"Uh huh.''

"And instead of them dumpin' on me and you, they should give us some kind reward. A bonus. Or a big dinner.''

I nodded, smiling. We started upstairs with Stoney insistent, "At the very least, a ceremonial dinner.''

I couldn't help laughing a little. Stoney nodded, excited.

"I'll take a nice thick steak, medium-rare, with everything on it. How does that grab ya?

"Sounds good.''

"With some fancy-assed mushrooms smotherin' it, and some nice thick gravy, and some of them big beefsteak tomatoes.''

"Corn on the cob," I added, in my mind putting on butter, and pepper.

"Yeah. And some bread to soak up that good gravy."

"You got it," I laughed.

"And of course, a little somethin' to wash it down with."

"Course."

I grinned mischievously to myself, then, keeping my face serious, casually added, "I'll call Finster and see what he recommends."

Stoney stopped abruptly.

"What Finster recommends, huh?"

I nodded solemnly. Stoney nodded, both of us trying to keep a straight face. We kept nodding, looking like we were listening to jazz, until neither of us could hold it any longer, and we both burst out laughing.

have to laugh at it all — if you take it too seriously, you go crazy. I feel like shit all the time

Autumn Leaves

In the pre-dawn darkness the tiny window was a dark blue square. I waited for the alarm to hit six a.m. My roommate Pete snored in the upper bunk. I pictured myself: washing up, dressing, making eggs and coffee, leaving our tiny dump, walking along the hushed Cambridge streets to the train. The day loomed: the locker room, the ward, Linc, Stoney.

I shuddered just as the alarm rang. The floor was chilly. On Pete's wall calendar a sexy redhead announced November —a stirring upper body shot.

Dressing, I remembered Linc's quip, "Another day, another half-a-dollar"—I threw cold water on my face and made breakfast in the kitchen barely big enough to stand in, rereading yesterday's mail.

You're working on a CANCER ward? That's rough. What's that got to do with film-making?

Are you taking care of yourself? How's Boston? Such a rich city. How is it being on your own? You know we worry.

Saw *Wild Strawberries* last night. Bergman's strange. Thanks for telling me about 'Don't Think Twice It's All Right'. I liked it, but it scares me. Can a song scare you?

The CORE chapter here is picking up. You should really join when you come back.

I finished another cup of coffee, bolted down the eggs, and tried fighting my dread of going to work—the pained faces, sheets, smell of alcohol and urinals, the coughing and groans of ill men waking. I sighed and went out, the morning chilly, dark. Shivering, I pulled my peacoat closer, teasing myself. The kid looks like a character in an Italian Neo-Realist film: dark brown eyes, small thin face, strong jaw, wiry build in peacoat, turtleneck, jeans, workboots—in the dark, in the city.

The lights were just coming on along the grey streets of the no-man's land between Roxbury and Dorchester. No fresh young Cambridge faces here. A vendor in an old leather jacket peeked out, his red weatherbeaten face framed by the newsstand's green dusty wood. "Paper?" I bought one. November 20. A day like any other day.

The locker room was empty. I changed into my orderly uniform, cursing, fighting—they'd starched the buttonholes shut. Up on the ward, Linc and Stoney waved calmly.

"Well, if it ain't the third Musketeer," Linc grinned.

"Hi. What's up?"

"Watch your language," Linc winked.

"Startin' early, huh," remarked Stoney. "You musta had yourself a good lovin' time last night." Linc rubbed his hands.

"Kid, you got the ward. I got the isolation cases. Linc's on house, but I'll help you out some."

"O.k."

It was pretty much a day like any day. There was a new patient, Smitty, who was sitting up, listening to the radio, and picking his nose.

"What's on the news?" Stoney asked.

"A murder in Revere."

Stoney shook his head.

"And Kennedy's visiting Texas. They're gonna have live coverage later on."

"Boy, I'd sure like to travel like that," Stoney yawned, looking around at the still-sleeping faces, and a few yawning and stretching.

Gradually, I started making beds, taking morning temperatures, giving baths, mechanically placing faces with diseases: O'Reilly: bladder cancer; Slattery: stomach cancer and infected legs; Devlin: prostate cancer; Reiner: multiple malignant lung biopsies; Ed: cancer of the throat. I stopped when Ed waved wearily, his other hand touching his heavily bandaged throat from his latest skin graft operation. As I served the breakfast trays and finished the baths, the beginning sun warmed the room through a bright grey sky.

"What's on?" Devlin asked Smitty.

"Mozart," Smitty smiled, his ear against the radio.

"Moe who?" asked Slattery innocently.

"Wolfgang Amadeus Mozart—one of the all-time greats."

"I hearda him," Ed nodded, as Reiner added, "He was one helluva genius. They say he was just a little tad. Picked up right off."

"Yeah," Ed nodded, "four years old and playin' the hell out of the piano."

"My, my," marveled Slattery, "this is like being at a convention of musicologists!"

"Musa-what?" O'Reilly sneered.

"That's a big word for people who like music, John," I said softly.

"You keep usin' those big words, Tim, and I'm gonna have to get you transferred outta here. Why can't you speak English, dammit?"

"Well put, John, well put," Slattery answered. "Give me a little time to think it over."

"Jesus," O'Reilly grumbled, turning on his side. I stared at his urine bottle by his bedside. It was blood-red.

"Too bad your show ain't on yet, O'Reilly," Reiner laughed, "O'Reilly's big on the mystery hour."

"Yeah," Ed nodded, "he's a fuckin' mystery all right."

"You know what you can do, Flanagan," O'Reilly mumbled.

Ed winked just as the nurse entered to change his dressing.

"How ya doin', Eddie?"

"Can't complain."

"Sleep all right?"

"So-so."

"Ready for a new ascot?"

"You're the boss, doll."

Smitty suddenly sat straight up, no longer picking his nose. He held the radio closely with both hands. Reiner stared at him.

"The president's been shot."

"HUH?"

Stoney bringing in some fresh linen, stopped in the middle of the ward; the nurse's hand froze on Ed's neck.

"What are you *talking* about?"

Out in the hall we heard a scream, followed by running steps, another voice—"It's Kennedy!", "WHAT? What!"

Smitty leaned into the radio as Slattery peered sharply at us. O'Reilly bolted up from his blankets. Ed's mouth dropped open. Devlin grabbed the siderails of his bed, his face white, a lock of black hair falling.

"What are they saying?" Stoney asked, "What are they saying, goddamit!"

Smitty leaned into the radio, waving his hand at us to shh, leaning like a safecracker—as if the closer he got to the radio the more information he'd have, as if the information lay hidden behind plastic, wires, and batteries.

"In the head. They shot him in the head!"

"Shit!" Stoney cursed.

"Jesus!"

"Mother of God!"

"Is he alive?" Stoney demanded. "Find out if he's alive."

Devlin groaned. "What's this world coming to?"

The nurse put her hand to her face and ran out. Slattery was trying to get out of bed; I motioned him back. Ed and Reiner shoved back their blankets.

"Just stay put, all of you," Stoney ordered.

O'Reilly stared furiously at Smitty, as if Smitty had just insulted his mother.

"Connally too," Smitty said excitedly. "They got Connally."

"Jackie? Johnson?"

"Jackie's fine. She's with him. Johnson's o.k."

Stoney nodded grimly.

"They're rushin' him to the hospital. Jackie has blood all over her."

"Oh God," Reiner moaned.

"In the head," Devlin brooded, holding his pillow, rubbing his temples.

"Jeez."

I could barely move.

"Jeez, well sometimes it looks worse than it is. If it's just a graze—"

"Stop mumbling," O'Reilly snapped.

"But if it was that, they wouldn't be rushin' him to the hospital, huh?"

"I just can't believe it," Slattery said to no one.

"Get back in bed, Mike," I said, taking Reiner's arm. "You're walkin' around in your bare feet."

"Don't tell me where to fuckin' walk," Reiner cried. "I'll walk where I wanna walk."

"Easy does it, old-timer, easy does it," Stoney crooned, taking Reiner's arm.

Smitty's face tightened. "They're gonna have to operate on his brain!"

"Jesus!"

Devlin frowned. "Jeez, that's very delicate. It's real touch-and-go."

"Someone knew just what they were doing," Slattery nodded bitterly.

"The brain—it's real small. But he'll have the best."

"Fry 'em," Ed blurted, "the rotten dirty bastards. Fry 'em to a crisp!"

"I just can't believe it," Devlin sighed.

"That's cause you're stupid," snapped O'Reilly.

Smitty looked up brightly. "Connally's o.k. He got it in the arm."

Reiner nodded dully, pulling back his covers, getting in bed, and shaking his head, whispering, "Mother of God." O'Reilly lay back in bed, staring at the ceiling.

"You o.k., John?" I asked, feeling numb, hot. He stared silently.

"Hey, Dov," Devlin sighed, "can you get me some water? I don't feel so hot." I got him a glass of water and held it up to his mouth, putting my other hand under his chin. He drank greedily.

"Don't gulp it too fast. It's not good for you."

"I know," he gulped.

Stoney walked out of the ward, saying over his shoulder, "I'm gonna check my patients. The rest of your linen's out here. We still got this dump to run, huh—"

"Check."

As I followed him out and grabbed the rest of the linen, Thelma, one of our aides, came running down the hall, her face wet.

"Did you hear, Dov? Kennedy? He's—"

"Yeah. I heard."

She hugged me, crying. "Why, Dov, why?"

Sheila, our wardclerk, had her head in her arms on the desk. Next to her, Gilly stood staring past the timecards. Three doctors were in frantic conference.

"*When?*"

"Just now! A minute ago!"

"No!"

"They're flying him to D.C. for surgery. Brain. Bad."

Thelma turned toward them in horror. "Oh God!" Stoney hustled over.

"Stay in the ward, kid. Some of those guys don't look so hot. No big thing, but just in case, you know?"

Stoney's jaw trembled slightly, his hand firm on my shoulder. He started to say something, shook his head, and moved down the hall, taking Thelma with him, nudging her, "Hey, beautiful, I need your help for a minute—"

"Why, Stoney?" she sobbed.

"Who knows?" Stoney grumbled, "The world's fuckin' itself by the minute."

I could hear a t.v.: "We interrupt this program to bring you a special news bulletin. President John F. Kennedy has been shot in Dallas, Texas. His condition is critical. He has been taken by ambulance to Dallas Airport where he will be flown to Bethesda Hospital near the nation's capital. A special team of surgeons from Walter Reede Hospital is on alert and will be there upon his arrival. Also wounded was Texas Governor John Connally..."

I stood frozen, no longer hearing, just staring at the linen cart. It was still there. It hadn't moved. It was a dirty white linen cart, piled up with fresh white sheets, pillowcases, and green army blankets.

"Minor wound in the right arm. No one else was injured."

Back in the room, the radio blared away. Reiner, Slattery, and Ed saw me, and, startled, left Smitty's bedside and hustled back to their own beds.

"Apparently, one of the bullets has lodged in the President's brain."

"We know that, you dumb sonuvabitch," Ed shouted at the radio.

"Now in a way," Slattery was saying to Reiner who was staring at his sputum cup, "this country is simply catching up with the rest of the civilized world." Slattery continued, bitter, ironic. "Look at Europe. The Roundheads and the Puritans. The Germans and the French. British and Irish. Basques and Spanish. Look at the Dark Ages. How far have we really come?"

Reiner spat a huge gob of bloody phlegm into his sputum cup. "Yeah," he winced, "History's one guy knocking off another guy. Oh Christ, I hope he's all right."

"The Chinese warlords. The British, French, and Belgium kin in Africa. Bang, bang, bang. And our country too—God bless it, I love it as well as the next man—but we let the bullets fly to make it ours."

I frowned and walked slowly towards the window. By Slattery's nightstand, the door was opened. I spotted what I was looking for. He'd smuggled in another bottle. The cap was off, the top of the neck gleaming wetly.

"Various assassinations of Indian chiefs, whole tribes in fact. Various assassinations of working stiffs, remember the Pinkertons—oh, they came *at* them, friend, they came with a vengeance."

"Can't you ever shut your yap?" Ed sneered. "You'd think you was still teachin', and not some run-of-the-mill, run-of-the-mouth wino."

"And the good ol' Robber Barons," Slattery winked, "let's not forget *those* fine fellows."

"ShutUP," Ed yelled.

I took a few steps towards Slattery's night-stand. "So, first you smuggle in another bottle. Then you sneak a—"

"I was upset, Dov, terribly. I AM upset, lad, I—"

I took the bottle, capping it. "No booze on the ward, Tim. Sorry."

"Give it here," Ed signalled. "I'll pour the sonuvabitch down the sink."

"He'll pour it down his own stinking gullet!" Slattery cried.

I kept walking with the bottle, and dropped it into the trash. When I returned, Devlin was scolding.

"—on his way to the *operating* room, and all you guys can think of is your goddam booze!"

"That's a lie," Ed sneered.

"We each grieve in our own way, Henry," Slattery said dully.

"Look," growled O'Reilly, "I'm trying to get some shuteye."

"At some point, John," Slattery muttered, "you're going to have to look this thing in the face."

"Why?" O'Reilly grumbled, burrowing into his covers.

"Why? Well, hmmm. Let's see now."

"I'm getting you some coffee, Tim."

"Are you implying that—"

"I'm going on break. If I come back and there's more of this bullshit, I'm calling Linc down."

"Oh please, Dov, please," Slattery begged, folding his hands in mock-pleading, "don't do it, son. I'll be good. Promise."

"Transfer the bastard," O'Reilly insisted.

"You guys *piss me off*," I blurted. "Kennedy may be *dead,* you *know?*" The ward hushed.

"He's right," Smitty whispered, "I didn't wanna say nothin', but. . ." He looked around, then hushed. Slattery slouched against his pillow and coughed, tears wetting the stubble on his face. Devlin looked down at his fingers. Ed rose.

"O.k. if I take a shower?"

"Do whatever you want, Ed."

Smitty lay shaking his head. "I just can't believe it."

"Let's pray for him," Reiner suggested.

Slattery shrugged. Reiner, coughing, cleared his throat.

O'Reilly angrily threw off his blankets. "I'm not gonna get any sleep with all this racket."

Reiner looked up at the grey sky through the window blinds. "Hello?" He paused, fingering his sputum cup. "Uhh, this is Mike Reiner. 2358 Shawmut." He paused again. The ward was silent. Ed was staring at Reiner, holding a bar of soap and a towel.

"Well," Reiner sighed, "it's a terrible day. I guess you heard. All I wanna say—is—uh, take care of him. He got it in the head you know. Do what you can. That's about it. Thanks."

The ward hushed. "Very nice, Mike," Slattery whispered.

"Jeez," Devlin murmured, "he talks to Him like he was His cousin."

"And another thing while we got you," Ed rasped, clutching his soap and towel, "find the suckers that did this, Lord. Remember the Good Book: an eye for an eye, and a tooth for a tooth." With that, Ed headed for the shower.

"And to think I was cussin' him out," Devlin moaned, "when the Bay of Pigs was goin' on. I was worried sick, you know, my kid's in the service. Jeez, I cursed him up and down."

"That was then, Henry," Slattery offered.

I froze, remembering sitting in my geometry class at high school, hearing the loud speaker announce the specially-called assembly, the special television setup—"the gravest situation since the Korean War, and in some senses much more..."—wondering, shuddering, it can't be happening, can't, can't, I'm only sixteen. I haven't even made love yet, traveled, done things, gone more to Greenwich Village, it can't happen. Just like that, BOOM—like the movie *The Day The World Ended*, like the *On The Beach* movie with Gregory Peck and Ava Gardner listening to "Waltzing Matilda" with their eyes welling-up, holding each other doomed waiting for the radiation—what would it do to you, can't happen now. How could I get home? How could I get to my sister Rachel five blocks away at the junior high school? And my mother working in Long Beach, how could she get back to Sandy Creek in time? And my Dad in Manhattan, if there was an atomic war, how could he get on the train back to our house? How could my mother drive home? Could me and my sister call up my mother and have her meet us at the train station so we could all be together, and make it to our house if our house was still there? And how could we do all that, and go over to my best friend Jordie's house so we could say goodbye before the radiation got us? Why did we have to live in New York, it would be an obvious target— one of the biggest cities and Metropolitan areas—why couldn't we live in North Dakota somewhere, and who was it pushing it all while I sat in geometry class? Who was pushing the buttons.

"Hey," Stoney shook me, "Hey."

"Yeah."

"I need your help for a minute."

"What's up?"

"That ol' guy in thirty don't wanna go to x-ray."

"Oh?"

"He's just starin' at the walls. Let's see if we can't move him."

In a single room, an old black man shook his head. "Tell me why," he enunciated very slowly, clearly, "tell me why I knew this was going to happen."

Stoney shrugged. "I'm not a fortune-teller, Pops."

The old man smiled bitterly. "You're not, huh?"

"No. What I am right now is the man who's supposed to take you down to get your chest x-rayed."

The old man's eyes moistened. "I can tell you what they're goin' to find. They're goin' to see a big hole. Left side." He rubbed his eyes.

Stoney looked at me, then looked away. "Well, maybe I can get them to do it later. We'll reschedule you."

"You do that, son."

"O.k. then," Stoney nodded, turning and motioning me to follow him out.

"Been on break yet?"

"No."

"Breakfasts done? Baths? Temperatures? Blood pressures?"

"Yep."

"Come on then. Let's get the fuck outta here."

Down in the cafeteria we spotted Linc holding forth among a crowded table. We got some coffee and donuts, and joined him.

"How do you see it?" Linc asked Stoney.

"See what?"

"The shooting!"

Stoney sipped his coffee, shrugging. Linc stuck his index finger out.

"It was that bastard Johnson. Texas sonuvabitch!"

I stared at Linc. "You're kidding!"

"You can't believe that, huh?" I shook my head. Linc leaned closer.

"He wasn't touched. His pal Connally got it in the arm to take the heat off. They planned it that way. Bet you a million dollars."

Stoney sipped his coffee.

"How's the ward? How's old O'Reilly and them takin' it? Ed? Mike?"

"They're upset."

"Fuckin' A-Right, upset! They should be! And it's all 'causa Lyndon Baines Johnson. That crook set it up with the CIA." Linc's eyes were red, wild.

"Now you don't know that, Lincoln," said Nadine, an older aide.

"The hell I don't. When you have a Presidential motorcade, you check out EVERYTHING. You think they got all those CIA guys with the shades and suits so they can just sit around with their finger up their ass? From what I hear, they had a clean shot. And tell me *this*, why was he in an open car?"

No one answered. Nadine frowned, thinking. Outside, the sky was full of sun, the buildings standing like old dogs soaking up sunlight. I thought: these buildings don't know anything, yet the people inside give them a pulse, an aura of ...of...I stopped and took a bite out of my donut; it felt like rock.

"Someone wanted to get him," agreed Larry, a young orderly from the psyche ward. "They didn't like all this New Frontier stuff. His stand on civil rights."

"He was a great man who would've done alot," Nadine said softly.

"You're talkin' like the man's dead," Stoney said.

"Hey," Linc put in, "the man got shot in the brain. Even if he does make it through, he might just be a vegetable."

"Hush," Nadine whispered, "don't talk that way." She rapped her knuckles on the wood table.

"Sure," Linc sped on, "don't talk about it. Don't ask questions. Don't think about it. Don't fuck with it. That's what they want. They want everybody to cry and shut up!"

"Take it easy," I said. "We're not the Texans, you know?"

Nadine and Stoney smiled at me; Linc lightly punched me in the arm.

"From the mouths of babes. Yeah. O.k. Christ, I could use a drink."

Stoney nodded, sipping down the rest of his coffee, and staring at the bottom of his cup.

Several people rose to go, leaving me, Linc, and Stoney.

"So the ward's not so hot?"

"No. Everybody's in a mood."

"Well, maybe I'll drop by later and say hello. If I get the chance. Everyone's all messed up."

"Tell me about it," Stoney sighed.

"People don't wanna eat, they don't wanna bathe, they don't want nothin'."

"They're in shock."

"Yeah," Linc grunted, "me too. I'm in fuckin' shock."

Stoney got up; I rose too.

"I'm just gonna stretch my legs a little, son. You can stay here a few more minutes if you feel like it."

I got some more coffee and came back, offering Linc some. He waved me off.

"No, I've had about six cups already, and it ain't even noon."

I sipped the coffee.

"Fuckin' Dallas," Linc muttered.

"Yeah. It's like before it was just a place, you know? A city somewhere, you know? Tallahasee, Denver, Trenton, Butte." Linc nodded listlessly. "Burlington, Keene, Springfield."

Linc dropped by later. Stoney was bringing Ed in a wheelchair. Ed was shaky, red-eyed.

"He's been barfin' up his breakfast," Stoney whispered. "Can't stomach all this, huh, old-timer?" Ed stared straight ahead.

"Hey, I'm talkin' to you, pal." Ed stared.

"Hey Lazarus," Linc smiled, "still kickin'?" Ed pushed Linc's arm away.

"Yeah," he rasped.

Stoney looked outside the door, then lit up a cigarette. Slattery and Reiner were sitting up, staring out the window. Devlin, Smitty, and O'Reilly were asleep.

"They should close this place up," Linc said. "Put the goddam flag at half-mast."

"He ain't dead yet far's I know," Stoney stated.

"A day of infamy," Slattery declared softly, waving quietly.

Linc moved toward the window, pushed back the blinds, and stared at the grey autumn sky full of hard white light.

"Whole goddam world's fallin' apart," Linc whispered, almost to himself. His face dropped its guard, sagging. The

blazing green eyes gleamed soft grey-green, tears on his
cheeks wetting the rough red skin. "Fallin' apart," he
murmured, his back to the beds.

"Watcha see?" Reiner asked. "Some nice ass?"

Linc didn't turn around. He picked up a towel from
Slattery's bedside and threw it at Reiner who caught it with a
hurt look.

"Hey!"

"Kennedy's shot, and all you can think about is ass?"

"I was just—"

Linc took a few steps towards Reiner. Stoney watched
carefully.

"You was just nothin'."

Reiner looked to me and Stoney for help.

"Linc?"

"What?"

"Uh, look, we're all upset, but we don't have to take it
out on each other, 'kay?"

Linc looked to the ceiling as if beseeching heaven.

"Christ, I wish I believed in God. I really do. Then I
could pray and ask him to keep all the Good Samaritans like
you in the seminary or some fuckin' place like that. As long
as it ain't around me. Yeah. Here. Look at this, Good
Samaritan—"

He was pointing to the t.v. Devlin had ordered, reviewing the news to the snoring Devlin.

"Do you realize, ol' Good Samaritan Sam, work-study
college kid Dov buddy, that the world, the town Dallas ain't
never gonna be the same again? Do you," he said, turning to
Reiner, "realize that, you old horntoad?"

"Take it easy," Stoney muttered.

"NEVER!" Linc yelled.

Stoney grabbed his arm. "Lighten up Jack."

"My name ain't Jack."

Just then Gilly walked in. "What is this, a convention?"

Linc smiled. "Just dropped in to say hello."

"Hello, Lincoln."

"That's all I wanted to hear. Thank you."

She studied him, an exasperated look on her face. Linc walked out, waving over his shoulder.

The rest of the day passed quickly. Linc wanted to go out for a few drinks, but neither me or Stoney were in the mood. When I left the hospital, walking with Linc, it was already getting dark.

"Sure you don't wanna stop off and have a few?"

"I'm tired as hell, Linc."

"Well, I'll just have a few for ya then."

"Fine."

The air was chilly. I saw the newspaper headlines in the darkening afternoon: JFK SHOT IN DALLAS. Coated men and women grabbed newspapers as fast as the old leather-jacketed vendor could pass them to the avid hands. He dumped a bag of change on a slab of wood to make change faster.

I walked slowly toward the train. The dilapidated red and brown smoky buildings seemed the same, the same the thin trees, their few orange-green leaves like skinny rumpled stars. The bars were packed. Usually, I could spot an empty stool, a table, part of a rail at the standups. Usually there was noise, joking. The bars, packed, seemed silent.

I trudged up the stairs of the El, and waited for the MBTA train to Cambridge. Along the platform, people stood reading, papers folded in half or spread wide, following the story with speeding anxious eyes and quivering fingers.

The crowded train was hot, grouchy. Everyone's newspapers got in the way. Some sat stunned, holding purses, lunchboxes. An elderly man in a black suit, white shirt, and grey tie, stared at his neatly folded newspaper, softly whispering, "John Fitzgerald Kennedy."

A middle-aged blond woman in a vinyl green jacket looked at the man. "Awful ain't it?"

The elderly man nodded absentmindedly. "Fitzgerald for a middle name. Interesting."

The woman caught me watching her. "Awful, ain't it?" I nodded.

"Fitz-gerald," the elderly man whispered.

Routine of death... somewhat unimportant... how alive opposed to... Kennedy

Behind me were other voices.
"Why does it always happen to the good ones?"
"Umm hmm. Always does."
"In the prime of life."
"Just starting out, umm hmm."

A lady in a heavy grey coat read with her finger to her friend, a heavy-set woman in a yellow raincoat with a blue and yellow kerchief around her head.

"Cerebellum...ooblong medulla. Where's that?"
"Here. There's a picture of it."

Through the train windows the sun glowed from gold to maroon-green against the darkening blue. The buildings began going ghostly, the lit ones like stony lions on fire, the shut ones sleepy animals. The Charles River gleamed softly, dazzled with streetlight reflections. We moved into Kendall Square. The sign was dark blue and white metal. (Jackie wears blue, the column announced. Me and Jordie snickered over the description of the refurnished White House, feeling good the Inauguration included Robert Frost. "That's class," Jordie nodded, "Get ol' Frostie up there. Have that crotchety ol' bastard read a few." Jackie wears blue. And the rumors he'd been sleeping around, Jackie wanting to leave him but for the Presidency, my mother sighing, "Well what's his sex life got to do with what kind of President he'd make? That's just dirt. So he's not Mr. Purity? That liar Nixon is?")

"He's got everything to live for. His country, his wife, his kids."

"He'll pull through. He's young, he's strong, he's healthy."

"And they have surgeons from Washington. They're the best."

"That's right. From Walter Reed Hospital, it says. That's where they all go, all the presidents go there. It's the best. It's even better than Mass General, and you know what a fine place that is."

"This medulla thing controls alota stuff."

"I never liked Texas. They're gun-happy down there. Shoot first and ask questions later."

"Trigger-happy. They think they're still fighting the Indians."

At Harvard Square, the streets were almost empty. I saw one couple holding each other, crying as they read the newspaper. On three stores were CLOSED signs.

My apartment was dark. I looked around the tiny bedroom, staring at Pete's desk—his police radio bought in a junk shop, his physics and botany books, his few others: Isaac Asimov's *Foundation and Empire*, a tattered copy of Robert Heinlein's *Stranger In A Strange Land*, and a copy of *The Art of Loving*. I stared dully at my desk: a tattered copy of Sergei Eisenstein's *Film Form* and *Film Sense*, my fall reading—*Moby Dick* and *Dead Souls*—along with old copies of *Uncle Tom's Children* and *A Portrait of The Artist As A Young Man*. Nearby were my few records: two Charlie Parker albums, and three gifts from Jordie—a Nina Simone album, a Joan Baez, and a Bob Dylan. I opened my desk drawer and took out the black leather book that I bought when I left for Albion College to make general notes, as well as plan films. I opened it, reading randomly:

Cambridge is beautiful. Many trees. Cobblestoned streets—remembering what feet? What grief?

The hospital is a hellhole. Smells of death, rubbing alcohol, phisohex. Will I ever learn to make a bed "Army" style? I'm not mechanical. I refuse to be. But there are siderails to fasten, oxygen tents to put up. A person's life depends on it! And breathing treatments. Will I get over being scared of the oxygen tanks?

Saw Ellen up at Radcliffe. Another world. Cream de la creme. I go to Albion, a good school in itself, innovative, bohemian, work-study, experimental, etc., etc., but no one is good enough for Ha-vid. Her friends look down on me. You work at a *what* they say. Hell with them. Ellen likes to show me off. She likes to brag about all her civil rights stuff. She's been up to Harlem a few times so she *knows*. And she made sure she made it back to Long Island but fast. You're being unfair, kid. Be charitable—she tries.

Took a body down today. An old man. I closed his eyes. His lids: like ice. No one claimed him. The area is full of old men. Many winos. Broken pieces. Like Slattery. Slattery taught college in the fifties. Refused to sign a loyalty oath. Blacklisted. Wife killed herself. Never recovered. I couldn't believe the body. Weighed a ton. Stoney did most of it. He smiled. Said you almost get used to it. Almost. I stood staring. I stared and stared. I know nothing. We put the body in the morgue freezer. The door was lemon-colored. Chrome handle.

Orange leaves of autumn like brooding orangeade. Red stone in houses expressing a grief beyond belief.

I want a love. Someone to hold. All over Cambridge they go arm in arm, camel hair coats, tweeds, long hair, blond, dark, shining eyes, laughing faces tilted to the crisp sun, alive.

Films to see: *Wild Strawberries, Bicycle Thief, Open City, Seven Samurai.* Note: see *La Strada* again, especially for the last scene with Anthony Quinn crying on the beach.

I closed the book and made some fresh coffee. I went back with my cup, opened a fresh page, and wrote: "November 20, 1963. Kennedy shot in Dallas."

I sipped the coffee. I sat there, clicking my pen. Then I wrote: "Ask not what your country can do for you, but what you can do for your country."

I paused, then wrote: "And what have you been doing? Going to the movies, reading, diddling yourself. Thinking, thinking (*that's what Madelie at Albion said, 'Dov, you think too much.' 'Get out,' Jordie advised. 'Take walks. You like to walk—that Brooklyn duck walk—I can hardly keep up with you.' He started laughing when I sashayed into the Charlie Chaplin walk, 'How's this Jordie? How's this?'*)

I stopped, drank the rest of the coffee and poured another cup. I went over to the kitchen, got four Lorna Doones, and returned, munching. It was good and dark now, the tiny square black with gold slivers. I opened the book, turning to a fresh page, blank as snow. The door opened. I looked up. The clock numbers, ghostly, green, whispered six thirty.

Pete walked in, taking off his wool hat, his leather jacket

over his suit and tie. He didn't look like an apprentice physicist—wild blond hair, immaculately bearded ruddy face, wiry build. From a big brown bag, he pulled out two sixpacks. He opened a can, and took a long swig.

"Hi Pete."

He nodded, swigging. He wiped his mouth, smiling, "Ahh, hits the spot."

"Is that all you can do, Pete," I frowned. "Kennedy may be dead, and all you can do is drink beer?"

He glared at me.

"What the fuck am I *supposed* to do?"

I glared back.

"And what the fuck are *you* doing about it, Mr. Cecil Fuckin' B. DeMille?"

"None of your goddam business."

"Well, Mr. Liberal. You do what you wanna do, and I'll goddam well do what I wanna do. It's still a free country, and if I wanna get polluted, I'll get polluted. What's wrong with drinking beer, anyway?"

"Fuck off."

"You want me to sit here and cry? You want me to start beatin' my tits and go buy a paper and read all that shit about what happened? You want me to look at the fucking traffic route of the motorcade and all that shit? Yeah, he's shot in the head. What can I do? Not a goddam thing. And I don't *wanna* do a goddam thing. I'd like to be able to come home, and just sit and drink a fucking beer, that's what I'd *like*. But I'll be goddamned if I'm gonna run around crying like some fucking Harvard liberal beating my brains out and tearing my hair. Fuck *that* shit."

He stared at me angrily, and chugalugged the rest of his beer.

"You get such a kick out of playing redneck, Pete."

"Yeah, maybe I do."

"Forget it. Sorry to bother you."

"And don't lay that on me either. Save it for your civil rights friends."

"Drop dead."

"Same to you and twice over."

He drank and sat in the kitchen two steps away with his back turned. I closed my book, and went into the kitchen.

"I'm sorry, Pete. I'm upset. Pete, I'm sorry."

"That's o.k. Want a beer?"

"Why not."

He opened a beer and gave it to me. We sat, drinking.

"It's been really unbelieva—"

"I told you I don't want to talk about it, o.k.?"

I shrugged and drank some more beer. The beer tasted cold and sour. Pete wiped foam off his moustache.

"I'm going over to Sue's tonight. I'll probably stay there."

"Uh-huh," I said, half-wishing he'd stick around.

"Fuckin' world."

"Yeah."

"Sometimes I wonder why I'm going through all this. Just so one day some crazy asshole can walk up and blow my head off."

"Yeah."

"Or some psycho who don't know his ass from his elbow can crash into me on some freeway."

"Yeah."

"It'll probably be just when I'm all setup too."

"I hope not, Pete."

He laughed.

"Well, I'm gonna shower up and hit the road."

I stared at the apartment. It seemed smaller by the minute.

"Yeah, I'm going out too."

"Gonna see your Harvard friends?"

"Maybe."

"Sure you are. Well, whatever. Have a good time. I didn't mean to jump down your throat."

"Well, I sorta asked for it. You have a good time too."

"I will—if I can walk."

I laughed, and headed out the door, wanting to get away, walk, walk, and walk some more. I suddenly felt hungry and headed over to Donovan's, a restaurant bar. The waitresses called me Smiley: I did my brooding there, explaining I was just thinking. They'd answer, "Oh, I thought you lost your best friend. You wanna call that thinking, fine."

An old man in a brown coat walked slowly out of Donovan's, stepping along a precarious invisible tightrope. He bunked into me.

"Oof!"

"You all right?"

"Coursh."

He walked a few more steps, then lurched against a battered Ford. He leaned against the front fender, his face scrunching up.

"Johnny!" he sobbed, "Johnny!"

An evening paper fell softly out of his coat, the headlines bright black under the Donovan's neon: KENNEDY DEAD. I squinted at the picture-blurb, a blurred-rushed reading: Bethesda Hospital...this evening...hemmorrhage...everything possible was...

I stumbled into a packed Donovan's, and dropped into a seat near the bar, squeezing past a middleaged couple listlessly eating Yankee Pot Roast, string beans, and boiled potatoes. Four men argued at the bar, signaling the bartender.

"A bullet-proof vest. That should be a requirement."

The bartender nodded wearily, bringing out a bottle of Old Crow.

"Put it on first thing in the morning. Take it off last thing at night."

An older man behind me, crumbling crackers into his soup, nodded.

"Can't be too careful," he agreed, fastidiously making sure the entire crackers crumbled into his soup.

"I mean," the first man said, "if we can't protect the goddam President who *can* we protect?"

"Ain't what it usta be, that's for sure," said the second man, pouring himself a healthy shot from the Old Crow, "you could go anywhere, anytime."

"Bullshit," said the third man, the biggest, wearing a windbreaker over a blue and white flannel shirt and slacks.

"I'm telling you what I know, Pat," the second man argued.

"Bullshit, and double bullshit."

"Hey, what bug's up *your* ass?"

"Usta be ain't what we got now, Larry. Forget usta be. This here's a *sign.*"

"What sign?" frowned the first man, a balding man in a suit. "What the hell are you talking about?"

"It's a sign. A bad sign. Something funny's going on. You know—peculiar. When your top guy gets knocked off like this, well, it's a sign."

"Yeah?"

"As sure as I'm standin' here."

"It's the Russians," Baldy declared. "They're jealous. They seen we got a sharp young guy—youngest President in U.S. history. They knew how much John had on the ball."

"Balls he had," growled the biggest man. "Stood up to them sonsabitches. Take one more step in Cuba, and I'll blow you bastards outa the water!"

"Yeah," nodded the fourth man, the smallest. "By God, it was the Russians!"

"So," windbreaker continued, "the Russians couldn't stomach that. And all their guys are practically wheelchair cases you know."

"Come off it," argued the second man, a blackhaired man with glasses, "Khrushchev's healthy as a horse!"

"Well, Pat's right, Larry," said Baldy, "there's lotsa things we don't know. They could not be disclosing stuff. You know how they do it. Ain't like here."

"Yeah, I'll give you that."

"They knew they had nobody of Kennedy's quality. So they knocked him off. That's how I see it."

"Makes sense," Baldy nodded. "He was gettin' the space program movin' fullspeed."

"Openin' up jobs," Larry added, "better rights for the Negroes."

"Let's not get into that," Baldy muttered, "you know how I feel about that."

"Yeah, then how come you voted for him?"

"Larry, I vote the party ticket."

"You better. You ever vote Republican, so help me God—"

"Know what we'll do?" Pat grinned, "We'll get you banned from Donovan's. For life."

They drank silently for about half a minute.

"Cowards. Sittin' behind a fuckin' windowshade."

"Premeditated murder. Had the fuckin' balls to rent a room. Know what I mean? Makes me sick just thinkin' about it. By Christ, they went up to the desk clerk, paid good money—"

"And if they was slick, they had a woman with 'em."

"Posin' as husband and wife. Dirty bastards."

"Fuckin' commies."

"The commies or the Protestants, by God!" the fourth man blurted.

"No, Freddie. Watch it, buddy. No Protestant would shoot Jack."

"Then it was the JEWS, by God!" declared the fourth man, almost standing up.

"Oh yeah?" Baldy muttered, "well, I'm a white man, hundred psscent 'Merican and *I* voted for him. And I didn't have to go into no goddam Peace Corps to do it, either."

Baldy promptly proudly downed two shots of Old Crow, and pointed to the bartender to get another bottle. I stared. It was already empty.

The waitress, sweating, came over, breathless.

"Ready to order?"

"Hamburger, medium rare, fries. Just ketchup on the burger."

"Drink?"

"Bud."

Back at the bar, the fourth guy, Freddie, was about to slide down, but Big Pat boosted him up.

"What do you think, Charlie?" Larry asked the bartender.

"What do I think? I think you guys oughta slow down."

He pointed to the small fourth man. "Freddie's on his ass already."

"Thanks, Mom," Big Pat grinned, leaning over and patting Charlie's cheek. "Thanks."

"You're all talking a bunch of shit. First you're talking about Cuba, Russia, hotel rooms, and the goddam Peace Corps! Make no goddamn sense at all!"

Freddie burped.

"I make sense," argued Baldy. "I was talkin' about the Peace Corps purely in, in the figgerative metabolical sense."

He lurched and steadied himself.

"And what's wrong with the Peace Corps," Larry asked, "the kids wanna go help out, let 'em. Wish my kid would go. Save me a *hell* of a lotta money."

"Yeah?" drawled Big Pat, "And what if she came back married to some Egyptian?"

"Huh?"

"That's what happened with Berrigan's daughter. She married some guy in Cairo."

"I'll be goddamned!" Larry exclaimed.

"No fuckin' Egyptian's knockin' up my daughter," Baldy glared. "My Peggy comes home and tells me that shit, I'll go to Cairo or wherever the hell it is, I'll go there and say, 'Hey, Abdul, let's go out to where the mummies are—' "

The bartender wiped the bar disgustedly, shaking his head. The waitress brought my food; I barely saw it, listening.

"And I'll say, 'Man-to-man talk, Omar, just me and you. O.k. now, look out there, and take a good look, 'cause that's the last fuckin' pyramid you're EVER gonna see!' "

Baldy cracked up, cackling, as Larry shook his head. Big Pat poured another drink. Freddie stood up straight and peered into the bar mirror as if beholding a revelation.

"By God, it was the Egyptians!"

The couple next to me had left their plates full of food. My hamburger tasted good. The men were quieter now. Every now and then Freddie would mutter, "Who would ever'v thought it would be the 'gyptians? Not me, not on yer life."

I finished, left the tip, paid the bill, and walked out. Along the streets the streetlights lit a few figures. In the houses, behind trees, lights and t.v.s glowed softly. To-morrow the television would have all day specials, sudden programming reeling out profiles on Kennedy, Connally, Johnson, reviewing Kennedy's life and career. Politicians and governments would line up for condolences with telegrams, black suits, and mourning faces: "A great grief," "Loss to the world," "Shocked and dismayed," "A great man." In the distance a car zoomed.

By the Charles River the streetlights on the water seemed like shimmering imprisoned ghosts. I shivered, staring at the black water. Along the riverbank, on a bench sat an old man, collar up, staring deeply into the Charles. A slight move of his face below his eyes acknowledged my presence.

"Terrible," he murmured, his voice softer than the Charles.

I nodded, wondering if he could see or sense me. He was staring straight ahead, as if quietly matching the Charles depth for depth. I kept walking. The streets were empty, except for an occasional couple, a motorcycle shooting around a corner. The stars shone, their light sharp, intense; intense too was the sharp silver light from the streetlamps against the trees, an icy green here, a frosty brown there.

Up at Radcliffe, a hush pervaded the ivy-covered red buildings, and the entrance hall and stairs up to Ellen's dorm room. She was sitting with her roommate who was lying down smoking, the evening paper spread out, an ashtray full of cigarettes, an electric coffee pot perking. A Peter, Paul and Mary album played.

Ellen was looking, without reading, at a book: *Issues In American Hisory*.

> Where have all the flowers gone
> Long time passing

"Hello, Dov."

"Ellen."

"I was in the neighborhood, and I thought I'd—"

She rose, putting a finger to her lips, and hugging me, cried a little. I smelled brandy. The bottle sat atop a copy of *Nobody Knows My Name*.

"Dov, I feel like the world's caved in."

"Yeah."

"I'm numb."

Her roommate smoked in silence. The black disc, hushed, circled again. Ellen raised a finger to her lips and sat down cross-legged on her bed, motioning me to sit down. I listened to the record, feeling a warmth glow through my chest.

> Someone's cryin' lord, Kumbaya
> Someone's cryin' lord, Kumbaya
> Someone's cryin' lord, Kumbaya
> Oh Lord, Kumbaya

"All classes are canceled tomorrow," Ellen whispered, softly pushing back her wheatblond hair, her grey eyes moistening. I nodded.

"Are you going to work?"

Outside, the night was deep black. The window sill was dusty. I thought of the dust on the ward window sill, sun on beds, siderails, Devlin's sleeping face, Ed refusing to fill out his dinner menu, "Don't talk to me about EATING!"

"Yes, I'm going."

"How *can* you, Dov?"

(Slattery, Reiner, Linc, Stoney, O'Reilly blinking, "He won't make it.")

"I have to, Ellen."

"Just like nothing happened."

"Come on, Ellen."

She looked down, and put my hand in hers.

"Was it rough today?"

"Very."

"Were people upset?"

("Fucking A Right!" Linc said, his face wild, red.)

"Very."

Her roommate stubbed out her cigarette, turned the record over, and lying back down, lit a new one.

"I wonder what Johnson'll be like," she mused, staring at her smoke.

"He'll continue the civil rights programs," Ellen said hopefully.

I wanted them to be quiet so I could hear the record, the song one sung on marches for the Freedom Riders in Alabama, and on vigils.

Michael Row the boat ashore, halleleujah
Michael Row the boat ashore, halleleujah

The door knocked; a woman entered with a gallon of cheap wine.

"Wanna drink, El?" her friend Summer grinned. "I bring you the best of the bestial Bacchus."

"I have some brandy, Summer, but come on in. You know Dov?"

"*Hi*, Dov," Summer winked. "Let's drink to good times," Summer laughed bitterly, "wonderful times."

"You look like you've had enough Summer," Ellen frowned.

"How can you *say* that, El? Frown, frown. Come on — it's such a *beautiful* world. And wine makes it even more beautiful. If you don't believe *me* ask the Greeks. Ask the Africans. Ask *everyone*. Lovely."

She began weeping, falling into Ellen's lap. "Shit shit shit shit."

"Fuck," Ellen smiled wearily, stroking Summer's head, "fuck fuck fuck."

"What is this? A pornographic chicken farm?"

Summer eyed me as if I'd just landed from Pluto.

"Dov was our high school comedian and resident angry-young-man," Ellen remarked dryly. "He tries."

"Of course, I wasn't good enough for Harvard," I snapped, "but maybe that's 'cause they're known for their non-sense of humor."

"I was just kidding, Dov," Ellen cooed. "Oh, you're such a little duck. You get your feathers ruffled so easily."

"Hmm," I said, trying to hear the end of the song, the surge:

Jordan's river is chilly and cold
Halleleujah
Chills the body but not the soul
Halleleujah

Staring into the night:

Remembering another dark night full of lights from passing towns   from the bus windows   the bus taking us to the March on Washington   August Summer 63   dark night the lights of sleepy Ohio towns leaving Albion at sunset   sleeping farm towns grey mining towns   Wheeling West Virginia   sagging porches under mountains slag heaps   the tired grumpy dawn along the freeway   signs Haggerstown Maryland   eyes coats sleepy eyes stretching arms   the cool dawn starting and almost disappearing at the same time   the August heat early

Lookit, I can see the CAPITAL! Lookit!

Big Deal

I don't CARE if I'm lying here in the aisle. If I don't lay-ooohhh-if I don't stretch out, I'm gonna DIE! ohhhh.

We stopping for coffee?

Ask the driver

I NEED some coffee

Make mine ham and eggs, and hashbrowns

How can you think of EATING—we're here! we're HERE!

And suddenly our bus, one of a thousand buses, bus after bus pulling in the signs BOSTON KANSAS CITY CHAPEL HILL DETROIT ATLANTA PHILADELPHIA HOUSTON CHICAGO PITTSBURGH LITTLE ROCK HARTFORD NEW YORK, people getting off, stretching, in suits and Florsheim's, dresses and flats, jeans and sandals, chinos and workboots, skirts and sandals, skirts and flats, jeans and desert boots, more suits, white short-sleeved shirts and slacks, straw hats, a few derbies, church hats with the veil and fruit on top, all walking slowly towards the pool at the Lincoln Memorial tens then twenties then hundreds elbow to elbow young· and old mothers holding their children's hands   it was getting hotter by the minute elderly couples proudly head-high arm-in-arm on a special promenade   fathers with their kids on their shoulders   and hotter the smell of powder sweat perfume shaving lotion   starch shoe polish

The signs SNCC CORE NAACP LADIES GARMENT UNITED AUTO WORKERS ELECTRICIANS URBAN LEAGUE TEAMSTERS

STUDENT GOVERNMENT HOSPITAL 1199 DISTRICT 65 GUILD WAR RESISTERS LONGSHORE   men and women with union buttons, bluewhite, redwhite, and paper hats with the union local number, a contingent from the Southwest in sombreros and serapes, American Indians in full tribal dress, signs: SOUTH DAKOTA, WASHINGTON, someone giggling as people stared or cheered open-mouthed, "South Dakota!" as if Mars and flying saucers were nearer as I went over angrily, "Yeah, and that's 2,000 miles away!" and the person stopped giggling, a contingent of singers harmonized at the pool:

> *Black and white together, we shall not be moved*
> *Black and white together, we shall not be moved*
> *Just like the tree that's standing by the water*
> *We shall not be moved*

as people walked faster to join in the singing coming up and linking arms   the song swelled camera crews rushed to film it t.v. reporters looked along the head of the pool going from cluster to cluster seeking Martin Luther King and the other speakers and leaders.

And earlier vigils at the Statue of Liberty supporting the Montgomery Bus Boycott   the Freedom Riders   the vigils the fasting.

"Here, have some salt tablets," Rona smiled, an arm-band on her pale arm. I shook my head.

"A fast is a fast."

"It's o.k., silly. Your body needs salt."

The speaker above the crowd below the Statue of Liberty's rising green figure, the clean sharp sting of seaspray and salt in the air. "And this movement is going to grow and grow—all over this land!" Like the song

> *I'd hammer 'bout a love between*
> *My brothers and my sisters*

And hearing the song I felt we'd grow, we'd become the ham-mer the bell

And at Albion Brownie who loved to be cynical drawled, "That's pretty tricky there, putting the hammer into the song. That's communism, you know. The hammer. They probably put the sickle into some other song. Though maybe not. No one uses a sickle in the United States, so if you sang it in a song, people wouldn't know what the hell you were talking about." And Brownie came to the March on Washington, joining the singing chorus, his eyes getting shiny,

The August sun baking the thousands with sudden shock realizing all the colors of faces like some incredible iridescence, black and white in different shades, not black or white but rosy-blond, jet black purple black blue-black charcoal slate chocolate-brown red-brown darklemon tan creamy fleshy-pink brightpink orange-white pale white green-tinged blue-tinged silvery, sandy-red dusky ebony flushed rosy-white, salt-and-peppered.

Near a fountain a large black woman laughed among a group of older men and women looking like they were going to church under a sign ATLANTA SOUTHERN CHRISTIAN LEADERSHIP CONFERENCE, standing patiently happily in the high heat, some wearing white gloves in suits, dresses, hats fanning themselves with copies of the program handed out by armbanded shirtsleeved barearmed men and women moving slowly but surely through the packed crowds.

As small groups of young people and a few oldtimers went up and down the poolsides offering newspapers, flyers, Women For Peace, DON'T PATRONIZE THESE ANTI-UNION, SANE, Urban League, something about Indochina, NAACP membership, Fund-Raising Drive for..., DON'T BUY THESE ANTI-UNION PRODUCTS, and the glare of the sidewalks making foreheads crinkle, eyes burn, drinking water at the fountain, an older salt-and-pepper woman laughing to her friend—

"Come on, Jean, you can drink the water here. No cracker gonna bust your head in."

"Mabel, honey, I'm gonna live 'til I can drink from every fountain from here to Corpus Christi. I'm gonna drink that water every which way. If I wanna stand upside down, I am."

Her gathered friends laughed as an older man sucking on a pipe remarked, "Then you better get some of these people to come back with us, sister, 'cause from now on Jesus is gonna be workin' him some OVER*time.*

"And what's he been doin' all these years?"

"Ummm hmm."

"That's the truth."

A young man in a green army jacket and an armful of papers approaching smiling to himself.

"Too bad Jesus isn't around. Looks like we're gonna have to do it ourselves. Like a copy of Labor Vanguard?"

They stared at him, growing quiet. In his back pocket was a worn copy of Existentialism: Nietzsche to Camus. *The young man grinned.*

"You know, some people say Jesus has been asleep for a long long time."

"Yes," an older black woman put in, "but when a sleeping bear hibernates and you wake him at the wrong time, well you don't want to be standin' near the mouth of the cave, hear?"

The young man sighed patiently. "What's God ever done for anybody? Assuming that he—"

"Yes, hearing is what he needs," someone else put in, mildly angry.

"Wellll," the old man in the suit said thoughtfully, "we're all here together and that what's most important."

"We united," declared Mabel.

The young man with the newspapers smiled wistfully, walking away, then turned and pointed up the the hot sky, "There's no help up there," and kept walking.

The old man took a step after him saying, "We each walk in our own particular light, but we all want to get out of the darkness."

"That's right!"

"Amen!"

"Those are the words!"

"Like Jesus might have said."

"From his heart!"

The old man sucked on his pipe smiling, " 'Course, Jesus can always use help." The gathering watched the kid continue up the pool. One of the women frowned angrily.

"If I was that boy's Mamma I'd whip his atheistic behind for him."

"Now, now, Sister Green, we're all God's children."

"That's what I'm saying. There's always some juvenile delinquents."

"Dov, Dov."

I blinked my eyes. A hand was on my arm. Through the window, past huge elms dark green against black night, a streetlamp lit a clock tower: midnight. Ellen's roommate was asleep. Summer had gone.

"Oh."

"Where do you *go* when you do that?"

"Do what?"

"You just disappear. Go off. Are you all right?"

"Yeah."

Ellen yawned.

"I guess it's time for me to go home."

She nodded.

"Thanks for coming over. I'm sorry I wasn't more, well...."

"Yeah, me too."

She hugged me, her body felt tired, tense.

"Bye Ellen."

"Give me a call in a few days, o.k.?"

"Sure."

I stumbled into my apartment without turning on the light, and slipped off my clothes. The alarm clock gleamed a ghostly green. I put on my Dylan album, barely able to move the needle to the particular song I wanted—Don't Think Twice, It's All Right—then lay back in the darkness, listening, listening long after the last note echoed and fell away. The room was hushed, still. Soft. Soft pillow. Light airy blue. Smell of dust somewhere. Remember: do your laundry. Wash. Do your wash. Shhh. Water. Black water. Shhh. Charle-s-shh. Black water. Terrible. Terrorble. Shh. Light's somewhere. Walkin' down the road. Faraway. Hey. Shh. Water. Blacknight. Nightlight water a river out to sea all rivers run into yet the sea not full unto sea black horizon falling over overlover over edge of world lie likeakiss like lielay shhh water waves blackgreengreen set the clock get up oh no so soft soft likeakiss waters shhh easy soft z zzz zs easy shhh z end of alphabet bye bye bet your bye bye by and by in the sweet honey bee beecomb become what will become of us us uh shh beecomb buzz zzz beecomb honey oh honey there there sha shhh there hair beecomb be shhh beee buzzzzzzbuzzbz BZZZZZT! BRAAABLAHBZZZZ!

I stumbled out of the soft bed; the floor like ice, BZZZZ, ghostly green numbers SIX AM SIX AM GET UP GET UP GET UP! I bashed the back of the clock.

"SHUTUP!"

"Fuck you," the clock snapped crabbily. "Get the fuck up and get to work."

"Up yours," I answered, scrambling back under the covers. The room was dark, colder. In the darkness eight beer bottles lined up along Pete's desk stared, perched on top of two torn up sixpack boxes, ripped and methodically folded into fat squares.

"Fuckin' Pete."

I dressed quickly, and drank old coffee—it tasted like a combination of licorice and wet cement. I gagged it down, grabbed my coat, and left the house. The cold air stung me. People were puffing little iceclouds. The newspaper had the same headline: JFK DEAD. On the train a young man read to his girlfriend.

"Oh God, he didn't make it Steven," she was crying. "He didn't. Steven."

Steven shut the paper and held his girlfriend. He was crying too.

Along the streets, in the alleys toward the hospital, a few winos were turning over, newspapers at the bottom of their pants legs peeking out from stuffed pants and shoes. "Kennedy, at least you'll be remembered," I whispered up at the sky, thinking of the Morgue at the hospital: the closed lemon doors shutting on bodies me, Linc, and Stoney brought down. Men and women unremembered, unclaimed, marked for a grave outside the city, a tiny plot with wind on it. A Clay. A Smith. John Doe. Jane Doe. Uncalled for, gone.

In the locker room, Linc and Stoney dressed. Stoney briskly buttoned his uniform with one hand, and smoked with the other. Linc was lacing his workboots and reading from a newspaper sprawled open on one of the benches.

"Funeral services at Arlington Cemetery. Hah! I know that place. That's where all the dead heroes go. They got stones there that could feed the three of us for a fuckin' *year*."

He turned to me. His breath stank.

"How're you?"

"So-so."

"Get a paper?"

"No."

"You can read mine. I'm gettin' the whole story."

"Uh huh."

"It's important, but you gotta know how to do it."

"Do what?"

He poked me confidentially in the ribs.

"How to read it. How to read between the lines so you know what the sonsabitches are really sayin'. Look."

He was pointing to an article about Johnson, reading out loud.

"President-to-be Lyndon Baines Johnson expressed his overwhelming heartfelt sorrow about the national tragedy. O.k. Translation: we pulled it off without a hitch!"

"Linc."

"Hey—the only time that crook is overwhelmed is when Ladybird gives him a blowjob."

I laughed despite myself.

"All these cocksuckers expressin' their heartfelt grief and sorrow. Bull. They haven't felt anything with their hearts for twenty years!"

"Well, you're gonna feel somethin' in your wallet if you don't get upstairs soon," Stoney drawled.

"Yeah, but *look* at this Stoney. Look at Connally. See how he's standin'? He's makin' sure he stands so you can get the best profile of his arm in a sling. Get that camera angle, boys."

Linc kept talking as we went upstairs.

"I haven't even been home, understand? Closed the bar you wouldn't come to me with, and three others. Went over to Mary's. She was all broken up. Cried all night."

"Too bad," Stoney muttered.

"What's wrong with you, today?" Linc snapped.

"Nothin'."

"Hungover, huh?"

Stoney looked at him.

"No. Bad dreams."

"Huh?"

"You heard me."

"So wha'd you dream, old man?"

"If you're nice and polite, young fella, I just might tell you. Not now. I need some coffee. Shake this whatever it is I got."

"I didn't sleep so hot either," Linc nodded, " 'cause you know what the hell happened? I went over there, figurin', o.k., I'll stay with Mary. It'll be nice, drink a little, get some, drink a little more, get—"

"Yeah, we got it," Stoney said.

"But you know what? I didn't feel like fucking. Maybe it was when she said, 'Just hold me, Lincoln.' And that was all right. I didn't even think about it in terms was I goin' queer or anything. And it's fuckin' strange just lyin' there without your clothes on. I mean, you seen her, but she's kind of deceptive. She's got a damn fine body. She's kinda shy about showin' it off. She don't wear no tight sweaters or tight skirts or nothin' like that, and she fools alotta guys, which is good, 'cause I'm the one I want her to fool around with. Just lyin' there. It was funny. Not like we were kids or anything, but in a way sorta like we were. You guys don't understand a fuckin' thing I'm sayin', do you?"

"I do," I said.

"And I kept tryin' to think, what a fine body, Linc old man, and I kept seein' Johnson's face, and that ugly bitch of his, that Ladybird vulture bitch. And I'd get mad as hell all over again, and Mary would whisper, 'Are you mad at me, Linc?' and I'd hafta say, 'No, no Mary.' It was swirling all around all mixed up. When I got up, shit—don't ask me how the hell I got up—I just got out the ol' tomato juice and pepper. I lucked out—she had some cayenne too—I poured that in. Then I was really up."

"But you didn't get any sleep?" I asked as we walked down the ward.

"Not a wink. You?"

"I got home around one."

"See your Radcliffe friends?"

"Hey," Stoney snapped, "let's get to it. It's ten to seven."

"O.k. O.k."

"Same as yesterday," Stoney said, studying the schedule, "Linc on house, me and Dov down here."

On the ward Devlin motioned me over.

"Hey, Dov, can you change my sheets?"

I could smell urine. There was a puddle from his waist to his ankles.

"What happened?"

"I couldn't find the urinal. I wasn't feelin' so hot, and then it—ohh, I'm like a baby. I can't hold it, Dov. I can't. I think it was all that water I drank. I called for the nurse, but it was real late, musta been three or four in the morning. I don't know. I heard them sayin' something about they were short-handed again."

"And you've been lying like this for three hours?"

He nodded. I changed his bed as the other men began waking up—O'Reilly grumbling, Slattery yawning, Reiner coughing as he woke, Ed sitting up picking at his bandage, bleary-eyed.

"How's everybody?"

No one said anything. Stoney came in with the breakfast menus. "O.k. fellas. We're gonna fill these out real fast and give 'em back," cursing under his breath, "I don't know what happened last night, but there's shit backed up for miles, all sortsa stuff. Just what we need."

Ed pushed the menu away. "Nothin' for me."

"You're gonna eat something," Stoney growled, turning toward him, "I heard you didn't eat supper."

"You heard right."

"I'm puttin' you down for bacon and eggs, toast, and some o.j."

"Good. You can eat it."

Stoney shrugged. When the trays came, I brought Ed's over.

"This is the third time: I don't want NOTHIN'."

"This isn't going to do a thing for—"

"Get outa here."

"Look, Ed. You're upset, o.k. But this isn't—"

Reiner coughed, spilling his coffee all over himself, cursing as the hot liquid splashed his arm. I ran over to clean him up, and out of the corner of my eye saw Ed nudge his tray off his nighttable. It crashed to the floor in a jangled slosh of silverware, bacon, eggs, broken glass, toast, and orange juice.

"Goddamnit!"

Ed just glared at me.

It continued through the morning. No one wanted baths. No one wanted anything. Slattery read the paper out loud to the ward, like Linc, trying to read between the lines. O'Reilly kept ordering him to shut up.

Around eleven o'clock I took a break, again with Stoney and Linc. The cafeteria was fairly empty. Linc stared sullenly, his uniform wet grey in the armpits.

"Let's hope this day goes fast. Everyone's in a pure shit mood."

"Mmm, hmm," Stoney nodded, blowing smoke rings. Linc stared at the newspaper.

"The best always get it early."

He looked up at us.

"Know who's next?"

Stoney's eyes narrowed.

"Who?"

"King. That's who."

"What makes you think that?"

"You have to *ask*?"

"Well," I put in, "someone has to stand up. You can't go runnin' scared your whole life."

Linc laughed, sneering. "Listen to his Jimmy Cagney shit! *You* were scared to put up a goddamn SIDERAIL, or don't you remember that?"

"That's different."

"What the hell do you know about it?" Linc snapped. "You ain't even got your dick wet."

He saw me redden, and leered, "Or *have* you?"

"Lay off the kid," Stoney drawled.

"O.k. I just don't want him gettin' a swelled head hanging out with all those Cambridge snoots. You walk around with a swelled head, and sooner or later someone's gonna crack it. Know what I mean?"

"Nope. Never had a swelled head. Hard head, maybe."

"Huh!"

"Now you," Stoney continued, lighting up another cigarette, "young fella, you walk around with two heads. But that's 'cause you buy cheap booze."

"Funny."

"Anyway," Stoney said, his eyes suddenly serious, "we got off the point. Here we are fuckin' off, and the goddamn world is about to drop over the edge."

"Edge of what?"

"Edge of everything."

"How do you mean?"

Stoney leaned back, tapping his ash, playing with his empty coffee cup.

"All I know is this. A lotta folks are tired and fed up. They WANT, and are determined to GET. It's in the air. You can feel it, smell it. Shit, you can almost touch it."

I stared at Stoney.

"Now I don't pretend to know what the hell's comin'

down. But it's comin'. As sure as we're sittin' here. It's comin'. It's overdue. And one more thing—"

"Yeah?"

"Gonna be blood. Maybe I don't want it, maybe you don't want it, but there is."

Linc looked straight at Stoney, nodding very slowly.

"And that's what your dream was about?"

"Not exactly."

"No?"

"No. But it was powerful. Woke me up."

Stoney put out his cigarette and looked out the window.

"What I dreamt was that there was a fire. In Roxbury. Only it wasn't just any old fire. This fire was takin' everything. You couldn't see the bricks in the building. Flames—all of it."

I whistled. Linc watched Stoney.

"And there was sirens, police, firemen, ambulances, all of it. And for a second I said 'Whew.' I don't know where I was in all this, but I remember going, 'Whew.' "

We listened.

"And then—and here's the part just before I woke up—I got this cold chilly feelin'. Real cold. 'Cause I suddenly realized that all the police cars, fire engines, and ambulances, was goin' the other direction. They was goin' away from there just as fast as they could, like the devil in a rocket was after them."

"Damn!" Linc breathed.

No one spoke. Stoney lit another cigarette after staring out the window, muttering, "Well, time to get back."

The rest of the day passed quickly. I found a relief in taking care of the men, washing them, changing bandages, taking temperatures. The men were morose, pensive. Ed finally drank a little beef broth. Linc and Stoney were paged throughout the day. Four of those times were to take down bodies to the morgue. I saw them after work in the locker room, wearily resting on the benches.

"How about goin' out for a few?"

"Where?"

"Dew Drop Inn?"

"Shit. You ain't gettin' *me* in there."

"Well, you ain't gettin' me to go drinkin' in Roxbury."
Stoney shrugged.

"Hey," Linc grinned, "there's a new place I heard
about—it's up a ways—mixed bag: college kids, some peons
like us, and some old gasbags. How about it?"

"Sure," Stoney yawned, "I'll have one or two, but then
I gotta get home."

"Dov?"

"Sure."

We walked in the darkening afternoon without speaking. Linc stopped by a food truck and got a cup of coffee—
his tenth of the day.

The bar was a large converted stand-up, now sporting
eight tables leading to a restroom past a large jukebox. When
I saw the jukebox, I grinned.

"Order me a bud. I'll be right back."

"One bud, for my buddy," Line shouted at the bartender, "a rye and beer for me, and a—Stoney?"

"Gin."

"The best gin you got. Got it?"

"Hey, you don't—"

"This one's on me."

The jukebox had Sam Cook, The Platters, Frank
Sinatra, Acker Bilk, Hank Williams, and—I had to look
three times—"Blowin' In The Wind"-B7—sung by Peter,
Paul, and Mary. I put in a dime and hit the button.

"Wha'd you play?" Linc asked, drinking his beer.

"You'll see."

"What's this?" Linc asked, leaning slightly to hear
better.

"Good song," I said, "Dylan. Someone else is singin'
it."

A few tables over, a young couple listened to the song,
and held each other's hands sadly.

"Hmm," Stoney grunted. Linc downed his rye shot,
wiped his mouth, listening. Stoney stared at me, sipping his
gin.

"You play this?" Linc frowned.

"Uh huh."

Two young men stumbled in.

"Hi, Sean."

"This place looks dead. Guess maybe we'll have to do somethin' 'bout that."

"What's the number of that?" Linc asked.

"B-7."

"Be right back. If he comes over, order me another of the same."

I ordered another round at the bar. Stoney held up my empty bottle, and I ordered him gin and beer. One of the young guys looked at me.

"Hi."

"Hi."

"How's it goin'?"

"Not bad. So-so."

"Kennedy's *dead*. You know that?"

"Yeah, I—"

"Everybody knows that, Dave. You know, right?"

"Yeah."

Dave took a step closer.

"Then how can you say 'not bad.' Me, I'm real bad. Real bad."

"Easy, Dave," his friend said, touching Dave's shoulder.

"O.k. O.k."

Linc was busy pressing buttons at the jukebox. He came back.

"This for me?"

"No," I said, "it's for your grandma."

Stoney laughed as more music came on. I looked at Linc.

"Why not," he said, downing his rye in one gulp, "it's a good song. I want to get it down. Shh."

Dave went over to the jukebox, took out a dime, and pressed a button. After "Blowin' In The Wind," Linc looked at the jukebox, waiting.

"Good song, right Stoney?"

"What I heard sounded good."

The soft whoosh of Acker Bilk's "Stranger On A Shore" filled the bar. Linc scowled impatiently. I started my second Bud, feeling the lights gleaming around me, the music soft. Linc watched me drinking.

"We're gonna teach Dov how to hold his liquor."

"You can't hold liquor," I giggled, "it's liquid."

"Get a load of this shit," Linc laughed. Stoney lit up another cigarette. Another song came on the jukebox.

"That you again?" Stoney asked.

Linc nodded, sipping his beer.

"ANY song that's worth a fuckin' DAMN, is worth hearin' three times." At the bar, Dave glared at Linc. Then he stared at his friend, walked outside, stood there sniffing for a second, then came back in.

"Hey, Bobby," Dave laughed, hitting his friend on the shoulder, "Bobby, buddy."

"What?"

"Guess what, Bobby, buddy."

"I give up. What?"

"I just went outside, and it, it's *windy*." He glared at our table. "Well, so I stuck out my hand, and I stuck out my ears. And you know what?"

"What, Dave," Bobby said wearily.

Dave glared at our table. Linc's eyes narrowed.

"I didn't hear a goddamn *thing*!"

Dave cracked up laughing. His loud laugh grated against the song. Linc pushed his chair back. Stoney reached for him, but he was already quickly moving toward the two men, his hands tensed at his sides.

"Hey, buddy, I'm trying to hear the jukebox."

"I ain't your buddy. Bobby's my buddy. I never saw you in my fuckin' life."

"Fine with me. Just keep your yap shut while my song's on."

"Why—"

Bobby grabbed Dave.

"Let's go home, Dave. Come on. It's dead here anyway. Come on. There's nothin' goin' on here."

Stoney was standing up. I stood up too.

"Come on Dave."

"Don't rush me. O.k. Yeah, you're right. Ain't *nothin'* in this place."

They walked out slowly, Dave with his back to the door. Linc sat down.

"I'll buy this round," Stoney said quietly, "then I'm goin'."

"Stick around," Linc smiled, "just gettin' warmed up."

"Yeah, was almost a little too warm," Stoney grinned. "You always take on guys two feet bigger'n you?"

"That punk? He wasn't shit. I coulda knocked him from here to the pisser with one punch."

"Well, I'm glad you didn't have to try, 'cause his buddy was no midget."

"We coulda sicced Dov on 'em."

Stoney laughed.

"See you clowns tomorrow."

Me and Linc drank Stoney's round. The young couple stared at us.

Linc waved merrily. They turned away. We drank quietly for a while, then I got up.

"I'm gonna go too, Linc."

"What have I got, fuckin' leprosy or somethin'?"

"No, it's just time to go. I'm tired."

"Yeah. I'm kinda tired myself. Well, I'll walk you to the train."

In the dark, people rushed home from work. Even in the rush, people seemed to move more slowly, numbed, worn-out. Linc yawned.

"Wooo, it's finally catchin' up with me. Just gonna go home and rack it."

"See you tomorrow Linc."

"Yep. There's always tomorrow. Ain't there? For some people."

He was standing there, yawning sleepily. I nodded.

"Crazy world," he yawned, covering his mouth. "Hell, I better get home before I fall out on the street. See ya, Dov."

"So long, Linc."

At home the apartment was dark. There was a note:

Staying at Sue's again. See you in a day or so. I looked in the refrigerator and cupboard, pulled out a can of cream of mushroom soup, and made that and a bacon, lettuce and tomato sandwich. The two beers had dizzied me. I ate and drank slowly, listening to the Dylan song again, "Don't Think Twice It's All Right."

I went out and walked, feeling strange, tired, and suddenly returned home. On Pete's desk was a newspaper I hadn't noticed, opened to a picture of Jackie Kennedy in black, weeping. I stared at it, then took it over to the bed, kicked off my shoes, and lay back, staring at it, not reading words, but just looking at the picture.

Jackie in black. Sad, grief-stricken. Stricken by grief. I'd become a famous film-maker, up-and-coming. She had dark hair, pale skin. Like Rona.

It's so strange, Ellen said, she got married so suddenly. She met him this summer, huh?

In CORE in Chicago. They fell in love. See, if you hadn't broken up last year, well, Dov, I didn't mean that. Who knows about these things?

It's o.k. Ellen. I didn't have any big plans. I really hope she, you know. I'm glad she found someone—oh shit, you know—"

Sure.

Walking with Madelie in the woods around Albion. I don't want to think so much, Dov. Why can't people just... why can't everybody just get along. I get so upset. I don't want to get upset. There's so many nice things.

I spread the blanket on the grass, and the cheese, wine, bread, sardines, and oranges. Her blond hair, the long slender body, tan face, deerlike brown eyes, and Jack-O-lantern grin. Her laugh.

Are you trying to get me drunk?

I wouldn't dream of it.

Hmmmm.

Hmmm yourself.

You are.

No, I'm just thirsty.

This cheese is good. I like it. Yummy cheese.
My friend Jordie calling, I'll go to Hooten for one more
year to keep the old man happy, then I'm off. Go some-
where. Maybe New Orleans, maybe San Francisco. This
painting teacher up here told me about a stained glass ap-
prenticeship out there in North Beach, one or two of its kind
in the whole country. Maybe they need someone. Even if it's
just carrying stuff at first. If I had the guts I'd say, I'm a
painter and that's that. You don't learn painting in college.
Or maybe I'll go back to New York. Look up DeKooning.
Tell him I think his stuff is fantastic, and does he need a
canvas stretcher? Who knows.
    Letters from home: We feel you could communicate a
little more, Dov. We know you're busy and hopefully you are
enjoying living on your own and taking advantage of all that
Boston and Cambridge have to offer. Look, we don't want to
interfere, but we would like to hear from you once in a blue
moon.
    I rubbed my eyes in the dark and looked at the picture
again. Black hair. Pale skin. Grief. I could become a famous
film-maker, help her, meet her. I lay back on the pillow,
wanting to stroke that face, hear her, "Oh God, God."
(When I rubbed Rona's breasts she moaned, "Oh God!"
pressing closer.)
    I'd stroke her, the exquisite elegance melting, she would
tell me about her agonies, then turn slightly, "Oh it's all
wrong, you're so young, we're in two different worlds," and
daring the world I'd stroke her, whispering, "It's all right,
it's all right, shhhhh, shhhh," her elegant hands pushing
back the dark hair, "I hate all those people, Dov," and I
heard Jordie's voice, "She *is* your type, Dov—dark hair,
pale skin, intelligent—no, you're not crazy, forget all that
stuff, it's a crazy world," Jackie's voice, "I've been so
alone," her eyes shutting, her face quivering. . . ."
    I stopped, and looked around the room to see if anyone
was watching. I put away the newspaper, and put on a
record, yawning. Eight o'clock felt like midnight. I pushed
the needle on the Joan Baez record to the last song.

> I live one day at a time
> I dream one dream at a time
> I live one day at a time

I felt my chest glow, my face trembling. As my eyes shut, I could taste salty wet on the corners of my mouth. After listening to the whole song, I stripped, put the song on again, and lay down, listening. Dream at a time. Dreams, dreee, dreamycreamy. Yesterday's dead? "That's a lie," I yawned, the pillow cool, "and in a way it isn't." Yesterday: deep pockets in the heart. Sew 'em up. Forget 'em. They're empty. Or: warm your hands there now and then. Reach in when you have to. And tomorrow turning corners down unknown streets with — who knows? Yes. LIVE one day at a time. Because, like that, GONE. Quick. Shut lemon door... Never again. Chrome handle. Gleam: gone. Piece of dirt. Wind on grass. Bye. Unclaimed. No name. Lie, lie there. So soft. Unseeing   sea out to edge falling off edge'v everything sea out to black horiz her eyes her risin'.

Hurry. Going maroon moon coming lie ok hey beautiful song worth hearing three TIME beautiful ull lull BULLETS SUDDEN PING! Gone GONE nothing lll left Thatsit. That's it — Bugs Bunny like Bugs Bunny Loony Tunes ending too speeding Th-d-d-duddle d-duddle du-duddle th-luddle rolling calliope THATS ALL FOLKS   sss shh women in black sh whirling whirworld whirl of shh   ssongsdreambullets PING! songs how long PING! bullets   and dreams.

Long songs so long on oh honey on dreams shhh shhhh dreams bullets GONE bullets
                    and dreams.

Webb's Scar

Ever since I met Webb, I've wanted to ask him about his scar. Webb's scar cuts from the northeast corner of his forehead jaggeding down his right eye across the bridge of his nose to just below his left eye, then slants down his cheek just below his ear: a full-face scar. When Webb smiles, his cheek looks weird, as if possessing two or three levels. When Webb's angry, the scar glistens.

Me and Webb get along well because we both love baseball and hate the Dodgers. I hate them for moving from Brooklyn. Webb hates them because he hates anything to do with Los Angeles. We also get along because we hate working at the Medical Center and are both active in the union, trying to get things done. Webb's been trying longer than me; he's been at the Medical Center for fifteen years, considers himself one of the "mid-range old-timers", and tells me who to trust and who to watch out for. He takes quiet pride in telling me, "I just do my job. Don't no one mess with me."

I recently found out why no one messes with Webb.

153

One slow Sunday we were standing around talking when one of the housekeeping supervisors passed by, and glancing at Webb, nodded off-handedly, "How's it going?"

"It's goin'," Webb replied.

"Everything cool, blood?"

Webb didn't blink.

"Yeah."

The supervisor left, staring straight ahead. I looked at Webb. Unsmiling, he lit up one of his cigars and stood there with his mop and bucket.

"Hate that sonuvabitch," he muttered.

"Who? Woods?"

"Yeah. Callin' me blood and all that. I don't dig that, man. That sonuvabitch goes round callin' everybody blood, and as sure as you and me are standin' here, he'll turn right around and write your ass up 'cause he thinks you're takin' too long on break."

"Huh."

Webb stared at the parking lot through the glass windows, down the sides of the building.

Up on the sixth floor, we could see a good deal of the city, sitting on the benches by the windows, or just standing around. Webb, in "greens", works in surgery, cleaning up the blood from the operations. I'm the floor's clerk, doing the general paper work, handling the phones and the surgery waiting room—telling family and friends when their people will return from the operating and recovery rooms, serving them coffee, tea, and juice, as well as listening to them talk away their fear and anxiety while they wait. Except for a few emergency surgeries, however, Sundays go slowly.

Webb smoked on his cigar, and laughed, short and sudden.

"Now he might think of writin' me up, but I don't think he will," he grinned.

"How come?"

He looked at me and smiled, as if mulling something over, then leaned his hands on his mop. "So, kid, who do you like for the pennant this year? Think anyone can take them Dodgers?"

"Cincinnati, if they get some pitching."

"Maybe," Webb frowned.

"And the Giants," I kidded, "if they can get nine starting players."

Webb laughed. "Giants, huh? Nine starters, huh?" He laughed some more.

I was just about to go back to work when Webb said, "You know why that sonuvabitch Woody won't write me up, now or ever?"

"No."

"Got a minute?"

"Yeah."

"Won't take long. Sit down."

I sat down. He relit his cigar, and offered me one.

"No thanks."

Webb puffed his cigar, flicked it, and stared out the window.

"Woody wasn't always a supervisor, you know. 'Bout a year or so ago he was just a plain old worker, just like you and me, and no big thing. He was o.k. He did his job, didn't push his work off on nobody, know what I mean?"

I nodded.

"Well, I don't recall just exactly when it all happened, but one day I hear him talking to this head honcho they had here to crack the whip over us in housekeepin'. He ain't here no more, but, man, he was somethin' else. A lifer who was the lifer to end all lifers. I mean, he's the kind of sonuvabitch that was just plain born mean; the kind of man—if you want to call him a man which technically I suppose he was—but mean anyway—"

"Uh huh," I said.

"Anyways, knowin' all this—'cause it wasn't like you could hide the fact that that dog was a dog since the man did not let up for a second—knowing all this, Woody starts reportin' people to this lifer, sort of on the sly, slidin' up to the man and givin' him different kinds of information and lowdown on folks, and not just on this floor, but a coupla other floors too."

I whistled soft and low.

"Yeah. Well, at first, a couple of us tried to be cool about the thing and talk to the man. You know, 'Hey Woody, what's goin' on, whatcha tryin' to do?' Annie, she don't work here no more, but she was here for a long long time, one tough cookie she was, Annie ask him straight out —'You buckin' for the bigtime, Clyde?' Mmm, that Annie she could get like ice, mmmf. Sayin' to him, 'Whatever you lookin' for, honey, you better find it quick 'cause I don't tolerate no finks or fibbers anywhere in my vicinity.' Vicinity! Ooo, she was somethin' else. But even that didn't stop him. He just kept on, runnin' to the man like that. Then one day they up and made him assistant supervisor for two floors —this one, and five.

"Wow," I whispered.

"Well, if you had had any thought in your mind about him just bein' misinformed or fucked up or whatever before, you shoulda seen him when he got that promotion. You woulda had no doubts whatsoever. All of a sudden he was King Shit. And first day to work King Shit wore a suit."

Webb began laughing; the laughter grew louder; he roared.

"And that ol' Annie, she fixed his ass good. She accidentally—accidentally now—bumped into him and poured coffee all over that sucker. Ruined that suit forever. And wouldn't let it go there neither. Just stared at him, didn't blink an eyelash, not a one, and smiled, 'You look nice today.' And I swore right then and there I thought he was gonna hit that woman with everything he had. And you know, I wish he had. Cause then we never woulda hadda worry about him, or the hassles like the one I'm goin' to tell you about, 'cause Annie woulda killed him right then and there, or come close to it. She was somethin' else that Annie was. Finally met this guy who worked out at Bethlehem Steel, and moved down to Houston. But that's gettin' away from what I want to tell you about this dude."

I nodded.

"Well, he started gettin' slicker—he thought—and bein' nice to all the black folks and savin' up his shit for the Filipinos, 'specially the womens 'cause he knew the womens wouldn't sass him whereas the men he could never be sure about 'cause he knew about some of 'em—from the last strike he seen 'em on the line. They know that karate and Kung Fu—that Guillermo cat runs a whole school—and Woody was scared to death they was gonna wipe the floor with his ass, which, believe me, some of them could do in a minute. I wouldn't wanna tangle with 'em myself, and I can take care of myself, know what I mean?''

"Yeah.''

"Anyways, Woody started really hasslin' the Filipinos and then sort of chippin' away at the rest of us, all the time suckin' up to that lifer bastard. But one day that lifer up and drops dead—heart attack—like that.''

Webb snapped his fingers.

"I'd bet any amount of bread it was 'cause he was such a tightass. Seemed like he had a hard-on for the whole world; he was one of those people that keeps it all inside when he ain't breathin' down someone's neck, know what I mean?''

I shrugged, "I think so.''

"Well, after that, they got a new guy, another lifer, only a little smarter. This boss gave Woody a fancy title—some bullshit like Operations Assistant, like they was on some destroyer or some shit like that—and he just ate it up. Started gettin' into some new shit—gettin' on us about doin' more buffing. Every day he'd come around yappin' about how the floors weren't clean enough, how they should shine. And he'd walk along the floors like he was Sherlock Holmes, or some huntin dog lookin' for little pieces of whatever bullshit he could find.''

I laughed. Webb glared at me, "Think that's funny, huh?'', then motioned to me.

"C'mere.'' I followed him out to the desk and looked down the hall.

"Look down this hall.'' The long linoleumed hall gleamed smoothly, almost glossy, wherever unencumbered by wheelchairs, guernies, linencarts, and chairs. The light shone off the floors.

"How's that look to you?''

"Pretty nice.''

Webb spat. "If that was a rink we could skate on it."

We went back.

"That's how my floors always been—I make a point of it. I don't need to buff every day to get them that way either. Well, when I told Woody this he had a bird. Started blabberin about there's too mucha this and too mucha that, and all other kinds of bullshit."

I nodded.

"Then he asked me if I was refusin' to do assigned work. And I said 'since when is buffin' every day assigned work, since when and where?' And he says 'It's goin' to be in the new job description on all floors', and I said, 'Not if I can help it. You gonna have the floors where there's only women workin' buffin' too? You gonna put some of them itty bitty Filipino women behind them big buffin' machines—is that your idea of some kind of joke or are you just a plain asshole?' And he said 'Don't call me no names, I'll report you.' And I said, 'Report away, man, if that's how you want to play it. But I ain't about to let you get away with this, not if I can help it.' "

I nodded.

"And then he comes on to me with this, 'Look, if you just stay cool and stay outa my way, I'll let it slide for you.' "

"Uh huh."

"Can you imagine him thinkin' he can run that on me? Well, I didn't hear nothin more about it until I heard they was havin' the Filipina women on the floors pushin' them buffers. Soon as I found out, I took my lunch break and went to see for myself. Sure enough, there were the buffers, and the women pushin' them, and one of 'em pregnant at that, which he knew too, that sonuvabitch. Cause what he told me later was, 'Well, she shouldn't be workin' if she's that far along,' which mighta been one of the few things he said that had any truth to it. Anyways, I went to find him and he says, 'Can't talk now, Hawkins'. And all this time, he's always ready to talk—baseball this, how's the family that. And him stupid enough to be thinkin' he's foolin' me! But what he don't know is, I'm like the kettle on the low flame. You heat the water, and it don't do nothin' at first. But you keep that fire lit and soon there's steam. And don't open the top too quick, or you'll get burned—bad! So, I went and told them women not to touch them buffers and wait 'til we talked with the union. Then Woody came to find me. You bet your ass he did. Which is when he made his BIG mistake, 'cause it was on the swing shift and that sucker came while I was eatin' my dinner.''

Webb paused, lit up his cigar again, and whooshed out the smoke. He watched the cigar glow, puffed, and continued.

"Now, you know how it is. You work all day, you work hard, and the one decent break you get—a whole half hour, none of this fifteen minute shit—you wanna eat. You wanna get somethin' in the blood, somethin' good, and you wanna have some time to eat it. See, I'm one of these people that really don't like to be disturbed when I eat—"

"Me too," I smiled.

"Then you understand what I mean. Well, Woody comes in and I'm sittin', you know, with a couple of other people—not many, it's a weekend like this one—Alberta, Jonesy. We're eatin', and talkin', you know, relaxin'—or tryin' to—and all of a sudden in slides Clyde with his hand on his hip which makes me mad. Just him standin' there with that hand on his hip like he's the King of the Shitpile.Which is what I say to him. I look up and say, 'Look who's here. The King of the Shitpile himself. How's the flies treatin' ya?'. and he tries to laugh it off, but I can see he's all bent out of shape and workin' himself up into somethin'. Then he starts in: 'You a shop steward, Hawkins?', knowin' goddam well I ain't, you know what I mean?' "

"Yeah," I said.

"But I cut him off right then and there cause I'm not standin' for this. I say 'Hey, don't say another fuckin' word. I'm on break, you know what that means. That means I don't hafta say diddley to you. Better go read that contract.' And he ain't smilin' but sort of grindin' his teeth and sayin', 'I want to talk with you outside, Hawkins,' givin' me this look like he's supposed to be bad, which made me even madder. And I say, 'Are you deaf, man? I'm on break. You wanna talk to me, you gonna have to wait until I'm through eatin'. Now get off my back 'fore you ruin my digestion. If you want to make yourself useful, why don't you go check the floors for lint?' "

I laughed.

"Well, Alberta and Jonesy and a clerk all start laughin' and Woody looked pissed, but I was so fed up I just turned my back on the man."

"Uh huh."

"Know what that sonuvabitch did then?"

"What?"

"He waited for me. I seen him standin' there in the hall waitin' for me with one of the head nurses, and I knew right away what he was doin'—tryin' to set me up. Thought he was so smart. Only thing is, I'm smarter than he'll ever be. I went and called Johnnie up on seven and got her to call the girls in the phone room and have them page that head nurse for the nursery three floors down. Then I went to my locker and got a little friend of mine, understand?"

I didn't completely, but nodded anyway.

"Then I walk real slow past him. I can tell he's tryin' to make up his mind if he should mess with me without a witness which is what he had that head nurse for, since he knows no one eatin' with me is gonna side with him on anything. Well, he decides to do it himself, he's such a honcho. And he sneers 'You off break, finally, Hawkins?' And I come right back with, 'Yeah, what of it?' He pussyfoot around a little then whine, 'You ain't shop steward' again, and I stared him straight in the eyes and say, 'You said that already, what else you got to say to me.' and he say it again, 'You ain't shop steward,' and I get up closer and say, 'Like I told you before. That's right. I ain't. I am a union member in good standing and I do what I think a union member's supposed to do when he sees something come down that ain't right. And I do that anywhere, anytime, and I don't ask permission from you, your boss, or your boss's boss. Now, if you got somethin' on you chest, get it off quick, cause I'm supposed to be workin' now.' "

"Well, that really riles him. He hisses, like the snake he

is. 'You got no call at all to be tellin the women on the floors anythin' about the buffers. You goin' against my orders, and the man downstairs, and you countermanding innovations.' "

I looked at Webb.

"Yeah, I couldn't believe my ears him talkin' that shit. If I hadn't been so mad, I mighta laughed myself to death."

I nodded.

"And he goes on, 'If you don't cut it out, I'm gonna have to write you up. Give you a warning. After two warnings, well, you know the rules—you can consider this here a verbal warning.' And I stopped him right then and there sayin', 'You wanna write me up huh?' And he says, 'I don't want to, but you're forcing my hand,' and I say, 'Well, we can just grieve this mother. I want to see where it says anything in the contract about buffing the floors, 'cause if it's there it must be in invisible ink.' And he says, 'It's there, and if it ain't, it's gonna be. It's new. You're buckin' the new, Hawkins.' And him callin' me this Hawkins shit, when I been knowin' him since I don't know when—that got to me too. And I says, 'It ain't in the contract, and you're a goddam motherfuckin' liar. And he gets real quiet and says, 'That's insubordination. I can have you fired for that.'

Webb paused.

"And that's when the steamkettle blew. I mean, I been really tryin' to be cool, calm, and collected like they say, but the way he said that like he was this little snotass snitch talkin' about firing me when I been here over ten years goin' on twenty. And I thought of that, and my family, and my little diddly shit check, which ain't much but which is all I got, understand, and that did it. I got that big red in front of my eyes, and next thing I knew I had that sonuvabitch right up against the elevator, with my forearm against his Adams apple and my little friend that I carry around for protection in my other hand. I put that blade against his throat, and I said—and meant it, and he knows I meant it—and I said, 'You ain't gonna do a goddamn thing, understand? Cause— and listen good cause I'm only gonna say this once—even if you do get me fired outta here, I'm gonna come after you. I'll come after you wherever you are. And I'll find you. Nowhere won't be far enough. I'll find you, and I'll slit your fuckin' throat from ear to ear—if it takes me my whole life, I will.' "

I took my breath in.

"And just like that I wasn't mad at all. I was even a little perturbed at myself for blowin' up like that, only there's so much a man can take, understand? And there was people around too—Jonesy, Alberta, five or six others. When I started to go back to work, everyone got out of my way. It was like the Red Sea partin' for Moses. It was kinda funny. And Woody he was kinda glued to the wall there by the elevator, like my blade put a spell on him, and nailed him to the wall."

Webb wiped his mouth and looked at his long unlit cigar. He relit it, and puffed on the cigar to get it regoing.

"Anyways, that's the last time he ever hassled me. Ever since then he's been real nice."

"And no one found out what happened."

"Nope. I thought for sure there might be someone who woulda said somethin'—other than Woods, that is—cause he knew I meant what I said. But the others, either they were on my side to begin with, or else they was scared 'cause they could see I meant business. Who knows? I'm just glad things worked out o.k."

"Yeah," I laughed, "they worked out o.k."

"I'm tellin ya," Webb frowned, "what you gotta put up with around here is somethin' else."

He walked away, whistling. I returned to my floor realizing I still hadn't found out about the scar. I figured maybe another time, after we talk more about the Dodgers.

A Slap in the Face

I. Concerning Assissi Gardens

If you want to understand why Rainey Smith worked so hard, laughed so deep, and at twenty eight had ulcers, you should know a little bit about Assissi Gardens, the private hospital where she worked with me, Mac, Dot and Wilma. I'd only been there eight months when the Chocolate Drop Explosion took place; but at Assissi Gardens, in five minutes you could get the picture.

Originally run by nuns, Assissi Gardens elegantly perched half-way up a heights, with its back to the seedy section of town. Down in the Tenderloin, dubbed by doctors Medicare Mecca, lived pensioners in hot-plate rooms, immigrant Filipino and Arabic families, and the night crew of prostitutes, junkies, and the melancholy lost. To all these people, Assissi Gardens offered its back door Emergency Room exit, literally looking the other way: up the hill.

Up the hill sat luxury apartments and old brick carriage houses covered with ivy. Assissi Gardens greeted these with its immaculate front: a modern, post-Frank Lloyd Wright

163

four-story wall of naked concrete and frosted glass looking down on huge double glass doors flanked by fountains, azalea bushes; and, in keeping with the official colors of royal blue, two dark blue-suited doormen on the outside doors, and on the inner doors two dark blue-suited men with gold breast inscriptions: SECURITY.

If you talked with the doctors or head nurses, or were lucky enough to find the seldom-seen Administrator, or the nearly invisible Board of Directors, you got a warm and wonderful feeling for Assissi Gardens. Even among private hospitals, it had a reputation for well-being and absolute cleanliness: spotless walls, beautiful rubber plants, wall-to-wall carpeting throughout, freshly painted rooms, color t.v.s at every bed, free phone service.

There was a new dialysis unit, a new radiation therapy department, and a brand new burn unit. The true pride and joy was each floor's deluxe suite, complete with kitchenette, tiled bath and Simmons hideaway sofa bed enabling a family to stay overnight for a nominal charge of three hundred dollars. One surgeon called Assissi Gardens "A marvel—truly Heaven on earth." Wilma Higgenbotham, the older aide who worked Dot's side, put it, "More like hell on wheels."

Rainey charmed everyone. It wasn't simply her stunning beauty: her long five-six, the immaculate Afro, the strong slim legs, the wiry arms. Nor was it her beautiful sculptured face: the wide high forehead, high cheekbones, delicate nose and highly expressive thin-lipped mouth with perfect teeth over a delicate squarish jaw, or her black mercurial eyes. New interns and residents, before they knew Rainey better and knew of her fiance, Royal, drooled, "How I'd like to get into *that*," winking and poking each other, and making buttocks-grabbing, breast-rubbing motions, breathing, "I'd ride that bitch all night." Yet more than her physical beauty, Rainey's nursing ability dazzled the doctors.

A spectacular event secured Rainey's reputation. One night, Wilma went home sick, leaving Rainey as the only aide. An acute alcoholic went into dt's, climbed out on the window ledge and threatened to jump, screaming to the gathering people six stories below to remove the green horses. He loved animals and didn't want them to get hurt. He clung to the tearing window curtains. His roommate fled to the nursing station where I was simultaneously answering phones and charting. I called Mac and we rushed into the room. The young guy warned us back, his pocked face and scraggly beard trembling, "Don't come near me. Not another step. Stay where you are, goddamnit! Bastards! Get back!" don't bring no priest! I'm burning up! Bastards! Get back!"

Suddenly Rainey strolled in. "Hey, turkey, you're gonna get sick standing out in that cold. Your nose gonna get so stuffed up you ain't even gonna be able to TASTE the big roast beef dinner tomorrow afternoon. All you can eat, too."

"Fuck you, and fuck your roast beef," screamed the guy, as Rainey added, "Not to mention the bottle they gonna have."

"B-b-b-bottle?" The guy turned instinctively towards the room. Rainey grabbed him gently just as three security officers rushed in, yanked him from her grasp, wrestled him to the ground and straight-jacketed him.

Afterward, she bawled out the security guards, but felt personally responsible for "that poor sucker" being man-handled. When we reminded her, "You probably saved his life," she shrugged.

The older doctors respected Rainey's phenomenal timing. She knew when to coax, taunt, ignore, kid, get tough. She received more patient letters than any other employee. Patients returned to visit her, irking many of the nurses, including Dot Finch, our head nurse.

Dot Finch, the other participant in the Chocolate Drop Explosion, was a credit to Assissi Gardens, as much a part of it as the plumbing. A retired Army nurse, Dot had come to Assissi Gardens in the late fifties. Over her twelve years' service, she doted on rich patients, catering to their every whim and need. She loathed the MediCal and Medicare patients, manipulating the bed assignments so that such patients would up on Mac and Rainey's side. Rainey swore Dot hadn't given a bedpan in ten years: "If she was drownin' in the ocean and somebody threw her one to hold onto, she might put her hands on it. Mind you—might.''

Dot possessed the waxy yellow sheen of the unloved spinster. Her thin, birdlike body fussed and fidgeted. Always cold, she wore a light blue or light yellow sweater. Her hands, strangely mottled, fluttered. She lived with her birds— parrots, canaries and wounded sparrows found in parks. She called the birds her children. They slept on her chest, warming her on cold nights. It was Charlie Silver, her doctor, who suggested the birds were aggravating her asthma. He urged her to ditch them.

Dot obliged stubbornly, retaining her few precious parrots who were "like my own flesh and blood, the babies.'' Wilma claimed Dot once owned a talking mynah bird, but that after three weeks with Dot, the bird had gone completely mute and starved itself to death.

Dot adored comparing notes with patients. Upon finding a fellow bird-lover, she brought in carefully clipped-out articles on new discoveries in nutritious birdseed, safer cages, and healthier litter, as well as sharing her copies of the National Audubon Society's latest endangered species list. She did this from a genuine desire to share, unlike other actions designed to obtain a hoped-for tip, which the rich patients invariably seldom gave, leaving Dot seething with resentment, and ready to pounce on the nearest victim—me for not answering the phones and lights quick enough, or Rainey and Wilma for anything. We took it, except Rainey. She'd stand, hand on hip, sneering, "Get off the rag, Dot.''

Sometimes Dot even snapped at Mac, Mary McGregor. Mac was a tough fifty-year-old woman with a vital healthy body, a head full of long white hair she refused to touch up, ("I like it—it looks like fresh snow. Besides, who would I be fooling anyway?'') and a bright brisk manner that covered thirty years of working in nursing homes and hospitals. At fifty-five, she was going through a divorce and supporting a seventeen-year-old daughter and a sixteen-year-old son. She constantly got phone calls that began with her patiently listening, then gradually shifted into her frowning, twisting paper clips, then finally saying firmly, "We'll talk about that

later," "You can't do that, forget it," "Absolutely not,"
"O.k., but if you're not in by midnight, I'm calling the
police," "Do what you have to, Harry, and I'll do the same.
Fine, you'll be hearing from my lawyer too," or "Don't talk
to me that way. I told you, I won't have it." Often, Mac
slammed the phone down, or let it gently drop, sighing,
"Those kids!" or "Idiot!"

II. How Certain Events Led Up To The Incident

It was Mac who kept Rainey and Dot from going at each
other's throats. Rainey hated Dot for shunning the MediCal
and Medicare patients. Dot hated Rainey's free and breezy
manner with doctors and visitors; and her bawdy joking, like
the night before the Chocolate Drop Explosion when she
came up to me winking.

"Hey, Josh—"

"What?"

Rainey swayed her hips suggestively. I waited, assuming
a complete deadpan. "What kind of smokes you carry," she
snickered, staring at my crotch quickly, "KINGSIZED,
regular, or what?" She jutted her hip provocatively.

My forehead hot, I felt my comeback snap alive. "I
smoke a pipe."

"A pipe!" Rainey spluttered.

"Or else," I began.

"Or else, what?" She giggled, trying to keep a straight
face.

"A good non-filter cigarette. I don't like anything
getting in the way of the, uh, taste."

Rainey grabbed her sides and ran past the nursing
station, laughing into the medicine room where we kept our
stocks, i.v. bottles. Dot stared at us crabbily.

"Jesus Christ, when you're not talking politics, you're
fooling around. Don't you ever *work*?"

I was sitting in front of a stack of five charts, with
another five I'd just finished. "You don't understand," I
smiled, "I can work and talk at the same time."

Rainey came back, frowning. "Who's not working?"

"Well, it seems to me you have time to fool around, that means something else isn't getting done."

"Don't worry your pretty little head now, Dot," Rainey crooned, "just saying a few words to my favorite wardclerk."

Mac ran over. "Quick, quick, Rainey!"

Rainey ran off with Mac into one of the rooms. Mac returned shortly. "That Rashad again. Can't hold down a thing." Sweating, Rainey came out, dragging a smelly bright red garbage bag. She stared sourly at Dot. "Yep," I said softly, "a pipe." Rainey's eyes gleamed. "Now why you keep doin' me like that, Josh, when you KNOW I got an ulcer. A pipe!" She snickered. "Hoo—it ain't too good for me to laugh like this, ooo, my stomach."

"You clowns," Mac scowled, as Dot spotted Dr. Silver coming up the hall.

"Charlie! You didn't!"

She scooted over to him.

"Oh it is, a new leather bag, let me see. Ohh, it's beautiful!"

"Glad you like it."

"Like it? I love it! Mmmm, real leather, I can smell it. I think it's Brazilian; Brazilian or Italian. If I didn't have this cold, I could tell you which. Isn't that a WONDERFUL smell? Mmm. New leather. Nothing like it in the world!"

Rainey was wiping her face with a towel. Mac was preparing her medicines.

"Here you go, Josh," Dr. Silver said, sliding still another chart over to me. "Thanks," I grumbled.

"Don't you have anything to do?" Dot asked Rainey.

"I was just leavin'," Rainey winked, "now that I'm finished discussin' the dangers of smokin'." She walked Dr. Silver to the elevator, sliding her arm through his. "So when you gonna make an honest woman of me, Doc?"

"When you start getting honest," Silver answered, starting Rainey laughing all over again. Dot frowned and stared at my pack of Marlboros.

"Are you smoking again on duty, Josh? I warned you about that."

"No, I'm not smoking. We were just, skip it."

"If you ABSOLUTELY NEED to smoke, then go back into the medicine room. But only if you're all caught up. And you're not, are you?"

"I'm doing o.k."

"What bugging you, Dot?" Mac asked gently.

"Nothing's bugging me," Dot snapped. "Why does something always have to be bugging me?"

"Now, Dot, come on!"

"I talked to Dr. Gould just before I came in today."

"Yes?"

"Freddie's going in for surgery. At 4:15. That's in ten minutes." Dot bit her lip. Her eyes moistened.

"Oh, I knew I should've taken the day off. I just knew it."

"Who's Freddie?" I started to ask, but Mac poked me.

"I'm sure everything will be fine," Mac smiled softly, "he's in good hands."

"The best. There's not a doctor in the city like Dr. Gould." I frowned, thinking Gould, Gould. I thought I knew all the doctors at Assissi Gardens.

Dot bit her thumb. "Oh, I hope so, Mac, I hope so. If I lost Freddie, I just don't know what I'd do."

I stared at Mac questioningly, trying to find out if Freddie was a brother, an old friend, an old lover.

"I just don't know," Dot sniffed, grabbing a kleenex from a small green-gray tissue box.

"Would it help to talk about it?" suggested Mac, "I can spare a minute or two."

"His poor tummy."

"Yes?"

"It's all puffed up and horrid. He won't eat."

"Tsk, tsk," Mac clucked.

"They say it's an incarcerated egg."

My neck bolted forward. Mac put her fingers to her lips, scowling fiercely.

"It's an extremely delicate operation. And no matter

WHAT Dr. Gould tells me, I just know the good Lord didn't intend this.'' Dot dabbed at her eyes with the kleenex, then blew her nose. I could feel laughter rising. I clenched my teeth.

"The greatest danger is the potential blood loss.''

"Yes?'' Mac nodded politely.

"Oh, there's a million things that can go wrong. I should be there!'' Dot bolted up. "I should be there!''

"Nonsense,'' soothed Mac, "what could you do except worry yourself sick?''

"I suppose you're right,'' Dot sighed, "I wouldn't be much help, would I? They probably wouldn't let me into the operating room.''

"Probably not,'' Mac yawned.

I couldn't stop the laughing, and muttering "Excuse me,'' bolted into the medicine room. Rainey came in, wiping her forehead and shoving another bright red bag of dirty linen down the laundry chute.

"What's with you, *turkey*?''

I cracked up.

J.J. passed through the open door, bringing up a patient on a guerney, signalling Rainey for help. They both returned a few minutes later.

"Thanks, Rain,' J.J. said.

"No problem, main man.''

Rainey started playing with J.J.'s wedding band. "I see you don't want me to live long, messin' with my mind like this.''

"Ain't your MIND I'm interested in.''

"Oh no?'' J.J. grinned.

Rainey laughed. J.J. shook his head. "You and Royal better hitch it up soon, so you don't lead any good church-goin' fool into temptation.''

"I'm gonna find out who your minister is and tell on you.''

"The man you just helped into bed is a Baptist Minister upstate. He told me he's in God's hands now. I told him, 'You in God's hands, and Rainey Smith's, so you can't lose.' ''

"You didn't say that either."

"Go ask the man."

"Oh sure. You don't think I'm gonna fall for that pack of lies, J.J. Thompson?"

"Suit yourself. Got to run," J.J. smiled. "Ask him, you'll be surprised."

"Me or him?" Rainey laughed, just as Wilma came in and dumped a bright red bag down the chute. "I saw they had some beans for lunch today, but this is too much."

Dot came in, checking her watch. "What is this, a convention?"

I moved back towards my desk.

"Can we get some new linen, is that all right?" Rainey snapped. Silently, Wilma grabbed some sheets and left. Older, wiser, Wilma always advised us to ignore Dot and hope she took some temperatures.

Mac bustled in. "That Rashad can't hold down a thing! I'm worried."

"Told you," Wilma said over her shoulder, "they should kill them beans."

"No," Mac replied calmly, "this man is throwing up when he has nothing to throw up. Now his sputum's bloody."

"Who?" Dot asked.

"You wouldn't know," Rainey said sourly.

"Mr. Rashad."

"That Arab, with the army of kids," Dot said.

"The man," Mac scowled, "with the G.I. bleed."

"Well," Dot said, "you want to call his doctor?"

"I think I better."

Later that evening, a young black woman was admitted to our floor, accompanied by her mother. Her papers read: VIRGINIA LOCKETT. Age: 13. DIAGNOSIS: THERAPEUTIC ABORTION. DILATION AND CURRETAGE. She was a Medicare patient. Shyly and sadly, she walked towards me. Her mother carried her luggage—a small overnight bag and a large bag of food whose warm smells took over the counter of the nursing station. Her mother, a heavy-set, brown-skinned woman with very clear skin, stared me straight in the eyes. "Virginia

Lockett for room—" She quickly glanced at the papers, "624, I believe."

"Welcome to Assissi Gardens," I smiled. "My name is Josh Singer. I'm the ward clerk. If you need anything at all, feel free to ask. If you could just have a seat in the waiting area over there, the nurse will be right with you."

The mother deposited the papers on the counter, and took her daughter to the area by the elevator. There were two large armchairs next to a long couch with a long cocktail table full of magazines—National Geographic, Time and Newsweek, U.S. News and World Report. Virginia studied the wall-to-wall carpeting, the pictures on the walls of evening oceans, and stared glumly up at the Muzak box above the elevator. The tune was the theme song from Dr. Zhivago. Virginia flounced, straightened her skirt, then clasped her hands. She unclasped them, and clutched a small radio and her other belongings: a geography textbook—Many People From Many Lands—and a movie magazine announcing: Why Liz Can't Forgive Dick.

Dot stared at the papers, then briskly dialed the phone, her finger snapping off the nursing office number. "Since when are we getting D and C's?" She waited, listening. Her face hardened. "You know I prefer not to get these patients, Lucy." Lucy Quinlan was the evening shift supervisor. "Well, if we're all filled up, we're all filled up. I guess there's nothing I can do. O.k., yes. You have a nice one too." She hung up the phone and glanced at the papers. "Thirteen. My God!"

I handed Dot the papers, expecting her to show Virginia Lockett to her room. It was on her side of the floor, and Wilma was at dinner. She shook her head. "Go get Rainey."

"She's helping Mr. Lucas with his shower."

"I'll help Mr. Lucas. Get her." She spotted my reluctance and sighed: "Never mind. I'll get her myself."

Soon Rainey stomped out, her eyes hot and black. She spotted the girl and her mother on the couch and her face changed into a big smile. She strode around the nursing counter, grabbed the papers off the top and, glancing at them, bopped up to the mother and daughter. "Hello, Mrs.

Lockett, Virginia. I'm Rainey Smith and I'll be looking after you.''

The mother rose slowly, taking her daughter's elbow.

"We gonna make you just as comfortable as we can,'' Rainey smiled. "We even have some heavy duty soul music, as you can see.'' She was pointing to the Muzak box.

The mother grinned grimly. The daughter nodded. Rainey took the overnight bag as they moved down the hall. "Virginia Lockett. Mmm, sounds like a movie star name, don't it? How about it, Ginny? You gonna grow up to be a movie star? You're pretty enough.''

The girl's face drooped as the mother, remembering something, went "Hmmph.''

Rainey shrugged. "Well, you never know, do you?'' nudging the mother. "And I can tell where this young lady gets her good looks from.''

The mother, still hummphing, cracked a slight smile. Virginia stared at the carpeting, as Rainey chattered on, "Mmm, something in that bag smells gooo-ood.'' They walked further down until I could only hear Rainey's last words, "What kind of radio you got there?''

Dot returned from the shower room, livid. "Thirteen years old! I'll bet she's twelve.''

Mac joined us, sitting down wearily and pulling out a chart and writing in nursing notes. "Now don't get started in tonight, Dot. Please.''

"We just got an abortion. Thirteen years old! You know what I keep telling them downstairs—''

"I also know you're worried about Freddie, so why don't you just try and relax.''

"O.k.'' Dot bit her nails. She arranged some papers near her, turning in her chair. "She's twelve and not a day older. I'm positive.''

"Is that why you didn't want to take her to her room?'' I snapped.

"Don't butt in.''

"I'm trying not to, but you're ruining my concentration.''

"Listen to that! I'm ruining his Highness' concentration! I work here too, buddy. In fact, I'm your immediate supervisor!''

"Dot! Calm down," Mac sighed.

"You're lucky I am too. I let you get away with murder.... What's taking Rainey so long? Josh, call into the room and see what she's doing. It shouldn't take this long." I pressed the button on the intercom and spoke into the holes. "Rainey?"

"Yeah?"

"Dot wants to know what's happening."

"We're shootin' up."

Wilma came by with a tray full of water pitchers and began filling them up. Rainey walked up the hall, leaned on the counter and glared.

"You got a problem?"

Dot backed up in her chair, squinting. "It just seemed you were taking an awfully long time."

Rainey's eyes shone hard, brilliant. "I'm explainin'. You know how stupid us black folks are. It takes a long, long time to show us how to work a t.v., push buttons and figure out where the john is."

"Rainey," Wilma frowned, "that's not funny."

Rainey folded her arms. "Anytime you think I'm goin' too slow, Dot, you do it. I know how fast you can move when you want to. And you'd probably be outta there in no time flat."

"Well, honestly," Dot scowled.

"Well, well," Rainey mimicked.

Wilma wrung out a towel, twisting it dry.

"Well," Dot sighed, "maybe it was a long time, maybe it wasn't."

"If you can't tell time with your watch right there on your hand and that clock above the elevator, either you need new eyeglasses, a new watch, a new clock, or all three."

"Well!"

Rainey leaned a little over the counter, her breasts bulging against the edge. "And if you want to start *timing* me, you better say that straight out so I can call the union right now and see what they say."

"Come on now, Rainey," Mac said.

"Come on yourself! Or maybe, Dot, you should go over to Sears and get yourself one of them three-minute egg timers."

I giggled and Wilma turned away so Dot wouldn't see her grin. Dot shuffled some papers, murmuring, "Honestly!"

"Now," Rainey said, tossing her head, "if there's nothin' else buggin' you, I'd like to go back and do what I'm paid to do." She pranced off proudly.

"I can't understand that woman for the life of me."

"She's mad about you not taking that Medicare patient," I said, watching both Wilma and Mac walk off. Dot studied me, frowning hard.

"You just love 'em, don't you?"

I looked around to see who I loved. "Who?" I thought she was going to say black people.

"All these Medicare and MediCal hustlers. Living off the fat of the land."   _welfare_

"Malarkey."

"Doesn't it _bother_ you that you work forty hours a week and so much of your money goes to take care of people who don't have the slightest ambition or inclination to do something with their lives?"

"I get angrier when my money goes for military spending, Welfare for the Pentagon."

"Now stick to the point."

"I am! I'm for Welfare for people that need it."

"So, any bum that doesn't want to work can get a free ride, is that it?"

"Lots of people WANT to work. There's no jobs."

Dot slapped her forehead. "You are incredible! WANT to work?"

"That's right! When I was out of work, before I came here, I met a lot of people at the Unemployment Office who would've loved a full-time—hell, even a part-time job. Anything." Even as I was talking, I could remember that winter —the endless waiting crowd under the low grey sky, young black longshoremen knocked out by containerization, middle-aged Chinese women, young Chicanos studying the want ads, an older white man in a suit, a young longhair like myself carefully filling out a possible placement form.

"Then what's stopping them. I see ads in the papers every day."

"Yeah! For microbiologists. Too bad they don't train you. I'd apply for it myself."

And I remembered the food stamp counselor, smiling sadly, "I know you're going to find this surprising, but you don't have enough money to purchase your food stamps. I'm really sorry."

Dot sighed. "You think that little girl wants to work?"

"I don't know," I snapped, "why don't you go *ask* her?"

Dot fidgeted, shuffled some papers, then dialed the phone. "Yes, I'm calling about a patient of Dr. Gould's. Yes, I'll wait." She straightened up, tense. "Still in surgery?" She hung up the phone, muttering, "This is going to cost a small fortune," and, catching herself guiltily, pressed her lips, "Well, money's no object," wiping away a quick tear. "Oh God!" She noticed me studying her. "What are you looking at?"

"Nothing."

Rainey returned and put some notes in Virginia Lockett's chart. "Dot, the patient wants to know if she can eat her own food."

"Fine. Is it soul food?"

"Just keep it up."

"For Heaven's sake, I just asked!" Dot dialed the phone again, got a busy signal, and hung up.

Wilma came over and nudged Rainey. "Girl, I want to talk with you when you got a minute."

Mac came by. "Any word yet, Dot?"

"Still in surgery. It's been over an hour and a half now."

Rainey and Wilma looked at me quizzically. I gave them my "later" look. Dot moved over and peeked at Virginia Lockett's chart. "You know, I think maybe Planned Parenthood should have some kind of mass advertising campaign. Try something new. Put Diana Ross on t.v. or something."

Rainey chuckled. "Sure. Maybe they could lure Aunt Jemima out of retirement too."

"Rainey," Wilma hissed, "come here."

Rainey cowed, accompanied Wilma into the medicine room. I mumbled something about checking supplies, grabbed a sheet of paper, and went back to listen. Wilma spoke slowly, anger taking hold of her. She was a light-skinned rocklike woman with a big frame, glasses and straight hair in a bun.

"What's bugging *you* now?" Rainey grumbled, "seems like the whole floor's going off the hinges tonight."

"I just don't like the way you be puttin' us down in front of Dot. It's not right. What you said before about us, talkin' about that poor child what come in with her mama, that's none of her business. And not a word of truth to it. Shootin' up junk! You're just reinforcin' lies she already thinks. You think you're gettin' the best of her, but by sayin' what you're sayin' you're lettin' her get the best of you."

"Wilma, Wilma," Rainey laughed, her eyes angry, "you shoulda been a preacher."

"Well, I don't know about that," Wilma stated, "but what I do know is you ain't gonna change how that dried-up old bitch out there—"

"Wilma Mae!"

"thinks. Uh, uh!"

"What could change her?" I asked.

"Broken jaw, maybe," Wilma blurted, raising her eyes suddenly as if shocked at her own words.

"Well, all I know is this," Rainey replied, "I gotta say somethin' when she starts gettin' funky like that. I mean, girl, she wouldn't even take that poor little kid to her ROOM. Couldn't even walk down the *hall*! Now, tell me, can't we *do* somethin' about that? Josh, can't we do something? I mean, that's racialist. What's that if it ain't that? I'm feelin' like I oughta be callin' the Panthers or the NAACP or the Better Business Bureau or SOMEbody. I mean, that's low down to the ground."

"Happens all the time," Wilma said. "You been here long as I have, you almost get used to it."

"Well, you got a lot more patience with it than I do, girl." Rainey shook her head. Wilma frowned.

"Well, I gotta get back to work."

When we came back out, Dot was hanging up the phone as Mac reassured her. "Dot, they'll call. You don't want to get too far behind on your medicines. It's getting late."

"I know. I know." Dot spotted Rainey. "Make sure that little girl gets nothing to eat after midnight."

"You think I don't know that?"

"Well, she might stay up and snack."

"How's that?"

"Just remind her."

Rainey's eyes glittered. "Maybe you think she's gonna stay up all night watchin' t.v.?"

"I told them downstairs I don't like these kind of patients."

"Well, maybe you don't, but she's here, so tough!"

Dot flounced in her seat. Wilma stuck her index finger out at Dot. "Now, look. I'm gonna say this once. That child is our patient. O.k.? And basically there's not a lick of difference between that little girl and Mrs. Edmunsen's daughter—"

"What?" Dot gasped. "How dare—"

Faith Edmunsen was the nursing supervisor for the day shift and the real head of the Nursing Service, propping up a wimp named Lance Wiggin, the figurehead Director. Even Mac whistled.

"That's right," Wilma persisted, "no difference between that young girl and Faith Edmunsen's daughter what went on vacation for a few weeks last summer. Mmmm-hmmm. And we know what that vacation was all about, too, don't we?"

"That's none of your concern!" Dot blurted.

"That's true," Mac reddened, "I don't see why you're bringing that up, why that's gossip of the worst—"

"No," Wilma interrupted, "now I don't see it that way at all. The thing of it is is that this girl's family, Mrs. Edmunsen and her husband, could afford to send her away. She got that abortion, everyone in this place knows that as a fact, and no one can say different. Can they?'' Her glare challenged all. None answered. "See, I'm only gonna say this once, then I'll shut up, because it really is none of my business. Just like what that Lockett child is here for is none of anyone's business either. Now, Edmunsen's little girl, her mamma and daddy had enough money to call her abortion a vacation with nobody to say anything about it. She went off to the country somewhere, like what folks with money do. But this child has no money. So she comes here, or if not here to General, and her business is there for everyone to see. To see and to judge. Which is what you're doin' right now. And I don't recall seein' anything about qualifications for being a judge on this job, either in the nurse's aide description or in the registered nurse job description. Judgment yes, but that's just common sense. But you don't got no license and don't wear no robes makin' you judge and jury of who comes in here. So you got no call to be sayin' what's wrong with that child over there, whether you think she should be here or not. This girl is our patient and we're suppose' to care for her. That's the main reason why we here in the first place.''

Wilma stomped off without looking back. We all just sat there. Rainey and Mac went back to work. I just looked at the charts in front of me, dully seeing doctors' orders in tangled handwriting ordering new treatments, discontinuing old medications and advising new ones, walking exercises, labwork, x-rays, breathing treatments.

"Happy now?'' Dot said.

"Huh?''

"You'd love the whole world, wouldn't you?''

"I like to give people the benefit of the doubt if that's what you mean.''

"Well, I've seen a lot more of the world than you have, kid, and let me tell you, it's a pretty rotten place.''

"The world is what you make it.''

"Would you tell that to the little girl in 624?''

"Sure, I'd tell it to anyone.''

"And I suppose you'd make it like Cuba or Russia or China?''

"No, not necessarily. I'd take parts of all three. Take the

good, leave the bad. Cuban seafood is out of this world.''

''I don't understand.''

''I didn't think you would.''

''What kind of answer is that? Explain to me—do you want me to understand you or not?''

I stopped. Did I really want Dot to understand? I thought of my small collective of radical friends working in hospitals. What would they say? Jack would say, ''Why waste your time on such a reactionary old bitch, Josh? Fuck it.'' ''Work around her,'' Sandy might suggest. ''Try and neutralize her,'' Karen would advise. Barbara would shrug.

Dot dialed the phone again and recited mechanically, ''I'm calling concerning Dr. Gould's patient.'' She straightened up suddenly. ''Yes?'' She listened, gasped, then slumped back in her chair.

''Dot?''

She gasped, holding the phone. I could hear the drone of a dead phone on the other end. Mac spotted us and hurried over. ''Dot?''

Dot blinked at us, then burst into tears. ''He, he, he didn't make it,'' she said in a tiny voice. ''He died on the table.'' Her face fell apart. ''Ahoooo, ahoooo, huh, huh,'' she bawled, lightly bouncing up and down in her chair.

''I'm sorry,'' Mac said gently.

''Ahooo, hooo, huh.''

''Sorry,'' I added.

Dot wiped her eyes and kept crying. ''He was so g-gentle when he ate. He ate right out of my hand.''

''He sounds,'' Mac began, then stopped, not knowing what to say and unable to say ''Wonderful.''

''L-l-lots of b-b-birds eat right out of your hand, but F-Freddie was so kind—ohoo hoo. Do you know what I mean? Do you understand?''

''You've had a terrible shock,'' Mac crooned, patting Dot's shoulder.

''Some b-birds when they eat out of your hand, they don't m-mean to, but they h-hurt you,'' Dot sniffed, swallowing. ''They're hungry—poor things—and sometimes they m-miss and peck your palm and th-that h-hurts.''

"Yes," Mac agreed.

"But w-with F-Freddie, it was like he knew, it was like he had m-m-manners and," Dot gripped Mac's wrist, "he l-l-loved me, Mac."

"I'm sure he did."

Dot looked up, her face contorted. "He n-n-NEVER hurt me, Mac—not wu-wu-once!" Her choking voice rose to a wet squeal.

Wilma and Rainey hurried over. "What's the matter?"

"Her parrot Freddie died," Mac said quietly, still patting Dot, who was sobbing uncontrollably.

"Poor thing," Wilma sympathized, "he was with her for a long time too."

Rainey stared at me dully, as if to ask "*Parrot*?"

"I'd heard he was feelin' poorly," Wilma said, struggling to find words, and slowly moving backwards so that she could quickly return to work.

"Well, he's with God now."

Dot, hearing the words, looked up, her tear-wetted face spotting Wilma and Rainey. She winced painfully. "Thank you, Wilma. Yes, he is. I know he is."

"That's right," I put in, "God takes all creatures, great and small."

Mac poked me hard in the ribs. "Why don't you go home," she suggested, "I'll finish up here."

"Ohhh, hoo, hooo."

"Go home, Dot. You've given all your medicines?"

Dot nodded weakly.

"Well, that doesn't leave much else. Go ahead. Go home."

Dot wiped her cheeks, reached for a kleenex, and blew her nose. "I suppose you think I'm acting silly."

"Nothing of the kind."

"I knew," Dot said, "I knew when it was taking so long. I knew it in my bones."

"Go home," Mac repeated.

"I don't know. It might be worse at home."

"You have to go there sooner or later. It may as well be now."

"Everywhere I'll look, I'll be reminded."

"It won't be easy," Mac said softly, patting her again. After a while, Dot straightened up and went to get her coat. She left shortly.

About an hour later, I passed J.J. downstairs. "Hey, Josh."

"Hi, J.J."

"What's with Dot, man?"

"Huh?"

"I seen her run out of here cryin' her eyes out."

"Oh yeah. Her Freddie died, man."

"She had an old man?"

"No."

"Kin?"

"No, he was her parrot."

"*Parrot*!"

"Parrot."

"You're shittin' me!"

"Nope."

"A motherfuckin' *parrot*?"

"Yep! It underwent a very delicate operation. Didn't make it. Kabooshed on the table."

J.J. whistled. "Operatin' on a bird. Man, I heard some shit in my time, but this is somethin' *else*. Mmm-mmmm."

"If you'd like, I'll let you know about the funeral service."

J.J. stared at me as if sizing me up. "You do that, Josh. You do that."

He burst out laughing.

"Shouldn't laugh about these things, J.J."

He kept laughing, and left muttering, "I didn't even know they had people could DO that."

III. The Slap In The Face

Dot returned the next day. She was sitting in the conference room, staring like a zombie, red, baggy-eyed. Below her hands was an unopened Cosmopolitan.

"Hi, Dot. How ya doing?"

She didn't answer. Mac entered, holding a Macy's bag. "Hello, Dot, Josh."

"Shopping?"

"Picking up my daughter's clothes." She frowned. "So what else is new? Just what she needs—another thirty dollar sweater. Can't go get it herself—she'll be late for cheerleading practice. I'm lucky my hair's already white." She looked at Dot again. "Feeling better?"

Dot nodded, barely.

"Are you all right?"

"Of course I'm all right," Dot snapped.

Mac shrugged and took off her coat and hung it up. She went over and poured herself some coffee from the Mr. Coffee machine we'd bought for the floor. "You don't sound all right," Mac said, slowly sipping coffee and blowing on it.

Dot looked down, her eyes moistening. "I'm still very upset about Freddie." She sniffed. "It's hard getting used to. I even cleaned his cage last night."

"Yes," said Mac. "Sometimes you have to wait these things out."

Rainey and Wilma entered, took off their coats and went right to the leather-bound patient care plans to get their assignments and check their patients.

Dot remarked, "Lockett's going home, I hear." Rainey glared at her.

The day went smoothly, busily. About four o'clock, Wilma came down the hall with Virginia Lockett and her mother. The girl sat in a wheelchair, her fine brown-skinned face pale and taut. At the elevator, Virginia rose. "I'm o.k. I don't need this thing."

"You sure?" asked Wilma. Virginia nodded weakly.

"I can handle her," the mother put in proudly. Virginia leaned against her mother.

"You sure you're o.k., Ginny?" Wilma asked again.

"I'm fine," the girl groaned.

"Get back in that wheelchair," ordered the mother. Virginia half sat, half slumped into the chair. The elevator opened, took them in and shut. I began taking apart the Virginia Lockett chart.

"So," Dot said, "so that little chocolate drop in 624 went home." I stared at her, shocked. Her tightly-pressed lips made her face hard and small.

Rainey almost bunked into Dot who gave a little jump.

"*Who* went home?"

Dot reddened.

"Who?" Rainey was about an inch away from Dot's face.

"Don't talk to me in that tone of voice."

"Who?"

"Rainey," Mac cautioned, bustling over.

"Stay out of it," Rainey snapped, pushing my arm away. "Both of you."

I hadn't even realized I was trying to stand between Dot and Rainey.

Wilma, spotting the two tight faces, rushed up. Rainey tensed. Dot trembled.

"Rain—" Wilma began.

"I said *who* went home, Dot?"

"I don't care to discuss it."

"Well, I DO!"

"If you want to talk," Dot gulped, "we can go into an empty room or talk about it later. It's—"

"No," Rainey interrupted, stamping her foot. "We goin' to talk about it RIGHT HERE AND NOW. I got nothing to hide about what I got to say. What I got to say can be said right here. I plain don't like you talking like that and I don't want to hear any more of it."

Dot walked away. Rainey followed her, close.

"I told you," Dot turned, breathing rapidly, "we'll talk about it, woman to woman if you want. 628's empty—we can go in there. Otherwise, I'm not going to discuss it with you."

"Good enough then," Rainey growled. She pushed past Dot into the room, slamming the door open so hard, it banged shut. Dot had to reopen it. We could hear their voices getting higher.

"Now, what's your problem, Rainey?"

"You know goddamn good and well what it is, and I would say it's not MY problem at all, but one big funkey problem YOU got!"

"Don't talk to me like that. Don't raise your voice to me. Don't push my friendship, Rainey."

We heard a loud slap, slap, slap—a silence, a groan. Rainey stomped out of the room, her stethoscope bouncing. "I'm goin' on break. I'm gonna call Royal. He got a shotgun. Blow that bitch's turkey head off."

"Hush," Wilma whispered carefully, studying me and Mac.

"Gonna call the union, then go down to the cafeteria. Too bad they don't got any whiskey down there. I could drink a case all by myself." She headed towards the elevator, grabbing a cigarette from Mac's pack of Marlboros. Mac grabbed it out of her hands. "You're not supposed to smoke. You can't have that."

Rainey stared at me wildly. I gave her one of mine. She stormed out. "Very nice," Mac said, "That's really going to help her ulcer. A fine friend you are."

I craned my neck to see where Dot was; Mac and Wilma looked too. Dot slowly stumbled from the room, red-faced, holding her left cheek. Her hand dropped, revealing on both cheeks hand imprints covering both sides of her face. "Sh-she assaulted me," Dot gasped, astonished.

"Sit down," Mac advised, putting her arm around her shoulders. "Sit."

"Mary, she HIT me," Dot sobbed into Mac's chest. "Ahoo, ahooo. I think my cheekbone's broken." Dot wept, then spotting me and Wilma, stopped abruptly. "Happy?" she asked.

"No," Wilma answered.

"I'm sorry this whole thing happened," I said.

"BA-LONEY," Dot cried, "you're glad, I can tell."

"Why don't you rest for a few minutes," Mac suggested.

"Rest?" Dot stared, studying Mac as if she was crazy. Mac nodded.

"Wait just a minute now. I want you to call security. I want you to call the police. The police! I want that bitch arrested! I want her out of here! She's fired. I fired her. I want her off the premises!"

"Really, Dot," Mac clucked.

"Really?" Dot shouted, "Really? My cheekbone is probably broken and all you can say is really! Oh my God, am I crazy?"

Mac rubbed her sides in frustration. "I know you're upset, Dot."

Dot spun towards me. "Call security. And call downstairs. See if they have a typewriter they're not using. As soon as I'm finished, I want you to type up all that's happened."

"Don't call security," Mac advised.

Dot slammed a chart on the desk. "Don't tell him not to call security, Mac! What is the *matter* with you?"

"Dot, I want you to calm down."

"I am not a child! Can't you get it through your thick skull that I have been *assaulted*!" Dot rose, quivering from head to foot with the indignity of it all. Wilma had already turned to go back to work. "And just *where* do you think *you're* going?" Dot demanded.

"Someone got to do some work around here," Wilma answered.

I began looking at charts.

"Look, I know you're very upset," Mac said, "but you're not going to be able to talk to anyone in the state you're in. I think you should first calm down before you decide anything. Would you like some tea or coffee?"

"Tea or coffee! I'd *like* some duplicate copies typed. One for me, one for the Nursing Office, one for Mr. Shields, my lawyers, her lawyers—if she can get any—and the union. That should be enough. How many is that?"

"I wasn't counting," I said softly.

"She thinks she's so smart and sassy. We'll see how smart she is on the foodstamp line."

"Dot, I told you to calm down," Mac repeated, her voice sharper.

Dot clutched her chest and raised her eyes to the ceiling. "God give me strength!"

Mac wearily muttered, "Make that a double."

"I want everyone to write a report," Dot insisted. "You heard her slap me, didn't you?"

I shrugged. Mac looked at Dot carefully, silently.

"Mac!"

"I heard a sound, that could have been a slap," Mac said.

"Josh?"

"I'm not sure."

"WHAT?"

"I said I'm not sure. It sounded something like a slap."

"We heard something," Mac added uncomfortably, "but we didn't SEE anything."

"SEE?" Dot fumed. "See? Did you SEE my face? Did you SEE the imprint of her hands on my face?"

Mac stared at her pen, as if trying to guess its weight, then sighed heavily. "I wish you'd settle this among yourselves—you and Rainey. Why drag all of us into it?"

"I don't want anyone 'dragged into this'. The point is— she slapped me. That's insubordination, physical assault. I can not only have her fired, I can have her arrested."

"So go call the police," Mac said wearily. "File a complaint."

"Josh, dial police emergency."

"It's not an emergency call."

"*Dial* it!"

I began dialing. Dot grabbed the phone and slammed it down. Then she dialed the page operator. "Sheila? This is Dot Finch on seven. I want you to page Lucy Quinlan for seven. Stat. Yes, it's an emergency."

"Dot," Mac warned. Dot stuck her tongue out.

Within minutes, the evening shift Nursing Supervisor hustled off the elevator. "What gives?" Lucy smiled. She was a big brown-haired woman, six feet one, from a small farm in South Carolina. Her reputation was: tough and tolerant.

"Rainey Smith slapped me. I want her fired."

"Now, hold your horses. Why don't you just sit down and tell me the whole story, now. People just don't go around slapping each other, do they?'' Her Southern accent was warm and slow, and her sharp grey eyes took us in.

"Where's Rainey and Wilma?"

"Wilma's with her patients and Rainey's at supper," I said.

Lucy took Dot's arm. "How about we talk about what happened in the conference room over some coffee, Dot? You can tell me all about it."

"She could use a good stiff drink," Mac said.

"Couldn't we all," Lucy smiled.

Several minutes later, she came out, sighing. "Mac— I'm sending Dot to x-ray to see if her cheekbone's broken. Think you can keep on top of things here?"

Mac nodded.

"I want all of you to write down what you heard and saw on the Unusual Occurrences Form. Josh, you'll bring these to me by the end of the shift."

I nodded.

"Now, if I send an aide up from five and come up and help you later with meds, Mac, how would it be if I just sent Dot home?"

"Fine. She's overwrought."

"Have Rainey show the aide from five around."

"Rainey has ten patients of her own."

"Please, Mac, for me?"

Mac nodded. Her eyes grumbled.

Several minutes later, Dot emerged from the conference room. "Well I'm taking your advice after all."

"Get some rest, Dot," Mac smiled softly. "You've had a difficult two days."

"I feel like the whole world's collapsed."

"You'll feel better tomorrow."

Dot sniffed, following Lucy who had her arm around her.

Mac shook her head. "What a mess this is going to be!"

"Can I go to dinner?" I asked, aching to go downstairs and talk with Rainey.

"I prefer it if you stayed here, Josh."

I must have made a great face because she waved her

hand. "Oh, go ahead. Just make sure you're back in half an hour. Please.'

"Thanks, Mac."

Down in the cafeteria, Rainey was at a table with J.J. and Lester, an older black housekeeping aide. Lester smoked a pipe calmly, listening. J.J. and Rainey argued.

"I ain't ashamed of what I done. I hit that bitch and I'll hit her again she keeps goin' like that."

"That ain't the point here, Rain," J.J. argued. "You hit her, but you don't got to shout it out to the whole world, know what I mean? Everyone around here gonna know, but you want to make sure they know only 'cause they heard it somewhere and not from you."

"I'll tell 'em. I got nothin' to hide."

"Do you hear what I'm sayin' to you? God-damn! You keep on runnin' your mouth, you gonna be out of a job, out of seniority, out of benefits. And your stomach ain't in the best shape to be walkin' around with no medical benefits."

"That's right," Lester puffed.

Rainey turned to me. "What's goin' on up there?"

"Lucy sent Dot home."

"Yeah?"

"First she's going to get her cheek x-rayed. It might be broken, they think."

Lester nodded, impressed. J.J. cursed.

"I *told* you I hit her!" Rainey beamed, "She's lucky she ain't in traction."

"You're lucky I came in here when I did," J.J. grumbled, "before you got on the page mike and told the world!"

"Well, they can fire me, I'll just go on unemployment. Have myself a ball. I been paying for it, now they can pay me."

"Sure," J.J. said steadily, "You actin' like you're out already."

"Just tryin' to make a point."

"Well, you keep makin' points, they gonna boot your bootie outta here."

"Um, hmm," Lester nodded.

"Yeah, you should be cool, Rainey," I said.

"Cool, huh? I been cool. I been cool for five years workin' with that bitch. I'm like you, Josh, ol' *college* boy. I got me a Ph.D. in patience."

"Sure don't sound like it," Lester drawled.

"Well, Les, you shoulda seen that little girl and her momma. And she treated them like they was dirt, less than dirt."

Lester's eyes, already dark, darkened further.

"Well, there's lots of ways of dealing with that shit," J.J. said.

"And mine's one," Rainey smiled, flexing her arm.

J.J. frowned. "You don't seem to understand. A whole lot of shit is gonna come down, and we sure as hell better be together."

"I think Rainey was right to hit Dot," I said. "What she did was completely intolerant."

J.J. twisted a fork so it bent double. "Don't talk to me about intolerance. They are not gonna tolerate what happened, and they gonna line up behind Dot like the Green Berets behind John Wayne."

Rainey winced.

"You feelin' o.k.?" Lester asked, softly, looking carefully at Rainey.

"I'm fine, Les."

"Umm."

"All I want you to understand, Rainey, is this—" J.J. said, "Don't talk anymore about you hittin' Dot. You tell me, you tell Lester, fine. Still, the less folks you tell, the better."

"Well, I just don't like lying."

"Think of it as lying low," Lester drawled.

"Uh, huh," Rainey nodded, looking around the room carefully.

"O.k.? Don't want to lose you," J.J. smiled. "Who else would I have to make my ol' lady jealous?"

Rainey winced, and grabbed her side, her fiery eyes going ashy. She doubled up. I could see her face gritting with determination, leaning to find a position with the least pain. If she could just lean that way, she could get enough strength to rise, finish her shift, go home, and try to sleep. She could rest and get up next morning early enough to have plenty of time to go see her doctor before coming back to work. She whispered, "And I was supposed to go see my sister tomorrow." She cursed the hospital, cursed Dot, cursed it all. Still, the pain was too great to care about anything, teeth clenched, her hands now held by J.J. I rose like I did when she had attacks on the floor, searching for milk or Maalox. Some doctors stood up. One came over. "Something wrong?"

"I'm fine," Rainey gasped, as I handed her a cup of low-fat skimmed milk.

"Fine? You don't look fine."

"No big thing."

The doctor, puzzled, looked at us and shook his head. Lester motioned him back, but Rainey wincing, grabbed Lester's arm.

"No, Les."

"You're sick. You need to get somethin', or else see someone."

"I know what's wrong with me. Just more of the same-old, same-old."

"Drink your milk and shut up," J.J. said.

Rainey drank it, sighed, and lay back in her chair, just as Wilma came in.

"Is it that late?" I asked. She nodded grimly.

"I'm holding court," Rainey smiled weakly under a milk moustache. "These here are my suitors."

"Some queen," I laughed.

"I AM a queen, only a whole lot of folks around here don't realize that."

"Well, this queen better get herself checked up real good," J.J. advised, "before your King-to-be visits his queen and find a whole lotta blood in the palace."

"Black blood," Rainey winked.

"Black and red."

Rainey sobered up a little.

"Yeah, black and red," J.J. repeated, "like the last time

you got to drinkin' and worryin' and takin' coffee and
cigarettes and alla that shit. Betcha you been eatin' that junk
food too, huh?''

Rainey shook her head.

"Rainey," Wilma said.

"Rainey, *what*?''

"I suppose I didn't see you eat them hostess cupcakes
when you came in today?''

"Girl, you a fink! I have lived to see the day when
Wilma Higgenbotham turned snitch!''

"You ate them cupcakes, girl.''

"The worst kind of shit,'' J.J. said, disgustedly. "Now
you know what the man told you.''

"He ain't my MAN, he's my doctor. Royal Green's my
man. I'm gonna have him bring his gun. Blow that bitch up
into the sky. She likes birds so much, she can take all her
birdshit birdseed and feed the angels.''

We laughed.

"Yeah, she can give them angels all that fancyassed stuff
she buys at $4.40 a pound. And even up there, she'll say,
'Hey, now, I don't take care of any old angel. Don't let me
near them Medicare angels. They smell SO BAD, and they're
just SO NASTY.' ''

We cracked up.

I suddenly realized Mac was alone on the floor and rose
to go. Rainey got up too. Wilma motioned her to sit down.
"Stay here 'til you feel better. I'll just grab me somethin' and
bring it back with me.''

"That's what you think,'' Rainey grinned. "You gonna
sit your grandma behind right down here and have a hot
dinner. I'm ready to go back.'' She gulped down the rest of
the milk, breathed in deeply and flexed. Her arms revealed
hard lean biceps. "This here's the arm that broke the birdy's
beak.''

Wilma laughed, and me and Rainey took the elevator
up.

As the doors opened, we saw Mac with the phone in one
hand and in her other, a full medicine tray. A part-time aide
was dragging a bag of dirty linen to the medicine room chute.

Mac hung up. "Am I glad you're back. The phones are ringing off the hook. Look, if my son or daughter calls, tell them I'll call back. We're swamped." She turned to Rainey. "Lucy Quinlan wants to talk with you. Page her and she'll come up."

"Where's Dot?"

"Dot went home."

"Who's takin' her patients?"

"The aide from five and you."

Rainey bit her lip bitterly. "And me. Uh huh."

Mac said nothing.

"Dot gets to go home and watch t.v. and I get her patients."

"I doubt if she is going to watch any television."

"You white girls really stick together, don't you?"

Mac stiffened. "I wouldn't know. All I know right now is I'm glad you're both back from supper. I'm behind enough as it is."

Mac walked off with her medicines. I wrote up my version of the Chocolate Drop Explosion on the Unusual Occurrence Report:

On March 25, 1972, I noticed Rainey Smith and Dot Finch talking about a patient. They seemed to have a difference of opinion regarding this patient. Since the patient had already gone home, I thought it was no big thing. However, Dot called the patient, a young black woman, "A little chocolate drop," a remark which I considered then, and now, derogatory and out of line. It angered Rainey greatly, and she and Dot had some words. They continued their conversation privately in an empty room. I heard some sounds. Shortly after, Rainey came out and announced she was going on her dinner break. Dot followed, alleging she had been slapped three times by Rainey.

Just before shift's end, I took down the Unusual Occurrence Reports in a manila envelope. I stopped off on the next floor, slipped into the men's room and read them. Mac's was very short:

At approximately 5:15 March 25, 1972, an argument occurred between Rainey Smith and Dorothy Finch, registered nurse. They went into an empty room to further discuss it. I heard a sound that sounded like a slap. I heard this sound three times. Miss Smith came out and said she was going to dinner. Several minutes later, Miss Finch came out. Her face was red. She said Miss Smith had hit her and began crying. The Nursing Supervisor for the evening shift was notified.

Wilma's was longer than Mac's:

Around 5:15, I was bringing some dirty linen towards the medicine room laundry chute when I saw Rainey Smith and Dot Finch engaged in heated conversation with Josh Singer and Mary McGregor watching nearby. Rainey was upset concerning a remark made by Dot that consisted of her calling a black teenager a chocolate drop. Rainey said she didn't care to hear that kind of language being used. Both expressed their opinions on this. They went into a room to discuss it further. Several minutes later Rainey went to dinner. Dot came back and said Rainey had hit her three times. I had heard some sounds coming from the room, but since the door was nearly completely closed, I couldn't tell what kind of sounds they were.

Down in the Nursing Office, Lucy Quinlan studied the envelope. "Next time this happens—and hopefully there won't be a next time—could you do me a big favor, Josh?"

"Sure," I said, staring straight into her sharp grey eyes.

"Seal the envelope."

"Sure."

"Sure," she smiled, sealing it. "Thank you."

Before going upstairs, I slipped into a telephone booth and called my girl friend. She knew the people, had met everyone on the floor two or three times; we'd gone to a few parties with Rainey and Royal.

"Hi, Fran."

"Hi, honey. What's up?"

I told her. She listened, adding a few "Gods."

"I don't know what to do."

"Well, for starters, you should get everybody's story straight."

"That's more or less been done."

She sighed.

"Are you busy?" I said. "Are you working on a painting?"

"I'm fine. Joshie, Joshie. My little organizer. Why don't you just quit all that and go back to trying to make films."

I wondered how I could film this. I could show five versions of the incident, like Kurosawa did in Rashomon. I sighed, wishing I'd never joined S.D.S., or when S.D.S. dissolved that I'd not joined a collective around "hospital work" and "health care organizing." "Well, maybe there's not a whole lot I can do until tomorrow."

"How's that?"

"Well, I'm sure that either tomorrow or at the latest the next day they're gonna call us all in, one at a time, and ask us our stories. They'll put the pressure on."

"How much does Dot calling the girl a chocolate drop come in? That's pretty outrageous!"

"I don't know. Rainey has to say she didn't touch her or that's that."

"Wouldn't they just suspend her for a few days? She's worked there a long time."

"No," I snapped irritably. "Don't you under*stand*? A *black* aide slapped a *white* nurse. Three times. They can't let that get around. They just can't."

There was a silence. "Hello?"

"I'm here."

"So?"

"I know I'm just an apolitical painter, but—oh, skip it."

"Come on, Fran—"

"Why don't you go call your organizer friends? They could tell you all the things you SHOULD do."

"I called you. Your instincts are better."

"I see. So now, I'm just an instinctive woman. Terrific."

"Fran."

"Well, it serves you right for using that condescending bullshit about how I 'don't understand'."

I stood there, holding the phone, admitting she was right. Fran, who during the Cambodian bombings wrote a letter to Nixon, suggesting he write his will. When the F.B.I. came to our apartment, she served them tea—oolong and Misty Mountain, asking them where on earth they found their beautiful grey suits, and gorgeous black shoes, cooing over to me, "Wouldn't you love a pair of shoes like these, Joshie? They're so-oh, I just can't find the words."

The older F.B.I. man sipped and smiled proudly, "Florsheim's." And Fran telling them she'd just had a fit of hysteria, gotten carried away after a rabble-rousing demonstration. She liked Nixon, found him cute for such a pudgy little fellow. She didn't tell them about her painting with red moons and Vietnamese women in rising maroon and green boats over a sea of torn silver helicopters full of skeletons with helmets pouring out of an orange chaise-lounge where Nixon was giving a G.M. executive a blow job.

"You're right, Fran. I'm sorry."

"Well, o.k.," she sighed, adding, "it sounds—rough."

"Thanks."

"Let me think about it some more and we'll talk about it when you get home."

"Fine."

"I'll make some popcorn so we can really concentrate."

I laughed, "You're crazy, gotta go." I chuckled, remembering Fran's remark, "It's all fine and dandy to like Marx and Lenin, but this country has its own setup. You're thinking of factories in Leningrad, and they've got Mission Impossible and Kentucky Fried Chicken."

I dialed the phone again, this time to a member of the health collective. I told Sandy the story. "It's simple," Sandy laughed, with his veteran optimism. "You defend Rainey to the hilt."

"That I know."

"You'll kick ass on that racist bitch."

"They're going to bring a lot of pressure down. And they might push Rainey—make her mad enough to the point she blows it."

"Struggle with her not to."

"Easier said than done."

"Always is."

"Yeah."

"Will anyone side with Dot?"

"I don't know."

"What kind of force is Mac?"

I sighed, hating the word "force."

"I really don't know. It's hard to tell. She likes both of them. She's known Dot for over ten years."

"She's probably right-center."

"I don't know," I repeated, feeling angry.

"Well, look—I don't think I'll call and get everyone together tonight, but if you just want to come over after work and discuss it, I'm available."

"Fine."

"We'll have a few beers if you feel up to it."

He was offering to stay up. In his own way, Sandy worked. He worked very hard at going to meetings, attending all the demonstrations he could, and studying.

"I'll see."

"Maybe I can set up an emergency meeting for tomorrow," he said, his voice picking up enthusiasm, "around eleven."

"You know I spend the day with Fran, Sandy. Besides, Jack and Barbara are both working days."

"Shit, that's right. Well, how about we get together for dinner tomorrow?"

"Yeah, that'd be o.k."

"Where should we meet you—if people can make it?"

"There's a place down the street. Bob's Donut Shop. But tell everyone to be there at 6 sharp. I get half an hour. Maybe I can stretch it, but I doubt it."

"Fine."

When I returned to the floor, Mac was busy answering phones. "Where the hell have you been?"

"Down at the Nursing Office."

"Wha'd you do? Read Lucy *War and Peace*?"

"Sorry. I'll just make the time my break time."

"Why don't you skip that, and set up some *work* time."

"Sorry. I made a few phone calls."

"You're lucky they weren't long-distance. You'd be broke by now."

"Sorry."

Rainey came over. "What did downstairs say?"

"Not much. She just took the reports."

Rainey poured herself some Maalox. "Well, one more hour and we can get the hell home."

"Home sounds great to me."

At home, Fran was working on a painting, scowling and humming. She kissed me quickly, "Ten minutes." I left her alone. She came out and hugged me. She was sweating, warm; I could smell her—salty, and kissed her warm pink flushed face, smoothing her long black hair, feeling her through her smock, her body alive from the painting, like when she had worked well, like when we made love.

"How's my little Vladimir?" she teased, rubbing my belly. The phone rang. It was Sandy.

"Hi. What's happening? I got a six-pack of Michelob here."

"Oh, I'm sorry man, I forgot to call back. Listen, I'm beat. Let's just get together tomorrow, o.k.?"

"No problem. I'll just save this stuff."

"O.k. See you manana."

"Manana. Say hello to Fran."

Suddenly feeling drained, strange, I showered and got into bed with Fran.

"Tired?"

"I guess so. I don't know what the hell's gonna happen at work."

She began rubbing my shoulders. "Maybe you should think of something else." She rubbed my hips. I felt drowsy and pleasantly electrified.

"What something else? Algebra? Fellini?"

"Fellini over Algebra."

I put my arms around her waist. She felt warm. She smelled like soap, fresh sheets and toothpaste.

"Maybe I shouldn't think at all."

"Or think like a moon thinks."

"Mmmm."

We kissed and I began to think like the moon thinks.

IV. After The Fact — Percussions and Repercussions

The drowsy warmth blew up with the shrill. I saw, not a moon, but Fran's face, yawning angrily.

"What *time* is it?"

The shrill continued. I reached for the phone. It was 7:45 a.m. The Nursing Service secretary wanted to know if I could come in for an informal meeting at 9 a.m. with the Nursing Director and his assistant concerning the incident of the night before. If I had plans they'd understand, but they wanted to get to the bottom of things as soon as possible. I wouldn't be paid for coming in, but it would definitely be greatly appreciated. I weighed the pros and cons. If I didn't come in, they'd be mad, but they couldn't do anything to me officially. I decided not to show, hoping neither Rainey, Mac or Wilma would either.

Only Mac came in. She briefly mentioned it that afternoon. Dot avoided everyone but Mac, openly giving Rainey the silent treatment. Rainey blithely strolled up and down the floor. "Hello, Dot baby. How's the world treatin' you today?"

Dot grimly pressed her lips together.

"Hey, hey, I'm gonna do my very best to see you don't get any abortion patients."

"Rainey," Mac warned. Rainey pranced down the hall, almost bunking into Faith Edmunsen, the dayshift Nursing Supervisor.

"Good afternoon, Rainey," Faith smiled, "you're just the person I wanted to see."

"*Well, well,*" Rainey grinned. "What a treat! Look who's here! It's Miss Faith everybody! Missy Faith!" Her best Aunt Jemimah Gone-With-The-Wind voice was so thick it startled everyone. Wilma scowled.

Faith motioned everyone over. "I want to see all of you in the Nursing Office conference room this afternoon. Rainey, I'll see you right now. Wilma, you'll come at 3:30. Josh at four. Is that clear?"

"Is this about last night?" I asked.

"No," Faith sighed. "It's about the Johnny Carson show. Yes, it's about last night."

"Aren't you going to talk with Dot and Mac?"

"I talked with them earlier."

She saw me frowning and added, "SEPARATELY, if that makes anyone feel better."

I shrugged, but I was relieved.

"Let's go, Rainey. I don't have a whole lot of time on this."

Rainey returned in half an hour and headed straight for one of the rooms. I hustled over. "How'd it go?"

"How does it always go with them bitches?" she whispered; then in a louder voice, "Josh, can you help me?" She winked. "Come in here and help me lift this patient."

"Yeah."

It actually was time to turn Mr. Rashad. We gently, firmly pushed on his 250 pounds. Rainey talked as we worked. "They took me through hot coals. Boy, I thought I was gonna blow it right then and there."

"Who was there?"

"Lucy, Faith and Wiggin. To think they call him the head of Nursing Services. He's a nothin' to end all nothins. Talkin' 'bout 'Violence appalls me!' I'm afraid to sneeze around the man—'fraid he'll go through an open window. Punk! But that Faith, mmm. She's somethin' else!"

"You didn't tell them you hit her?"

"Almost. But I kept cool."

"Good."

"I almost wished I had told 'em, Josh. I got nothin' to hide and here I gotta lie. Ain't a thing I hate worse than that."

"Well, sometimes it's necessary. Did they ask you anything about Dot calling Virginia Lockett a chocolate drop?"

"No. They didn't mention it at all. Wanted to know about the slappin' mostly."

"Not a word, huh?"

"No. Hmmm."

"How about that."

"What you suppose that means?"

I felt disturbed and elated as if I was a big-game hunter and had spotted dangerous prey. "They don't want to talk about that part," I said, feeling my blood quicken, "because they know Dot said it and they know that's why you slapped her. So they want to leave that part out entirely because it puts them in a defensive position, defending Dot."

Rainey beamed. "You are worth something more than just sittin' behind that desk, ain't you?"

I shrugged, embarrassed. Rainey sidled over to Mac. "How'd your big interview go, Big Mac?"

"O.k." Mac grunted.

"What's o.k.?"

"That's my business."

"Ain't it my business? Ain't it about ME?"

"Yes, it's about you."

"So tell me, then. You got nothin' to hide from your ol' Rainey now, do you?"

Mac seemed preoccupied. "I came in this morning and talked with Lucy and the others. I said what I had to say. Let's leave it at that." Her dark green eyes darkened.

"No sweat," Rainey laughed, hurt. "I know you got a lot on your mind—your husband, your kids, and, hey—ain't you goin' on vacation soon?"

"Hopefully."

"I thought it was all set," Rainey asked, her eyes searching Mac's face.

"It was, but—Let's skip it for now, o.k.?"

Mac briskly walked away. Rainey whistled. "Been workin' with her eight years and that's the first time she ever did *that*."

"Maybe she's just in a bad mood. She really doesn't want to be involved in all this, you know."

"Maybe."

"Well, I better get downstairs."

"Have fun, Josh. We gonna be havin' meetings up the butt. They want us to come down tomorrow too. Meet with the Man."

"Shields?"

"You got it, honey. The top."

"Is the union gonna be there? Were they there today?"

"No."

"Well, then it's all unofficial. They can't use anything that happens in that meeting unless the union rep is there. Or a shop steward." I hesitated, then looked at the clock and went to the elevators. "Be right back."

"Give 'em a big French kiss for me."

The Nursing Office consisted of four doors that increased in size as you went down the hall: Nursing Office, Nursing Services Coordinator, Assistant to the Director of Nursing, Director of Nursing. Opposite these four doors was the conference room with a long table surrounded by chrome chairs. On the table was a percolating Mr. Coffee machine, a stack of styrofoam cups, packets of sugar and Hi-and-Lo, along with several packages of Viennese Ladyfinger cookies. Sitting in the room, near the Mr. Coffee machine were Lance Wiggin, Faith Edmunsen with her glacial blue eyes and chipmunk cheeks. As I stared at her and Lance Wiggin, Lucy Quinlan walked in. I felt like I'd walked into a vanilla no-man's land. "How's everybody," I grinned.

They smiled politely.

"How's it going?"

"We know 'How it's going,' Faith Edmunsen smiled. "That's why we want to talk with you."

"Uh huh." I smiled. They smiled. We were all smiling. Faith's eyes narrowed. "There was an incident on your floor the other day."

"Uh huh."

"Between Miss Smith and Miss Finch. Miss Finch was struck."

I took a deep breath and jumped in. "Allegedly struck."

Mr. Wiggin cleared his throat. "We've read all the reports so we know your version, Joshua."

"Uh huh?"

"We basically want to hear everything you saw or heard." They had the incident reports in xeroxed sets. They were trying to see if our verbal stories matched our written ones. I was way ahead of them; I'd made a copy of my report and already gone over it.

"Check."

"Go ahead," Lucy Quinlan smiled warmly.

"Well, there was this young black woman who came in the night before for a therapeutic abortion. And—"

Lucy reddened. Wiggin coughed. Faith Edmunsen, unblinking, interrupted me. "We're not interested in that part. We mainly want to concentrate on what happened."

"As far as I'm concerned, this is part of it. An important part."

"Try to be helpful," Lucy drawled. Edmunsen shuffled some papers, then lit up a cigarette angrily. She was smoking Virginia Slims.

"Would you like some coffee?" Lucy asked.

"Love some."

"Cream and sugar?"

"Two creams, no sugar. I'm sweet enough as it is."

Wiggin nodded like he was my best friend. I suddenly felt a contempt, recalling Sandy's words. "They are basically a bunch of clowns." I agreed and disagreed. Clownish, they could fire Rainey. They could fire me. It wasn't Ringling Brothers, though at times it seemed like a circus. Lucy handed me my coffee. "Thank you."

"You're very welcome." Faith tapped her papers, "Now, we don't have a lot of time."

I cleared my throat. "Well, Dot didn't like this abortion patient." Edmunsen started to say something, but Wiggin motioned her off. He crossed his pantsuit legs and took a cigarette from Faith's pack. "She made Rainey admit the patient while Rainey was giving another patient a shower." Although she tried to control her eyebrows, Lucy couldn't; one shot up. "This made Rainey mad to begin with, and then all evening Dot kept saying things about people on Welfare and Medicare. I argued with her about this too."

"Did you hit her?" Faith asked.

"Let him talk," Wiggin said.

"Anyway, the next day, shortly after we came on, the patient was discharged and Dot made this remark, saying 'Well, that little chocolate drop went home.' "

Wiggin reddened slightly, but recovered. He tapped his

ash away. "That's harmless enough, an expression of opinion."

"Maybe yes, maybe no. But when Rainey expressed *her* opinion, they started getting into it. Rainey thought, as I do, that it was a very racist, prejudiced expression of opinion."

"That's a term not to be used loosely," Wiggin began.

"We are not a section of the Civil Rights Division," Faith said quickly, "These matters are really not our responsibility."

"Yes and no," I replied. "The hospital does have a stated policy of treating all patients regardless of race, religion or creed."

"I think we're getting just a little out of hand," Wiggin smiled. "It's always in this day and age a complex and *important* issue, but I don't think this is really the time to discuss it. We could—any day you wish to come in early, just sit around and chew the fat, of course."

"Of course," I said softly.

"However, we mainly want to find out about what happened between 5 o'clock and five fifteen on a certain Tuesday evening." He stared at his watch. "And it *is* getting late."

Faith tapped a pencil on her reports. "Josh, just concentrate on what happened when Rainey and Dot went into the room."

"Sure. Like I said, they were arguing about the Medicare patient, then Dot suggested they continue the talk in an empty room. The floor, at the time, was relatively quiet."

"Rainey was not on break?"

I paused, feeling a trap open. "Not that I recall, not to my knowledge. She might have been, I can't say for sure one way or the other. I'm not sure if Dot was on break or not either."

Faith's eyes narrowed. "Go on."

"Rainey went in first, then Dot. The door was practically completely shut."

"You couldn't see inside?"

"Not a bit."

"Go on."

"Well, I sorta heard their voices, though they were muffled. Then I heard some kind of sound."

"Slapping."

"A sound. I couldn't tell if it was slapping or not."

"It wasn't a horn beeping was it?" Faith asked.

"No, it wasn't a horn beeping," I said, looking her straight in the eyes, "or a rooster crowing. Not that kind of a sound. More like a hard, short sound."

"Like a slap," Wiggin nodded.

"I don't know."

"Come, now, Josh," Wiggin smiled. "You, a college graduate with a Masters Degree, aren't intelligent enough to distinguish sounds?"

"I have ear problems. Recurring cysts." I leaned over and poured myself more coffee. There was a silence. They glared politely. I smiled, sipping. "This is *good* coffee."

In the silence, there was a scream. I fantasized Faith standing up yelling, "We know that bitch hit Dot, and we know you know, and we KNOW you know we know, you snot-nosed radical little shit, sipping our coffee and smiling at us when you plot with your little goddam phone calls to overthrow our government!"

Instead, she smiled politely. "I made it myself." Tee-hee

"Do you understand, Josh," Lucy said, "the seriousness of the situation?"

"Yes."

"That we can't have employees slapping each other around."

"I'm all for peace, you know that."

Faith snorted. She'd seen me passing out anti-war leaflets at a supermarket one Saturday morning, leaflets supporting the Vietnamese. Often, I had to remind myself that I really was for peace, that in order to get peace, though, you had to get rid of the violent people. Sandy could explain it at times, and Marx, Lenin, Mao and Che could explain it even better. Mac had hit on it once, saying, "Basically, I would just like to rest and not have to worry about anything."

Wiggin shuffled his papers. "Well, I don't see much value in pursuing this further right now. We know your opinion on the matter Josh and of course respect it, and I guess that's that."

"Is that it?"

Wiggin looked at Lucy who waited his eye-instructions, then glanced at Faith, who, deciding something, nodded back angrily and lit up another cigarette—her sixth since we'd started talking. Wiggin rose. He looked like a penguin, pudgy, all white, with a questioning chin-tilted expression attempting pensiveness.

"You have to understand, Josh. Everything that goes on on the floors is our concern, and more, our responsibility. We have to answer for it. Do you understand the position we're in?"

"Yeah. It's hard."

"You should only know the half of it."

He rubbed his forehead and, for a split second, seemed weary. "This is an informal talk, but tomorrow, it will be a different situation. Mr. Shields will be here, as well as someone from the union."

"So it's tomorrow for sure?"

"Yes."

"Fine," I said, "I'll look forward to seeing Mr. Shields. As far as the union goes, I'm all for it—you know me, I'm all for the—"

"We know," Faith sighed, "we know."

They all rose. Lucy began gathering up the styrofoam coffee cups. Wiggin stuck his hand out. "Thanks for coming down, Josh."

I shook his hand hard. His grip was like a fried smelt— limp and gritty.

Back on the floor, Rainey rushed over. "How'd it go?"

"Fine."

"What does that mean? Wha'd they ask you? They get on you?" She seemed anxious, breathless.

"The real fireworks will be tomorrow. They want us all down there. How they're gonna do that is beyond me."

Mac, overhearing, fidgeted.

"We've told them everything and written our reports. For God sakes, what more do they want?"

"They wanna see us squirm," Rainey jeered.

"They wanna catch us in a lie," I added.

Mac reached for her cigarettes and lit one up.

"What's there to catch? It's over with. Why don't they just forget it and let us all go back to work. Enough is enough already."

Walking up, Wilma nodded grimly. "Takin' us off the floor like we had all day. I feel like I been behind for three days now. They think we got all the time in the world. They got the time to sit around drinkin' that coffee all day with that Joe DiMaggio Mr. Coffee machine, and they think everybody got that kind of time, just 'cause they do. Sit around havin' meetin's all the time. I'd love to have a job like that."

Mac puffed. "I doubt it, Wilma."

Wilma leaned towards her. "You do, huh? Well, don't. Sit on my fanny, holdin' a bunch of papers and gettin' paid a thousand clear a month, and drink coffee? When I take home half of that? Don't doubt it, girl, don't doubt it for a minute."

"Don't hold your breath, either," Rainey laughed.

"There's more to it than meetings," Mac put in hotly. "There's a lot more to running a hospital than meets the eye. It's a tremendous amount of headaches."

"Well for a thousand a month clear," Wilma answered, "I'd go buy me a whole *lot* of aspirin."

"You have to deal with the personnel. You have to deal with the families. You have to deal with the Board of Trustees, and all kinds of people not to mention the shipping and delivery and replacement of equipment, the food, a million things."

"So how come you never took supervisor?" Rainey asked suddenly.

"I have enough headaches of my own without looking for new ones."

"So that's why you turned it down *four* times?"

"Exactly right."

"But the money's good."

"It's not enough for what I'd have to do. If I thought I could do it. I don't like ordering people about, checking up on people. I have enough to do just to keep my own life together. And from what I've seen, once you go downstairs, you soon forget all the nursing you ever learned. You're away from the patients. You're away from the floors. I don't like that. I'm a nurse. I'm not a politician.''

Mac stubbed out her cigarette grimly.

"Well, different people like different things. All depends on what you're cut out for.''

"And you're just a farm girl," smiled Rainey, "what left the farm and went into nursing.''

"I'm happy right where I am," Mac scowled.

"And where you at?" Rainey teased. "Startin' life fresh again, huh? Ditchin' that dead-ass husband of yours, and your kids gonna leave home soon—''

"I *hope* so."

"Be a whole new world. Gonna paint the town red.''

"Go on. You make me sound like Betty Davis or somebody.''

"Nah," Rainey said. "You're better lookin' than her. Better tits, bigger ass.''

"Like you, huh?''

Rainey laughed. "You're too much, Mac.''

"Yes, I know. About thirty pounds too much.''

Wilma laughed along with me and Rainey as Mac rose and began setting up her injections in the medicine room.

Later, Lucy Quinlan posted the vacation schedules, then left quickly. Mac's vacation space was blank. Rainey, Wilma, Dot and I stared at it. "I thought you had your vacation all settled, Mary," Dot said.

Mac took one look, went and poured herself some coffee and lit up.

"There's some problems," she stated absent-mindedly, her eyes furious, "they said I might get my vacation and I might not.''

Rainey pulled me over to the side. "What gives?" I asked, completely confused.

"You don't think they're holdin' Mac's vacation over her head to make her add more to her story?''

"What?''

"You heard me.''

"Damn!"

"I'll bet that's what it is," Rainey whispered. "Hold on."

She went over to Mac, who motioned her away crankily.

"I'll swear on a stack of bibles that's what it is."

"Could Wilma find out?"

"Lemme ask her." Rainey caught Wilma as I was leaving for dinner and my meeting. "Wilma, honey, go ask Mac if this vacation thing's being held over her pretty old head."

"Ask her yourself."

"I already did."

"And what makes you think she gonna tell me what she wouldn't tell you."

"You one of her peers."

"Peers my ass," Wilma mumbled.

"What's *your* problem, girl?"

"I'm just sick and tired of the whole thing. And now it's gettin' ugly."

"It was ugly from the git. Or don't you remember that little girl?"

" 'Course I remember. Look, why don't we just wait and see what happens with the union. Maybe after all this blows over, they'll still give her time comin'. They ain't *that* evil."

"Oh no?"

"They're just tryin' to see how far they can push. It's the only card they got to play."

"Just find out from Mac is it true or not?"

"I'll see."

As I left for dinner everyone had their back turned to each other.

V. Meetings and More Meetings. What Is To Be Done?

The restaurant, Bob's Donut Shop, was two blocks away. At a big orange booth sat the other members of my Health Care Collective—Sandy and Karen, Jack, who worked in housekeeping at Garden Crest Convalescent and

Barbara, a registered nurse at the Veterans Hospital. Sandy
was sharing a Marlboro with Jack; Barbara was knitting.
Karen waved to me. I slid into the booth, into peering faces,
napkins and silverware.

"Hi."

"Hi."

"How's it goin'."

"Hi."

The waitress came by and took our orders. Sandy
started, "O.k., so what have we got?"

"You told everyone the basic story?"

He nodded.

"Well, what I think we should do first is," Barbara
began, just as Jack said, "Anything new happened? Sometimes these things take off, you know." "Wait a minute!"
Karen smiled, "I think we need a chair."

"You chair, Karen," Sandy smiled.

"O.k. Let me take prerogative here. Anything new,
Josh?"

"Well, they're meeting with all of us separately today.
And that's not that big a deal. But what I wasn't expecting at
all was I think they're holding Mac's vacation over her head.
Get her to change her—"

"Point of clarification," Barbara interrupted, "Mac is
the other r.n.—the right-center one?"

"Right-center, right-shmenter," I growled, staring
angrily at Sandy and at Barbara, at their horrible habit of
categorizing people like news analysts or generals; as if working people were one undistinguished mass and not older
women who slept with birds and young women who ate cupcakes and had ulcers, served oolong tea to the FBI, wore
yellow sweaters, underwent divorces.

"Well, where *does* she stand?" Sandy asked.

"I don't know. So far she hasn't sided with Dot, let's
put it that way. I think she has a lot of principles around
this."

"But," Barbara pointed, with finger raised, "you don't
know that as a fact."

"Not as an absolute—"

"What's her class background?" Barbara asked.

"She's working class. Grew up on a farm. Worked all through high school picking peas." I was remembering a conversation one late slow night with Mac and Rainey. "We had peas for breakfast, peas for lunch, peas for dinner. We cooked peas more ways than I ever want to remember. Talk about hard times. That was a depression. Today, people say 'I'm depressed.' You should have been around then. You would've seen depression."

I'd asked her about farmworker organizing. She laughed. "I was right there. We struck in Salinas. My God, it was awful. They sent goons with clubs and shotguns. Beat one man to death. Burned down the homes of the Mexicans and Filipinos. Killed an eight-year-old child."

"And how'd it turn out?"

"We were out thirty-three weeks. We won. If you could call it winning. Look at it now. They have to do it all over again."

I found myself staring, not at a Salinas lettuce strike, but at Barbara, knitting in Bob's Donut Shop.

"And you know, Josh," she was saying, "I don't want to get off the point here, but I think it's fairly key, I think you've always had a certain reluctance, a kind of hippy disdain, for using political terminology. Yes, *like* right-center, *like* working-class background. And if we don't use it, who will? And if this woman isn't right-center, let's argue it out, *politically*." She bit into her roastbeef sandwich and wiped some gravy off her lip. Sandy waved to Karen who waved him off.

"Barbara still has the floor."

"All I meant to say was, that I don't think there's anything wrong in describing someone that way, that's all."

"Mac was involved in some big strikes in the thirties," I blurted, "Does that make you happy?"

Karen's eyes lit up. "What kinds of strikes? Where?"

Sandy cleared his throat, staring at Karen.

"Excuse me, Sandy—" Karen started.

"I think we're getting really off the subject," Jack grumbled, "We're supposed to be helpin' Josh figure out what to *do*."

"Well, Karen's the chair," Sandy said, "not me."

"Let me make this point," Karen put in. "Let's not focus on Mac." Sandy shook his head in disagreement. Karen held her ground. "At least let's not get off into a discussion of Josh's strengths and weaknesses. Let's get back to what Jack was saying. We don't have lots of time."

Jack raised his hand. "Jack."

"What will this thing with her vacation do to Mac? Which way might it make her go?"

Everyone looked at me. I shrugged. "I think it'll just make her madder. She can be real stubborn. I think right now she's just amazed and really pissed that they would do this to her. She's been working there for fifteen years. It's very possible they've made a really bad mistake. I think also that she'll get her vacation time."

"That's not the point." Barbara interrupted.

"Well, she should get her vacation, Barb," Karen blurted.

"Come on, come on now," Sandy cautioned as Karen and Barbara quieted down. "She'll get her time if we win."

"If." Jack muttered.

Sandy raised his hand, Karen nodded. "How would you assess the situation as it stands right now?" Sandy asked.

"Well," I answered, "I'm not sure how far to push."

"Like?" asked Karen.

"Well, I had this idea. We got this meeting tomorrow, a big—"

"What meeting?" Barbara snapped testily.

"We have this big meeting. They're bringing the administrator, Ike Shields—top man, real sharp."

"Yeah? So?"

"He's very good at intimidating people."

"What's his background like? Lifer in the Army? Navy?"

"It's a little more complicated than that. He went to Harvard after getting out of the navy with a commission. He's worked his way up. He's the one who initiated the whole area-wide Hospital Administrators Association. His big thing is pushing labor relations classes and industrial engineering techniques and studies."

"Speedup," Jack said.

"Just another ruling class flunkey," Barbara said.

"Well, he's a little more than that. He's dangerous."

"Your favorite word."

"We're getting off the point," Karen sighed. "Josh, what's your idea? Do you have a plan?"

"Yeah. We push hard on the racism around this. We threaten to bring charges against Dot."

Jack whistled, then grinned. Karen clapped her hands.

"It's what Marx said," I smiled. "Be bold. Be bold."

"Can you *do* that?" Karen asked, a little breathless.

Sandy was leaning back in his chair, calmly smoking and studying me. Barbara picked up her knitting.

"We can try," I said, growing excited. "We can say that the hospital has a stated policy of being open to all people regardless of race, creed, or religion. We can threaten to go to the Panthers, the NAACP, the Lawyers Guild—"

"Hold on," Sandy cautioned. "It's fine to take advantage of certain contradictions in a legalistic manner, but I'm not sure this is the time. Besides, I doubt if they'll let you. If you do this, also, you're in their ballpark, apart from the fact that they control the courts and any forum where there's mediation, *you* have to *prove* Dot said what she said. She could deny it. And from the reports you told me about, the only ones who will acknowledge that she said that are you, Rainey and Wilma. Maybe Mac. See, it comes back to her again. Will she say Dot said that? And, even if she does, they'll probably minimize it—they probably won't even allow it admitted in the meeting."

"But just *saying* it may make them back off."

"You're dreaming."

"Well, I think you're dead wrong," Jack said. "I think it's basically a great situation. Fuck it, Josh, go for the throat. Do it!"

Karen nodded shyly. Sandy frowned, exasperated.

"You don't just 'do it.' That's Jerry Rubin. That's the hippy dippy Yippies. And it's a complete overemphasis on spontaneity, Jack. It's *exactly* what Lenin said not to do in *What Is To Be Done*."

"You do need some kind of plan," Karen added softly to Jack.

Jack tapped his spoon on the table. He didn't smoke.

"Yeah, well sometimes you can plan too fuckin' much."

"Look," I put in, "even if it is just me, Rainey and Wilma pushing it, that's three out of five. They'll have to pay some attention to it. And I'm white, so isn't like it's all white against black."

"You're a radical," Sandy observed. "That makes you not white in their eyes."

"That's kind of a weird thing to say," Barbara said. She had her hand raised, and kept talking. "I think Josh is right. With these nursing office creeps the best thing is to throw them off guard."

"They're probably having their own meeting right now," Jack said.

I looked up at the clock. I had ten minutes left.

"Shit, it's almost time for me to split."

"So what have we got?" Sandy smiled, looking around at everyone.

"We got diddly," Jack mumbled.

"Come on, Jack. Have patience," Karen said.

Except for Sandy, they all looked tired. Jack, Karen and Barbara had worked full shifts. Barbara still had her nursing outfit on. Despite my frustration, I felt a warmth towards them. They'd all come to have supper, and help me figure out what to do. I looked at them and recalled past demonstrations, a picket line in the early morning rain at the VA Hospital where Barbara worked, her picking me up in her car at 5:30 a.m. sharp. All of us marching against a meeting of Thieu and Kissinger, running from the Tac Squad charging at us and three thousand other people, Karen grabbing Jack away from the path of a panicking horse and Sandy grabbing both of them. Ducking into a doorway as the police swept down the street at the same time I ran through the same door —the four of us finding ourselves in the lobby of a fancy hotel and sitting down shakily ordering coffee that cost each of us a buck fifty. I recalled Fran scoffing, "*They're* gonna make a revolution?'' and me answering, ''You may not think they're much, but they're all I've got.''

''You got me. You have me. You've HAD me.''

And me hugging her, ''Yeah. I have you, and I'm glad as hell I do.''

''You do-do.''

''No, do-do.''

''You're silly. You're too silly for that bunch.''

''Silliness is an important source, a sauce of dialectics. The Dionysian ability to laugh. Dive with the hips. Sense of humor. Or as they say in Arizona, a sense of Yuma.''

''Sense of bullshit.''

''I'm serious.''

''Yuk, yuk.''

''Seriously, Fran. You like Karen.''

''I like Karen, and sometimes Jack. The others you can keep.''

''Well, the world's not perfect.''

''It's a tangerine ellipsoid.''

''*That's* your latest painting.''

''Right—the world.''

When my coffee came, I dumped in some cream and sugar. ''For a health care worker, you sure don't eat correctly,'' Barbara observed. ''Why don't you have a little coffee with your sugar?''

I shrugged.

''That's not helping Josh prepare for his meeting,'' Sandy said, and without taking a breath, added, ''Well, should Josh push the racism angle?''

''It's not an angle. It's what I think is the best thing to do.''

''Yeah?''

''I'll talk it over with Rainey and J.J.''

''Who's J.J.?''

''He's the chief shop steward. Works in the E.R. Good guy, real good guy. If I suggested that we push them on what Dot said, I think he'll go for it.''

''Why?''

" 'Cause he was really pissed when we told him what Dot said."

"Push then," Sandy said, "for all it's worth. You'll probably have to take some leadership in this though. And I wouldn't say too much about going to the NAACP or any of those liberal groups. We don't want to get into legalisms."

"It's just a tactic," Barbara argued.

" 'Just a tactic' can sometimes change into a whole strategy. Naturally, we have to work within the system, that's the objective situation right now, and we do use legal channels *sometimes*, but I think that on the whole, given the lull in the movement these days, there's a danger, a tendency for everyone to get real liberal, and minimize the fact that we work at the point of production, and that that's essentially illegal work."

I smiled. Jack looked thoughtful and played with his spoon. Karen looked down. "Illegal work" was a favorite expression of Sandy's, part of his misjudgment of the moment, his fanciful vision of undergrounds. I thought of the Bolshevik undergrounds, then looked around, wondering what a black woolen Russian hat and red stars would look like in Bob's Donut Shop, especially near the front counter that offered jelly donuts and maple bars.

"Essentially," Sandy continued, his voice picking up, "all socialist work is illegal. In India, Nicaragua, and Zimbabwe, Iran—we could be shot for what we're doing right now."

"But we're in Bob's Donut Shop," I said.

Jack and Karen giggled.

"Yeah, we're here!" Jack declared.

"What does this have to do with what Josh is gonna say tomorrow?" asked Karen, as Barbara poked Jack. "You shouldn't laugh, Jack, it's not a joke, it's an important point."

"I'll *tell* you," Sandy put in, slightly flustered. "For Josh to lie, for Rainey to lie too, that's basically in the spirit of illegality. If we were all honest and legalistic, we would admit Rainey slapped Dot, and we would add she was provoked. We might push for a suit, providing we could prove that the civil rights of the young black girl were violated. And that's providing that the girl and her family—since she's a minor—would want to sue, which I highly doubt. It's a ticklish situation. She probably just wanted the abortion done and over with."

"Probably," Barbara said, her face tightening.

"See, I'm not talking about going around in cloaks with microfilm in sandwiches, or any of that *I Led Three Lives* anti-communist shit," Sandy sped on. "What I mean by illegality is a whole way of being, thinking, trying to stay one step ahead of the ruling class wherever it is."

He gripped his empty coffee cup, hard.

"Including Bob's Donut Shop."

Karen rubbed Sandy's forearm. "Honey, I think it's time for Josh to go."

It was. I had two minutes left. "Look," I said, "You've been very helpful, really. So I push on making them defensive?"

They all nodded, Jack slapping me on the back. "Go get 'em."

"I'll talk it over with Rainey and J.J. and Wilma too, and see how Mac takes it."

"Who's J.J.?" asked Jack.

"The chief shop steward," Barbara groaned, "He told you, dummy."

"Uh huh."

"Go ahead, Josh," Sandy said, "we'll get yours and you can pay us later."

"Thanks again, all."

Outside, in the spring evening, I did a little dip, then ran. I pretended we were storming Assissi Gardens, and had three minutes to get inside. I saw the traffic light flashing yellow and, speeding up, zoomed across the street on a halfback diagonal. I sped through the open doors, past both the doormen, cautioning, "Hey!"; and the security guards, "Slow it down there!" I made the elevator doors, pushing them back, entering and feeling the floor rise and my stomach churn the remains of a cheeseburger, fries and two coffees. As the doors open and I saw Mac, Dot and Rainey arguing. I wished

I could film them. Especially to show Sandy and Barbara that these were flesh-and-blood people, who talked about Arabs, Tammy Wynette, the price of beef, the Supremes, picking up kids, leather bags and a million other things—so that they would stop talking about "right-center" and "illegality."

"I don't want to talk about it," Mac was grumbling, "and I don't want anyone asking me about it anymore. Let's drop it for now."

"But I don't *understand*," Dot said, "You put in for this vacation three months ago. You *need* it with all your problems with Burt."

"Of course I need it. But I don't care to discuss it any further."

"Fine," Rainey said angrily. "Just trying to help."

Mac patted her arm. "Let me handle it in my own way."

"I just don't understand," Dot sighed.

"Hi, Josh," Rainey waved.

"Where have you been?" Dot griped.

"Dinner—where'd you think I was?"

"God only knows where you've been."

"Good. In that case, this Sunday you can ask him."

Wilma frowned. A steady churchgoer, she deplored all of my anti-God quips. Rainey laughed. "You chat with the Man Upstairs on Sundays, Dot?"

Wilma smiled, despite herself.

"That's between me and Him," Dot replied.

"Next time, ask him what he thinks about Medicare folks."

"Stop it," Mac said.

I moved over toward Dot. "Where I go on my dinner break is my business. If I wanna fly to Montana and back, I'll do that. Got it?"

"You don't have to be rude. I just asked."

"Just trying to get a few things straight."

"That's the problem around here," Dot muttered. "Everyone's always trying to get a few things straight. That's probably why everything's so out of whack."

She handed me a notice officially announcing the meeting next day.

Later that evening, J.J. came upstairs and slipped into the medicine room, motioning to me and Rainey, who announced we were going on break.

"So, how's it goin'?" J.J. asked.

"Fine," Rainey said, pouring herself some Maalox.

"You look fine," J.J. answered. "For a cadavar."

"Don't get on me now."

"All set for tomorrow?"

"Sure! No big thing."

"Uh huh."

"I have an idea," I said quietly, looking to make sure Dot wasn't within hearing distance. I could hear her voice, chatting with Mrs. Crawford about the merits of cable t.v. Mac was sitting on the couch near the elevators, charting and chain-smoking Marlboros.

"Shoot!" J.J. said.

"Let's take it to 'em. Emphasize Dot calling Virginia Lockett a chocolate drop."

"Yeah?" J.J. said carefully.

"Take some of the heat off Rainey."

"Maybe."

I waited. Rainey poured herself more Maalox. "I get uptight just thinkin' about it."

"Thought you were just fine," J.J. kidded.

"We can sort of threaten to take it to the papers, sort of sue them for racial discrimination."

"Now, wait a minute, Josh. You don't just 'sort of' sue somebody. You do it, or you don't."

"You know what I mean. We *bluff* 'em."

"Even when you bluff, you gotta have your shit together."

"Well, we can say we're going to check into it. Check what happens when the hospital's policies are being violated."

J.J. nodded, still cautious.

"And we can bring up the clause in the contract *we* have," I said suddenly, "that an employee shall not be discriminated against regardless of race, religion or creed."

"How's that now?"

"We can say they are picking on Rainey. Turn it around. They *are* picking on her because she fought against Dot's remarks."

"Just watch how you say 'fought.' You say fought, that's admittin' she slapped ol' Birdlady. That'll blow the lid off."

"O.k. We'll say she strongly OBJECTED."

"That's better. Some of that Perry Mason shit."

"Hit 'em with that. They're scared to death of that stuff."

"Yeah," J.J. smiled, thinking it over. "We hit 'em with some of that Perry Mason shit."

"Just pretend Shields is that D.A.-Hamburger."

J.J. laughed, then stared at Rainey who was grimacing. "You o.k. Rain?"

"Fine. You men just go right ahead makin' plans for me."

"Aw!"

"Really. What I hear sounds good. Go on, Josh."

" 'Course, a lot depends on us sticking to our stories no matter what."

Rainey nodded.

"They're gonna try and trap us."

"TELL me about it," snorted Rainey. "They tried that all day, every which way. Three on one."

"It'll be worse tomorrow."

"No, it'll be better—'cause we'll all be there together."

Rainey suddenly spat out her Maalox and grabbed her side. J.J. rushed over. I grabbed a pillow from the linen cart and placed it in back of Rainey's head as she slumped down on a chair. "I'm o.k.," Rainey groaned.

"What did you have for dinner?" J.J. asked. Wilma passing by, rushed in.

"Stand back," Mac ordered, appearing out of nowhere. "Give her some air."

"I'm getting Dr. Attaway. He's on."

"No you *ain't*." Rainey gritted.

"The hell we ain't," snapped J.J. going over and dialing

the phone. I could hear the page operator, "Dr. Attaway, 4998, Dr. William Attaway, please call 4998."

Dot peeked in. "Oh dear!"

Rainey glared.

"I got to go," J.J. said, studying his watch quickly. "I'll check back later."

"Don't make a fuss," Rainey said, teeth clenched.

"Josh," Mac advised, "stay with her until the doctor comes."

"You're going to worry yourself to death, Rainey," Dot said.

"When I need *your* help, I'll ask for it," Rainey snapped. "And don't hold your breath."

Dot stalked out, talking to herself. "You try and help and what do you get for it?"

The room grew quiet.

"How have your bowel movements been?" Mac suddenly asked.

"None of your beeswax."

Mac nodded to me and Wilma. "Are you having black stools again?"

Rainey shook her head. Just then, Dr. Attaway strolled in briskly. He was a tall, well-built, balding black man, dressed very conservatively in a three-piece charcoal grey suit, blue shirt and silvery tie. Rainey had nicknamed him The Reverend. He was the only black doctor at Assissi Gardens, hired under pressure from civil rights groups in the late sixties.

"How's my favorite girl?" he smiled, his eyes severe.

"Not so hot, Rev."

"No?"

"Just nervous."

"You keep getting 'just nervous,' you might have to find yourself a new job, so you can be less nervous."

He took her pulse, then felt her stomach. His touch looked gentle, firm. Behind his elegant reverend look, was an exquisite mind and a national reputation as an internist, specializing in diagnosing gastroenterology problems. Even

Dot respected his skills, once declaring, "That man has forgotten more things about the digestive system than most ten people will ever know."

"Tell me when," he smiled. Rainey nodded obediently. Attaway began pushing lightly with fingertips along Rainey's belly. He touched the middle, right side, just above her womb and below the belly-button on her left side. She gasped, gripping his elbow so hard, fingermarks showed on the white jacket over his suit. He didn't blink. "Mm, hmm! That's the one we wanted to keep an eye on."

"Whatcha gonna do?"

"The first thing I should do is slap you around for eating whatever you have been eating. Then, I should put you in the hospital—tonight—and run some tests."

"You can't do that. Not now."

"Rainey, I'll only put you in if you promise me you'll stay put."

The last time he'd hospitalized Rainey, she'd left to go to Royal's sister's wedding.

"I want you to stay home for two days. See how you feel. How's your sick leave?"

"I got a few days and that's about it."

She bit her lip. "But I can't stay home. After tomorrow."

"I *strongly* advise you to stay home, Rainey. Before you're out for a much longer time."

Rainey shook her head.

"For heaven's sake, Rainey," Mac exclaimed, "they can postpone the meeting. What's the matter with you!"

"Your health comes first," Wilma added, anxious.

"That's what I'm *thinking* about," Rainey pouted. "I want to get this over with, outta the way one way or the other."

"I don't think you've heard what I've been saying," Dr. Attaway said calmly, his voice picking up a little. "You have an *active* ulcer that is presently flaring up. As it stands now, it's simply flaring up. Nothing a little rest, Maalox and the *proper* strictly observed diet can't cure—temporarily. Now you can aggravate it to the point you may need surgical intervention."

Rainey winced. "Look at it this way: if I can get this stuff over with, I'll be less aggravated."

Attaway fiddled with his bag. "It's your life, Rainey. I wish I could say that you know what's best, but right now I don't think you do."

He began writing out a prescription. "Take this four times a day. At the SPECIFIED times."

Rainey nodded.

"That doesn't mean you take it twice at eleven o'clock at night to 'make up' for not taking it earlier because you were out. Four *separate* times."

"Yessir."

"Feeling a little better?"

Rainey nodded.

"Good. One more thing."

"What?"

"Promise me that after this 'business' you have tomorrow, that you'll take off a few days."

"Promise."

"O.k. Now, I'll be on call all night if you need me again for anything."

"Thanks, Doc."

"The best thanks you can give me is to follow what I've said and do it."

Rainey finished the shift. Everyone, looking towards the meeting, seemed tense and nervous. Just before I was about to leave, Sandy phoned.

"Anything new?"

"Rainey got sick."

"Yeah?"

"She has ulcers."

"Wow!"

"Yeah."

"Well, I mainly called to wish you luck tomorrow. Any last minute, uh, things?"

"Not really."

I waved goodby to Rainey and Mac. Wilma and Dot were putting on their coats.

"Give 'em hell, Josh."

"We will."

"Don't be nervous."

"I'm as calm as a dog on a roller coaster."

Sandy laughed.

At home, Fran said, "You seem jumpy."

"I'm uptight about tomorrow. My stomach's doing somersaults."

"I'll make you some oolong tea."

"If it's good enough for the FBI, it's good enough for me."

Fran laughed, yelling over her shoulder, "What I wanna know is when are you getting those beautiful black shoes?"

She made me some mushroom soup along with the tea, and dished herself out some strawberries and sour cream, her favorite midnight snack.

"You'll do fine," she said.

"I hope so."

"How was your meeting with the Red Army?"

"Fran."

"Now, I know you're jumpy. Can't even take a little teasing."

I kissed her; she pushed me away. "Swallow before you kiss me."

"Good strawberries. Yum."

"You know, the whole thing might turn out easier than you think."

"How so?"

"Well, it seems to me, non-political as I am, that Dot's alone. No one really supports her."

"Maybe."

"She's alone."

"The supervisors support her."

"Well," she smiled slyly, "they know what happened. But—" She bit into a strawberry, "they can't prove a thing."

"Yeah."

I told her about Mac's vacation. "That's disgusting."

"Yeah."

"Ooooh, that makes me mad!"

"Yeah."

She began doodling with my pen on a napkin. Soon four

fat chickens appeared pecking each other in the ass. The last chicken held a car in its beak.

"What's this called?" I grinned.

She wiped her mouth. "Stuffed Fowl."

I repeated her words, "Stuffed Fowl" as I took the elevator up to the meeting next morning. I stopped in the men's room on the first floor and studied my good-luck outfit in the mirror: maroon corduroy pants, blue shirt, blue blazer and pink tie. I winked, "Get 'em kid."

In the Nursing Conference Room, Rainey and Wilma were sitting on one side; Dot was on the other. I took a deep breath and sat down in the chair next to Rainey. On the table were three pots of coffee near the Mr. Coffee machine, and four plates of cookies: Ladyfingers, Vanilla Wafers, Fig Newtons and Oreos. I winked at Rainey and Wilma, and began psyching myself up. I thought about Rainey grabbing her side. I thought about Virginia Lockett clutching her radio, her Geography textbook and her fan magazine. I thought about her drawn face as she slumped into the wheelchair. I thought about Mac's face when she saw the vacation schedule.

They came in all at once: Faith Edmunsen with Lance Wiggin, Lucy Quinlan and Ike Shields, the Head Administrator for Assissi Gardens. A big man, six feet four, he wore a deep black three-piece suit with a white shirt and an ivory tie, and black shoes. He was broad, with thick brown hair and metallic grey eyes, that looked frigid. There was a remote touch of blue in them.

"I think you know everyone," Mr. Wiggin smiled. Ike Shields nodded briskly, frowning slightly. "Where's Mary?"

We all looked around for Mac. She wasn't there. Lucy rose, "I'll go check."

The door opened and Mac almost bunked into Lucy. "Sorry," she said breathlessly, "I had to get my daughter. My husband was supposed to pick her up, but—"

"Fine," Ike Shields said warmly, rising. "Come in and have a seat."

Mac bustled in, catching her breath, taking off her coat and nodding to everyone. She sat down near Dot. Rainey poured herself a glass of milk. Ike Shields smiled, "Go on, Rainey, make yourself at home."

He smiled at me next. "How are you, Josh?"

"Fine."

Faith, Lucy and Wiggin all sat next to each other, Faith the nearest to Ike Shields, who was sitting near Wilma and Rainey.

"Where's J.J. at?" Wilma asked suddenly.

"Oh, I forgot!" Faith exclaimed. "His little girl fell off a swing at school. They're bringing her into the Emergency Room."

"Jesus!" Rainey groaned as Wilma gasped and Mac shook her head.

"That poor child!" Dot exclaimed as Faith and Lucy nodded.

"Possibly someone from the union headquarters may come," Wiggin said. "But they told us not to wait."

Rainey gulped more milk down. "We can handle it," I whispered. She nodded tightly.

A silence took over the room. Lucy Quinlan broke it. "Who all would like some coffee?"

She poured to the raised hands, passing the cream, sugar and Hi-and-Lo. The cookies circulated. "Vanilla Wafers— my favorite!" I joked. "Mmm." Faith Edmunsen stared coolly at me, as did Shields. There was the sound of sipping, stirring and a few crunchings.

Shields nodded to Wiggin. "Shall we start?"

Wiggin cleared his throat. "We all know why we're here today."

Mac lit up a cigarette and blew her match out.

"A serious incident occurred the other day that we want to clear up as soon as possible. Mr. Shields has kindly consented to come here and be with us today, taking time from his very busy schedule to participate and give what input he can."

Ike Shields carefully sipped black coffee.

"Did you want to say a few words?" Wiggin asked.

"Yes." Ike Shields' eyes took us all in. He had excellent eye contact. "As you know, Assissi Gardens has one of the finest reputations in the area, if not in the entire state. We particularly pride ourselves on our Nursing Service and like to think we have the best personnel possible working for us. We also like to think that our stress on discipline combined with a very finely-honed sense of team nursing is what makes us among the best in the field.'' There was utter silence. His eyes fell on me, then on Rainey. ''Now, when we hear of incidents, occurrences that seem to run counter to our conceptions, it's only natural that we grow concerned.''

He smiled thinly, his jaw tight. ''Of course, in every kind of group situation there are always little kinks and quirks, personality conflicts. We expect that. We are dealing in the real world after all. We—'' He flickered a quick look at me, ''are not Utopians here. But—'' Everyone tensed. Even Faith Edmunsen, who'd been nodding proudly, tensed in the middle of sipping her coffee. ''when it comes to our attention that there has been something as contrary and unconducive to our concepts as physical blows, we grow *extremely* concerned.''

There was not even a touch of blue in his eyes now. ''And the fact of the matter is,'' he continued with intensity, ''we won't have it. Period.''

Rainey gulped down her milk and reached for another carton. Dot was staring wide-eyed at Ike Shields. Wilma's folded arms tightened. Mac lit another cigarette. So did I.

''The contract itself is quite clear on this matter. Physical assault is grounds for immediate termination. As it should be. There is no place here for people who can't work things out in a rational manner. That's what our concept of teamwork is all about. We rationally help each other out so that the patient can get the best care possible.''

''Hmmph!'' Shields focused on Wilma. ''I'll be finished shortly, Mrs. Higgenbotham, and then everyone can speak their piece.''

Wilma sat up straighter in her chair.

''As I was saying,'' Shields continued, ''there are enough problems without compounding them. Now I've read all the reports and have talked with Mrs. Quinlan, Mr. Wiggin and Mrs. Edmunsen, and I am far from satisfied. I want to get to the bottom of this thing, and I want to get to it today. And when it's over, I want it over. I want all of us to be able to go back doing what we were hired to do."

There was a dead silence. Wiggin coughed, smiled and stared at Faith Edmunsen, who was smiling nervously.

"I think Mr. Shields has said pretty much what's on all our minds," Faith said. "And said it well, I might add. We don't enjoy this any more than you do—let me add that also."

No one spoke. I tried to think of something to say. I didn't know where to start. I took a deep breath and raised my hand. "So does this mean it's an open discussion now?"

Faith looked to Ike Shields who nodded. Still no one spoke. I felt like I was on the top of a steep cliff. I looked at Wilma, who sat with folded arms. Rainey was reaching for a cigarette and I let her take one. With a sigh of relief, she blew smoke through her nostrils. I took another deep breath, clinging to Fran's face, remembering J.J.'s laugh, "A parrot?": and Virginia Lockett's mother carrying the bag of food.

"Uh, yeah," I began. "well, I think everybody here is for teamwork. I'm all for it, I know that. But that means you also have to have respect."

"Excuse me," Ike Shields interrupted, staring at Rainey. Rainey met his eyes head-on. "Did you slap Dot?"

Rainey didn't blink. "No, I did not." Dot gasped.

"You did not?"

"Right!"

"Dot?"

Dot, breathing rapidly, held her Adam's Apple. "Oh yes she did!" she exclaimed, turning to Rainey. "You did too!"

Shields suddenly turned to me and said, "Go on, Josh. Finish what you were saying."

I took another deep breath. "Well, in terms of respect, I think Dot has certain weaknesses. This is also in terms of teamwork. I mean, the whole thing started out when a young black woman was admitted to our floor for a therapeutic abortion."

"We're not talking about that!" exclaimed Faith.

"Really, Josh," Lucy added.

"Now, now," Ike Shields said. "Let's let him talk."

"Well, Dot wouldn't even admit the patient and it was on her side."

"Is this true?" Shields asked. Dot nodded, gulping.

"Well, that shouldn't have happened. Go on."

"She got Rainey to admit her. Then the next night when the girl went home, she said, "Well, that little chocolate drop went home."

"An ill-advised figure of speech."

Shields turned to Dot. "You said that?"

"I really don't remember."

"Sheee!" exclaimed Rainey, as Wilma flounced in her chair. "You said it," Rainey argued. "You said it, Dot, as sure as I'm sittin' here!"

"Now, wait, wait! We're getting just a *little* out of hand," Wiggin cautioned meekly.

"*I* got somethin' to say," Rainey blurted out, her hand raised.

"Wait your turn," Ike Shields advised.

"I'd like to say something if I may," Wiggin said.

"Yes, Lance?"

"There are always attitude problems," Wiggin smiled placidly. "In fact, I have them myself. We all try and deal with them in an adult manner, adjust and go on. What Dot said or didn't say may have, indeed, been out of line—if she did indeed say that. In this particular case, as you know, abortion is a very inflammatory issue, often passionately so. Some people, and I would include Dot in this category, so love life that the very idea of abortion is repugnant to them. I feel this way myself, as does my Mrs."

Ike Shields sighed.

"My point is this," Wiggins smiled kindly; "Attitudes can be talked about—whatever they are." He leaned back, smiling. "Talked out, not fought out."

Rainey slammed her empty milk carton on the table. "Well, now, you talkin' like I DID slap her, like I'm guilty until proven innocent. I thought this was the United States, where it's *supposed* to be the other way around!"

"You misunderstand me," Wiggins smiled nervously.

"Maybe *you* misunderstood what Josh was just sayin'. Dot's a racist. She don't like black patients. In fact, she don't like no kind of Medical or Medicare patients a lick, and that's the damn truth of it."

"Let's watch the language, Rainey," Faith Edmunsen said. Shields lit a cigarette. He was smoking Navy Players. "That's a very serious allegation, Rainey."

"And it's NOT true," Dot pouted.

"What we're mainly trying to focus on," Faith said, "is the best manner in which we can maintain maximum teamwork—for patient care. I think in our little family, we tend to forget that. The patient is our prime concern."

"*Patient*, huh?" Rainey snorted. "So tell me that girl wasn't a patient?"

"I don't think you understand," Faith said.

"Oh, I understand just *fine*," Rainey shot back. "But understand *me*. What we're here for, as you say, is to take care of all these people. And that means ALL. We ain't supposed to just take care of all the *rich* folks and ignore the other ones."

"No one's saying that!" Lucy groaned. Shields nodded, his eyes sharper.

"But we ain't," continued Rainey, "the judge and jury of who comes in here. Everyone *supposed* to get equal treatment and equal time—that's the way it's *supposed* to be. Now if that ain't the way you see it, and you want to change THAT, well let me know right now, because I'll be outta here so fast, you won't HAVE to worry about firin' me—" She paused for breath.

"No one's said a word about firing you," Lucy Quinlan said softly.

"Yeah, let me know, because I'll be outta here before you can say Wait. Really. I need this job, but I don't need it THAT bad. I need my self-respect more. And I ain't ABOUT to give that up, not for you, or anyone!"

"We know that," Wiggins said, abashed. "We know you're one of our best—"

"I *know* what I am. You don't have to tell me who and what I am."

Everyone sat stunned. Rainey opened another carton of milk and swallowed.

Wilma cleared her throat. "See, you're sittin' in your offices talkin' about patient care and what not, but you really don't know what's goin' down on the floors. You think you can get a little taste from meetin's and reports and things, but that don't do the job. Not by a long shot. You all oughta spend a little more time on the floors and see things for yourself."

I sat, surprised. Both Rainey and Wilma were now leaning forward in their chairs. Mac was stifling a small grin; her eyes, hooded the whole time, sparkled. Dot was staring, slouched in her chair, holding a Fig Newton in mid-air. Wiggins fidgeted in his chair. Faith met Rainey's stare eyeball-for-eyeball, while Lucy looked away. Ike Shields calmly puffed his cigarette.

"Well, that is an interesting idea," Faith nodded curtly. "It is something we could possibly look into."

Wilma ran her tongue along her upper lip. "Shouldn't be too hard. All you need to do is get on the elevator."

Mac covered her mouth with her hand. In the tense silence, Shields tapped his cigarette ash, smiling.

"You know, you may find this surprising, but you've actually read my mind, Wilma." She stared at him. "I've been thinking about this for quite some time, and you've expressed it rather well." He paused. No one said a word. "I think what you've expressed is a genuine concern for more supervisory participation in patient contact. And I think it would be an excellent idea to set up a viable form in which this could take place. They're right," he said, turning to Wiggin and Faith Edmunsen. "Many times, we're so swamped with paperwork, conferences and a million and one different things that I guess there becomes what I would call an alienation factor."

"Whatever," Rainey muttered.

"Speaking of which, you haven't said much, Mary," Shields said softly, looking at Mac. She shrugged. Ike Shields smiled kindly. "Did Rainey slap Dot?"

I whistled. I couldn't help it. Mac studied a Ladyfinger

cookie. "I heard what sounded like a slap," Mac said very slowly, "but I didn't see a thing. It could've been a lot of things."

Rainey grunted and looked down as Shields quickly looked at her, then at Dot, then at Faith. Mac popped the entire cookie into her mouth.

"Well," Ike Shields said slowly, "to get back to what we came here for, I think the best thing for all concerned is to let the matter drop. For the time being. If any personality conflicts develop, I'll consider transfer requests at a later date. Faith, you'll be in charge of that." Faith nodded. Ike Shields stared into his empty coffee cup and slid it towards the center of the table where Lucy Quinlan instantly poured him another cup. "How does that sound to everyone?"

Faith and Lucy nodded, as did Wiggin. Rainey shrugged, I nodded, Wilma simply folded her arms, eyeing Rainey and trying not to smile. Mac lit up another cigarette.

"Well, I'm not satisfied!" Dot declared.

"I didn't expect everyone to be satisfied," Shields said calmly. "What I _do_ expect is to maintain a situation where there's as little conflict and pressure as possible. I don't want anyone leaving this room feeling something's being held over their head."

I took a deep breath and whispered to myself, "Be bold." "Does that mean," I said, as matter-of-factly as possible, "that the problem with Mac's vacation will be straightened out?"

"Pardon?" Ike Shields said, his face reddening just a tinge.

"That's already been taken care of," Faith said quickly.

Mac's eyebrows shot up. "That's news to me."

"I was going to mention it to you before the meeting, but you were late. It was just an oversight."

"Huh," Mac said, studying Faith.

"Will someone please fill _me_ in?" Ike Shields snapped.

"I'll tell you later," Faith smiled.

"Fine," Shields nodded, checking his watch. "So does that about wrap it up?" No one said anything. Wiggins sighed, "I guess so." The tension eased from the room like a balloon letting out air. It returned with a brief motion of Ike Shield's hand, motioning us to stay seated. "One last thing I might mention."

We waited.

"I hope I made myself clear about how distasteful even the rumor of such occurrences are to me. Remember, there's a recession out there, and there are many people on the street just aching for a chance to work, more than ready to make the effort it takes to avoid such personality conflicts as we've been talking about today. Now, you're all excellent employees, in my opinion, and we don't want to lose anyone we don't have to lose. At the same time, as I said, there are many people waiting on line. Keep that in mind." Without a further word, he rose slowly, pocketed his Navy Players, and left.

Everyone sat dully around the table. Rainey looked drained, as did Mac and Dot. Wiggin rubbed his forehead. Faith Edmunsen and Lucy Quinlan began gathering up the coffee cups, napkins, creams, sugars. Dot helped them. As Rainey, Wilma and I left, Mac waited for Dot. "Coming, Dot?"

"I'll be up in a few minutes," Dot said, running a napkin along the table, wiping up some spilled milk.

V. Finale

The four of us piled into the elevator. As we shot up, Wilma burst into a huge grin. "Well, I guess we took care of business."

Mac stared at the floor buttons.

"Took care of business, girl," Rainey grinned, "and then some." She did a little dipsy-doodle hip strut. "Did you see that sucker Wiggin's face when I said 'Understand *me*' "

"I saw it," Wilma chorused. "He looked like a groundhog that woke up under a tractor!"

"And did you see Shields' face when ol' Josh asked him about Mac's time?"

"You *know* I saw *that!*" Wilma laughed.

"That was a miracle itself. Josh honey, you cracked the great Stoneface!"

I laughed.

"Thank you very much, Josh," Mac said softly.

As the doors opened, Rainey pranced out to the nursing station where a float nurse and two aides began getting ready to leave.

"And did you see that Edmunsen bitch just about choke to death on her cookie when I gave her what for?"

"Girl, you almost made her swallow that thing whole," Wilma snickered.

"And when you said 'Hmphh' when ol' Shields was layin' it out," Rainey chortled.

"I couldn't help myself!" Wilma blushed.

"And did you see Shields eyeballin' Josh when he got the ball rollin' with that talk about RE-SPECT!"

Wilma looked at me and laughed. "If looks could kill, honey, you'd be in the freezer right now."

"But that Shields is somethin' *else* now, ain't he?" Rainey whispered.

"He sure is," agreed Wilma.

"Comin' in slick."

"Like a greased hog."

"Tried turnin' us around but fast."

"Mmm-hmm."

"And can that man dress?"

"Can't he though."

"He goes shopping with Wiggin," I said innocently. They both cracked up.

"Ol' Wimpy with his wimpy-assed self!" Rainey laughed.

"You're terrible," Mac said. She was writing in her days on the vacation schedule.

"You about ready to crack a smile now, grumpy?" Rainey laughed.

Mac turned. "Almost. Don't push me. You heard what they said about pressure."

Rainey laughed hysterically. "Old Mac. Mac the Fox."

"Is that 'cause I have such a big tail?" Mac asked, finishing her vacation days with a flourish, pushing her silvery hair back.

"That and 'cause you're so sly."

"Sly?"

"Sittin' there not sayin' a thing. Cool as ice."

"Cool as ice nothing. I thought I was going to urinate all over myself."

"*Tell* me about it," Wilma said.

"I find these things very unpleasant," Mac said, "and it wasn't very pleasant for Dot."

Rainey and Wilma stopped smiling.

"Maybe we can all chip in and buy her a new parrot," I kidded.

"Sheeee!"

"Let her get her rich patients to buy her a new bird," Wilma said. "I got better things to do with my money."

"Hey, I'm just kidding, kidding you know—joke?"

"Yeah," Rainey said, her eyes recalling and lighting up, "Like when you said 'I just LOVE Vanilla Wafers.' That ol' Lucy looked at you like you was cra-zee."

"He is." Mac said, starting to get her medicine cards in order.

"Well," Wilma replied, "back to work, I guess."

Rainey was reaching into her black purse and pulling out a red flyer. "We gonna CELEBRATE tonight!"

I stared at the flyer—a menu from Lee's, Rainey's favorite take-out place. It announced wonderful, inexpensive food: Oyster Loaf, Ribs, Chicken, Fried Shrimp, Louisiana Catfish and Buffalo Fish, greens, potato salad, cornbread, blackeyed peas and the specialties of the house: Pecan Pie, Sweet Potato Pie, and Peach and Apple Cobblers.

"Who's gonna help me celebrate?"

I licked my lips. "I'll have the ribs, greens and pecan pie."

"Those pecan pies are gonna kill you, Josh," Mac said.

"Love 'em, just love 'em."

Rainey winked, nudging Wilma.

"Josh sure does love his pie, truly."

Wilma blushed. "Girl, you're terrible."

"Let's see, I'm gonna have me some Oyster Loaf—a DOUBLE, and some greens and blackeyed peas, and some cornbread. And, how about some Sweet Potato Pie," she grinned in Mac's face, " 'cause I'm so sweet."

"Hmmm," Mac said, pursing her lips. "Just go easy on the sauce. Remember, you haven't been feeling well."

"Sure, Mac, sure."

Wilma studied the menu. "Hmm, the fried chicken sounds good. Some chicken and potato salad."

"No pie?" Rainey asked.

"No." Wilma replied.

"Wilma," Rainey sang, taking Wilma's arm and slowly stroking it, "don't you want some nice hot sweet potato pie, Wilma?"

Wilma frowned harder.

"It's a special occasion, you know."

"Well, o.k. Put me down for one piece."

Rainey turned. "Big Mac, what are you gonna have?"

Mac shook her head. "Nothing for me, thank you."

"Don'tcha wanna eat with us black folks?"

"Is Josh an honorary black now?"

"C'mon, Mac. We *celebratin'*. We gonna party down."

"You're not going to have those wheelchair races like you did the last time, are you?"

"Mac."

Mac sighed. "Oh, all right. What was that fish you had the last time? That wasn't half bad."

"Here we go!" Rainey shouted. "Now there's someone with taste! Mac the Fox orders one heapin' plate of Lewweezeeanna Buffalo Fish!"

"And some vegetables please."

"Don't got no *vegetables*. We got greens, blackeyed peas, and potato salad."

"Greens will be fine."

I smiled. "As long as there's no peas in it."

Mac laughed. Rainey dialed the phone. "Hello, Lemme speak to Sarah. Yeah."

There was a brief pause. Rainey winked at us, giving us the high sign. "We gonna have us a FEAST!"

"I wonder what's keeping Dot?" Mac said. "Maybe she'd like something."

I was wondering too, wondering if she wasn't having still another meeting, if maybe they'd waited for us to leave and were not planning further strategy. I suddenly remembered J.J.'s kid. "Hey, I wonder what happened with J.J.'s kid?"

"Sarah," Rainey was saying excitedly. "Fine, and how are you? Great. And how's that fine old man of yours? Uh huh. The kids? Good, good. Yeah, he's fine. Finishin' law school. Yeah, I caught him all right. June. June bride. Sure, you're invited. Hey, listen, Sarah, we havin' a little party here around 6. You think you can send us over some food?" Rainey laughed, talking past the phone.

"Does the bear shit in the woods?"

"O.k. We want one order of ribs—" She looked at us. "How hot, Josh?"

"Medium."

"One medium order of ribs, one big Double order of Oyster Loaf—with plenty of sauce—"

"Rainey," Wilma called. Rainey waved her off. "One order of fried chicken for my lady Wilma here, and one big order of Louisiana Buffalo Fish for a young thing gonna eat with us." Mac curtsied. "And one order of cornbread, three orders of greens, two sweet potato pies—"

"Three," Mac said.

" 'Scuse me, three. And one pecan pie."

Rainey listened, nodding. She turned to us. "Anyone want chicory coffee?"

Wilma nodded. I shook my head, as did Mac.

"One chicory coffee. Thanks, Sarah. Yeah, see you soon too."

Rainey hung up the phone and clapped her hands.

"What about Dot?" asked Mac.

"They don't sell birdseed. Sorry."

Mac shrugged. I dialed the Emergency Room, and asked for J.J.

"He's not here," the receptionist said, "He took his kid home."

"How is she?"

"She's o.k. A mild concussion."

"She's o.k." I said to Rainey, Wilma, and Mac. Just then the elevator doors opened. Dot entered with an armful of packages.

"Sorry I'm late. I just ran across the street to get a few things at Simpson's."

Simpson's was Dot's favorite gourmet dessert store. She opened her packages. There was a huge dark blue tin of Danish Butter Cookies, a yellow-green metal box of Chinese ricepaper-wrapped milk candies, and some Polish orange-flavored wafers.

"Friends?" Dot smiled warily at Rainey, holding out her right hand.

"Hm," Rainey said, not extending her hand.

Dot fidgeted with the packages, chattering.

"As Mr. Shields said, 'It's all over and done with,' so I thought I'd bring a few little peace offerings. Something to nibble on."

"Peace offerings—that's what they gave the Indians," Rainey muttered.

"That's very nice," Mac said, stepping close to Dot. "Thank you, Dot."

Dot looked at Mac gratefully, her face hurt, as Wilma nodded at the packages, particularly the Danish Butter tin.

"That's a whole lot of cookies there."

"Not the way Josh eats them," Dot remarked, "for a skinny kid he can really pack it away. I don't know where he puts it. Honestly!"

"I worry alot," I grinned.

"Oh God!" Mac said, "now I've heard everything!"

I walked off with Rainey down the hall.

"Hmmm," she said to me, "who does that bitch think she's foolin'—bringin' in them cookies and candy and shit? Peace offering. She can kiss my ass."

"I don't know if she'd do that."

Rainey laughed, then disappeared into one of the rooms.

As I walked back, I saw the red emergency call-light flash from Mr. Rashad's room.

I rushed over and grabbed Dot.

"Rashad needs help quick!"

"Get Mac," Dot spluttered, "hurry!"

I ran up the hall looking for Mac, and saw her bringing a medicine tray out of another room.

"Mac—Rashad!"

She ran; I was right behind her. Inside the room, Dot was fussing with pillows while Mr. Rashad spat up blood. Mac ran out, returned with a syringe, and gave him a shot. The choking lessened. He wheezed, his eyes large and weak.

"Everything's going to be fine," Dot nodded nervously. Outside, Mac sighed, "I'm calling Dr. Kalantari. This is his third attack this week." She dialed the phone; soon the page operator's voice rang out, "Dr. Kalantari, Dr. Kalantari, please call 4998."

Just then the food arrived from Lee's. I got everyone's money, paid and tipped the delivery man, then took the huge hot bag.

"What's that?" Dot frowned, "Soul food?"

"Yeah!"

Rainey came up the hall, rubbing her hands.

"Now I could smell that if I was in China!"

Mac kept a straight face and walked up to Dr. Kalantari who was walking off the elevator. As she took him to the room, I could hear his voice, "Has he been getting those breathing exercises I ordered?"

Dot covered her mouth.

"Oh, Jesus, I forgot to call that inhalation therapist and tell him to come up here last night! I blew that whole order!" She turned to me.

"Josh, did you write in Dr. Kalantari's note about Rashad's pulmonary treatments?"

I flipped the patient care plan to Rashad's name. "Yes."

"Well," Dot sighed, "At least he had a few treatments today then."

"If he did," interrupted Dr. Kalantari, "They were very short. These treatments are important. If there isn't a thera-

pist available, I want one of you to do them. Is that understood?''

Dot and Mac nodded.

''I've known the family for many years now, and I'd like
to keep him alive. All right?''

Dr. Kalantari was one of the few general practitioners at
Assissi Gardens, taking many of the Arabic patients from the
Tenderloin area, as well as the handful of storeowners in the
city. He took a very reserved attitude towards the richer
Arabic patients, although he treated them with skill and dili-
gence. Reportedly, he'd been forced to leave Iran in the early
fifties, a rumor his reserve neither dispelled nor verified.

Wilma and Rainey had unpacked and set up the food.
The ribs smelled hot and spicy. Kalantari wrote some orders.

''I think he'll be fine for the rest of the night.''

''How's he breathing?'' asked Dot, adding, ''Maybe
some of the sheiks that are coming here will set up some
schools where we can learn Arab so we can better understand
the Arab patients here.''

''He's breathing,'' Dr. Kalantari murmured, his eyes
darkening. ''He's breathing like most Arabs breathe. Oi-yul.
Oi-yul.'' I snickered, as Dot watched Dr. Kalantari briskly
leave, passing up the elevator for the stairs.

''Honestly! I'll never understand that man.'' She saw me
grinning and jutted her skinny neck at me.

''And how do Jews breathe, Josh?''

''We're used to holding our breath—from the concentration camps,'' I shot back. Everyone tensed.

''How's the ribs?'' I asked Rainey, turning my back on
Dot.

''Fine. You won't find barbecue better than this,
honey.''

''Beef or pork?'' asked Dot.

''Want some?'' interrupted Mac, offering Dot some
Buffalo Fish.

''No thank you. I had a huge lunch today.''

''These ribs are pork,'' Rainey pronounced.

''I didn't know you were allowed to eat pork, Josh,''
Dot said.

I stared at her, wondering if she were just stupid, or if she was going to start leaning on me from now on. Then I smiled to myself.

"Well, Dot, we're allowed to eat pork that's been specially treated."

The food smelled wonderful, and I felt silly, crazy.

"We are allowed to eat pork that's been bagelized."

Dot screwed up her face.

"Bagelized! Come on now!"

"Here comes another one of Josh's tall tales," Wilma laughed.

"Uh uh," Rainey shook her head, winking at Wilma and Mac, "this one's true."

I turned and stared at Dot. "I know it sounds ridiculous. That's the first thing everybody says. But it's an ancient tradition. The term bagelized of course is taken from the ancient Hebrew, so it loses a little in the translation." Dot's face, still skeptical, relaxed; she was almost hooked. "See, in the past they had no methods of freezing pork, or really, re-frigerating any kind of food—"

Dot nodded wisely.

"That's one of the reasons the Jewish dietary laws came into existence. Pigs, being cloven animals of course, were ver-botten. However, among some of the Hassidic sects that later became quite popular, pork was allowed with certain pro-visos."

"This is fascinating," Dot breathed.

"If the PIG," I stated, staring straight into Dot's face, "was surrounded with a special ritual food that would purge it of its undesirable qualities, it COULD be eaten!"

"Yes."

"Now, this special ritual food, believe it or not, turns out to be what we call today—the bagel!"

"My God!" exclaimed Dot. Rainey almost spat out a mouthful of Oyster Loaf.

"Or should I say, a series of bagels."

"A *series*?" Dot breathed.

"You know the hole in the bagel?"

"Of course! I'm not that stupid!"

"Well, that hole, within the purification rite, was considered to be a sacred portal through which the rotten spirits could leave. Now, what they would do is, they would take the pig—" I made a sweeping motion with my hands as if scooping up a suckling pig, and stared directly into Dot's face. "Yank open its mouth—" I made the yanking motion inches from her nose. Rainey stifled a giggle while Mac, chewing, shook her head. "And then surround the pig with bagels. Through all the sacred portals the evil spirits would flow out. The tricky part was that all the bagels had to be touching each other. It's the same idea as electrical circuiting—if they weren't all touching each other, it would fuck up the flow of the current."

"Astonishing!" Dot marveled, turning to the others, "Isn't that the most *amazing*—" Suddenly she saw their faces, and blushed furiously.

"Oh, *Joshua*! You're pulling my leg *again*!"

I shrugged. "History is history, Dot, what can I tell you."

"Honestly!" She looked around. Rainey was holding her sides.

"Well, someone should go around and check on things while this big supper's going on, so it might as well be me," Dot said, pulling her black sweater closer to her body.

"Might as well," Rainey muttered. Dot walked up the hall, shaking her head.

"How about tradin' me some of your ribs for some chicken, Josh?" Wilma winked.

"No problem."

Rainey brought out a radio, turned it on, and danced to the song:

Hey, Mr. Bigstuff
Whoooo do you think you are

"Sacred portals, huh?" she laughed, winking at me.

"Sacred bullshit," Mac said, wiping her lips daintily

with a napkin and searching, "Where are those greens?"

"Food and sound, food and sound," danced Rainey, Oyster Loaf in hand.

I reached for the pecan pie, but Wilma slapped my wrist. "Finish your food first."

Mac dug into the greens.

"Lookit, ol' Mac," Wilma laughed, "Next thing, she gonna do the funkey chicken for us."

"Anything's possible," Mac smiled, without turning her eyes up from the greens.

I Looked Over Jordan

The brightness of the whiteness astonished Josh. His eyes gobbled up the Emergency Room Lobby action. The walls, the white sign announcing PLEASE REGISTER AND BE SEATED, the long hall lined with stretchers and wheelchairs— all gleamed white and silver, as hospital people dressed in vanilla moved, and had to do something. He felt like he was inside a gigantic refrigerator. Bells rang. A lady with a cold boomed out "CODE BLUE ICU CODE BLUE ICU"; and three doctors in long white coats, with the thing they listened to your chest with around their necks, sped down the hall as if racing each other.

The lack of many colors frightened Josh. He had never been in a hospital—only down the hill where he went for "checkups" at the clinic and the doctor smiled, "Well, I think you're gonna live." But now his sister was hurt. It was his fault. His sister had fallen off a swing. He had dared her to bail out. He could still see her flying through the air grinning, then landing th-ack on her arm and crumpling into a scream and his mother running over. If she died... But his mother said she wouldn't die. His Mom said she had probably just broken her arm—how *great*—*just* broken her arm —just what she needed. That's what his Mom had said driving them here, and now seeing the doctor "to make it good" his Mom had said to him, "Now you wait right here. And I mean *wait*. I don't want you getting into any more trouble— *any* more trouble, or it's no t.v. for a week. And that's just for starters, understand?" Josh had whispered "Yes". His mother had studied his face, then hugged him—he could smell her coat—and put her hands through his hair whispering, "Now your sister is very frightened, so you be good. You be my big strong man, o.k.?" and then left with his sister down the hall.

Josh looked out the plate glass window. Under a sky about to rain a black man was huffing and puffing up the hill. He looked like he was having a fight with the sidewalk, head leaning forward, hands prizefighter-held. Just as he approached the Emergency Room entrance, there was a long scream. The scream grew closer; up the Emergency Room ramp a zooming white and orange ambulance screeched to a halt, red lights flashing. The black man, startled, grabbed his hat and jumped out of Josh's vision as the doors flung open and two dark green attendants pulled out a stretchered old woman with a maroon blanket strapped around her. The two attendants rushed her into the lobby. The old woman's eyes were open and still, and, wide open, was her mouth, as if she had been about to take a bit of food and stopped. A plastic band was around her wrist. In her arm, a tube rose up into a bottle on a pole carried by one of the attendants—a young Mexican man moving fast in a semi-crouched position, concentrating on holding the pole and bottle straight. Bustling past the patients waiting to register, through the dark brown doors reading AUTHORIZED PERSONNEL ONLY, an attendant gasped over his shoulder to the clerk, "Transfer from General" as Josh leaned forward squinting. From her forearm to the bottle, the plastic moved dark and bright red. Suddenly into the lobby burst a worried-looking woman in

curlers with two small children crying, "Grandma." Josh
wondered about his grandma. His grandma was o.k. His
grandma did not have a tube in her arm or a plastic band
around her wrist. His grandma had a timex watch. His
grandma had a ring too, a red ring with a gem called car-
nelian. His grandma was o.k.

Just then the black man walked into the Emergency
Room lobby, registered, then plopped down next to Josh.

Mose was tired as hell. He wiped his face with his handkerchief, breathing deep. His lunged screamed, "Give us a
break." He was mad at himself for not taking a cab, always
having to hold onto that extra coin and not admit that nowa-
days his lungs needed a cab, even though in 61 years cabs had
not really entered the picture. The ambulance had gotten to
him bad.

Mose had a distinguished-looking face. Friends bragged,
"A face that comes right at ya," the face of a fine dark black
made lighter by age and work, like a rich sunbaked loam or
long-used ebony, only it was neither wood nor earth, but the
flesh of 61 years. Mose, as always when he came to the hospital, wore his carefully-pressed dark blue double-breasted
suit, a pink shirt (his concession to the changing times), a
light turquoise tie, and topped it all off with his black and
white checkered fedora with a green feather. He hadn't really
needed to register since the Emergency Room clerk, a home
girl from New Orleans, recognized him right away.

Yeah, the ambulance had gotten to him bad. Fear
grabbed his guts, the fear everytime he returned to remembering the night of his attack. It rushed back—passing out in his
room first feeling his lungs terribly wrong couldn't get no air
no air at all though he always kept his window open liking
fresh air. And how suddenly it seemed his whole body was
jumping on his lungs feet first, and the pain like a cable
wrapped around his chest cutting his shoulders and squeezing
like baling wire into cotton as he HAAAA KHAAA KHAA
clutched and he had called MAY even knowing somewhere his
MAY was passed away and put into the earth two years that
April clutching for her in the photograph on his night stand
as he dropped crashing the voices the pounding on the door

he smelled dust the people rushing in as he fought the no-air trying to grab that killer cable set it straight "OH LORD!" and he could smell the smelly hotel rug wool and dust "Give him air goddamit, give him air" his neighbor's faces above in the light "Call an ambulance" the astonished faces a hand under his head the "Tsk tsk" whispers "Green, it's Moses Green" as the ambulance sheets down the stairs red green lights flashed by the night the scream suddenly in the Emergency Room white and brighter lights white coats the smell of metal alcohol sheets the voice "Don't fight me old blood, you'll be all right. You may not know it now bro', but I'm here to help" and the "Get Intensive Care" "Blood gases stat" "Valium 10" and the voices went away and his two weeks in the hospital and the breathing machines and them explaining how they wanted to cut on him explore his chest take a piece of his lung (a very small piece) and check it out. "Check for what?" he'd asked, and they said check for to make sure it wasn't worse, and worse meant cancer. And his daughter flying out from Louisiana, having to take off work, and just lying there with tubes and machines, not being able to do a damn thing.

And he had what they called Chronic Obstructive Pulmonary Disease and Asbestosis. He had written it down and knew it like he knew his social security number. He'd even looked it up. And the asbestosis part—what it was was his lungs, like he had told folks years and years ago, which was what made him so goddamned mad, his lungs had gone pure rotten from the shipyards in the holds wrestling that insulation and laying that grating in the engine and boiler rooms and that white dust they all usta choke on in Biloxi his friend made a bitter joke calling it Klan Breath. That white dust was a sight worse than even they all thought 'cause once that asbestos got down there in the lungs it stayed. It stayed worse than a relation wearing out their welcome, cause the difference was you could throw them out, but that white dust stayed forever. Only supposedly no one'd known this at the time. They didn't have the information down. So that asbestos dust had stayed in his chest and worked out, hardening

up his lungs like blocking up a street so you couldn't get past.
Now he practically had to haul ass just to breathe.

And today he was to find out about his piece of lung
they'd taken and studied on.

Moses noticed next to him a thin white child staring at
the old woman from the ambulance. Mose grinned at the kid,
who, lock-eyed on the emergency room doors, suddenly
turned and regarded Mose.

"Hi."

"Lo there'."

"Is that old lady gonna die, Mister?"

"Don't rightly know, son," Mose smiled. "You
frightened?"

"No", Josh replied, "Nothing scares me. Not a stupid
hospital, that's for sure."

"I see."

"You're sick, huh?"

"I could be better."

"Are you *real* sick?"

Mose stared at the child. "What makes you think that?"

"I saw you coming up the hill. You were walking real
funny, I mean slow."

"Well now," Mose laughed, "you a regular Sherlock
Holmes."

"Uh huh," Josh grinned.

A shriek of pain came from behind the Emergency
Room doors. Josh jumped out of his seat.

"What was *that?*"

"Dunno. Pretty sick peoples behind that door, son.
Need help right away." He snapped his fingers twice. Josh
sat back down, hushed.

"You sure this place don't scare you, son?"

"Maybe a little. But they'll never get me in here."

"Oh?"

"I'll run away."

"Is that right? Where you run away to, son?"

"To the woods. I'll live on roots and berries."

Mose chuckled. He looked around.

"Know what, son?"

"What?"

"This place scares *me*!"

"Really?"

"That's right."

"Why? Are you gonna die?"

Mose trembled. His superstitious side wondered if this strange little kid wasn't meant as a sign. His experienced side laughed. A sign—a kid with a yellow sweatshirt bragging I'VE BEEN TO MAGIC MOUNTAIN, green jeans, and red and white tennis shoes. Mose chuckled to himself.

"Well, I might and I might not. I plan on living long as God sees fit."

"You could get Marcus Welby for your doctor. He'd save you."

Mose looked at the kid to see if he was teasing or not. The kid nodded with serious sympathy.

"That's on t.v., son." Mose said softly.

"Yeah," the kid nodded, "get him and Steve Kiley."

Mose shook his head, wondering.

"What's your name?" Josh asked.

"Green, Moses Green."

"That's neat. Are you related to Mean Joe Green?"

"Ha—no. But he'd be a good relative to have around."

"Moses," Josh said, as if to himself.

"And do you know about Moses, son?"

"Yeah! He led the people out of Egypt and walked through the Red Sea and he got to the promised land, but he couldn't go 'cause God said no and he was sad and he had to just watch at the river of Jordan."

"You know it real good."

"How come you got the name Moses?"

"Well, I reckon it was pretty popular down South," Mose paused, "and I guess you might say there's lots of Egypts."

"Huh!" Josh studied Moses' face, as if searching for Egypt.

Moses thought the child hadn't understood and smiled kindly at him. "Yep, you know Illinois?"

"Sure," Josh replied. He excelled at geography, leaping

at any chance to show off. "Illinois—Capital: Springfield. Biggest city: Chicago. Most people think Chicago is the capital, but it isn't—it's Springfield."

"Uh huh. And there's another town in Illinois, called *Cairo*. See?"

"Yeah," Josh said delightedly.

"And—guess what else," Mose smiled, remembering years ago a union picnic after he'd moved to the coast up outside of Reno in the mountains.

"What?"

"In Nevada there's a place outsida Reno in the country called Pyramid Lake. See?"

"Yeah!" Josh exulted.

"So, there's lots of Egypts."

"Yeah," Josh said, "but that isn't what you meant."

Mose gasped and wondered if instead of him playing with this kid the kid wasn't playing with him.

"And what's your handle, son?"

"Handle?" Josh asked, thinking: this guy is silly.

"Your name. What they call you."

"I'm Joshua," Joshua said, proudly adding, "Josh is my handle."

"Now there's a good name too. Joshua, he was something else."

"Yeah." Josh wondered if he should tell Moses his secret.

"Guess what Moses?"

"What?"

Josh leaned closer, whispering, "Sometimes I fight the battle of Jericho."

"Is that right now?"

"Wanna know how?"

"Sure. Love to hear about a good fight."

"Well, my Dad doesn't get home until 5 and sometimes even later, and my Mom she goes to school sometimes so she can get a better job and she don't get home until 5. And I get back from school at 3."

"Uh huh."

"So me and my sister fight the battle of Jericho. In the

living room.''

"In the living room. How about that.''

"I'll show you,'' Josh whispered, delighted, "even though it isn't the same here.''

"I understand.''

Rising, Josh positioned himself, bracing his body, his face assuming a ferocious expression. He bent his head low, swaying, crooning "Ohhhhhhhhhh'' slowly; then suddenly strode around the lobby darting left and right, thrusting hands out in imaginary sword thrusts as he sang: "Joshua fought the battle of Jericho-O Jericho-O Jericho-O'' With each O, he slew another enemy, thrusting his imaginary sword,

> Joshua fought the battle of Jericho-O
> And the walls came tumbling down.

He ran back breathlessly to Moses; his eyes lit up, whispering, "And when we sing 'And the walls came tumbling down', we charge the couch.'' Darting again into the middle of the lobby, Josh struck a pose and on the emphasis, flung his fist out:

> You can *talk* about your king of Abraham
> You can *talk* about your king of Saul
> But there's none like good ol' Joshua
> At the battle of Jericho — Whoa!

Mose clapped softly as a nurse bustled over.

"Little boy, you're going to have to quite down.''

"Oh.''

She was middle-aged, looked in charge, and smiled while nervously straightening her hat.

'Did you see the sign outside that says 'Quiet Zone'?''

"No.''

"Well, the hospital is a quiet place. All the sick people need their rest. And they can't rest if you make lots of noise.'' She smiled—she looked like she was going to bite him. She turned to Mose. "Isn't that right?''

"Oh, that's right. Hospital is a quiet place. Uh huh.''

The nurse minced down the hall, paused, then stopped a dark gray security guard. She whispered and motioned towards Moses and Josh, then strolled away. The guard sauntered over. He was chubby, youngish, wore an oversized hat, and seemed half-serious and half-asleep. His pants sagged, loaded down from his gun, blackjack, and handcuffs. He looked at Josh, his blue-grey eyes bored and irritable.

"You making noise, sonny?"

"No."

The guard scowled at Moses. "He with you?"

"Mm."

"Well, keep an eye on him."

"Mm."

Irked, the guard leaned down towards Josh and said, "You make any more noise and I'm gonna run you in."

Josh wanted to say, "You'll never get me copper," but thought better. In the movie on t.v. the gangster from the slums, who grew up bad because he couldn't help it and nobody loved him sneered, "You'll never get me *copper*."

Josh sat back down next to Mose, following the guard with his eyes. The guard ambled down the hall, turning into a small station where another security guard sat with a radio. They had a little police station in the hospital! Josh wondered why. Why should they have a police station in a place for sick people? Maybe there was a dope ring? That was it. A dope ring. On t.v. there had been a doctor who was a dope addict.

The security guard stared at the old man and the little pipsqueak. He wondered how to make their relationship. Kid didn't have any Negro—no, black—that's what they wanted to be called—anyway, the kid didn't have none he could tell. Maybe an inter-marriage, with the old man Gramps, or some fucking thing like that. God, he was sick of all these sick, whining, creepy people groaning, or worse—passing out, vomiting, bleeding on the floor. Thank God he didn't have to clean that crap up. He could call Housekeeping. Yeah, a shit job he couldn't ditch soon enough. He regretted screwing around so much in high school, hanging around his father's hardware store, getting such a late jump. But now he was on his way: junior college, and going on to Criminology and Sociology. But for now he had this punk $2.50 an hour. People who mopped floors got $4.50—for mopping a floor—union shit—when he could get shot by a

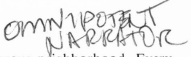

junkie, a nut. This was a dangerous neighborhood. Everybody said so. Right on the ghetto. He was damned glad he lived in a residence hall. Good guys. Life was simple. Lots of friends. Lots. But even if the old man and the kid weren't family, what in hell did they have in common to yak about?

Josh touched Mose's arm. "Are you gonna tell my Mom on me?"

"No," Mose said, surprised. "What's to tell?"

"I got in trouble."

"What you take me for," Mose snorted. "I never finked in my life and ain't about to start now."

"You like my secret?"

"It's fine."

"Moses Green—MOSE!" A young black woman dressed in white with a stethoscope around her neck smiled over. Moses rose, instinctively tipping his hat, beaming with his entire face, and it seemed like his entire body, as he took her outstretched hand. "Hey, Johnnie, hey gal."

Johnnie was a strikingly beautiful woman with a large Afro, a long full body, and a finely chiseled face marred slightly by a small scar on her left cheek. She'd told Mose it was a kiss from her first lover; his experienced eye made out a razor.

"What you doin' draggin' your carcass around here?" she smiled.

"Came to see you, what else?"

Johnnie had cared for Mose his whole time in the hospital. She reminded Mose of his daughters—sassy and sweet, and when she got mad, no bull, you did what she said and no two ways about it. He saw her face soften, like his daughters', beautiful to behold. He saw this softening often in women who worked hard. Often work made their faces hard, life made their faces hard. It was almost like a percentage, a ratio: the harder they worked, the more when they got a chance to take a breather, rest with loved ones, the more their faces turned soft and warm.

"How you been, Mose?"

"Oh, you know."

"Yeah, I know," she smiled, as if knowing better.

"Can't complain."

"How's that ol' breathing machine workin' out? How's that ol Mose Green machine?" That had been their little joke, her easing him into it, him grumbling, fussing, saying he'd be damned if he was going to be hooked up to a machine for the rest of his life.

"It's all right."

"You get your wind back so you can take me out on the town."

Mose laughed. "Awww, what you want with an old man like me? You got yourself a man. Ain't you goin' to hitch it up soon?"

"I might just do that," Johnnie grinned, "He ain't half bad. I just been waitin' to see if you got better."

"Come on," Mose laughed, clutching his side, "don't make me laugh too hard—I still got some stitches might just bust open."

"Can't have that now, can we? Who's your little partner?"

"Oh, excuse me. This here's Josh. Josh, this is Johnnie, one took care of me when I was sick here. Best nurse in the hospital."

"Hi," Josh said, squinting, "you're a nurse?"

Johnnie blushed, then smiled, and knelt down.

"Well—"

"Well now, son," Mose interrupted, "Johnnie is just the best nurse in the hospital, the healingest—"

"Mose," Johnnie frowned, then turning to Josh—"I'm an aide. I ain't a nurse yet—and might not ever be. There's a head nurse on my floor who's in charge, but," she smiled proudly, "I run the floor."

"Oh," Josh said, smiling shyly.

"Josh here fights the battle of Jericho," Moses winked, "in his living room."

"What you men wanna be fightin' all the time for?" Johnnie frowned, half-laughing.

"I'm *Joshua,*" Josh declared. "Joshua and Jericho, you know."

Johnnie's eyes twinkled. "I guess so. So you fight the

battle, huh?''

"Yeah! Wanna see?" Josh took his Jericho stance, then peeked down the hall to spot anyone in sight.

"Maybe when I get back. I got to take me a shot in here.''

"You can't get a shot. You take care of people who are sick. *You* give *them* shots.''

"Well, my little smarty man, that's true. But some dingaling upstairs threw away some dirty needles used on a hepatitis patient, and I got stuck.''

"Dingaling," Josh giggled.

"And hepatitis ain't nothin' to be messin' around with.''

"What's heptightis?" Josh asked.

"It's a bad sickness.''

"As bad as what Moses got?''

Both Johnnie and Mose grew quiet. Johnnie knelt down, whispering, "Hey, now, Mose got a bad sickness," lowering her voice, "worse than hepatitis, o.k.? Don't be askin' so many questions now. Be cool. You know how to be cool, don't you?''

"Sure," Josh smiled.

Johnnie turned to Mose, whispering, "Want me to take this kid back up with me? I can take him to the pediatrics lounge and leave a message with the receptionist here for his mother.''

"No, it's o.k.''

"Sure now?''

"It's o.k. I said.''

"All right—well—maybe I'll see you in there, or when I come out.''

"O.k.''

Just then a nurse walked over.

"Mr. Green?''

"That's me.''

"Dr. Middlebrook will see you now.''

"Well," Mose drawled, rising, "guess this is it. If I don't see you when I come back out, it's been real nice passin' the time with you.''

"You're my friend," Josh said staunchly, sticking out his hand.

Mose shook hands with the child, the kid's grip strong with affection. "See ya son." Without looking back, he strolled through the doors.

Josh watched him go. The lobby seemed shrunken. He hoped Moses would be o.k. But his Dad had come back from the hospital the time he broke his leg trying to break up a fight at his high school. Josh had been just a little kid, but he remembered his house then, as if a big part of the house disappeared.

Inside the emergency room nobody noticed Moses enter. On a nearby stretcher lay a middle-aged white woman in a waitress uniform with her chest goldenly embroidered: Hamburger Palace. She bit a pillow, her forehead sweating. From thigh to foot her exposed left leg glistened with raw circles swelling and shining like a large piece of bacon beginning to bubble and curl. Further away, a straining, struggling group of orderlies and nurses gripped an elderly Filipino man intent on jerking his entire body, his torso arching as if ready to rocket into space. An intern shouted,

"Where's that Dilantin?"

Johnnie, her sleeve rolled up, waved.

"Quit followin' me, you hound dog."

Mose grinned.

A nurse pointed. "Could you please go into room B— right there—and strip down, Mr. Green? The doctor will be in in a few minutes."

Room B was a small room with a green curtain for a door. Two big steps took Mose across the room. The walls were immaculately white, the floors cheap linoleum, the ceiling glitter-stucco. The rest of the room contained a porcelain scale, two chairs, a sink, a table, a medicine cabinet, and a chrome guerney with a white-papered leather top.

Mose took off his suit jacket, placed it on a hanger on a hook, then unknotted his tie, and draped it neatly over his jacket. He topped it off with his hat, grinning at the thin likeness, "You losin' a little weight there, ain't you?"

He sat down to wait, smiling, determined. He'd be

damned if he'd strip down 'fore the doc came. Freeze his ass off in a cold room waiting on a doc who was gonna step in later than sooner. That much Mose knew. First came the nurse with the thermometer—as if thermometers told all. He could tell them he had no fever. He always knew when fever hit. Still, he'd have to sit there like a damn fool with that thing in his mouth.

A nurse he didn't recognize popped in. "Mr. Green?"

"Uh huh."

"The doctor will be right in." She hustled over to the white table, opened a drawer, began shaking the thermometer. "Take your temperature—and he'll be right in," she smiled brightly, "and how are you feeling today?" as she stuck in the thermometer.

"Mmmff."

"I'll send Dr. Middlebrook in shortly."

Three minutes later the first nurse returned, took out the thermometer, shook and studied it all in one motion. "Well, so far so good." Her eyes fell on his clothes. Mose smiled. He could tell she was trying to figure out if she should ask him again to strip down for the doc. "Kinda drafty in here," he winked. The nurse nodded, and, caught between frowning and smiling, left. Mose, grinning, settled down.

Dr. Middlebrook moved away from the elderly Filipino man, followed by his intern and his resident. "What's next?" he asked. The intern glanced down a long writing pad full of tiny scribbled notes, names, and room numbers. "We have a burn going to room C, a possible appendectomy in D, and the asbestosis from two weeks ago. The asbestosis is ours— Green."

"Green," Middlebrook repeated dully.

"Yeah, the old guy."

Middlebrook winced.

"Ahhh," the resident smiled, "Mose the question man." That had been their nickname for Moses. The resident's eyes shone from twelve straight hours of overnight duty.

"Where's his chart?"

"Got it right here," said the intern, "Want us to see him

with you?"

"No, I'll see him myself. Why don't you and Mike check the appendectomy, then the burn. I'll come over in about twenty—wait—make it half an hour."

As Middlebrook walked off, the resident and intern began scrubbing their hands at a nearby sink. "Think he'll show him that article?" the intern asked the resident.

"I don't know. He's got enough to do in there as it is."

"It blows my mind he's even considering it."

"Well, maybe Laura jumped all over him. She does that sometimes."

"What do *you* think?"

"I don't know. You?"

"I think he should," the intern declared.

"Do you," yawned the resident.

"Yeah, it's taking a chance, but with a guy like that, you should just put it all up front."

"Maybe."

Middlebrook opened the chart, paused at the article stuck inside, and cursed. He wished that Laura, the Industrial Claims interviewer, had never given his intern the article. Why complicate things? They all knew how terrible asbestosis was. Goddamn pushy bitch. No wonder. Laura was from Detroit. He'd never met a patient person from Detroit. She knew her stuff, though—knew it, he admitted, grudgingly, better than most interns and residents. And, admitting deeper, better than most staff doctors. A clerk with a B.A. But she was definitely pushing, going beyond her bounds, xeroxing articles. Middlebrook pushed the article aside, and thumbed through the chart.

Moses Green. Middlebrook stared at the Emergency Room sheet shorthand: 61 yr. old BM with acute sob, chest pains. He turned the page to Laura's neatly typed, fully worded industrial interview:

Sixty-one year old black man presented to Emergency Room via ambulance in severe distress with acute shortness of breath and severe chest pains radiating to shoulders, arms, and back. Patient has worked on docks and shipyards for over forty years: 1930s and 1940s (early) New

Orleans, Louisiana, and Mississippi (Biloxi, Passagoula). Patient an excellent historian. In Mississippi patient worked as shipscaler and laborer in enclosed spaces in the holds of various ships, as well as in various engine and boiler rooms installing insulation and laying gratings. Both the installation material and gratings contained asbestos used for fireproofing. Patient claims there was little ventilation and constantly "clouds of white dust". Often dust was so thick patient could not see his co-workers fifteen to twenty feet away. Patient claims they were given masks at times, but that these masks did not prove adequate for any great or even consistent period of time. Patient claims that the dust was "all over the place.", often remaining in the workclothes of himself and his fellow employees.

Patient worked in the Richmond-Oakland area from 1940-1944, when he was drafted into the army. Since returning he has worked in the Hunter's Point shipyard from 1946 (approximately) to the present. Patient has worked constantly around asbestos, as well as in hot, smoky environment for over forty years.

After staring at the pathology report, Middlebrook closed the chart. He gritted his teeth. Mike rightly called Mose Green the question man. Moses reminded the doctor of a bulldog: slow, but once the teeth sank in, forget letting go. He was unlike Middlebrook's other patients, who growing obsessed with their illnesses, became pathetic experts, writing elaborate letters documenting every little creak and pimple. No, Moses was something else Middlebrook had rarely encountered. During the hospitalization, Green asked if he could "read up on it." The surprised intern told him Mose planned a trip to the library. At first Middlebrook encouraged it—give Green a focus. Soon Middlebrook found it distasteful. The man obviously had limited reading skills, reading with his finger, following words. Why struggle and strain in a library? Irked, Middlebrook felt his medical judgement doubted. True, he always wanted his patients informed, yet Moses presented a different dimension with his unending drawl, "Can you run that by me again?" asking questions when Middlebrook was behind schedule with other patients to see, never being able to spend much time with his patients in the hospital and the clinic. Middlebrook also felt he had bent over somewhat backwards for Moses, genuinely liking the man, feeling bad for him.

He suddenly noticed the clock. He'd spent five minutes thumbing through a chart he knew by heart. Cursing himself, he strode toward Room B, and pulled back the curtain.

"Hello, Moses. How are you?" Middlebrook smiled, sticking out his hand.

"Fine," Moses said, shaking Middlebrook's hand, "fine, Doc."

"Your, uh, breathing machine working out o.k.?"

"Oh yeah. I got the hang of it."

"You had it when you left."

" 'Mazin' little machine," Mose said politely, staring at the doctor, trying to read the news. Middlebrook tried to stare at Moses' forehead, and lost as if fought by a stare made of magnets. His eyes locked into Green's, and Moses, staring him straight in the eyes, knew. It was forever if it was less than thirty seconds.

"Sit down, Mose."

"I'll stand if you don't mind."

Middlebrook hid behind the chart. Despite his shirt and the white coat over it, he felt nude. He took a deep breath, and plunged.

"Your report came back positive."

"Positive? The piece of lung you took?"

"It's malignant."

As if blind, feeling for a chair somewhere, Mose pulled it over and sat down. "Lord." He breathed deep, as if he could feel by breathing the place where the cancer lived. He breathed short, labored, wondering what exact part of him breathing was full of that... A great urge gripped him—to tear off all his clothes, reach inside his lungs, and grab that malignancy out—get ahold of it—every last bit of it and tear it outta there—go deep as need be to get it all out, like blood leeches in swamp water, he wanted to get it offa himself—he shuddered—where else was it, how far was it in—he shuddered and smelled his fear—strong, sour.

"Often," he heard the doctor saying, "Often it develops in patients with asbestosis. Not always, but often."

"Not always, but often," Mose repeated.

"It's called mesothelioma—a tumor in the lining of the lungs."

"Run that by me again?"

"Meh-so-theel-i-oma," Middlebrook enunciated.

"Even sounds bad." Mose wanted to ask exactly where it was. He was being attacked. He wanted to attack back.

"Yes."

"And how much of my lungs is mesotheliomed up?"

"It's hard to tell. But it seems fairly, uh, advanced. We could try further surgery."

"Cut some more?"

"But I'd rather wait."

"And you say it's the lining of the lungs—like in a house or like a ship where the insides are rotten?"

"Something like that."

Mose thought for a minute, his hands hanging down over his knees. Could they cut it all out, or was it in there for good—sounded like for good. He sighed, "Well, I didn't really 'spect nothin' would change. I just thought... Ahhh, I don't know what I thought... Maybe some mistake..." He looked up, his eyes hopeful, "You know, maybe they got the reports mixed up or somethin' like that," knowing as he spoke there'd been no mistake in this case, but holding out, like playing a big hand with two jacks.

"I wish it was a mistake, Mose, believe me, but it's not."

The sky cracked open. The rain poured down, the windows suddenly alive with streaming water. Middlebrook tried staring out the window, but Green's eyes, with a loud silence, forced him back.

"So how long I got to live?" Mose asked softly, jutting his face forward.

"It's hard to say. A year. Maybe two. You could go on for quite a while. Sometimes there's a remission and it's longer."

"Re-what?"

"Remission. You're healthy for a spell."

"Healthy for a spell. Year or two, huh?"

"Industrial Medicine is a relatively new field."

"Mm."

"It's a relatively new field, and there's lots being done in it."

Mose nodded.

"There's new things every day. At least we'll find some ways to make you more comfortable."

"Comfortable."

"There's therapy, different kinds of therapy, treatments, medications."

Mose suddenly turned around. "But it's more or less too late. Right?"

Middlebrook winced. "Well, cancer, in particular industrial cancer, well, there's a tremendous amount of valuable work being done."

"Right?"

Middlebrook didn't answer.

"It's real late. Like, don't even bother to knock."

"I'm sorry Mose."

It was quiet. Mose rose from the chair. "Anything you want me to try out now?"

"Not right now."

"I just keep goin' like I been goin' "

"I'm sorry Mose."

"Ain't your fault."

Middlebrook rose, clutching Moses' chart. "Look, I want you to come see me next Tuesday. We'll talk more then. I'd like you to think about, well, going back to stay with one of your daughters. Being with your family."

Moses glanced sharply at him. "You mean go live in New Orleans."

"That's right. That's what I mean."

Hell, Mose snorted. He'd known that was coming. But what did this Doc know about bein' a burden, probably never worried about pulling his weight—just heal people up in time to tell them they was never going to heal up again, hold back the clock hands, palm a trump card to fool you into thinking you had more playing time plus a shot at the kitty. Don't do it, Mose, a voice warned. Don't blame. But he thought of lying in a room, getting greyer, thinner... He heard people with cancer smelled bad, had their own special smell. Soon he'd have that smell on him. No talcum powder, no cologne could keep that smell offa him. His grandchildren would remember him as the man in the room who smelled bad. He, who at the bottom line, showered daily. His face twisted. He felt like he could puke for a thousand years.

The rain streamed down. A car went by with its lights on even though it was only four o'clock in the afternoon.

"Well, think about it, Moses. And we'll talk more about it next Thursday."

"I'll think on it."

Middlebrook pretended to study a chart. Moses dressed, fixing his tie, knotting it carefully, slipping into his suit jacket.

"Mose."

"Uh huh."

"How'd you get here?"

"Bus."

"I'm going to write you out a taxi voucher. Just present it to the clerk outside, and they'll have a taxi take you home."

"Thanks."

Middlebrook watched Mose put his hat on, stroke the green feather for luck, and slowly walk out to the Emergency Room lobby. When Moses was out of sight, Middlebrook went over the the sink, splashed cold water on his face, slicked his hair back, and, plopping down in a chair, took out the article.

Well, he hadn't given Green the article. His serious doubts seemed justified. What Moses needed now was rest and support. That's why he recommended Green return to New Orleans—he had family, lots of friends, and could be treated at any one of several excellent medical facilities. It was not at all necessary to show him the article. He had taken things, on the whole, very well. Just as, a voice inside him whispered, thousands of other Moseses walking around not knowing what they had would take it once the disease burst out in them. Middlebrook grabbed the article and began leafing through it angrily.

The asbestos industry still in its infancy in the early 1900s began its rapid growth during the post World War I construction and automobile booms of the 1920s. During the 1930s the John Mansville Company, giant of the U.S. asbestos industry, began developing a strategy that was to serve it well for 30 years... weave asbestos into the matrix of the economy so that it would become indispensable... fund medical research that would discredit reports of asbestos hazard...

Such control galled Middlebrook — that medicine could be interfered with in such a manner. He read on:

Asbestos insulation for ships came into widespread use during the shipbuilding boom of World War II, endangering several million shipyard workers. Today the estimated 30,000 industrial uses for asbestos include products as varied as insulation for Apollo space rockets, roof shingles, siding, brake lining, clutch facing, linoleum, electric wire casing, draperies, rugs, floor tiles, ironing board covers, potholders, and fireproof clothing...

John Mansville sales grew from 40 million in 1925 to 685 million in 1971. Today asbestos manufacturing employs 50,000 people... Insulation workers in the building trades number 40,000, and an estimated 5 million people work daily with asbestos containing products...

Middlebrook went on to the part that grated him the most:

In 1929 Metropolitan Life Insurance Company was commissioned by asbestos industry to conduct a study of asbestosis... Medical examinations were conducted on a total of 126 asbestos workers... Sixty-seven of the 126 workers examined were classified as positive cases of asbestosis, 39 doubtful, and only 20 as completely free of any sign of asbestosis. On their face, these figures represented an epidemic of disease. Calculated as percentages, the findings showed 53 percent of the workers having asbestosis, 84 percent with some signs of the disease (positive plus doubtful), and only 16 percent with no signs of asbestosis at all. However, the authors did not publish these percentages. They simply listed the number of workers in each category and hurried on without comment... In addition to minimizing the incidence of the disease, the authors also played down its severity. They dismissed workers' complaints of coughing, shortness of breath, typical early symptoms of asbestosis, with the response, "Too much emphasis should not be placed on statements of subjective symptoms."

By 1942 other case studies followed, showing that asbestosis victims suffer a high incidence of lung cancer. Two scientists from Saranac dismissed the conclusion, because, they argued, asbestosis victims might be especially susceptible to lung cancer. What was clearly called for was a large-scale plant wide study, in which workers employed at some particular date were followed for a period of years. . . In fact, it was not until twenty-one years later that the study was performed. In the interim the Saranac paper was industry's proof that no link existed between asbestosis and lung cancer.

By 1960 medical research on asbestos was at a watershed. A total of 63 papers on the subject had been published in the U.S., Canada and Great Britain. The 52 papers not sponsored by industry, mostly case histories and reviews of case histories by hospital and medical school staff, indicated asbestos as a cause of asbestosis and lung cancer. The 11 papers sponsored by the asbestos industry presented polar opposite conclusions. . . The difference was dramatic—and obviously dependent on the doctor's perspective. . .

Middlebrook put the article down, breathing rapidly. Perhaps the writer knew Laura. Much of the article he knew. The rest was familiar too—the 1972 asbestos hearings, the fine work being done in New York, some other places. Everyone in the field was coming to know about it. But what if he showed Green the article and Green sued? Malpractice? Could he claim he hadn't been warned or told until too late? No, the odds were against Green suing his employer—the government, or the hospital. But, a voice whispered, what if he hooks up with a lawyer? How could a man like him meet one of those ambulance chasers? Friends, contacts. In the hospital Moses' room overflowed with people. The man knew people by the carloads it seemed—from his union, his church, his hotel. And what if he just raised hell? He seemed quite capable of that. Hadn't he called Middlebrook's office daily since leaving the hospital to find his biopsy results, forcing Middlebrook to see him in the Emergency Room? Yes, Moses might raise hell. Still waters ran deep. Dying people changed, often drastically. Some shrank, withdrawing. Some grumbled, cranky, irritable. Others raged. Which was Moses?

Suddenly his mind saw Moses' face when he suggested exploratory surgery—Moses nodding, "See if you can't arrange to put me under local—so's I can watch the whole thing." Middlebrook tried to tell him over and over that the operation was way too painful. Moses persisted, "I just don't like the idea of bein' under. I want to see whatcha all doin' and follow it." They compromised. Middlebrook said, "If there's too much pain, we put you under," knowing full well the pain's intensity. Yet Green astonished them, lasting a frighteningly long time before they put him out. Impulsively, Middlebrook rose,and clutching the article, strode toward the lobby to find Moses. He stopped at the door.

Suppose Green sued? A California asbestos worker won a settlement for 400,000 dollars. Suppose Middlebrook's colleagues scorned and jeered him? He pictured Fitch, the Medical Chief, staring like an amused iceberg, "So you showed him an article, article from where? *Science for the People*—what's that? Documented? Who wrote it? Where'd he intern? Where'd he do his residency? What Medical Center is he with?" Middlebrook scanned the article. The writer didn't even have an M.D. after his name. At the very least... The hell with it. He opened the door. At the very least he should write the magazine—he looked at the masthead, then glanced inside to a Cambridge, Massachusetts address. He imagined Fitch sneer, "Harvard radicals! What else!" Definitely, he would have to write, somehow verify the report's veracity. There were no two ways about it. To give Moses the report would only disturb the little time left. He also needed to take into account that the man was dying—a big subjective factor. Besides, Mose could raise a stink, misinterpreting his treatment. Why it could possibly border on unprofessional conduct. He'd been crazy to consider it. His hand seemed frozen on the doorknob.

"Dr. Middlebrook?" A nurse studied him curiously.

"Yes?"

"Dr. Wagner wants a consult on a patient up on 7."

"I'll be there shortly. Thank you."

And to a certain extent one could say Moses knew the job's risks. He knew the dust was bad for years. Granted, many workers in industry incurred illness, but look at their salaries. Some earned more than interns and residents. Street-sweepers made 14,000 dollars a year! For sweeping a street! Some even lived in the suburbs, although Middlebrook held nothing against blacks living in the suburbs—blacks or anyone else for that matter. Some of them worked extremely hard for their money. But any profesion and trade entailed risks. And medicine was not, Middlebrook frowned furiously, required to perform miracles. Doctors were not medicine men with fetishes, but scientists. It was so easy for some interns and the world's Lauras to wax idealistic, and boldly believe in hiding nothing from the patient, jarring the entire doctor-patient relationship that hung on such a delicate thread in the first place. Well, they'd learn. He'd learned. They wanted to risk scrapping the vital objectivity without which they would crack. He'd seen it, seen the doctors who left themselves overly vulnerable, who lost insight, clarity, distance. Some drank. Others grew overly fond of Demerol. Still others burnt out, grew overwhelmed, demoralized, unable to realize they were just one person in a growing and difficult field. Why for their own health . . . Middlebrook stood there with his hand froze on the doorknob.

*   *   *   *   *

As Moses slowly walked into the Emergency Room lobby, he ran into Johnnie.

"You still followin' me?" She stopped, seeing his face. "Mose?"

He recognized her, and stared, his eyes full.

"Place plays a mean hand, chile," he whispered hoarsely, "turned me up the ace of spades."

Although she was standing right next to him, Johnnie had to lean closer to hear him, and hearing him, her heart filled up into her eyes, aching. She took his hand. His hand was big, extraordinarily calm. Moses smiled, his eyes still full. "You tell your man to hitch it up soon so's I can come and make sure everything run smooth." Johnnie nodded, trying to control her face. Mose touched the green feather of his hat. "Remember me tellin' you I was shop steward for nine years and deacon of the church for seven? You know I know how to keep things runnin' smooth."

Johnnie nodded, "I'm sure you do, Mose."

"I rate. They callin' me a taxi."

She nodded again, feeling her face muscles tremble. Mose shook her shoulders gently, grinning, "You send me the invite and take care of yourself."

"All right," she said, feeling small, forcing a grin, adding, "but you gonna have to rent a tux." She watched him go, then quickly turned into the Emergency Room, stumbled past a nurse into an empty room, and leaned against a wall.

*   *   *   *   *

Moses found Josh reading *U.S. News and World Report* upside down. As soon as Josh spotted Mose, his eyes lit up. He dropped the magazine.

"You're back!" Josh smiled enthusiastically, then stopped, seeing Mose sink into a chair.

A young teenager entered. Rainy wind blew a smell of wet sidewalk and cold air. The teenager had a radio growing out of his ear; the song too seemed to come in from the rain:

> Yeah, well I heard it in the Want Ads
> Extra Extra read all about it

Mose gazed past the big glass window. Wrong song. He wasn't a young man. No one would want him. A blue-white neon sign announced: EMERGENCY ROOM ENTRANCE.

"You're not feeling better?" Josh asked softly.

Moses grunted.

"You feel bad, huh?"

Mose replied as if with his whole body, as if hearing an old deep song:

> All of me
> Why not take all of me?

"I feel *blue*."

"Blue."

"BL-OOOOO. On Moses' lips the bl sounded like blood blurted, the oooo like someone crying without caring who heard, or the end of a disappearing train in the country late at night.

Josh had heard of feeling blue before, but suddenly his eyes lit up. *Feel* like a *color*!

"Yeah," he marveled, mulling it over, "when I'm happy sometimes I feel, I feel, uhh, orange." Josh beamed. "Yeah, I feel *orange!*"

Moses stared at the kid, as if finally recognizing him. Orange! Orange! He felt like the kid had walked into his house uninvited. Orange!

Josh thought he had done something wrong. He couldn't figure out what or why—maybe Moses didn't like orange. He sense a deep sadness. "Didn't the doctor fix you up?"

"Sorta," Mose muttered.

"What's wrong with you?"

"I got bum lungs."

"How'd you get your lungs bummed?"

Mose laughed, shortly. "I got my lungs bummed 'cause my job."

"Were there bad people there?" Josh frowned.

"Yeah, you could say that. But it mainly was this stuff I worked with, these particles and dust and stuff."

"What's particles?"

"Well, let's see." Mose thought, scratching his head. He looked at the rain. "Well, particles is like little bits, kinda like raindrops only they ain't wet and they don't fall outta the sky. Sometimes you can't see 'em, 'cept they's part of the dust."

"You mean dust like when you don't sweep the floor?"

"No, lemme see now—you ever go out to the country

with your family?''

"Yeah."

"Well, you know how when you go up a dirt road you look behind and the air is all brown from the dust, and you can't see nothin' in back?''

"Yeah."

"Well, that's what it was like where I worked most of the time.''

"Oh, did you work on a dirt road?''

"No, son. Where I worked *inside* was like working on a dirt road outside, far's the dust full up with particles.''

"Oh, I get it.''

"Good.''

"But what's particles got to do with you having bummed lungs?''

"Well, these particles got in my lungs. And they ain't never comin' out.''

"Ecccchh!''

"Exactly.''

"They must have tasted awful,'' frowned Josh, scrunching up his face.

"Yeah, that dust leaves a bad taste, all right.''

"And *then* what happened?''

"Well, the particles bummed up my lungs.''

"Lungs?''

Mose looked at him angrily. "C'mon, you know what those are? You got two of 'em, left and right. They pump the air. Sorta like a music box — you know.''

"*Music* box?''

Mose made music with his hands, squeezing two imaginary ends. 'Like so.''

"Hmmm.''

"Music box, or an accordion. You know? They play 'em at weddings? It's black and white, you carry it on your back, and you put both arms around to play it.''

"Yeah.''

"Well, that's what lungs do—go in and out, back and forth—only they pump air, not music.''

"And they're right here,'' Josh said, striking his chest.

"That's right. One on each side. Hopefully."

"That's my chest. I got a chest. My sister and Mom got titties."

"That's right too, son," Mose smiled, his eyebrows raised, "Men's different than women's." Josh giggled.

Mose stared out into the rain. Yeah, there had been some "bad people." In Mississippi over half the foremen were in the Klan. The boss man you never saw because the boss man was Uncle Sam—or as the joke ran with some— little boss man Sam and the shipping companies run Sam. But there were good people too, and staring out into the rain, Mose remembered—Thomas, Gordon, Hayes, Jones, Stokes, Robinson, Bob and Lee, wondering if they were still around. Yeah, then they lived for any job. Work in the shipyards was steady money, and more, a lifetime of security. Everyone would give you that. You walked with pride and respect when you spoke to folks, "I work for the government," or "Yeah, he got that government job,"—a lifetime of security, respect.

"So, it was dusty?" he heard Josh saying.

"Yeah." And he remembered writing stuff up, sweating over grievances. It was hard work and in all the places whether it was just an on-the-spot committee or a company union or a union that was what a union was supposed to be and even out here they finally moved on cleaning things up, a man in a suit arrived to check dust levels.

Some of the younger men shouted, "Levels! Levels! Are you crazy? Just look around, man! Ain't no levels! It's damn near solid!" cracking, "What you gonna do? Take a tape measure to it?"

The suited expert smiled, clucking, "I hear you. I hear you," explaining how they didn't understand. Certain levels were hazardous and they were trying to get the hazard level down to two asbestos fibers per cubic centimeter—that was progress, a standard to be *enforced*. This, as opposed to five asbestos cubic centimeters they'd been working with for years. The Joker walked up, shook hands with the expert, smiling, "Appreciate it, man, you savin' my life, you really are." The expert smiled gratefully as the Joker added, "But

what about these older brothers? Whatcha got for them?''
The expert started talking about yearly checkups and
disability forms.
   "Why didn't they clean it up?" Josh asked.
   "Good question, son."
   Many of them hadn't even been told. They knew it was
some bad shit. While back once a bunch of them had decided
to write a letter to Roosevelt. Roosevelt would understand.
They worked hard on the letter:

> We, employees of the Oakland-Richmond area, feel it
> is ironic that while we build Liberty ships for the freedom
> fight, we are subjected to hazardous conditions...

   And many resented signing. Some refused outright.
Others, astonished, pointed out, "Be glad you have a job
period." Others said it was the least they could do for the war
effort—put up with a little dust. Still others argued, "Next
thing you'll be wantin' a Cadillac pickin' you up at your
house." Mose argued with one Church board member who
called him Judas. Boy, he had to turn the other cheek that
time, and told him real good no he was not a Godless man. It
was just God had a whole lot to do, and you couldn't just sit
on your hands and let God do it all the time. Sometimes,
maybe more times than most folks knew, He needed some
helping out. Mose had gotten too hot—he admitted it later
—but he would be damned if he would stand by and see
brothers and sisters hack and choke to death, war or no war,
job or no job. Word got out; they laid him off to teach him a
lesson. He'd wound up going overseas—not that he hadn't
been ready to go. He fought with honor, and when he
returned they'd been sorta forced to take him back, although
they dropped him down to laborer, shooting down the tubes
eighteen years of seniority.
   And it had taken another twenty years to get to where he
got to try for a welding spot. In the late sixties after Detroit
and Watts burned to the ground they looked around and
asked him to take the welding test and his friends jeered,
"About time" and "Overdue". When he passed (having
done the job for years at laborer's pay), they wrote him up in

the newsletter—the employee of the month, a pillar of the community, all just before his cough worsened, worse than anything May had been able to do with her teas roots and barks which kept him o.k. for years and helped keep the cough down to where he figured it might even quit.

"Why didn't they give you a mask?" Josh asked.

"A mask?" Mose drawled, dreamily.

They had. Cheap little masks amounting to nothing but a filter on the face. They spent more time unclogging the dirt and dust out of it than in actually wearing it. He'd tried every which way to fix it to keep the dust out: he'd plugged cotton into it, and took pliers and squeezed the metal squares tighter to keep the dust out. When exasperation set in, Mose made folks laugh by taking off his mask and mock-walking out the door, declaring, "Be back 'bout half an hour. Got to go over to the five-and-ten and pick me up another one of these". The fellas cracked up, adding, "That's the truth too," and "Listen to the man," and "Take mine with ya."

And the time his best friend Carver cracked them all up when he came in with a Halloween goblin mask, saying he'd found himself a double duty mask to keep the dust out and scare off all the evil spirits. The foreman hadn't thought Carver was too funny, threatening to send him home, but then the man couldn't take a joke noways. Mose sidled over, smiling, "Can't send Carver home"—real soft— "I'm Carver's ride, and if he leaves, then I'll have to leave too 'cause I'm the one he's dependin' on to get home." Several of the other fellas had come over and sort of surrounded the foreman, smiling, saying, "Yeah, we'd have to go too 'cause we came with Mose." The foreman glared, "Are you threatening me?", and Mose said softly, "No, it's strictly a transportation problem."

"Moses?"

He saw Josh's face staring at him.

"Sorry, son, I was off somewhere."

"Are you all right?"

"Sure."

"Why didn't they give you a mask?"

Moses laughed, thinking of Carver again. "That's a

good question. That's a great question. Fact, that's the question of all questions." He laughed again, a big gut laugh, full, edged.

"How come?"

"Son, you sure ask alot of questions." Mose realized it was not exactly some game this child was playing. Not exactly. He also wanted to know. Some kids just kept asking away to tease. Or like when his own daughters, anxiously wanting to be soothed to sleep asked just to hear his voice and know their father was there and everything was all right. Yeah—there was something too of this in Josh asking all these questions.

"How come?" Josh persisted.

How come? How come he was dying? How come he'd fought the good fight 61 years trying to do as his Ma and Pa raised him—to do right and do in wrong? And how he had always fought against bitterness, especially making a point to find good in all, telling people how bitterness was a dead-end street—get you nowhere but in a trash can if you don't love your fellow man. Yeah, bitterness is like a termite—it eats the foundation of your house. It's like a big lemon—make your face small and your body small. Yet how many times had he heard the angry voices, the wailing voices, the stunned voices, and the clenched teeth voices: why? how come? HOW COME? WHY? NO! Like when his daughters had gone to Mississippi with his and May's blessings, when Malcolm was shot, Medgar Evers, Luther King, why? And the many people he knew, folks known only to family, kin, neighbors, shot at, fired, hounded, driven out of town, out of a neighborhood, a job, and trying to keep going like the song One More River To Cross, just wanting to get it done if it could be done by getting people with people.

"They gave Kojak a mask," Josh stated.

Moses stared at the child.

"See, there was this guy and he worked in a place like you, Moses, where it was dusty and hot and lots of noise. Well, he got in with this wrong crowd of bad guys, you know—"

"Kojak," Moses muttered.

"Yeah, and these bad guys were blackmailing him 'cause he killed this guy by accident and they saw it and he didn't think anybody would believe him because he'd been in prison for something he did dumb when he was a kid and the guy got in with these bad guys even though he didn't want to, but see he had a real sick wife, she was in the hospital even and he really loved her and they had a little girl—"

Often Mose worked extra hard to save for his daughters so they could get that education, and now he pointed with pride to one daughter nursing in New Orleans, Doris, and another, Rainey, teaching in Baton Rouge, even though Rainey had had to fight to get the Baton Rouge job, and his Doris told stories about some patients and doctors in New Orleans still seeing a black nurse as if belonging in maid service or the kitchen, as Doris, a spitting image of May, grinned, "Guess they're not *accustomed* to seeing a black woman without a mop and bucket, but *I'll* change *that*," yeah, and he'd seen change come a long long ways, yet when he saw mobbed buses in Boston he feared yesterday returning.

And staring at Josh for a minute he remembered Emmet Till and Little Rock, wondering why was it they always went after the children, working them over as soon as they were ready to walk almost? Was it to let them know early where they stood in life—sock it to them quick, or was it that plus more—that cowards prefer children?

"And this guy drove a truck for this plant, and the bad guys told him to keep his eyes and trap shut, and they didn't tell him they were smuggling heroin into the plant in his truck, but he had a best friend who ate lunch with him *every* day and he got wise and saw the bad guys and investigated, and they caught him and said he was too smart for his own good—"

Too smart—yeah, there had been the time he designed, on his own time, what Carver called the Green Dust Bowl— a machine to remove the dust from the air, especially from the engine and boiler rooms, since the blower machine there, supposed to help, only spread dust everywhere. Moses designed a machine on the vacuum cleaner effect—a dust-sucker. He showed the blueprint around. May was proud. The men admitted, "Looks good," adding, "if it works."

He gave it to the foremen, who came back later and quietly said, "Supe wants to see you in his office."

The Supe, sitting behind his huge oak desk, studied the blueprint, his face serious.

"Sit down, Green, sit down."

The Supe muttered, then suddenly looked up. "What's your classification?"

"Laborer."

There was a silence. The Supe's eyes narrowed. "Not draftsman?"

Mose stared at him. The Supe's face reddened. "I said —not draftsman?"

"No." And in his mind: "Not yet."

"How about inventor?"

"No."

"So you're not a relative of Thomas Edison?"

"Mm."

The Supe lit an Old Gold cigarette, puffed, snapped the match into the ashtray, and blew smoke angrily.

"Green, we pay you to install grating and installation." He blew more smoke, then pointed to the blueprint. "We don't pay you for this."

"I know," Mose stated, "I just thought—"

"That is precisely my point," interrupted the Supe, his voice even, "you thought. We don't pay you to think." His eyes narrowed. "We pay you to use common sense." He ground out the cigarette into the ashtray. "And to my way of thinking, for you those are two different things."

Mose stared, feeling a tremendous urge to grab the desk at both ends, and shove the desk and the Supe across the room, through the wall, and let the devil ride him out the rest of the way.

"Got it Green?"

"Got it."

"Good. You can go."

Mose looked at the blueprint on the desk, then looked at the Supe.

"I'll just hold onto this for a while," said the Supe.

"And anyway, they really fixed his friend who was too smart—a beam fell on his head and killed him on the spot. You knew 'cause they all ran over and they said, 'Don't look', so you knew it was real gooshy, and then the guy who loved his sick wife and killed the other guy by accident he got real mad 'cause this guy was his pal and he called up Kojak and told him everything and wanted justice for his friend—"

Mose remembered those sudden deaths: a crane on overload, a snapped cable, a heap of razor-sharp metal in oil, the screams, the running the rushing a mass of blood, the "JESUS!", and the hospital the sirens the faces: a wife, a child, a brother, mother, girlfriend; the services, Rock of Ages, We Shall Gather By The River, and he'd stood like a rock all these years not knowing inside the rock—HA!— dust piled up inside a mask those masks pieces of tin chicken- wire for all the good—

And he remembered the piece of writing—Langston Hughes' "Minstrel Man", his daughter Rainey'd showed him once, touching him deep, and he had her type it out for him and he'd put it to memory:

> Because my mouth
> is wide with laughter
> and my throat is deep with song
> You do not think
> I suffer after
> I have held my pain so long
> Because my mouth
> is wide with laughter
> you do not hear
> my inner cry
> because my feet
> are gay with dancing
> you do not know
> I die

Only he hadn't wanted to die, didn't want to die, wanted LIFE, and he felt his bile like a river rise up his throat   a mask and now he had a machine to breathe with to put over his face one more thing to put on the face   another mask   the

mask you wore when they said go slow   the mask when they
said hey you   the mask when they said get out   and even the
mask when he fought at times wishing damn wish I could rest
knowing he'd get none til this fight was finished nor would
that end it for sure   and he'd never minded facing something
straight out   but something that hiding crept and snuck up
that waiting snuck around snuck up slowly   what kind of
face—like the Klan like this mesothelioma—what kind of
face was that that had no face.

"Soooo, when Kojack came to investigate, they gave
him a mask. So why didn't they give you one, Moses?"

And he found himself shaking in the middle of the lobby,
standing full height, heard his voice taking over the entire
area: "THEY NEVER GIVE YOU A MASK, OH THEY GIVE YOU
WHAT THEY WANT YOU TO WEAR, BUT IT AIN'T YOUR FACE,
IT AIN'T EVER YOURS THEY GIVE YOU NOTHING THEY GIVE
YOU SHIT AND DON'T YOU EVER FORGET IT!"

Josh's mouth dropped as if a river crashed over the falls
and the full-force fury smacked him full-face. He saw Moses'
eyes: full, powered, flowing, the thick arms outstretched.

The security guard ran down the hall, hat flopping. A
few waiting patients backed up, others froze. Josh, staring
open-mouthed, knew something awful had happened to
make Moses with his whole body like that, only Josh didn't
know what to say or do.

The security guard grabbed Moses, "Easy now,
fella—". Mose, turning, gritted, "Get your hands offa me,"
pushing the guard back like a sack.

The guard, knocked backwards, thought, "He's run
amuck! He pushed me!" Frightened by Moses' strength, he
grabbed his blackjack from his back pocket as he saw Loyd,
the black security guard, running, motioning. He raised the
blackjack; Mose grabbed the guard's wrist, powerfully
wrenching, the force pulling the guard across Moses' body.
The blackjack flew against a wall and bounced off, clattering
down the hall. Mose hooked a fast left to the guard's belly.
The grunting guard caught his gut with his hands, jutting his
jaw forward just as Mose threw a roundhouse right catching
the guard square in the jaw and dropping him.

The black security guard grabbed Mose, "Easy now, man, easy, hey!"

"You leave my friend alone!" Josh yelled, pushing on the guard.

"Easy now, easy."

For a second the dumped guard groped for his gun, but Johnnie, another aide, an intern, and several patients broke it up in a swarm of arms, coats, and faces. The two guards left down the hall as Johnnie's voice soothed Moses, "It's me, Mose, me, Johnnie, c'mon now, let's sit down Mose."

Mose gasped, gripping Johnnie's arm; he felt like he'd swallowed fifty razors. "They don't give you shit."

"You're right, baby, hundred percent right," Johnnie soothed, "just set right down here," and her voice faroff, "go on folks, it's all over. No, I got him—no need for a doctor. He's fine. He's all right."

Josh sat down at the far end of the lobby. It was all his fault. His Mom would be furious. Mose would be mad. Johnnie too. The police might arrest him. They were probably drawing up charges right now: interfering with an officer, assault maybe—he had pushed the guard! They'd put handcuffs on, take him Downtown, book him, do fingerprints. Then the mug shots—three pictures, his face, left and right side. Well, he would tell them nothing. Maybe he should make a run for it. Run home. But his Mom would worry. He sat, quietly.

Johnnie took Moses' handkerchief from his breast pocket and wiped his face. "You o.k.?"

"Yeah," Mose blushed, gasping for breath, "I'm fine, just fine."

"What you tryin' to do—train to fight Ali? You gonna go to Zaire?"

"Never been to Africa," Mose laughed.

"Me neither," Johnnie smiled. She looked over to Josh. "And how are you?"

"Fine," Josh answered, "just fine."

Moses squinted at him. "What you sittin' over there in the boondocks for?"

Smiling, Josh rose, came over, and sat down next to

Mose and Johnnie.

"It's o.k. for me to sit here?"

"Sure it's o.k."

Through the door strode a slickered cabbie, his raincoat streaming. "There a Green here?"

"There's my ride. Yeah, here," Mose motioned, rising. Johnnie still held his arm. "Hey, you sure you're o.k. now? We can ask him to come back, or you can wait for another one."

"No, I'm fine. Really."

"O.k., then, you take care of yourself, Mose."

Mose nodded, then looked at Josh. "Well, son," and couldn't think of a thing to say. He smiled and thought for a second, and grinned, "Thanks for helpin' me out."

"You're gonna be all right?"

"Sure am."

"You have friends?"

"Lots."

"Know what?"

"What?"

"I got a book at home. It's my book. No one else's. When I get home I'm gonna put your name in it."

Moses turned to Johnnie. "You hear that?" He smiled to himself. "Well now, you do that. You do that and you gonna beat St. Peter to the punch."

"I am?"

"That's right. 'Cause if and when I make it up to heaven, St. Peter's the one puts your name down—so they say—so's to make sure you got a room. Only the thing of it is is that you'll beat him out 'cause you'll have my name down first."

"Yeah," Josh smiled.

"Take care son."

" 'Bye, Moses."

Josh watched Johnnie escort Mose out, staring as Mose, moving slowly, crouched into the wet cab. The cab slid out of the neon light. Josh watched until he couldn't see the head-lights' beam. Turning, he saw his mother and sister down the hall. The security guard was talking to his Mom. She quickened her pace, furious. Rachel was trying to keep up, her arm white and huge.

"What have you been up to?"

"Nothing," he replied, half-hoping.

"Don't nothing me! I heard you were in a fight! Nothing! And you upset that man who just left! I *told* you." She suddenly realized that everyone in the lobby was watching her. "Oh, take these keys and get in the car. And put your hood up. Can you do that? You think you can walk to the car without all hell breaking loose?"

"Yeah."

"*What?*"

"Yes, Mom."

She gripped his shoulder. It hurt. "Get in that car and don't let me hear a peep out of you." Josh left, silently.

*   *   *   *   *

Johnnie started back to her floor, then turned, looking at Josh's mother.

"Is that your boy?"

"Yes," Josh's mother sighed, "I'm sorry if he caused any trouble."

Johnnie smiled her special smile. "That's a fine son you got there. Little wild maybe, but a fine son."

"Why, why thank you," Josh's mother said, puzzled.

"Little incident. No big thing. Your son did right— overall."

"Well, but—" Josh's mother started to ask more of Johnnie who was already walking down the hall. Josh's mother shook her head, then took Rachel's hand, "Come. Let's go home."

Johnnie passed the security guard-room. The guard, rubbing his jaw, glared. "I'm writing you up," he sneered. Johnnie's eyes leveled on him. "That's a dying man you hassled back there, hero."

"Dying?" whined the guard, rubbing his jaw.

"That's right," she snapped, stepping closer. "Go ahead, write me up. I'll just add it to all my other ones. And don't forget—I can write too, sucker. I can write about you attacking a patient. Don't think for a minute I can't write *that*."

"You interfered and obstructed."

"Ooooo—you're so *bad*." She leaned closer, and stuck her finger at him. "Look. That's my patient. Don't you ever, *ever*, mess with my patients."

"You talk big now. We'll see what your supervisor says."

"I don't give a good goddamn what she says. You can tell the whole world for all I care." Walking away, she stuck her behind out, and slap-patted it. "Put *this* in your report."

The black security guard followed her. "Easy, sister."

"Don't worry about me, and don't sister me. Just keep that jerk outta my face, and keep on protectin' this place from all the ba-aad dyin' folks." Johnnie kept right on walking.

*   *   *   *   *

Josh's mother, after putting Rachel in the back seat, watched Josh stare down the street. She still couldn't understand why the aide mentioned her son so warmly. Well, they were all tired. She'd wait until they got home. She just wanted to get home, eat, and take a nice hot bath.

"Hi Josh," Rachel smiled.

Josh looked at his mother.

"Go ahead, talk to your sister."

"Hi Rach."

"Lookit. The doctor gave me his autograph." She held out her cast.

Inscribed in red magic marker an autograph read: To My Favorite Bravest Patient, Rachel. Your Friend, Dr. Aaron Blake.

"See?" Rachel grinned.

"Neat," Josh yawned.

"I have to wear this a long time."

"Yeah."

"Then I have to come back and they'll take it off and my

arm will be all new.''

"Yeah,'' Josh yawned.

Toward evening at the small house in Visitation Valley, the whole family was exhausted—Josh, his mother, and Rachel from the day at the hospital, and Josh's dad from all-day conference about the schools—he was teacher representative for his high school. After coming home, Josh had been immediately sent to his room. Rachel took a long nap after Josh's dad, calling her his "walking wounded,'' insisted on signing the cast. Then Josh's mother and father talked.

"No t.v. for a week seems pretty stiff, honey.''

"He's got to learn.''

"True, but it sounds from what you've told me that more happened that we don't know about.''

"I guess. I'm just beat.''

"So, you want to keep him in his room all evening.''

"He can have dinner! Christ, I'm not an ogre!''

"Well, why not let him watch some t.v. and I'll talk with him in the morning.''

"Now that's what you always do. Reverse my decisions. You'll spoil him silly.''

"Ahh, c'mon.''

Tired, she relented, telling herself this was the last time. Surprisingly, Josh didn't want to watch television. He barely spoke during dinner.

"Something is definitely going on,'' his father said, loading the dishwasher.

"He's overwrought.''

Josh went up to his room after dinner. At different times, his father and mother drifted upstairs to check on him. Josh's father spotted him deep in concentration at his desk. His mother, passing, heard Josh softly singing. They later found Josh asleep fully clothed on the bed. Undressing him, they put on his pajamas, pulled back the covers, and tucked him in. On his desk the special birthday diary they'd given him had a page torn out, crumpled up, then uncrumpled with a concerted attempt to smooth it out. On the page was printed neatly:

when Israel was in Egipt land
let my peeple go
oprest so hard they cood not stand
let my peeple go

Underneath it was printed: Josh is stupid. Josh is dumb. This
was all lightly crossed out. In the book, on a fresh page, carefully printed in big words was a single sentence, all in caps:
I MET A MAN TODAY. All over the rest of the page was a name
printed in different sizes, and a few attempts at script:
MOSES.

*   *   *   *   *

Before going back to his motel, Mose stopped off to buy
some food. He saw a family bustling about, and felt a warm
surge, remembering Josh. A great urge gripped him to see his
daughters, his sons-in-law, and, especially, his grandchildren.

Walking through the rain, he reached his hotel, holding
a medium-sized paper bag containing a chuck steak, spinach,
rice, and apples. The hotel sign gleamed wetly on and off:
REGENCY. He entered the lobby and waved to the few folks
sitting in the old armchairs and reading magazines near the
potted plants, then took the elevator up to his studio. The
hallway was chilly. Mose checked the thermostat—it was all
the way down. He scowled and turned up the thermostat,
muttering, "A sick man deserves a little warming up."

Entering his room, he put down the brown bag and
stretched out on his sofa. Through his window he could still
see the rain: softer, still steady. Sitting up, he took out his
wallet and began thumbing through the pictures of his
daughters, their husbands, and his grandchildren. A song
came to mind:

Well I'm walkin' to New Orleans
Yes I'm walkin' to New Orleans

Through the walls someone coughed. Mose shivered. What
held him here? May was gone. True, he had many friends,
especially Carver, him and Carver'd come a long ways together. He had many friends in New Orleans too, plus family.
He rose as if trying to grab at something. Scratching his head,

he went over to his refrigerator and took out a can of Malt Liquor. He opened the top and sat back down, sipping. Yeah, he had lots of friends. Words flashed in his mind. Friends. Were there bad people on your job? Dust and particles. Friènds. He stood up suddenly, as if in shock.

He remembered two years ago, a man his own age— Flood, Carl Flood—who suddenly took ill and three months later died. He hadn't known the man well, worked in another section, but he knew Flood did installation work. Other instances poured into his memory. He placed the can down on the table. What had happened to all the men he'd worked with? Beyond the "tests" and occasional checkups? They had gotten x-rayed. Mose had told everyone he knew to get x-rayed, but x-rays didn't tell all; Mose knew that much from some of his studying up. And even Carver and his friends visiting him in the hospital! What a damn fool he was! They had sat on his bed and he hadn't even figured out to tell them to get checked out—thoroughly checked out—the works— so concerned had he been with his own hide! He grabbed his keys and rushed outside and down the hall, jammed a dime into the telephone and dialed. It rang three times, got picked up on the fourth.

"Hello, is Carver there?"

"Hi," a child's voice answered, "This is Michael."

"Put Carver on, son."

"You want grampa?"

"That's right son. 'Lemme speak to your grampa."

"Grampa isn't here. He went to see Auntie in Houston."

"Damn, that's right. Well, 'lemme speak to your mother."

"Mama's at her sister's. I'm in charge here 'cause I'm the oldest."

"Well, look, can you have her to call Green. Mose Green."

"Green."

"She knows the number."

"All right."

"Tell her it's important."

"All right."

"Tell her it's *very* important."

"O.k."

Mose paced back to his room, and grabbed his phone book from a drawer in the table. Suddenly, he felt tired and sat down. It could wait until morning. But he would do it. Call Carver and all the fellas. Insist they get checked out, *tested*—not just a quick chest x-ray, but the works. Carver had a son in Mare Island. Gilliam had people in Norfolk, Virginia, where they struck in '68, duking it out with the National Guard. Those folks would see they got tested right. They deserved to know—if they didn't already. Mose smiled. Yeah, heard it through the grapevine, huh. And when he returned to New Orleans he'd go down there too. And make sure he'd hit Mississippi—have his daughters drive him there, or take a train—whatever way, he'd get there. If he couldn't go himself, he'd get the word there. He'd spread the word. He was going, but not without getting in some licks, and seeing to it that others didn't have to go so soon. Goddamn, he was dying, but he wasn't helpless. he pranced around his room, wheezing a little. How'd they put it at the union meetings? Secretary-Treasurer, I move we go on to the last two items of our agenda—Unfinished Business, and Good and Welfare.

He laughed out loud, rubbing his hands. He took out a pan, turned on the small stove, and put on some oil. He decided to splurge and do some pepper steak. He cut up the chuck steak, salt-and-peppered it, cracked an egg into some flour, then rolled the meat in it. He poured in more oil, turned it up hot—it sizzled and splattered. As he fixed the spinach and rice, he bit into a red apple, and bit off some more, murmuring, "Give me strength! Give me strength!" laughing to himself. Then he threw the meat into the sizzling pan. He took from the back of his cupboard the small bottle of Gordon's gin he saved mainly for friends. This occasion called for a little treat. He poured a small shot and drank it slowly, letting it relax in his mouth awhile.

The smell of frying·meat filled the studio. The spinach and rice mixed in. Mose strode around the room as if about to burst, beaming, saying out loud, "They don't know who they *messin'* with." He grabbed the photo on his night-stand, "*Do* they?"

May smiled. "They sure don't. They could ask me. I could tell 'em," she winked, "I could tell 'em just how *much* trouble they're *in*."

"Ha!" he laughed, clutching the photo to his chest, "you know, gal, you know."

He took off the food, pouring the spinach liquid and meat drippings onto the rice. He added salt and pepper, poured some hot sauce, and he was ready. He ate slowly, relishing each bite. As he ate, he took a piece of paper and a pencil, and slowly drew up a list of his closest friends. Before he finished eating, he carefully folded up the paper and placed it on his night-stand next to the photo of May.

After supper, he checked the time—he was due for his breathing exercise. From behind the small couch he took out his breathing machine, put on the respirator, and began his exercise.

He thought of Johnnie, Josh, his daughters, his grand-children. He smiled. What if he did go to New Orleans? He could talk it over with Doris and Rainey—about how much to tell the grandchildren. It was hard to figure what to tell—where fright ended and understanding began. He'd best let Doris and Ben, and Rainey and John judge that—after all, it was their children. Before it got worse, he would take the children down to the wharves and show them the ships, pointing, "See them ships? I'm in some of them ships." And they would ask, "How is that, Grandpa?" or say, "You're here with us, Grandpa." And he'd reply slowly, "I did the floor in the engine room of that one, and the floor in the boiler room of that one, and that's the room with the machines that help that ship move." And they would marvel how their Grandpa was in those ships, and be proud, brag-ging at school, "If you see a ship you see part of my Grandpa."

He breathed hard. His chest hurt. For an instant he felt sad. Well, he wouldn't know what to tell them exactly, but that was what he wanted to leave them.

He wondered where all the ships he'd worked wound up. All over the world. Or sitting in drydock like himself, old and wheezing, the insides goin' bad. Or, all over the world—Rio, Manila, Liverpool, Buenos Aires, Bangkok—all the fabulous places described by friends shipping out in the Marine Cooks and Stewards Union. He remembered the good-natured insistence, "You got to go to Rio, Mose. Rio is where it is—maybe a little too wild for you, but I think even a homebody like yourself could get behind it." And Mose answered softly, "After livin' and workin' in Louisiana and Mississippi, ain't nothin' too wild for me."

He yawned. He put away the machine, took off his clothes, washed up, and got into bed, tired. Yeah, it was time to think about going home, and getting ready. He'd call his daughters in a few days. He'd be able to tell a whole lot by their voices whether or not to return. He began to drift. . . ships. . . Josh asked him about masks. . . faces. . . kids. . . he wanted. . . to see his grandchildren. . . hold them in his arms . . . feel the young life. . . young life pushing masks away. . . tell them. . . he had to shave every day. . . he didn't want to smell bad. . . tell them. . . Drifting, he had a dream.

He was walking in a wide green field on a hot Louisiana day with the sun hotter than a picnic fire. Someone was having a big barbecue—hot meat in the air. People sang. Some wore church clothes, others still wore their work clothes. The sun was red hot like the barbecue fire. Someone said, "Charity." Someone sang, "Sweet Chariot." A gate swung; it was a rusty iron gate. He was in the shipyards, and the doctor, all grey, said, "I'm sorry." And Mose smelled a great stink and smiled, "Phew!", then shocked, realized it was himself as people smiled and sniffed politely, holding their handkerchiefs to their noses sniffing, "Sure nice seein' you again, Mose", and "See you 'round," and "Take it easy, man," then bolted out the door. The door was grey and it was raining and the sky turned grey-white then back again to a hot orange.

He heard a sweet voice sing "AND WHAT DID I SEE". Through the green grass toward him slowly ran people moving through the reeds—some folks he hadn't seen in years—his grandpa arguing with his Pa about crops, his daughters his grandchildren moving very slowly their arms outstretched, May his May strolling, picking flowers, and behind them followed Carver The Joker Thomas Jones Gordon — many of his old friends singing WHAT DID I SEE COMIN' FOR

"You the angels?" Moses asked puzzledly.

"Sheee," Joker cracked, "after all the times you told me to go to hell, you callin' me an angel *now?*" Carver, winking, held up his arms as if being frisked or getting ready to dance —his pits, rich, dark, wet, and smiled, "See any wings? C'mon, let's check the meat."

Mose excused himself—it was time to go on the breathing machine. As he breathed he heard laughter, shouts, clapping. People were singing again. In suits, dresses, overalls, skirts, the singing and clapping sounded like a chant, like work and harvest songs. At first it sounded like children teasing him:

> Old Mose Green and his breathing machine
> Old Mose Green and his breathing machine

He almost expected to see children thumb their noses at him, but then the clapping picked up; the suits and overalls and dresses began waving like long grass, including those holding full plates, eating and swaying at the same time, waving glasses and spoons, forks:

> Old Mose Green and his breathing machine
> I said
> Old Mose Green and his breathing machine

Josh darted into his Jericho dance, his face whirling closer and closer, laughing, turning into his daughters, then his grandchildren, and then into another small child extremely familiar, he squinted hard—it was himself smaller —he gasped as the clapping increased. The chorus shouted: "Who is that now?"

> Old Mose Green and his breathing machine
> Say what?
> Old Mose Green and his breathing machine

He breathed in and out. The machine turned lime-green, then

bright green. Out of the earth flew a bird, gleaming brown with green and maroon markings; it looked like two hands with their thumbs hooked and the other fingers fluttering— like when Mose imitated animals in the twilight—silhouettes for his daughters and May. The bird flew around the trees, flew up into the sky, then returning, flew back into the earth as the chorus returned:

> Old Mose Green and his breathing machine
> Oh!
> Old Mose Green and his breathing machine
> Yeah!

(Carver led a line of dancers, sweating freely, clapping)

> Old Mose Green and his breathing machine
> Amen

May singing held the sweet note long and low.

Mose grinned. He breathed—the sky was bright blue and bright orange—he felt warmer. He breathed, a warmth rose from his armpits and like two wings from his groin and from his ears and shoulders and back muscles emerged warmth like fire and from his legs breathing warm, and there was not a breathing machine as he breathed in a warmth almost a flame in the gathering faces he could smell pine and oak and sauced meat hot and lush honeysuckle perfume and as the air cooled and the sky grew dark blue with a blue green twilight and an orange moon May hugged him, whispering, "Time to turn in, honey" and his grandchildren jumped up and down tugging on his arms, "Carry me home, grandpa carry me home."

Other titles by South End Press

Fiction/Poetry

Tales I Tell My Mother / Zoe Fairbairns, Sara Maitland, Valerie Miner, Michele Roberts and Michelene Wandor. Fifteen stories, written as a collaborative project, involve Fifteen stories, written as a collaborative project, explore the experiences of contemporary women in a variety of short-story forms. Through it emerge five strong and distinct fictional voices, female and feminist, and testing both those definitions every step of the way. It is a book which everyone interested in fiction or politics must read.

Hand Over Fist / Henry Noyes. This is a Chicago story about life in the 42nd Ward in the final period of the Korean conflict. Sicilian immigrants and Black ex-sharecroppers who have settled on Chicago's Northside search for jobs, living and breathing space, and education for their kids. But the American Dream turns nightmare in the explosive tenant-landlord relations polarized in the life and death struggle of Anna Mae Green and Kathryn Bianchi. The shadows cast by the skyscrapers of the Loop where money is king fall like a blight over Little Italy.

LOUDcracks/softHEARTS / Jean Lozoraitis. A collection of feminist poems. The themes range from society, to the media, to food, to relationships, to street people, workers, and kids to fighting back..."the struggle will continue til the fear dies in the flame." *Jean Lozoraitis.*

Ecology/Science

Ecology as Poltics / Andre Gorz. In his first English-speaking work since the widely accalimed *Socialism and Revolution*, Gorz examines the relationship between ecology and politics—between ecological balance and our economic and political structures. A major premise of the book is that we cannot avoid the political nature of ecological issues. At the same time, the ecological movement is not an end in itself, but a stage in the larger struggle. Gorz shows that technology which has at its base the domination of nature can only lead to the domination of people; and he shows that only a fundamental restructuring of technology and society can reduce waste and inequality.

NO NUKES; everyone's guide to nuclear power / Anna Gyorgy & Friends. Explains the inner workings of nuclear plants, the nuclear fuel cycle, nuclear health and safety hazards, the economics and politics of nuclear power, and the activities of citizens groups around the world. It reveals the true costs and risks of nuclear power for workers and consumers.

The Sun Betrayed / Ray Reece. A behind-the-scenes history of the collusion between federal and corporate energy executives against small-scale solar energy development. Since 1971, a technocratic alliance of federal agencies, major corporations, utilities, and elite universities has aimed at placing control of solar energy in the hands of the U.S. corporate oligarches.

Politics

Critical Teaching and Everyday Life / Ira Shor. This is a unique education book. It develops teaching theory side by side with a political analysis of schooling. Written in the Freirian tradition, this book is committed to learning through dialogue, to exploration of daily themes, and to creating democratic culture. Shor poses alienation and mass culture as key learning problems, and develops critical literacy as a foundation for studying any subject. *Critical Teaching* challenges the social limits of thought and action.

The Crisis in the Working Class; an argument for creating a new labor movement / John McDermott. A straightforward, down to earth look at the position of workers in the U.S. today. McDermott begins with a telling indictment of trade unionism as it has been practiced in the U.S. in recent years.

go on to next page

We are led back through one hundred years of American labor history, reliving the lives of Frederick Douglass, Eugene Debs, and others, as well as great movements, such as the American Railway Union and the I.W.W. The history is vivid and detailed, and throughout, the author does not lose sight of its relevance to the present. He describes a new stage of U.S. capitalism—collectivized capital—and presents a proposal for working class organization today.

The Curious Courtship of Women's Liberation and Socialism / Batya Weinbaum. A theoretical guide to the shortcomings of Marxism and the pitfalls of socialism for feminist movements. The theoretical solution which emerges uses three major paradigms: the class struggle of Marx, the generational struggle of Freud and the struggle between the sexes of radical feminists.

Science and Liberation / ed. by Rita Arditti, Pat Brennan and Steve Cavrak. A collection of essays that discuss the role of scientists and science in the modern world—the use of science in supporting racial and sexual myths, in rationalizing capitalist technologies, in supporting big business' nuclear energy plans, and in war-related and policy research. For scientists and non-scientists alike.

The Politics of Eurocommunism / ed. by Carl Boggs and David Plotke. A collection of essays by Marxist activists and scholars from Spain, France, Italy, and the U.S. The contributors address critical questions raised by eurocommunism: Do the Communist Parties of Western Europe represent the interests of working people? Is it possible to achieve socialism through parliamentary means? this book also contains sections on the emergence of the women's struggle for liberation throughout Europe and how this struggle has affected the communist parties, the implications of Eurocommunism for the left in the U.S., and original documents from Italy, Spain, and France.

SOUTH END PRESS

Write to us for a catalogue of additional titles:
South End Press, P.O. 68 Astor Station, Boston, MA 02123